This first volume of

CRIMES AND MISFORTUNES

contains such mystery classics as

Frederic Brown's sardonic look at what makes urban decay, "Town Wanted". . .

Stanley Ellin's shocker about a man who made a legal living by killing, "The Question". . .

Robert L. Fish's zany Schlock Homes caper, "The Adventure of the Adam Bomb". . .

and a dozen more marvelous tales of murder, misdemeanor and mischance.

The Anthony Boucher Memorial Anthologies

SPECIAL WONDER (2 volumes)
CRIMES AND MISFORTUNES (2 volumes)

In Beagle Books editions

Volume 1 of
CRIMES
AND
MISFORTUNES
The Anthony Boucher
Memorial Anthology
of Mysteries

Edited by
J. Francis McComas

BEAGLE BOOKS • NEW YORK
An Intext Publisher

Library of Congress Card Catalog Number: 72-102341

This edition published by arrangement with Random
House, Inc.

First printing: April 1971

Printed in the United States of America

BEAGLE BOOKS, INC.
101 Fifth Avenue, New York, NY 10003

ACKNOWLEDGMENTS

COME INTO MY PARLOR, by Gloria Amoury. Copyright © 1967 by H.S.D. Publications, Inc. First published in *Alfred Hitchcock's Mystery Magazine*. Reprinted by permission of the author.

DEAD PHONE, by Poul and Karen Anderson. Copyright © 1965 by Fiction Publishing Company. First published in *The Saint Mystery Magazine*. Reprinted by permission of the authors and their agents, Scott Meredith Literary Agency, Inc., 580 Fifth Avenue, New York, N.Y. 10036.

A GOOD IMAGINATION, by Robert Bloch. Copyright © 1955 by Royal Publications, Inc. First published in *Suspect Detective Stories*. Reprinted by permission of the author and Royal Publications, Inc.

TOWN WANTED, by Fredric Brown. Copyright 1940 by The Munsey Company. First published in *Detective Fiction Weekly*. Reprinted by permission of the author and his agents, Scott Meredith Literary Agency, Inc., 580 Fifth Avenue, New York, N.Y. 10036.

THE GENTLEMAN FROM PARIS, by John Dickson Carr. Copyright 1950, 1954 by John Dickson Carr. First published in *Ellery Queen's Mystery Magazine*. Reprinted by permission of the author.

THE MOORS MURDER, an article by Miriam Allen deFord. Copyright © 1967 by Fiction Publishing Company. First published in *The Saint Mystery Magazine*. Reprinted by permission of the author.

THE COMPETITORS, by Richard Deming. Copyright © 1955 by Flying Eagle Publications, Inc. First published in *Manhunt Detective Story Monthly*. Reprinted by permission of the author and his agents, Scott Meredith Literary Agency, Inc., 580 Fifth Avenue, New York, N.Y. 10036.

THE QUESTION, by Stanley Ellin. Copyright © 1962 by Stanley Ellin. First published in *Ellery Queen's Magazine*. Reprinted by permission of the author.

THE ADVENTURE OF THE ADAM BOMB, by Robert L. Fish. Copyright © 1962 by Davis Publications, Inc. First published in *Ellery Queen's Mystery Magazine*. Reprinted by permission of the author.

This book is lovingly dedicated
to the memory of Anthony Boucher
1911-1968

Born William A. P. White in California, where he
was educated (B.A. from the University of Southern
California, and M.A. from the University of California) and lived all of his life. Author of seven novels
(five as Anthony Boucher, two as H. H. Holmes) and
innumerable novelettes, shorts, short-shorts, vignettes,
fact crime articles, translations in French, Spanish,
Portuguese, hundreds of radio shows (largely Sherlock Holmes). Editor of magazines and anthologies.
Famous mystery reviewer (as Anthony Boucher) of
the *San Francisco Chronicle, Ellery Queen's Mystery
Magazine, New York Times Book Review;* and
science fiction reviewer (as H. H. Holmes) of the
*San Francisco Chronicle, Chicago Sun Times, New
York Herald Tribune Book Review*. One of the
founding directors of Mystery Writers of America,
a permanent lifetime director of the organization,
national president in 1951, and recipient of their
Edgar Award for best criticism on many occasions.
Frequently recognized as America's foremost authority on the mystery story. Major non-professional
interests were historical vocal records, football, bas-
ketball, rugby, Elizabethan drama, food, Gibsons,
imported dark beer.

CONTENTS

"History is little else than a picture of
human crimes and misfortunes."
Voltaire's *L'Ingenu*

INTRODUCTION

The anthology you are about to read is truly a labor of love. Each writer donated his story without recompense, and the proceeds have been pledged equally to the Mystery Writers of America and the Science Fiction Writers of America. We of the Northern California Chapter of MWA feel sure that Anthony Boucher would have wanted it this way. Certainly the contributors agree with us.

Each writer has provided a short introduction, relating his story or his career to Tony. I venture to say that never before has a single book contained so many warm, glowing tributes to one man.

Anthony Boucher described himself as an editor and reviewer, but he was more than that: an authority on vocal music who was doing opera criticism at the time of his death; a linguist of ability who did translations from the Spanish, the German, the Italian, the Portuguese and the French (the Simenon in this volume is translated by Boucher); an ardent Sherlockian. He also was a wonderful amateur chef.

Despite constant illness, Tony took a profound joy in living. He loved to tell and hear stories; a devout Catholic, he especially delighted in jokes which ribbed the church and its clergy. His vast interests included the theatre and Shakespeare, and he was a rabid football, track and gymnastics fan with an encyclopedic knowledge of each sport's vital statistics.

Boucher took an M.A. with honors in German and Spanish at the University of California, but had no desire to become a college professor. Rather, he wanted to write plays. The pickings for playwrights were poor, however, in the post-depression thirties.

Finally, after strong urging by his friends, including me, he produced a novel. Because even then he was enamored of the detective story, it was a mystery titled *The Case of the Seven of Calvary*. The detective was one Dr. Ashwin, who was modeled on Tony's Sanskrit professor at U.C. Indeed, *ashwin* was the Sanskrit translation of the professor's English name. (Yes, Boucher was even fluent in Sanskrit.) He published *The Seven* under the pseudonym of Anthony Boucher, Anthony being his own saint's name and Boucher a family name.

For a period of about ten years Tony was an extremely productive writer, doing five full-length mystery novels under the Boucher name, and two more under the pseudonym of H. H. Holmes. He took a keen delight in the Holmes cognomen, for few of his readers realized that it was the professional name of America's most prolific mass murderer, a grizzly gentleman whose thriving business was conducted in a "murder castle" in Chicago during the 1890s. H. H. Holmes' real name was Herman W. Mudgett, which Tony used in certain correspondence and to by-line some of his poetry.

The sleuth in the two Holmes books was a nun-detective, Sister Ursula. After *The Seven*, the Boucher novels usually featured the ebullient private eye Fergus O'Breen. O'Breen also figured prominently in several science fantasy stories which Tony wrote for *Astounding Science Fiction* and *Unknown Worlds*. Another brilliant Boucher creation was Nick Noble, the Los Angeles ex-cop turned wino whose wits were sharpened by cooking sherry. The nonexistent fly on Nick's nose was as much a trademark as Archie Goodwin's identic memory.

In addition to writing crime, fantasy and science fiction stories, Boucher also collaborated on the Sherlock Holmes and several other radio mystery shows of that period.

During the 1940s Tony Boucher began his major lifework when he became mystery reviewer for the *San Francisco Chronicle*. After the end of World War II he reviewed mystery novels for *Ellery Queen's Mystery Magazine*, and ultimately for the *New York Times*. He loved writers, and he knew they had to eat; but as a reviewer, he felt his first duty was to the readers. Words of praise had value, he often remarked, only if there were also words of unpraise. But his unpraise was without malice, and he was especially gentle with first novels. Editors used more quotes from Tony's *New York Times* reviews on their jacket blurbs than they did from all other sources combined: impressive proof of his unique ability to write a selling review while still maintaining his scrupulous personal integrity.

In 1949 Mercury Publications launched the *Magazine of Fantasy and Science Fiction* with Tony Boucher and me as editors. Here Tony was at his finest, for he combined an unerring sense of what would be "commercial" with excellent literary taste. While editing *F&SF*, we also edited Mercury's ill-fated *True Crime Detective*. It was a magazine of literate fact crime studies, for we shared a complete rapport in our fascination with murder. Tony's two all-consuming artistic passions, in fact, transcending even the mystery story and science fiction, were opera and the study of actual murders.

His achievements of late years are well known: book and opera reviewer of national stature; radio and TV personality whom it was a pleasure to hear or watch; anthologizer of original and faultless taste; calculating and deadly poker player; wit, raconteur, delightful conversationalist . . . the attainments seem endless. In losing Tony Boucher, we all lost something that was dear and needful, for he was more than just the rennaissance "ideal man." Accomplished in the arts, the sciences and politics, he was, most important of all, accomplished in the ordinary decencies of living.

J. FRANCIS MCCOMAS
San Francisco
May, 1969

Acknowledgments

I certainly did not do all of the work on this anthology. I was ably assisted by various people, and I want to give them public thanks now. Reginald Bretnor conceived the original idea and handled the tremendous flood of mail connected with the project. Jack Leavitt donated his legal services, and served, along with Poul Anderson and Joe Gores, as trustees on behalf of the authors. Joe's lovely wife, Susan, did all of the clerical work and was indispensable in taking my dictation. Randall Garrett lent moral support, worked out a computer scheme whereby the initial solicitation letters were dispatched, and arranged for Rick Shorers to create our stationery. Dean Dickensheet, from his deep knowledge of Tony's literary tastes, selected the title. Most especially I must thank Phyllis White, Tony's widow, who made the project possible by insisting that MWA and SFWA, not herself, should receive the proceeds from these volumes.

J. F. McC.

CRIMES
AND
MISFORTUNES

COME INTO MY PARLOR

GLORIA AMOURY

When I became executive secretary of Mystery Writers of America in May 1965, I was simultaneously introduced to the field of mystery writing (my fiction credits, in Saturday Evening Post, Redbook *and other magazines, had been non-mysteries) and the name of Anthony Boucher.*

After a few perusals of his column, and a dealing or two with him over our awards, I grew to venerate the name, the man and the legend, as did our members. But I never dreamed my own writing would come to his attention.

However, shortly after my first suspense story, "Come into My Parlor," appeared in Alfred Hitchcock's Mystery Magazine, *I received what might have been the last letter Tony wrote to anyone. Dated April 13, 1968, it reads: ". . . Was 'Come into My Parlor' a first story? Don't remember seeing fiction from you before. In either case, I don't imagine you'll mind hearing that you've usurped the Abou-ben-Adhem-like place on the Honor Roll in my annual* Best, *usually occupied by Charlotte Armstrong. Best and Pascal love, Tony."*

IN THE LUXURIOUS HOTEL room overlooking the Bay of Naples glistening in the setting sun, two middle-aged ladies chatted pleasantly. Surface talk, their conversation gave no hint of their reflections.

The hostess, thin and dark in prim black, with the youthful

1

face of one who nibbles at life rather than devours it, appeared innocent and passionless compared to the other. Yet it was Marcia who regarded her guest as a spider might an unwary fly. Vivienne, in girlish pink which accented her plumpness, and with gray-black roots marring her yellow hair and the sensuous face of one who constantly participates in life and is soiled by it, seemed relaxed.

"What a coincidence that we met in the square," Vivienne murmured, as a small maid, olive-skinned and peasant-skirted, cleared the remnants of the *piccata* from the candle-lit table and brought in a bowl of apples and almonds.

"It's never a coincidence when Americans meet in Italy," Marcia answered. "We all cluster around the same squares and fountains. Too, I'd heard from home that you were touring near here. Your sister told Mother." She didn't add that she'd had her parents keep her posted on Vivienne's whereabouts, which they'd thought good sportsmanship; nor that during the past week she had been actively searching for Vivienne.

"Touring is a word used by the successful," Vivienne said wistfully. "Wandering is what I do."

The slight sympathy evoked in Marcia by the words evaporated at the sight of Vivienne's still round bosom and shapely legs. Possibly Vivienne had had it rough, financially, since Tom's death, while she herself had made money. Still, there were other ways of being successful than the most obvious, and a restless spirit, not a roaming body, made a wanderer.

"*You* tour," the guest went on, "with your music."

Marcia glanced at the talisman of every hotel room she occupied, her rented grand piano with the embroidered covering protecting its gloss, like a shawl a delicate person. Thanks to Vivienne, the piano had been a person to her through the years, the only constant companion, friend and mate she'd had. "I was lucky to click with it."

"I read about your last concert. The critic said you interpreted Chopin as well as Rosalind Turek does Bach. I don't know who Rosalind Turek is, but that's a compliment, isn't it?"

That compliment, like others about her singing tones and the nuances of her shadings, as always, whirled through Marcia's head meaninglessly. She suspected that musical talent, like other such gifts, was more admired by those who heard it from box seats than by those who, happening to possess it, had to use it as a life-substitute. "Let's not talk about music. Let's talk about us."

"That's the subject I've been hoping to avoid," Vivienne said, embarrassedly.

Marcia's expression hardened. "At this point, the—circumstances—are just something you and I shared."

Vivienne looked at her curiously. "I should have known a woman as—great—as you are, from the music, would feel that way. But when you stopped me tonight, my first thought was that you felt toward me the way most women in your place would and I—got scared."

"Scared?" Marcia forced a laugh. "Of me?"

"I harmed you long ago. Another in your place might think—of harming me now."

"Let's not use ambiguous words like 'harm.' You were a divorcee living next door to us, and my trusted friend. Somehow, possibly helped by such stimuli as the moonlight on the nearby Wabash, you managed to run off with my husband—"

"It didn't happen the way you put it," Vivienne said.

"How did it happen? I've always been curious."

"I can't explain it," Vivienne said, "especially to someone as—self-controlled—as you've always been. But Tom and I had to do what we did."

"If Tom was driven by a wild passion for you," Marcia said, "he successfully hid it from me."

"But from no one else," Vivienne said, artlessly. "I guess because you're the artistic type, with your thoughts always above the flesh, we did surprise *you*."

This artistic type, Marcia reflected, was now going to claim her revenge—a life for a life. Vivienne had taken hers and left the hulk to exhaust itself pushing an ordinary talent to an undreamed-of potential. For with Tom gone and no appetite for other men, what could she have done with her years but follow the instructions of piano coaches, practice eight hours a day, and finally smile woodenly over concert-stage footlights at the audiences of the world? She had planned this action for seventeen years. Now, the victim had been relatively easily found, had come with her readily and was unconsciously goading her to it. "Now that you realize my thoughts are always above the flesh," she said, disarmingly, "you trust me, don't you?"

"I came with you, didn't I?"

"Why? To find out how I've managed without Tom?"

"No," Vivienne said, in a low voice. "Because you talk

with the accent of home, and I was sure you'd give me good food. I haven't heard the one or had the other in some time. But now that I've heard your talk and had your good food, I hope Tom and I didn't hurt you too much."

"You didn't hurt me at all. Witness the piano. How many women pianists make it big? Dame Myra Hess, Turek, Novaes—only a few. With Tom I'd have been an ordinary housewife; without him I've touched the stars."

"I guess you have," Vivienne said.

Marcia shivered. Failures always had their dreams of success as an opiate against loneliness, but no one was lonelier than the successful, alone. What was hollower for a performer than a concert stage before an audience with no one in it cared for or caring? If she'd been a failure, she might have forgiven Vivienne, but success made the revenge more neccessary. "The past is past," she said, smiling. "Now, we're Americans far from home and you're visiting me. I've a treat for you." She rang for the maid.

The maid came in with a pitcher.

"Lemonade," Vivienne said, delightedly. "Made the American way. Lemony, with lots of ice."

"Made the Indiana way. I remember you loved lemons. You used to suck lemon halves with sugar."

"Imagine your remembering! The veal was flavored with lemon too. How considerate you are, and what a fool I was to worry."

"You were foolish indeed," Marcia agreed as she turned away from her guest and took a tall glass from the cupboard, a certain glass containing a few powdered grains which, when mixed with lemonade, Marcia knew, would kill.

It takes six weeks for the poison to close the kidneys of its victim and cause death from uremia, the book on poisons in the Rome library had said. By then she'd be safe behind the Iron Curtain on a Budapest stage, this encounter with Vivienne forgotten by its only other witness, the small maid.

Turning back to Vivienne, Marcia asked conversationally, "How long have you been in Europe?"

"Ten years. But we traveled around in the States before that."

Traveling with Tom . . . Marcia thought of sidewalk cafés in Paris she'd sat in, alone, of the car ride through the grandeur of the Amalfi mountains taken with a fellow passenger, a German woman who couldn't speak English but had smiled with irritating recognition that they were both those pitiable objects, women alone; she thought of Bavarian Alps, seen alone, of the Mediterranean at night, seen alone. Only once had *she* traveled with Tom.

"Tom and I," she couldn't help saying, "went to San Francisco on our honeymoon. We rode cablecars and ate at wharf fish-places. There was a baby-grand in our hotel lobby, which overlooked the Golden Gate. I'd play Debussy and he'd recite François Villon's poems to me, in French, to the music."

Vivienne smiled. "Those poems are effective even without Debussy."

"I should have realized," Marcia said bitterly, "that you'd be familiar with them too. Stupid of me."

"I had them fifteen years to your two," Vivienne said. "They sounded impressive in the States but ridiculous in Paris, with his American accent. But who could stop him from spouting the only French he knew?"

Marcia realized with a slight shock that she hadn't known Tom had had a poor French accent. That wasn't something one noticed when one was young and in love. What did a poor accent matter? She filled Vivienne's glass with lemonade. "Didn't Tom get a good job with an engineering firm in Kansas City right after—he left with you?"

"That's right. A good job."

Until Vivienne's sister had babbled that news to her one bright, hot morning as she'd dusted Tom's big chair, she'd convinced herself that it was a fling and that he'd be back. But the words "good job" made it permanent and had sealed her doom as this concoction would Vivienne's. "All the while he was a teller at the bank in South Bend, he talked about finding some opening in engineering. He was lucky to find one so quickly after he went with you."

"We'd driven off in the car, *your* car," Vivienne said, somewhat sheepishly. "It was summer, you remember. When we got to K.C., Tom bought a newspaper and saw an ad for an engineering trainee. He answered it in his shirtsleeves, with the sweat from the road on his face. Maybe if he'd cleaned up he'd have looked like the other applicants and he mightn't have got the job, but as it was, the boss probably figured he was so—dedicated that he put wanting-the-job even before cleanliness."

Marcia, too, had traveled that summer. Numbed beyond tears, she'd passed flat Indiana towns on the small electric train and then had made her way through Chicago to Professor Hoelick's studio overlooking Lake Michigan. Unawed by the giant grands back-to-back, or by the electric metronome sternly overhead—so different from Miss Claver's prim parlor-with-upright—she'd played a Beethoven sonata and then said, "I've studied the piano casually, under a local teacher, most of my life. I'd like to do something important with my music now. I've heard your name. Will you teach me?"

"The maximum talent, application, and luck," the bushy-haired German answered, "is still no guarantee that the possessor of them all will accomplish anything artistically. In your case, your timing is execrable and, obviously, you've never been taught that a sustaining pedal exists. Still, you have the beginning of a singing tone. If you can meet my price . . ."

Unhelped by Tom, she'd met it through her steno and typing.

"Tom clashed with his boss after three months in K.C.," Vivienne was saying, "and that ended the engineering. Then he tried sales promotion."

"I can't believe he gave up engineering that easily," Marcia said. "He kept talking about a series of tunnels he wanted to build some day."

Vivienne smiled. "If I didn't know which two years you had him, I could figure out the dates from that brainstorm."

"What do you mean?" Marcia asked uneasily.

"His notions lasted about two years apiece and produced their own job-kicks. I went through at least seven. I didn't mind the insurance salesman bit or the TV producer bit, in the States, but in Europe his ideas got wilder. The worst was the hotel in Yugoslavia in which he wanted to invest, without knowing the language."

Marcia glanced sharply at her guest, jolted by the words. After Tom had left her, she had continued to have images of him: Tom, a thin, dignified thirtyish, a gray-templed, distinguished fortyish, ever onward and upward in engineering and, recently, even wonderful in death. It was jarring to realize that Vivienne had so unsettled him. "I'm surprised he was so—unstable."

"He wasn't exactly unstable. Just restless in jobs. The two-and-a-half-year stint with that bank, when he was engaged to and then married to you, was the longest he ever had in one place, he told me."

She was lying, Marcia decided. Tom had been as solid as

stone in the old days, his head filled with dreams of one career, engineering. Still, a remark of her father's popped into her head. "He's as solid as a five-letter word beginning with 'S,' all right. Sieve, not stone. Your love's blinding you, daughter." Her father had been jealous of Tom. Weren't all fathers of their sons-in-law?

"I suspect he'd have exploded in some other way," Vivienne went on, "if he hadn't met me."

"I never saw signs that an explosion was coming."

"They just weren't visible to you. For example, you never got that fifty dollars back, did you?"

"What fifty dollars?"

"The money that was stolen from your purse the day of the picnic."

"Oh, that money. No. But our cleaning girl took it. She admitted it, and said she'd spent it."

"She was protecting Tom," Vivienne said. "She'd had an affair with him."

"I don't believe you!" Marcia burst out. "You can say anything here, after all this time and with Tom dead. You know the only way you can boost yourself in my eyes is by making him seem bad. Next you'll tell me that rotten Tom corrupted innocent you."

"No," Vivienne said, softly. "We deserved each other."

Marcia couldn't deafen herself to the ring of truth in the tone.

Shaken, she gathered memories once precious and suddenly seeming soiled, and searched for consolation in them. "The —fifty dollars. How did you know about that? No one but Tom and the maid—But of course. Tom probably told you about it later."

"No," Vivienne said. "At the time. *He* took it and spent it on me. We had a lovely drunk on it at the Three Bay Bar. You were awake when Tom got home, he said. He told you some tale about a lonely bank examiner promising him a promotion if he drank with him until three A.M.—"

In Tom's arms, Marcia remembered, painfully, despite the reek of his breath, she'd consoled him after the dead hours spent with the bank examiner. There'd been other nights when he'd said he'd been delayed with other bank examiners, or scouts for engineering firms. And times when he'd driven the cleaning girl home and had got lost on the way back, he'd said. He'd been such a silly, Marcia had murmured fondly, getting lost for an hour on a straight road. Other money had disappeared, and the pearl ring, an heirloom of her mother's. Once the memories started souring, Marcia, still holding Vivienne's glass, was powerless to stop them.

"You must have had quite a life with him," Marcia said, "because presumably when *you* lived with him, you knew him."

"It wasn't bad," Vivienne said, seriously. "We had our ups and downs, like most couples."

One's lot, Marcia reflected, was indeed tailored to suit one.

"When he didn't work," Vivienne said, "I did. I had some weird jobs, from hash slinging to hat checking."

"He let *you* work! He wouldn't even let me give piano lessons!"

"So he told me. But that was because he couldn't stand kids around. Which was why we never had any, and probably why you didn't have any."

The golden wraith of the child who might have been and whose coming, Marcia'd thought, had been only temporarily postponed by Tom, left its perch on her conscience and vanished into oblivion.

Vivienne was still talking of her jobs. "The one job I had that I never let him forget was the time *he* arranged for me to—well—It was very dignified. Tom had met a rich New Yorker in a London pub. We were broke, and the fellow wanted a date for the night. Tom told him he knew an English girl—I was so good with the limey accent that the guy never noticed my Midwest twang. But later, whenever Tom and I fought, I'd say, 'You've done the worst a man can do, by your woman.' "

For the first time, Vivienne's eyes clouded with pain. As insensitive as Vivienne seemed, Tom had hurt her, too.

"People are like icebergs," Marcia breathed, her hand tightening on the glass. "Nine-tenths submerged beneath the surface. I never knew Tom at all."

Vivienne shrugged. "He wasn't a bad guy. And shaved, dressed-up and sober, he had enough charm to win a queen, right to the end. With that baby face and tousled hair, he *was* handsome when he was young, wasn't he?"

"Yes," Marcia said, "he was." And she let her earliest and most sacred memories of him sour with the rest.

"He grew enormously fat before he died. In my opinion,

his weight brought on the heart attack, not the brawl he was in. But maybe you never heard how he died."

"No, I never did."

"He died in my arms," Vivienne said.

"Oh?" Marcia didn't resent it in the least.

"In Paris, some months ago. Tom had been drinking, and this fellow came up to him and said—It's a long story. Are you sure you're interested?"

"On second thought," Marcia said, "I'd rather hear it some other time. I've absorbed enough about Tom for one night."

"I guess a woman as—great—as you are, with the music, can't waste her time on small talk about a man she knew for only a little while. My throat's dry from all this talk. I suppose that gorgeous glass is for me. May I have it?"

"Glass?"

"The lemonade."

"Oh, *this* glass," Marcia said, staring at it. "There seems to be a spot on it. I'll get you a clean one."

"Don't bother."

"I insist." And Marcia poured the contents of the glass down the wash-basin drain.

Vivienne had three glassfuls of lemonade. Then she rose and said, "Guess I'll tootle off to my digs, as crummy as they are."

"Don't go!" Marcia cried, impulsively. The leaden feeling inside her for seventeen years had melted. She was appalled at what she'd almost done to this woman, this—human being, this fellow-sufferer at the hands of Tom. How could she make it up? "I have twin beds. Stay here while I'm here. My next concert isn't until next week, in Vienna."

"I couldn't bear to," Vivienne said. "It'd be too painful to leave it all when I had to. I'm not doing badly now. A friend I had left me a few lira to get by on."

Marcia studied Vivienne momentarily, then offered, "I can spare some lira too."

Vivienne protested, but not strongly, and then left richer than when she'd come.

Marcia stood at the window and watched the other leave the plushy hotel entrance and then walk tiredly past dusty street urchins and animals toward wherever cave-dwellers live.

"There but for the grace of God," she murmured, and quietly began to weep. Then, carefully, she took the covering off the piano, sat down and began to play Chopin nocturnes, all nineteen, followed by the lesser known twentieth, posthumous, in C-sharp minor, and never had her trill been so exquisite nor her crescendos and decrescendos so gradual.

DEAD PHONE

POUL AND KAREN ANDERSON

As a critic, Anthony Boucher was honest to the point of ruthlessness. Unlike some, he never tried to wound personally the author of a work he didn't care for; rather, he leaned backward to be kind. However, if his reaction was negative, you knew it and you knew precisely why. I tried to draw a lesson from his rather cool reviews of my first two mystery novels. Maybe I succeeded, because he did like the third—and that praise meant something! He also spoke well of this short story, and that is one reason why it is included here. The other reason is that it gives my wife, who collaborated on it with me, a chance to join in the contribution. He was a dear friend to both of us.

THAT WAS AN EVIL autumn, when the powers bared their teeth across an island in the Spanish Main and it seemed the world might burn. Afterward Americans looked at each other with a kind of wonder, and for a while they walked more straight. But whatever victory they had gained was soon taken away from them.

As if to warn, a fortnight earlier the weather ran amok. On the Pacific coast, gale force winds flung sea against land, day and night without end, and rainfall in northern California redressed the balance of a three-year drought in less than a week. At the climax of it, the hills around San Francisco Bay started to come down in mudslides that took houses and human bodies along, and the streets of some towns were turned into rivers.

11

Trygve Yamamura sat up late. His wife had taken the children to visit her cousin in the Mother Lode country over the Columbus Day weekend. His work kept him behind; so now he prowled the big hollow house on the Berkeley steeps, smoked one pipe after another, listened to the wind and the rain lashing his roof and to the radio whose reports grew ever more sinister, and could not sleep.

Oh, yes, he told himself often and often, he was being foolish. They had undoubtedly arrived without trouble and were now snug at rest. In any event, he could do nothing to help, he was only exhausting himself, in violation of his entire philosophy. Tomorrow morning the phone line that had snapped, somewhere in those uplands, would be repaired, and he would hear their voices. But meanwhile his windowpanes were holes of blackness, and he started when a broken tree branch crashed against the wall.

He sought his basement gym and tried to exercise himself into calm. That didn't work either, simply added a different kind of weariness. He was worn down, he knew, badly in need of a vacation, with no immediate prospect of one. His agency had too many investigations going for him to leave the staff unsupervised.

He was also on edge because through various connections he knew more about the Cuban situation than had yet gotten into the papers. A nuclear showdown was beginning to look all too probable. Yamamura was not a pacifist, even when it came to that kind of war; but no sane man, most especially no man with wife and children, could coolly face abomination.

Toward midnight he surrendered. The Zen techniques had failed, or he had. His eyes felt hot and his brain gritty. He stripped, stood long under the shower, and at last, with a grimace, swallowed a sleeping pill.

The drug took quick hold of his unaccustomed body, but nonetheless he tossed about half awake and half in nightmare. It gibbered through his head, he stumbled among terrors and guilts, the sun had gone black while horrible stars rained down upon him. When the phone beside his bed rang he struck out with his fists and gasped.

Brring! the bell shouted across a light-year of wind and voices, *brring,* come to me, you must you must before that happens which has no name, *brring, brring,* you are damned to come and *brring* me her *brring brring brrRING!*

He struggled to wake. Night strangled him. He could not

speak or see, so great was his need of air. The receiver made lips against his ear and kissed him obscenely while the dark giggled. Through whirl and seethe he heard a click, then a whistle that went on forever, and he had a moment to think that the noise was not like any in this world, it was as if he had a fever or as if nothing was at the other end of the line except the huntsman wind. His skull resounded with the querning of the planets. Yet when the voice came it was clear, steady, a little slow and very sad—but how remote, how monstrously far away.

"Come to me. It's so dark here."

Yamamura lay stiff in his own darkness.

"I don't understand," said the voice. "I thought . . . afterward I would know everything, or else nothing. But instead I don't understand. Oh, God, but it's lonely!"

For a space only the humming and the chill whistle were heard. Then: "Why did I call you, Trygve Yamamura? For help? What help is there now? You don't even know that we don't understand afterward. Were those pigs that I heard grunting in the forest, and did she come behind them in a black cloak? I'm all alone."

And presently: "Something must be left. I read somewhere once that you don't die in a piece. The last and lowest cells work on for hours. I guess that's true. Because you're still real, Trygve Yamamura." Another pause, as if for the thoughtful shaking of a weary head. "Yes, that must be why I called. What became of me, no, that's of no account any more. But the others. They won't stay real for very long. I had to call while they are, so you can help them. Come."

"Cardynge," Yamamura mumbled.

"No," said the voice. "Goodbye."

The instrument clicked off. Briefly the thin screaming continued along the wires, and then it too died, and nothing remained but the weight in Yamamura's hand.

He became conscious of the storm that dashed against the windows, fumbled around and snapped the lamp switch. The bedroom sprang into existence: warm yellow glow on the walls, mattress springy beneath him and covers tangled above, the bureau with the children's pictures on top. The clock said 1:35. He stared at the receiver before laying it back in its cradle.

"Whoof," he said aloud.

Had he dreamed that call? No, he couldn't have. As full awareness flowed into him, every nerve cried alarm. His lanky, thick-chested frame left the bed in one movement. Yanking the directory from its shelf below the stand, he searched for an address. Yes, here. He took the phone again and dialed.

"Berkeley police," said a tone he recognized.

"Joe? This is Trig Yamamura. I think I've got some trouble to report. Client of mine just rang me up. Damndest thing I ever heard, made no sense whatsoever, but he seems to be in a bad way and the whole thing suggests—" Yamamura stopped.

"Yes, what?" said the desk officer.

Yamamura pinched his lips together before he said, "I don't know. But you'd better send a car around to have a look."

"Trig, do *you* feel right? Don't you know what's happening outdoors? We may get a disaster call any minute, if a landslide starts, and we've got our hands full as is with emergencies."

"You mean this is too vague?" Yamamura noticed the tension that knotted his muscles. One by one he forced them to relax. "Okay, I see your point," he said. "But you know I don't blow the whistle for nothing, either. Dispatch a car as soon as possible, if you don't hear anything else from me. Meanwhile I'll get over there myself. The place isn't far from here."

"M-m-m . . . well, fair enough, seeing it's you. Who is the guy and where does he live?"

"Aaron Cardynge." Yamamura spelled the name and gave the address he had checked.

"Oh, yeah, I've heard of him. Medium-big importer, isn't he? I guess he wouldn't rouse you without some reason. Go ahead, then, and we'll alert the nearest car to stop by when it can."

"Thanks." Yamamura had started to skin out of his pajamas before he hung up.

He was back into his clothes, with a sweater above, very nearly as fast, and pulled on his raincoat while he kicked the garage door open. The wind screeched at him. When he backed the Volkswagen out, it trembled with that violence. Rain roared on its metal and flooded down the windshield; his headlights and the rear lamps were quickly gulped down by night. Through everything he could hear how water cascaded along the narrow, twisting hill streets and sheeted under his wheels. The brake drums must be soaked, he thought, and groped his way in second gear.

But the storm was something real to fight, that cleansed him of vague horrors. As he drove, with every animal skill at his command, he found himself thinking in a nearly detached fashion.

Why should Cardynge call me? I only met him once. And not about anything dangerous. Was it?

"I'm sorry, Mr. Cardynge," Yamamura said. "This agency doesn't handle divorce work."

The man across the desk shifted in his chair and took out a cigaret case. He was large-boned, portly, well-dressed, with gray hair brushed back above a rugged face. "I'm not here about that." He spoke not quite steadily and had some difficulty keeping his eyes on the detective's.

"Oh? I beg your pardon. But you told me—"

"Background. I . . . I'd tell a doctor as much as I could, too. So he'd have a better chance of helping me. Smoke?"

"No, thanks. I'm strictly a pipe man." More to put Cardynge at his ease than because he wanted one, Yamamura took a briar off the rack and charged it. "I don't know if we can help. Just what is the problem?"

"To find my son, I said. But you should know why he left and why it's urgent to locate him." Cardynge lit his cigaret and consumed it in quick, nervous puffs. "I don't like exposing my troubles. Believe me. Always made my own way before."

Yamamura leaned back, crossed his long legs, and regarded the other through a blue cloud. "I've heard worse than anything you're likely to have on your mind," he said. "Take your time."

Cardynge's troubled gaze sought the flat half-Oriental countenance before him. "I guess the matter isn't too dreadful at that," he said. "Maybe not even as sordid as it looks from the inside. And it's nearing an end now. But I've got to find Bayard, my boy, soon.

"He's my son by my first marriage. My wife died two years ago. I married Lisette a year later. Indecent haste? I don't know. I'd been so happy before. Hadn't realized how happy, till Maria was gone and I was rattling around alone in the house. Bayard was at the University most of the time, you see. This would be his junior year. He had an apartment of his own. We'd wanted him to, the extra cost was nothing to us and he should have that taste of freedom, don't you think?

Afterward . . . he'd have come back to stay with me if I asked. He offered to. But, oh, call it kindness to him, or a desire to carry on what Maria and I had begun, or false pride —I said no, that wasn't necessary, I could get along fine. And I did, physically. Had a housekeeper by day but cooked my own dinner, for something to do. I'm not a bad amateur cook."

Cardynge brought himself up short, stubbed out his cigaret, and lit another. "Not relevant," he said roughly, "except maybe to show why I made my mistake. A person gets lonesome eating by himself.

"Bayard's a good boy. He did what he could for me. Mainly that amounted to visiting me pretty often. More and more, he'd bring friends from school along. I enjoyed having young people around. Maria and I had always hoped for several children.

"Lisette got included in one of those parties. She was older than the rest, twenty-five, taking a few graduate courses. Lovely creature, witty, well read, captivating manners. I . . . I asked Bayard to be sure and invite her for next time. Then I started taking her out myself. Whirlwind courtship, I suppose. I'm still not sure which of us was the whirlwind, though."

Cardynge scowled. His left hand clenched. "Bayard tried to warn me," he said. "Not that he knew her any too well. But he did know she was one of the—it isn't fashionable to call them beat any more, is it? The kind who spend most of their time hanging around in the coffee shops bragging about what they're going to do someday, and meanwhile cadging their living any way they can. Though that doesn't describe Lisette either. She turned out to have a good deal more force of character than that bunch. Anyhow, when he saw I was serious, Bayard begged me not to go any further with her. We had quite a fight about it. I married her a couple of days later."

Cardynge made a jerky sort of shrug. "Never mind the details," he said. "I soon learned she was a bitch on wheels. At first, after seeing what happened to our joint checking account, I thought she was simply extravagant. But what she said, and did, when I tried to put the brakes on her—! Now I'm morally certain she didn't actually spend most of the money, but socked it away somewhere. I also know she had lovers. She taunted me with that, at the end.

"Before then she drove Bayard out. You can guess how

many little ways there are to make a proud, sensitive young man unwelcome in his own father's house. Finally he exploded and told the truth about her, to both our faces. I still felt honor bound to defend her, at least to the extent of telling him to shut up or leave. 'Very well, I'll go,' he said, and that was the last I saw of him. Four months back. He simply left town."

"Have you heard anything from him since?" Yamamura asked.

"A short letter from Seattle, some while ago." Cardynge finished his cigaret and extracted a fresh one. "Obviously trying to mend his friendship with me, if not her. He only said he was okay, but the job he'd found was a poor one. He'd heard of better possibilities elsewhere, so he was going to go have a look and he'd write again when he was settled. I haven't heard yet. I tried to get his current address from his draft board, but they said they weren't allowed to release any such information. So I came to you."

"I see." Yamamura drew on his pipe. "Don't worry too much, Mr. Cardynge. He sounds like a good, steady kid, who'll land on his feet."

"Uh-huh. But I must locate him. You see, Lisette and I separated month before last. Not formally. We . . . we've even seen each other on occasion. She can still be lovely in every way, when she cares to. I've been sending her money, quite a decent sum. But she says she wants to come back."

"Do you want her yourself?"

"No. It's a fearful temptation, but I'm too well aware of what the end result would be. So she told me yesterday, if I didn't take her back, she'd file for divorce. And you know what a woman can do to a man in this state."

"Yeah."

"I'm quite prepared to make a reasonable settlement," Cardynge said. "A man ought to pay for his mistakes. But I'll be damned if I'll turn over so much to her that it ruins the business my son was going to inherit."

"Um-m-m . . . are you sure he really wants to?"

"I am. He was majoring in business administration on that account. But your question's a very natural one, though, which is also bound to occur to the courts. If Bayard isn't here at the trial, it won't seem as if he has much interest that needs protection. Also, he's the main witness to prove the, the mental cruelty wasn't mine. At least, not entirely mine— I think." Cardynge gestured savagely with his cigaret. "All right, I married a girl young enough to be my daughter. We look at life differently. But I tried to please her."

Yamamura liked him for the admission.

"I've no proof about the lovers," Cardynge said, "except what she told me herself in our last fight. And, well, indications. You know. Never mind, I won't ask anyone to poke into that. Lisette was nearly always charming in company. And I'm not given to weeping on my friends' shoulders. So, as I say, we need Bayard's testimony. If there's to be any kind of justice done. In fact, if we can get him back before the trial, I'm sure she'll pull in her horns. The whole wretched business can be settled quietly, no headlines, no—You understand?"

"I believe so." Yamamura considered him a while before asking gently, "You're still in love with her, aren't you?"

Cardynge reddened. Yamamura wondered if he was going to get up and walk out. But he slumped and said, "If so, I'll get over it. Will you take the case?"

The rest of the discussion was strictly ways and means.

Rain pursued Yamamura to the porch of the house. Right and left and behind was only blackness, the neighborhood slept. But here light spilled from the front windows, made his dripping coat shimmer and glistened on the spears that slanted past the rail. The wind howled too loudly for him to hear the doorbell.

But the man inside ought to—

Yamamura grew aware that he had stood ringing for well over a minute. Perhaps the bell was out of order. He seized the knocker and slammed it down hard, again and again. Nothing replied but the storm.

Damnation! He tried the knob. The door opened. He stepped through and closed it behind him. "Hello," he called. "Are you here, Mr. Cardynge?"

The whoop outside felt suddenly less violent than it was— distant, unreal, like that voice over the wire. The house brimmed with silence.

It was a big, old-fashioned house; the entry hall where he stood was only dully lit from the archway to the living room. Yamamura called once more and desisted. The sound was too quickly lost. *Maybe he went out. I'll wait.* He hung coat and hat on the rack and passed on in.

The room beyond, illuminated by a ceiling light and a floor lamp, was large and low, well furnished but with the comfortable slight shabbiness of a long-established home. At the far end was a couch with a coffee table in front.

Cardynge lay there.

Yamamura plunged toward him. "Hey!" he shouted, and got no response. Cardynge was sprawled full length, neck resting across the arm of the couch. Though his eyes were closed, the jaw had dropped open and the face was without color. Yamamura shook him a little. The right leg flopped off the edge; its shoe hit the carpet with a thud that had no resonance.

Judas priest! Yamamura grabbed a horribly limp wrist. The flesh did not feel cold, but it yielded too much to pressure. He couldn't find any pulse.

His watch crystal was wet. On the table stood a nearly empty fifth of bourbon, a glass with some remnants of drink, and a large pill bottle. Yamamura reached out, snatched his fingers back—possible evidence there—and brought Cardynge's left arm to the mouth. That watch didn't fog over.

His first thought was of artificial respiration. Breath and heart could not have stopped very long ago. He noticed the dryness of the tongue, the uncleanliness elsewhere. *Long enough,* he thought, and rose.

The storm hurled itself against silence and fell back. In Yamamura's mind everything was overriden by the marble clock that ticked on the mantel, the last meaningful sound in the world. He had rarely felt so alone.

What had Cardynge said, in his call?

Yamamura started across the room to the telephone, but checked himself. Could be fingerprints. The police would soon arrive anyway, and there was no use in summoning a rescue squad which might be needed another place.

He returned to the body and stood looking down. Poor Cardynge. He hadn't appeared a suicidal type; but how much does any human know of any other? The body was more carefully dressed, in suit and clean shirt and tie, than one might have expected from a man baching it. Still, the room was neat too. Little more disturbed its orderliness than a couple of butts and matches in an ashtray on the end table next the couch. No day servant could maintain such conditions by herself.

Wait a bit. A crumpled sheet of paper, on the floor between couch and coffee table. Yamamura stopped, hesitated, and picked it up. Even dead, his client had a claim on him.

He smoothed it out with care. It had originally been folded

to fit an envelope. A letter, in a woman's handwriting, dated yesterday.

My dear Aaron—

—for you were very dear to me once, and in a way you still are. Not least, I suppose, because you have asked me to return to you, after all the heartbreak and bitterness. And yes, I believe you when you swear you will try to make everything different between us this time. Will you, then, believe me when I tell you how long and agonizingly hard I have thought since we spoke of this? How it hurts me so much to refuse you that I can't talk of it, even over the phone, but have to write this instead?

But if I came back it would be the same hideous thing over again. Your temper, your inflexibility, your suspicion. Your son returning, as he will, and your inability to see how insanely he hates me for taking his mother's place, how he will work and work until he succeeds in poisoning your mind about me. And I'm no saint myself. I admit that. My habits, my outlook, my demands—am I cruel to say that you are too old for them?

No, we would only hurt each other the worse. I don't want that, for you or for myself. So I can't come back.

I'm going away for a while, I don't know where, or if I did know I wouldn't tell you, because you might not stop pleading with me and that would be too hard to bear. I don't want to see you again. Not for a long time, at least, till our wounds have scarred. I'll get an attorney to settle the business part with you. I wish you everything good. Won't you wish the same for me? Goodbye, Aaron.

                                                        Lisette

Yamamura stared into emptiness. *I wonder what she'll think when she learns what this letter drove him to do.*

She may even have counted on it.

He put the sheet back approximately as he had found it, and unconsciously wiped his fingers on his trousers. In his need to keep busy, he squatted to examine the evidence on the table. His nose was keen, he could detect a slight acridness in the smell about the glass. The bottle from the drug-store held sleeping pills prescribed for Cardynge. It was half empty. Barbiturates and alcohol can be a lethal combination.

And yet— Yamamura got to his feet. He was not un-acquainted with death, he had looked through a number of its many doors and the teachings of the Buddha made it less terrible to him than to most. But something was wrong here. The sense of that crawled along his nerves.

Perhaps only the dregs of the nightmare from which Cardynge had roused him.

Yamamura wanted his pipe in the worst way. But better not smoke before the police had seen what was here . . . as a matter of form, if nothing else. Form was something to guard with great care, on this night when chaos ran loose beyond the walls and the world stood unmeasurably askew within them.

He began to prowl. A wastepaper basket was placed near the couch. Struck by a thought—his logical mind functioned swiftly and unceasingly, as if to weave a web over that which lay below—he crouched and looked in. Only two items. The housekeeper must have emptied the basket today, and Cardynge tossed these in after he got back from his office. He wouldn't have observed the holiday; few establishments did, and he would have feared leisure. Yamamura fished them out.

One was a cash register receipt from a local liquor store, dated today. The amount shown corresponded to the price of a fifth such as stood on the table. Lord, but Cardynge must have been drunk, half out of his skull, when he prepared that last draught for himself!

The other piece was an envelope, torn open by hand, ad-dressed here and postmarked yesterday evening in Berkeley. So he'd have found it in his mail when he came home this afternoon. In the handwriting of the letter, at the upper left corner, stood *Lisette Cardynge* and the apartment address her husband had given Yamamura.

The detective dropped them back into the basket and rose with a rather forced shrug. So what? If anything, this clinched the matter. One need merely feel compassion now, an obligation to find young Bayard—no, not even that, since the authorities would undertake it—so, no more than a wish to forget the whole business. There was enough harm and sorrow in the world without brooding on the unamendable affairs of a near stranger.

Only . . . Cardynge had wakened him, helplessly crying for help. And the wrongness would not go away.

Yamamura swore at himself. What was it that looked so impossible here? Cardynge's telephoning? He'd spoken strangely, even—or especially—for a man at the point of self-murder. *Though he may have been delirious. And certainly I was half asleep, in a morbid state, myself. I could have mixed his words with my dreams, and now be remembering things he never said.*

The suicide, when Cardynge read Lisette's ultimate refusal?

Or the refusal itself? Was it in character for her? Yamamura's mind twisted away from the room, two days backward in time.

He was faintly relieved when she came to his office. Not that the rights or wrongs of the case had much to do with the straight-forward task of tracing Bayard and explaining why he should return. But Yamamura always preferred to hear both sides of a story.

He stood up as she entered. Sunlight struck through the window, a hurried shaft between clouds, and blazed on her blonde hair. She was tall and slim, with long green eyes in a singularly lovely face, and she walked like a cat. "How do you do?" he said. Her hand lingered briefly in his before they sat down, but the gesture looked natural. He offered her a cigaret from a box he kept for visitors. She declined.

"What can I do for you, Mrs. Cardynge?" he asked, with a little less than his normal coolness.

"I don't know," she said unhappily. "I've no right to bother you like this."

"You certainly do, since your husband engaged me. I suppose he is the one who told you?"

"Yes. We saw each other yesterday, and he said he'd started you looking for his son. Do you think you'll find him?"

"I have no doubts. The man I sent to Seattle called in this very morning. He'd tracked down some of Bayard's associates there, who told him the boy had gone to Chicago. No known address, but probably as simple a thing as an ad in the paper will fetch him. It's not as if he were trying to hide."

She stared out of the window before she swung those luminous eyes back and said, "How can I get you to call off the search?"

Yamamura chose his words with care. "I'm afraid you can't. I've accepted a retainer."

"I could make that up to you."

Yamamura bridled. "Ethics forbid."

One small hand rose to her lips. "Oh, I'm so sorry. Please don't think I'm offering a bribe. But—" She blinked hard, squared her shoulders, and faced him head on. "Isn't there such a thing as a higher ethic?"

"Well-ll . . . what do you mean, Mrs. Cardynge?"

"I suppose Aaron praised Bayard at great length. And quite honestly, too, from his own viewpoint. His only son, born of his first wife, who must have been a dear person. How *could* Aaron see how evil he is?"

Yamamura made a production of charging his pipe. "I hear there was friction between you and the boy," he said.

A tired little smile tugged at her mouth. "You put it mildly. And of course I'm prejudiced. After all, he wrecked my marriage. Perhaps 'evil' is too strong a word. Nasty? And that may apply to nothing but his behavior toward me. Which in turn was partly resentment at my taking his mother's place, and partly—" Lisette stopped.

"Go on," said Yamamura, low.

Color mounted in her cheeks. "If you insist. I think he was in love with me. Not daring to admit it to himself, he did everything he could to get me out of his life. And out of his father's. He was more subtle than a young man ought to be, though. Insinuations; provocations; disagreements carefully nursed into quarrels—" She gripped the chair arms. "Our marriage, Aaron's and mine, would never have been a simple one to make work. The difference in age, outlook, everything. I'm not perfect either, not easy to live with. But I was trying. Then Bayard made the job impossible for both of us."

"He left months ago," Yamamura pointed out.

"By that time the harm was done, even if he didn't realize it himself."

"Does it matter to you any more what he does?"

"Yes. I—Aaron wants me to come back." She looked quickly up. "No doubt he's told you otherwise. He has a Victorian sense of privacy. The sort of man who maintains appearances, never comes out of his shell, until at last the pressure inside gets too great and destroys him. But he's told me several times since I left that I can come back any time I want."

"And you're thinking of doing so?"

"Yes. Though I can't really decide. It would be hard on us both, at best, and nearly unbearable if we fail again. But I do know that Bayard's presence would make the thing absolutely impossible." She clasped her purse with a desperate tightness. "And even if I decide not to try, if I get a divorce, the lies Bayard would tell—Please, Mr. Yamamura! Don't make a bad matter worse!"

The detective struck match to tobacco and did not speak until he had the pipe going. "I'm sorry," he said. "But I can't decree that a father should not get in touch with his son. Even if I did resign from the case, he can hire someone else. And whatever happens, Bayard won't stay away forever. Sooner or later you'll have to face this problem. Won't you?"

The bright head bent. "I'm sorry," Yamamura said again.

She shook herself and jumped to her feet. "That's all right," she whispered. "I see your point. Of course. Don't worry about me. I'll manage. Thanks for your trouble." He could scarcely rise before she was gone.

The doorbell jarred Yamamura to awareness. As he opened for the patrolman, the storm screamed at him. "Hi, Charlie," he said in a mutter. "You didn't have a useless trip. Wish to hell you had."

Officer Moffat hung up his slicker. "Suicide?"

"Looks that way. Though— Well, come see for yourself."

Moffat spoke little before he had examined what was in the living room. Then he said, "Joe told me this was a client of yours and he called you tonight. What'd he want?"

"I don't know." Yamamura felt free, now, to console himself with his pipe. "His words were so incoherent, and I was so fogged with sleep myself, that I can't remember very well. Frankly I'm just as glad."

"That figures for a suicide. Also the Dear John letter. What makes you so doubtful?"

Yamamura bit hard on his pipestem. The bowl became a tiny campfire over which to huddle. "I can't say. You know how it is when you're having a dream, and something is gruesomely wrong but you can't find out what, only feel that it is? That's what this is like."

He paused. "Of course," he said, seeking rationality, "Cardynge and his wife told me stories which were somewhat inconsistent. She claimed to me he wanted her back; he denied it. But you know how big a liar anyone can become when his or her most personal affairs are touched on. Even if he spoke truth at the time, he could have changed his mind yesterday. In either case, he'd have gotten drunk when she refused in this note, and if it turned out to be an unhappy drunk he could have hit the absolute bottom of depression and killed himself."

"Well," Moffat said, "I'll send for the squad." He laid a handkerchief over the phone and put it to his ear. "Damn! Line must be down somewhere. I'll have to use the car radio."

Yamamura remained behind while the policeman grumbled his way back into the rain. His eyes rested on Cardynge's face. It was so recently dead that a trace of expression lingered, but nothing he could read. As if Cardynge were trying to tell him something. . . . The thought came to Yamamura that this house was now more alive than its master, for it could still speak.

Impulsively, he went through the inner door and snapped on the light. Dining room, with a stiff, unused look; yes, the lonely man doubtless ate in the kitchen. Yamamura continued thither.

That was a fair-sized place, in cheerful colors which now added to desolation. It was as neat as everything else. One plate, silverware, and coffee apparatus stood in the drainrack. They were dry, but a dishtowel hung slightly damp. Hm . . . Cardynge must have washed his things quite shortly before he mixed that dose. Something to do with his hands, no doubt, a last effort to fend off the misery that came flooding over him. Yamamura opened the garbage pail, saw a well-gnawed T-bone and the wrappers from packages of frozen peas and French fries. Proof, if any were needed, that Cardynge had eaten here, doubtless been here the whole time. The refrigerator held a good bit of food; one ice tray was partly empty. Yamamura went on to the bathroom and bedrooms without noticing anything special.

Moffat came back in as the other man regained the living room. "They're on their way," he said. "I'll stick around here. You might as well go on home, Trig."

"I suppose so." Yamamura hesitated. "Who'll notify his wife?"

Moffat regarded him closely. "You've met her, you said, and know something about the case. Think you'd be able to break the news gently?"

"I don't know. Probably not. Anyhow, looks as if I'll have to tell his son, when we find him."

Moffat tilted back his cap and rubbed his head. "Son left town? We'll have to interview him ourselves. To tie up loose ends, make sure he really was away and so forth. Not that— Huh?"

Yamamura picked his pipe off the floor.

"What's the matter, Trig?"

"Nothing." The detective wheeled about, stared at the body on the couch and then out the window into night.

"Uh, one thing," Moffat said. "Since you do know a little about her. Think we should notify Mrs. Cardynge at once, or let her sleep till morning?"

It yelled within Yamamura.

"I mean, you know, theoretically we should send someone right off," Moffat said, "but even if she has left him, this is going to be a blow. Especially since she's indirectly re-spon—"

Yamamura snatched Moffat's arm. "Yes!" he cried. "Right away! Can you get a man there this instant?"

"What?"

"To arrest her!"

"Trig, are you crazy as that stiff was?"

"We may already be too late. Get back to your radio!"

Moffat wet his lips. "What do you mean?"

"The purse. Hers. The evidence will be there, if she hasn't had time to get rid of it— By God, if you don't, I'll make a citizen's arrest myself!"

Moffat looked into the dilated eyes a full second before he pulled himself loose. "Okay, Trig. What's her address again?" Yamamura told him and he ran off without stopping to put on his coat.

Yamamura waited, pipe smoldering in his hand. A dark peace rose within him. The wrongness had departed. There was nothing here worse than a dead man and a night gone wild.

Moffat re-entered, drenched and shivering. "I had to give them my word I had strong presumptive evidence," he said. "Well, I know what you've done in the past. But this better be good."

"Good enough, if we aren't too late," Yamamura said. He pointed to the ashtray. "Cardynge was pretty nervous when he talked to me," he went on. "He hated to bare his soul. So he smoked one cigaret after another. But here—two butts for an entire evening. If you look in the kitchen, you'll find that he made a hearty meal. And washed up afterward.

Does any of this square with a man utterly shattered by a Dear John letter?

"The dishes are dry in the rack. But something was washed more recently. The towel is still moist, even though the saliva has dried in the corpse's mouth. What was washed? And by whom?"

Moffat grew rigid. "You mean that letter's a plant? But the envelope—"

"Something else was in that envelope. 'Dear Aaron, can I come see you tonight on a very private matter? Lisette.' She came with a pretext for discussion that could not have been particularly disturbing to him. Nor could her presence have been; his mind was made up about her. But they had a few drinks together.

"At some point she went to the bathroom, taking her glass along, and loaded it with powder poured from the capsules. Then, I'd guess, while he went, she switched glasses with him. She'd know he used sleeping pills. Convenient for her. Still, if he had not, she could have gotten some other poison without too much trouble or danger.

"Of course, she couldn't be sure the dose would prove fatal, especially since I doubt if they drank much. Maybe she patted his head, soothed him, so he drifted into unconsciousness without noticing. He'd take a while, possibly an hour or two, to die. She must have waited, meanwhile arranging things. Washed both glasses that had her prints on them, fixed the one on the table here and clasped his hand around it for prints and poured most of the whiskey down the sink.

"If he'd started coming around, she could have returned the pill bottle to the bathroom and told him he'd had a fainting spell or whatever. She could even say she'd tried to get a doctor, but none could or would come. He wouldn't be suspicious. As things turned out, though, he died and she left. The only thing she overlooked was the evidence of the food and cigarets."

Moffat tugged his chin. "The autopsy will show how much he did or did not drink," he said. "Did that occur to her?"

"Probably. But it's no solid proof. He didn't *have* to be on a tear when he decided to end his life. The missing booze could've been spilled accidentally. But it would help plant the idea of suicide in people's minds. She's clever. Ruthless. And one hell of a fine actress."

"Motive?"

"Money. If Bayard testified against her in the divorce pro-
ceedings, she'd get nothing but the usual settlement. But as a
widow, she'd inherit a mighty prosperous business. She
married him in the first place for what she could get out of
him, of course."

Moffat clicked his tongue. "I'd hoped for better than this
from you, Trig," he said with a note of worry. "You're really
reaching."

"I know. This is more hunch than anything else. There
won't even be legal grounds for an indictment, if she's disposed of the proof."

"Do you suppose she was mistaken about his being dead,
and after she left he roused himself long enough to call you?
That sounds unlikeliest of all."

"No argument," said Yamamura grimly. "That call's the
one thing I can't explain."

They fell silent, amidst the rain and wind and relentless
clock-tick, until the homicide squad arrived. The first officer
who came in the door looked pleased, in a bleak fashion.
"We got the word on our way here," he said. "She wasn't
home, so the patrolman waited. She arrived a few minutes
afterward."

"Must have left this house—" Yamamura looked at his
watch. 2:27. Had the whole thing taken so short a while?
"About an hour ago, seeing I was phoned then. Even in this
weather, that's slow driving."

"Why, no. She said twenty minutes or thereabouts."

"What? You're sure? How do you know?"

"Oh, she broke down and confessed all over the place, as
soon as Hansen asked where she'd been and looked in her
purse."

Yamamura let out his breath in a long, shaken sigh.

"What was there?" Moffat asked.

"The original note, which asked for this meeting and furnished an envelope to authenticate the fake one," Yamamura
said. "I was hoping she'd taken it back with her, to destroy
more thoroughly than she might have felt safe in doing here."
More sadness than victory was in his tone: "I admit I'm surprised she spilled her guts so fast. But it must have affected
her more than she'd anticipated, to sit and watch her husband
die, with nothing but that clock speaking to her."

The discrepancy hit him anew. He turned to the homicide
officer and protested: "She can't have left here only twenty

minutes ago. That's barely before my arrival. Cardynge woke me almost half an hour before that!"

"While she was still here—?" Moffat contemplated Yamamura for a time that grew long. "Well, he said at length, "maybe she'd gone to the can." He took the phone. "We just might be able to check that call, if we hurry."

"The line's dead," Yamamura reminded him.

"No, I get a dial tone now," Moffat said. "They must've repaired it a few minutes ago. Hello, operator—"

Yamamura became occupied with explaining his presence and showing the squad around. When they came back to the living room, Moffat had cradled the phone. He stood so unmoving that their own feet halted.

"What's the matter, Charlie?" the inspector asked. "You look like the devil. Couldn't you find out anything?"

"No." Moffat shook his head, slowly, as if it weighed too much. "There wasn't any call."

"What?" Yamamura exclaimed.

"You heard me," Moffat said. "This line went down about midnight. Wasn't fixed till now." He took a step forward. "Okay, Trig. What really brought you here?"

"A phone call, I tell you." Yamamura's back ached with a tension he could not will away. "From Cardynge."

"And I tell you that's impossible."

Yamamura stood a while hearing the clock tick. Finally, flatly, he said: "All right. Maybe there never was a call. I was half asleep, half awake, my brain churning. I guess that subconsciously I was worried about Cardynge, and so I dreamed the message, even took the phone off the rack, it felt so real."

"Well . . . yes." Moffat began to relax. "That must be what happened. Funny coincidence, though."

"It better be a coincidence," Yamamura said.

The men looked simultaneously at the body, and at the phone, and away.

A GOOD IMAGINATION

ROBERT BLOCH

"A Good Imagination" is a story that Tony liked—and the approval of Anthony Boucher is an accolade any writer appreciates.

What I appreciate still more is Tony's friendship. Much as I admired him as an editor and critic and author in his own right, I remember him most glowingly and gratefully as a boon companion. Whether sharing parties and podiums with him at science-fiction conventions or enjoying visits in the privacy of our homes, just being with this man was an occasion for delight. Tony Boucher loved life—and we who were privileged to be a part of that life will always love Tony. His most lasting memorial is engraved in the hearts of his friends.

I MAY HAVE MY faults, but lack of imagination isn't one of them.

Take this matter of George Parker, for example. It finally came to a head today, and I flatter myself that I handled it very well. That's where imagination counts.

If it hadn't been for my imagination I probably never would have noticed George in the first place. And I certainly wouldn't have been prepared to deal with him properly. But as it was, I had everything worked out.

He showed up, right on schedule, just after lunch. I was down in the basement, mixing cement, when I heard him rap on the back door.

"Anybody home?" he called.

"Down here," I said. "All ready to go."

So he walked through the kitchen and came down the cellar stairs, clumping. George, the eternal clumper, banging his way through life; about as subtle as a steam roller. And with a steam roller's smug belief in its own power, in its ability to crush anything that didn't get out of its way.

He had to stoop a bit here in the basement because he was so tall. Tall and heavy-set, with the thick neck and broad shoulders that are the common endowment of outdoor men, movie stars, and adult male gorillas.

Of course I'm being a bit uncharitable. George Parker couldn't be compared to a gorilla. Not with that boyish crew cut and amiable grin of his. No self-respecting gorilla would affect either.

"All alone?" he asked. "Where's Mrs. Logan?"

"Louise?" I shrugged. "She's gone over to Dalton to close up the bank account."

The grin vanished. "Oh. I was sort of hoping I'd get a chance to say good-bye to her."

I'll bet he was. It almost killed him, realizing that he wasn't going to see her again. I knew. I knew why he'd come scratching on the door with his "Anybody home?" routine. What he really meant was, "Is the coast clear, darling?"

How many times had he come creeping around this summer? I wondered. How many times had he called her "darling"? How many times during the long weekdays when I wasn't home—when I was slaving away in town, and she was alone up here at the summer house?

Alone with George Parker. The steam roller. The gorilla. The ape in the T-shirt.

In June, when we first came up, I had thought we were lucky to find somebody like George to fix things around the place. The house needed repairs and carpentry work, and a fresh coat of paint. The lawn and garden demanded attention, too. And since I could only get away on weekends, I congratulated myself on finding a willing worker like George.

Louise had congratulated me too. "It was wonderful of you to discover such a jewel. This place needs a handy man."

Well, George must have been handy. All summer long, Louise kept finding new things for him to do. Putting in a walk to the pier. Setting up trellises. The neighbors got used to seeing him come in three or four days a week. I got used to it, too. For better than two months, you'd have thought I didn't have any imagination at all. Then I began to put two and two together. Or one and one, rather. George and Louise. Together up here, day after day. And night after night?

Even then, I couldn't be sure. It took a great deal of imagination to conceive of any woman allowing herself to become enamored of such an obvious ape. But then, perhaps some women like apes. Perhaps they have a secret craving for hairy bodies and crushing weight and panting animalism. Louise always told me she hated that sort of thing. She respected me because I was gentle and understanding and controlled myself. At least, that's what she said.

But I saw the way she looked at George. And I saw the way he looked at her. And I saw the way they both looked at me, when they thought I wasn't aware.

I was aware, of course. Increasingly aware, as the weeks went by. At first I contemplated getting rid of George, but that would have been too obvious. Firing him in midsummer, with work to be done, didn't make sense. Unless I wanted to force a showdown with Louise.

That wasn't the answer, either. All I'd have gotten from her would've been a tearful denial. And before she was through, she'd have twisted things around so that I was to blame. I'd be the brute who penned her up here in the country all summer long and left her alone to suffer. After all, I couldn't really prove anything.

So then I decided to sell. It wasn't difficult. Getting the place fixed up was a good idea; it added a couple of thousand to the value of the property. All I had to do was pass the word around to the realtor over at Dalton, and he did the rest. By the end of August there were three offers. I chose the best one, and it gave me a tidy profit.

Of course, Louise was heartbroken when she heard about the deal. She loved it here, she was just getting settled, she looked forward to coming back next year—why, she had even meant to talk to me about having a furnace put in so we could stay the year round.

She played the scene well, and I enjoyed it. All except the part about staying up here permanently. Did the little fool really think I was stupid enough to go for that? Staying in town alone all week, slaving away at the business, and then dragging up here weekends in the dead of winter to hear her excuses? "No, really, I'm just too bushed, honey. If you knew how much work I've been doing around the place! I just want to sleep forever."

I wanted to shout at her, then. I wanted to curse her. I wanted to spit it all out, tell her that I knew, then take her in my arms and shake her until her silly head spun. But I couldn't. Louise was too delicate for such brutality. Or so she had always intimated to me. She demanded gentle treatment. Gentle George, the gorilla.

So I was gentle with her. I told her that selling the place was merely a matter of good business. We had a chance to realize a handsome profit. And next year we'd buy another. In fact, I had already arranged a little surprise for her. After Labor Day, on our way back to town, I'd show it to her, even though it was a day or so out of our way.

"Out of our way?" She gave me that wide-eyed stare. "You mean you've got another place picked out, not around here?"

"That's right."

"Where? Tell me. Is it far?"

I smiled. "Quite far."

"But I—I'd like to stay here, on the river."

"Wait until you see it before you decide," I said. "Let's not talk about it anymore now. I imagine you're tired."

"Yes. I think I'll sleep on the day bed, if you don't mind."

I didn't mind. And we didn't talk about it anymore. I just completed the sale and got Louise to start packing. There wasn't much to pack, because I'd sold the furniture, too.

Then I waited. Waited and watched. Louise didn't know about the watching, of course. Neither did George.

And now it was the last day, and George stood in the cellar with me and looked at the mixing trough.

"Say, you do a pretty good job," he said. "Never knew you was so handy."

"I can do anything if I set my mind to it." I gave him back his grin.

"Is this the hole you want me to plug up?" he asked. He pointed to the opening underneath the cellar steps. It was a black shelf about two feet high and three feet wide, between the top of the basement blocks and the ceiling beams.

"That's it," I told him. "Goes clear back to the shed, I think. Always bothered me to see it, and I'd like to cement it up for the new owners before I go."

"Keep the mice out, eh?"

"And the rats," I said.

"Not many rats around here," George muttered.

"You're wrong, George." I stared at him. "There are rats everywhere. They creep in when you're not around to see them. They destroy your property. If you're not careful, they'll eat you out of house and home. And they're cunning. They try to work silently, unobserved. But a smart man knows when they're around. He can detect the signs of their handiwork. And a smart man gets rid of them. I wouldn't want to leave any opening for rats here, George. I'd hate to think of the new owner going through the same experience I did."

"You never told me about the rats," George said, looking at the hole in the wall. "Neither did Lou—Mrs. Logan."

"Perhaps she didn't know about them," I answered. "Maybe I should have warned her."

"Yeah."

"Well, it doesn't matter now. The cement will take care of them." I stepped back. "By the way, George, this is some new stuff that I got in town. I don't know if you've ever worked with it before. It's called Fast-seal. Understand it dries hard in less than an hour."

"You got the instructions?" George stared at the coagulating mass.

"Nothing to it. You use it the same way as the regular cement." I handed him the trowel and the boards. "Here, might as well get started. I'm going to dismantle this target range."

He went to work and I stepped over to the other side of the basement and took down my targets. Then I got the pistols out of their case and packed them. After that I took up the revolvers. I did a little cleaning before I laid them away.

George worked fast. He had the energy for tasks like this; energy, coupled with lack of imagination. Physical labor never troubles people like George, because they're not plagued by thoughts while they work. They live almost entirely in the world of sensation, responding aggressively to every challenge. Show them a hole in the wall and they'll cement it, show them a woman and they'll—

I steered my thoughts away from that and concentrated on oiling the last revolver. It was a big Colt, one I'd never used down here. Odd, that I collected weapons and used them so seldom. I liked to handle them, handle them and speculate on their potential power. See, here in this tiny hole lurks death; from this minute opening comes a force big enough to burst the brain of an idiot and emperor alike, to shatter the skull of sinner and of saint. With such a weapon one could even kill a gorilla at close range.

I held the revolver and stared at George's broad back. He was working swiftly with the trowel, closing off the opening entirely and smoothing it over.

I loaded the revolver, cocked it, and stared again. Ten feet away from me was a perfect target. It was an easy shot. The fool would never know what hit him.

That was the whole trouble, of course. He'd never know what hit him.

And I wanted him to know. Somewhere, deep down inside, even an ape like George had the ability to think, to realize. The trick lay in finding a method that would stimulate his imagination.

So I put down the revolver and walked over to him.

"Looks like you're finished," I said.

He nodded and wiped the perspiration from his forehead. An animal odor came from his armpits.

"Yeah. This stuff sure does a swell job. It's getting hard already. I just got to smooth it off a little more."

"Never mind." I stepped back. "You look as if you could use a beer."

He grinned and followed me over to the portable refrigerator in the corner. I took out a bottle of beer and opened it for him. He gulped gratefully. The bottle was empty before he bothered to look up and remark, "Aren't you drinking?"

I shook my head.

"Not around firearms, George." I pointed to the cases on the table.

"Say, Mr. Logan, I always meant to ask you something. How come a fella like you collects guns?"

"Why not? It's a fairly common hobby."

"But I never seen you shoot one."

I walked over and fished out another beer, uncapped it and handed it to him.

"Perhaps I don't collect them to shoot, George," I told him. "Perhaps I just collect them as symbols. Take this Colt, for example." I held it up. "My admiration for the black barrel has nothing to do with ballistics. When I look at it, I see a thousand stories. A story for every bullet fired. Scenes of violence and danger, of high drama and low melodrama."

"Sort of appeals to your imagination, is that it?"

"Precisely." I handed him another beer. "Go ahead, George," I said. "I've got to clean out the refrigerator anyway. This is our last day, you know. Might as well celebrate."

He nodded. But he didn't look as though he was in a mood for celebrating our departure. The ice-cold beer, downed rapidly, was beginning to take effect. Just a few bottles on a hot day will do the trick—particularly after violent exertion. I saw to it that another was ready before he had finished this one. He drank quickly, noisily, his neck bulging, his thick lips greedily encircling the mouth of the bottle. On his face was the absorbed look of an animal oblivious to everything except the immediate satisfaction of his appetite.

I picked up the Colt again and walked over to the cemented portion of the wall. With my left hand I rubbed the solidifying surface. "Marvelous stuff," I said. "Why, it's hard already. And perfectly dry."

He grunted. He put down the empty bottle and reached for the full one, his fifth. I waited until he had taken a healthy swig. Then I bent down and put my head next to the wall.

"What's that sound?" I asked.

He looked up. "I don't hear no sound."

"Mice," I said. "Back in there."

"Or rats, like you told me." He nodded.

"No, I rather think this is a mouse. The squeaking is so shrill. Can't you hear it?"

"I don't hear nothing."

He came over and stooped. His hand brushed the Colt and I drew it away.

"I still can't hear nothing."

"Well, it doesn't matter. This job is airtight, isn't it?"

"Sure."

"Then whatever's inside will suffocate in a few minutes or so." I smiled at him. "You must be deaf to the high tones, George. I heard that sound all during the time you were cementing the wall."

"What's the matter, it bother you, thinking about the mouse?"

"Not particularly, George."

"Anyways, there won't be no more getting through. This wall is already solid, now."

He thumped it with his fist.

"I done a pretty good job."

"Yes, you certainly did. And it's your last one, too." I went over to the refrigerator. "Which reminds me, it's time we settled up. But first, let's have another drink."

George glanced at his wrist watch. "Well, I dunno, Mr.

Logan. Maybe I better be running along. I got some business over to Dalton . . ."

Yes, he had business in Dalton, all right. He wanted to run over and see Louise. Maybe they'd have time to say good-bye again, the way they had last night before I'd arrived. Or before they knew I had arrived. But I saw them then, and I could see them now in my imagination.

It took a lot of effort for me to shut out the picture of what I had seen, but I did it. I even grinned back at George. And I held out the bottle and said, "Just one more, for old time's sake. And if you don't mind, I'll join you."

I took out a bottle for myself, opened it, raised it. With my left hand I picked up the Colt again.

He lifted his beer and belched. The sound echoed through the cellar like a revolver shot.

"A little toast might be in order," I said.

"Go ahead."

I smiled. "Here's to freedom."

He started to drink, then pulled the bottle away from his lips. I watched the crease form in his sweating forehead. "Freedom?"

I shrugged. "There's no sense trying to keep any secrets," I said. "After all, you're almost like one of the family, in a way."

"I don't get it."

"You will."

"What's this business about freedom?"

"Mrs. Logan," I said. "Louise."

He put the beer down on the table. "Yeah?"

"We've separated."

"Sep—"

"That's right, George." I turned my head. "Do you hear anything from behind the wall?"

"No. But what's all this about separating? You have a fight or something?"

"Nothing like that. It was all very sudden. You might say it was completely unexpected, at least as far as she was concerned. But I thought you might like to know."

"Isn't she over to Dalton, then?"

"I'm afraid not."

"You mean she went away already, today?"

"You might say that."

"Look here, Logan, just what are you driving at? What's the big idea of—"

I cocked my head toward the wall. "Are you sure you don't hear anything, George?"

"What's there to hear?"

"I thought she might be telling you good-bye."

He got it, then.

"Jesus, No! Logan, you're kidding me!"

I smiled.

His eyes began to bulge. I watched his hand curl around the mouth of the beer bottle. And I brought the muzzle of the Colt up until he could see it.

"Put it down, George. It won't do you any good. I've killed a mouse. What makes you think that I'd be afraid to kill a rat?"

He put the bottle down. The minute he let go, his hands started to tremble. "Logan, you couldn't've done it, not you. You wouldn't—"

I inched the revolver up higher, and he flinched back.

"That's right," I said. "I couldn't have. You and Louise were so certain about me, weren't you? You decided I couldn't do anything. I couldn't suspect, couldn't see what was going on right under my eyes. And if I did find out, I couldn't do anything about it because I'm a poor weak fool. Well, you were wrong, George. And Louise was wrong. I wonder if she can hear me now, eh?" I raised my voice. "Are you listening, Louise?"

George moved back against the wall, his mouth twitching. "You're lying," he said. "You didn't kill her."

"That's right. I didn't kill her. She was quite alive when I was finished. I merely saw to it that her arms and legs were bound tightly, so that she couldn't thresh around, and that the gag was firmly in place. Then I lifted her up into the hole and waited for you to come."

His face was whiter than the wall.

"You can understand why, can't you, George? Even an ape has enough imagination to appreciate the situation. Quite a joke, isn't it? You cementing up the wall, and all the while I knew you were killing her. And to make it even funnier, *she* knew it too, of course. She lay in that black hole, trying to cry out to you, while you sealed her up in an airless tomb, in a darkness that is worse than night, in the darkness of death—"

"You're crazy!"

I saw his muscles flex, his neck tighten. "Take one step," I said, "and I'll blow your face off."

He moved then, but away from me. He went to the wall and began to pound on it. The cement held.

"No use," I said. "It's solid. You did a good job, George. Your last job, and your best. Besides, it wouldn't be any use now. The air couldn't have lasted this long. She's gone."

He turned, panting. He held up his hands, and they were red. "Crazy!" he gasped. "No wonder she was scared of you, hated you. No human being could think of a thing like that."

I smiled. "Yes they could, George. Haven't you ever read any books? Did you ever hear of Edgar Allan Poe? *The Black Cat,* or *The Cask of Amontillado?* I guess not, George. You've always been too busy living, haven't you? And Louise was the same way. You believe in action, and you despise people like me. You say we've always got our noses buried in a book, while you're the practical ones, the go-getters. You're proud because you take what you want from life. And you laugh at us. I'll bet you and Louise laughed at me a lot. Now it's my turn."

"You—you can't get away with it!"

"Why not?"

"I'll tell. I'll get the sheriff on you!"

"No you won't. You're an accessory, George. Don't forget, you walled her up. And if you go to the sheriff I'll have my story. I'll tell him we were both in on it together, that I'd promised you half of her insurance. She has quite a lot of insurance, George. I'll tell the sheriff how you walled her up alive, while she writhed and kicked and tried to scream, knowing you were killing her. Not me, George. You!"

He almost rushed me, then. I took the first step forward and at the sight of the Colt he wilted. When I laughed, he put his hands over his ears.

"A pity she didn't listen to you last night, George, when you kept urging her not to wait until I came. You wanted her to drop everything and run away right then and there. You could get a ranger's job in Montana, wasn't that it? And nobody would ever know. Only she had to be practical. She wanted to stick around and draw the money out of the bank first. Wasn't that it?"

"You heard us?"

"Of course. I parked down the road and came up under the window. Then I went back and drove in, the way I always do. You didn't even have time to plan how you two would meet and arrange for your getaway, did you, George? You couldn't even say good-bye properly. Well, do it now.

There's a chance in a thousand that she can still hear you."

His eyes were glassy. It wasn't the heat and it wasn't the beer. He was shaking, whimpering.

"Hurry up, George. Tell the lady good-bye. Tell the lovely lady good-bye before she takes her last breath, before she gasps the last gulp of air into her lungs and feels them burn and shrivel. She'll die fast, George, if she isn't dead already. And then she'll crumble. She won't rot, because it's dry in there. There'll be no odor. She'll just mummify. Her limbs will turn to brown leather, and her hair will become brittle and drop out, and her skin will flake and her eyes will dry and coagulate in their sockets. But on what's left of her face you'll still be able to see an expression. You'll be able to see how she was at the moment when she died—with that last silent scream for mercy. She's screaming at you now. Can't you hear her? She's screaming, 'George, help me! Get me out of here, get me out of here, get me out—' "

George made a sound deep in his chest. Then he blinked and ran for the stairs. I didn't try to stop him. I let him thud up the steps, listened as he thundered through the kitchen, slammed the door.

It was very quiet in the cellar after that. I put the Colt away in its case, but first I took the precaution of unloading it and wiping off the barrel and the butt.

Then I took the empty bottles and stacked them neatly in the corner.

I finished George's beer and drank my own. And after that, I went upstairs.

There was nothing left to do now but wait.

I must have had two or three more beers while I was waiting. I got them from the big refrigerator in the kitchen and carried them into the front room so that they'd be handy while I read. I picked up my copy of Poe, and not by accident. I wondered if his treatment of the situation was as melodramatic as mine had been. Perhaps not, but then, I had my reasons. In retrospect, what I had said to George seemed a bit silly and overdrawn, but it served a purpose.

After a while, I got absorbed in my reading. Say what you will, Poe had a wonderful imagination, and I can appreciate that.

It was almost dusk when I heard a tapping on the door. I thought of Poe's raven, and put the book aside.

"Come in," I said.

It wasn't Poe's raven, of course.

"Hello, Louise." I smiled up at her. "Did you get everything accomplished?"

"Yes, darling." She sat down, and I noticed just the hint of a frown on her face.

"What's wrong?"

"Nothing. But something odd happened to me on the way back."

"So?"

"I was coming along the County Trunk, just about opposite the Beedsley place, when a state trooper pulled up alongside me."

"Speeding?"

"Of course not, silly. You know I never do over fifty. But he asked for my driver's license, and then he did a funny thing. He made me get out of the car and come over to the motorcycle. And he had me talk into the squawk-box. I think that's what he called it, anyway."

"What on earth for?"

"He didn't tell me. All I know is I had to give my name to the sheriff. And then he said he was sorry to trouble me, but I'd saved him a trip out here for nothing. And he let me go. I asked him what this was all about, and he just shrugged and said there'd been a little misunderstanding but this cleared everything up. Can you figure it out, darling?"

I smiled. "Perhaps," I said. "But maybe we'd better talk about it some other time. I don't want you getting all upset over nothing on our last night here."

"Darling, tell me. I insist!"

"Well, we had a little excitement around here, too," I told her. "Remember George Parker was supposed to come over and put in that cement?"

"Yes, that's right." She hesitated. I watched her. It was pleasant to watch her, to sense the way she was waiting for what I'd say next. If I could have, I'd been willing to prolong that particular moment forever. But finally I let it go.

"Well, he never showed up," I said.

I could almost *feel* the way she sighed with relief.

"So finally I went ahead and did it myself."

"Poor dear. You must be tired."

"You don't understand. That isn't the excitement I was talking about."

"N-no?"

Again I let her wait, savoring the moment. Then I went on, knowing there was a better moment to come. "But along about four, Sheriff Taylor called up, wanting to know where you were. Of course I told him, and I imagine that's why the troopers were out trying to locate you."

"But whatever for?"

"Are you sure you want to hear the rest?"

"Please."

"It's a rather unpleasant situation, apparently. It seems our friend George has suffered some sort of nervous breakdown."

"George?"

"Rather incredible, isn't it? Always seemed like such a stolid, unimaginative fellow, too. You've seen a bit more of him than I did, and I'm sure you wouldn't say he was the sensitive type, would you?"

"Tell me what's wrong, what's happened—"

"If you wish. As I get it, friend George came bursting into the sheriff's office with an utterly fantastic story. At first they thought he'd been drinking, but apparently he was in a state of actual hysteria. It seems he was accusing me of murdering you and walling your body up in the cellar."

"You're joking!"

"That's what the sheriff told George, at first. Until he realized the poor fellow was almost out of his head with fear. Naturally, the sheriff called me and I told him to try and locate you. I'm glad he did. I'd hate to have us involved in any trouble just as we're ready to leave."

I couldn't see her face in the dusk, so I got up and went over to her. She tried to turn away, but I held her and patted her shoulder. "There, there," I murmured. "I didn't want to upset you. Nothing to worry about. It's all over."

"George!" Her voice started to break, but she controlled it. "How is he?"

I sighed. "Stark staring, according to the sheriff. They called Doc Silvers right away. Unless he snaps out of it, he'll be committed. A pity, too—somebody said he was planning to take a ranger's job in Montana."

Louise was shaking, but her voice was firm. "Did he say anything else?"

"No. What more is there to say?"

"Why did he think you'd try to kill me?"

"I haven't the faintest idea. Funny about these strong, silent types. Once their imagination runs away with them, they can't seem to control it. They get keyed up to a certain pitch and then snap, all at once. I'm just glad it didn't happen

CRIMES AND MISFORTUNES, VOLUME I   43

when he was out here with you. There's no telling what he might have attempted." I laughed. "It may sound far-fetched to you, darling, but he could even have tried to assault you. Can you imagine being made love to by a lunatic?"

She shuddered and buried her head against me.

"Let's talk about something more cheerful," I said. "Here, have a beer."

I could feel her sob.

"Don't cry," I told her. "We're going away tomorrow, remember? Back to town. Just you and I. You needn't worry about George—they'll take care of him. You'll never have to see him again. Why, in a little while you'll forget all about him."

"Y-yes . . ."

"We're going to have a lot of fun together," I murmured. "That's a promise. I've got it all planned."

And I have, of course.

I wasn't lying to her.

I intend to have quite a lot of fun with Louise, tonight. She's in the bedroom right now as I write this, sleeping. I gave her quite a strong sedative, but it will wear off in another half hour or so. Then she'll be wide awake again. And I want her to be wide awake.

I want her to be wide awake when I take her in my arms, and I want her to be wide awake afterwards, when I hold her ever so gently, but ever so firmly, and tell her just what really happened. I want her to know how clever I am, and how strong, and how wise. I want her to know that I'm stronger and wiser than George could ever be.

She must realize the cleverness that brought everything to perfection. She must come to appreciate that I'm the better man after all. And of course I am.

It would have been stupid to confront them both with their guilt; what could I possibly have gained? And it would have been equally stupid for me to kill George and run the risk of discovery. As things worked out, as I *planned* them to work out, George is disposed of forever. I've sealed *him* up behind the walls of a madhouse for life. He'll live on and suffer, thinking Louise is dead and that he killed her. And of course the sheriff and the folks around here know differently. They know she's alive, and that there's nothing behind the cement wall. They'll remember talking to her and me, and that she was to go away with me. Neither the new owners nor anyone else will ever tear down that wall.

I'm going to make all this very plain to Louise. I'm going to tell her exactly what happened. In fact, that's why I'm writing this. I don't trust myself to find the exact word to convey the meaning of the moment.

I'll let her read what I've written.

Have you read this far, Louise?

Do you understand now? Do you understand what I've done?

And do you understand what I'm going to do, in just another moment?

That's right, Louise.

I'm going to bind and gag you. And I'm going to carry you down into the cellar, and tear the wall open once again. I'm going to thrust you into the darkness and let you scream away your life and your sanity while I wall you up again with fresh cement—wall you up forever, until your body rots to match your rotten soul.

I'll be standing right behind you when you've read this far, so you won't have a chance to scream. And you won't have a chance to beg, or plead, or try any of your stupid feminine tricks with me. Not that they would do any good. No use telling me I'll be caught, either. You know better than that.

The alibi is already set. I'll leave here alone in the morning. And you'll stay here forever.

That's because everything was planned, Louise. Because, you see, I *am* a better man than George. He was only an animal, really. And the difference between an animal and a man is really very simple.

It's all a matter of knowing how to use your imagination.

DONOGHAN'S WIFE

R. BRETNOR

Tony Boucher was a gentle man. He abhorred the reality of violence—and loved murder in the abstract. He never read "Donoghan's Wife," and so he never met Mrs. Donoghan, or Donoghan himself, or Mona Ramell, or the dark Gypsy and her son. Had he done so, I think, from what I know of him, that he might have detested or despised or pitied them. He would not, however, have made the terrible error of denying their essential humanity, with all its depths and darknesses, and desperate seekings, and triumphs and tragedies—as so many intellectuals do when they consider those whom they believe to be inferior. He was too good a Christian. I think he would have liked the story.

AFTER SHE BECAME AWARE that Mrs. Donoghan was sitting, silent and alone, in the too-silent shop, Mona Ramell waited an endless hour before she closed her door behind her and tiptoed down the hall. It was thirty feet to the Donoghans' apartment, another twenty to the shop's back door. She did not hurry; haste was the slayer of anticipation. Donoghan's wife would still be sitting there.

Sometimes, when the risen sun bathed the whole shop in love and light and warmth, quickening the Mary Gregory tumblers on their shelves, the glass bells, the Wedgwood, the Staffordshire dragoons, Mathilde Donoghan sang in her small, clear voice the simple songs of her childhood in the Camargue while she dusted them—as though the task could wipe away all the eroded years and return her there. Now she did not sing. Now there were storm clouds hanging over-head, as dark and deadly as a threat of war. Their gunmetal reflections left each bright object dull, lifeless, decayed. Even the four potted palms, along the tall French windows which formed the southern wall, hung their sad, wounded leaves in that killing light. And there among the slain she sat, in the huge Chinese chair which Donoghan always used himself when, sober and cheerful early in the day, he would play chess with his friend Ambejian, who dealt in rugs, or with the college boy from down the street. There she sat, gripping its black, curved arms, listening to the sounds that came to her through plastered ceiling and floor and carpet, the sounds of Donoghan and the Gypsy woman in the bedroom beneath her feet, the sounds that Mona Ramell had also heard. She listened to their laughter, in the betraying si-lences. She listened to the protests of the bed, for Donoghan was a powerful and tempestuous man for all his fat. She heard the occasional harsh comments of the bathroom. So intent was she that she never heard Miss Ramell's soft, soft knock at the hall door, or her softer entrance.

For a large woman, Miss Ramell was unusually silent; spike heels carried her as quietly as her blue, furred slippers would have done. Seeing herself unnoticed, for a moment she stopped dead still, taking the situation in, adding its obvious-ness to what she already knew. During that pause, she saw the tortured muscles at the corners of Mrs. Donoghan's tight mouth, and instantly a smile came and went, twisting the soft, white reaches of her face under the violet lids, beneath her piled blonde hair. She saw the bruised, plump wrists above the clutching hands—and thought of Donoghan's vast, freckled, hairy forearms, and felt the bruises which, eleven years before, his hands had left upon her pale, plump thighs. A dozen times, after she had first moved in, he had come to her in the small front apartment, and she, knowing that she was just one more among his many women, had let him sleep with her, reveling in his roughness and his strength, and bitterly—because she knew that it was so—resenting his vul-gar rape of her gentility.

"Mathilde?" Mona Ramell called, in her high, incongruous, girl's voice, as though she did not know just who was sitting there. "Mathilde? I don't want to disturb you, dear. May I come in?"

Mrs. Donoghan looked up, her poodle eyes as dead as all

the things surrounding her. "*He* is down there," she said, each word a drop of poison slowly pressed. "He is down there with *her*. He's with the Gypsy woman. In *my* house."

They knew each other well, those two. For ten years now, since Donoghan had tumbled Mona Ramell and moved on, they had been allies, equally hating, equally betrayed, their separate interests alone dividing them. Mathilde Donoghan was thoroughly familiar with the small town splendor, the social burden of being the Rich Man's Daughter which, long since, still rode Miss Ramell like an Old Man of the Sea; she knew about the brief and loveless marriage, the brief, loveless, desperate matings which had followed it. And Mona Ramell, on her part, was quite as well acquainted with the cold stream of nuns and maiden relatives by which Mathilde, orphaned again by her uncle's death, had been washed across the world to Canada and the United States, and across her flat, gray adolescence to maturity. Often she had shared the memory of Uncle Léonard's sun-drenched parlor, cluttered with clocks of porcelain, with music boxes and fringed and beaded lamps, with souvenirs of Verdun where he'd been wounded, with endless bric-à-brac. He had been a large man, had Uncle Léonard, as big as Donoghan—and, thinking of this now, Mona Ramell, as she always did, smiled very slightly to herself. As for the women Donoghan had had, they knew them all: some intimately—the Navy Warrant Officer's bedraggled wife had wept her sorrows out to each in turn; some only through a glimpse or two—like the gaunt, painted dowager, chauffeured and Cadillaced, pet-monkeyed, minked, the sort one would expect to see with dancing-studio call-boys, who quite improbably had driven him away for a long, drunken weekend in Tijuana.

Under their feet, the bedsprings wept aloud; there was a gasping cry, cut off; then Donoghan's short bark of laughter.

Mathilde Donoghan's hands whitened on the chair. "You do not understand," she said, as though a volume had been spoken. "This is not the same. She is a *Gypsy*—a Gypsy woman, do you hear?" For the first time, now, her vowels very faintly assumed their native shapes, as they often did when she spoke her uncle's name. "A Gypsy. They killed my mother. They killed her in the woods when I was four. Th-they cut her throat. *And now he brings this Gypsy woman here, into my house.* The house he bought with *my* inheritance."

Sometimes, hearing the story in the past, Mona Ramell

had ventured very softly to question whether Gypsies had
really been responsible; whether perhaps a tramp, a maniac,
a robber had done the deed? Always she had been told that
only Gypsies could ever be so cruel, for everybody knew the
things they did, cheating and poisoning, and maiming little
children, whom they had kidnapped from their homes, to
beg for them. But now she heard the voice of Mathilde
Donoghan as flat and dull and as intense as the invading
light; this was no time for reasoning.

"Why did he marry me?" Mrs. Donoghan leaned forward.
"I'll tell you why. He'd heard those stories about French-
women, that's why. And I was not like that—me, from the
convent in Quebec. I wanted a good husband, children. He
married me because I had some money in the bank, left to
me by my aunt. What was he? A cook aboard a ship, when
I was working for the Sisters in New London."

She paused, listening. Her breasts rose and fell.

"He had no education," she went on. "What, grammar
school perhaps? A year of high school? And still—he never
fails. It's now been almost twenty years, with antiques. He
never reads a book; he never pays too much; he always sells
for more than anyone. The same with women. Look at him—
fat as a pig, drunk half the time, but he can smell a pushover
like an old dog smells a bitch in heat—"

Miss Ramell dropped her eyes.

"—or maybe they smell him. What difference does it
make? I have said nothing. At least when he is with them he
leaves me alone. But this I will not stand. A Gypsy woman,
here. You've seen the sign?"

Miss Ramell had indeed—*Madame Zelda, Astrological
Forecasts, Character Analysis,* with a large drawing of a
palm, in the bedroom window right beside the street, a piece
of grotesque folklore out of place in that neighborhood.
Still, letting her hands wrestle with each other in her lap,
she said, "Maybe she's not a Gypsy *really,* dear. Her name is
Lopez. And that boy of hers—what's he called? Pete?—he
looks more Mexican."

"She is a Gypsy. Have you seen her eyes? The whites are
yellow, not like yours or mine. She is a Gypsy who has
left her tribe—probably for a man. Now, with the boy, even
her own people won't take her back." Abruptly, she leaned
forward. "Listen! They say that they are Christians, all these
Gypsies. Every year, in May, they come to the church of Les
Saintes Maries de la Mer, where Saint Sara is, their patroness.

There they spend the whole night in the crypt, without the priest. It is not consecrated. It is old, old. And the things they do there are not Christian things. Everyone knows, and everybody keeps doors and windows bolted till they have gone away. That was when my mother died, while they were there. *They* murdered her."

Far, far away, over the Coronado Islands south and west, lancets of lightning slit the sagging sky. Their ghost-lights flickered on Mathilde Donoghan's taut, bloodless cheeks. "*Never*," she whispered. "She shall *not* have him, even for a little while." Then suddenly she dropped into the language Donoghan had taught her. "Piss on him!" she cried. "*Piss* on the dirty, stinking bastard. I—I'll kill him first." There was a brass coal-scuttle by her hand, and in it, with a poker, tongs, a riding-crop, was a Gurkha *kukri* in its sheath. Now she took this, drawing it. The blade was eighteen inches long, heavy, curved, razor-edged. "I'll kill him. I'll kill him like his Gypsies killed my mother, do you hear?"

Mona Ramell's breath strangled in her throat. Fear surged through her—fear for herself, fear for—and of—her friend, and a strange, surprising, passionate fear for Donoghan, for his coarse, cruel, shamefully precious life. In that moist, deadly air, she struggled with her fear; then all at once its garrotte was broken; shrilly the panic-stricken words escaped from her.

"You mustn't—*mustn't*. Please! Please, Tilda honey—you mustn't say such things. Dear, you mustn't even think of things like that! No, *no*—no matter what they did. It was so long *ago*. You were just a little girl. *She* wasn't there. Maybe —maybe she wasn't even born—"

Mathilde Donoghan stared through her as she spoke; she stroked the weapon cradled in her hands. "—like they killed my mother, that is how," she said; and rivulets of sweat ran down her face.

Mona Ramell whimpered. Her lips drew back from all her large, flat teeth. "You want to punish him—of course you do. You want to stop him doing it with her. Well, I would too! Why, she's almost black. And in *your* house, as you said. But that's not how. Not by c-committing murder, dear. You'd ruin your own life and—and—well, anyhow—" She caught her breath; her hands seized one another, held each other still. "Anyhow, there's a better way to—to break them up, a *much* better way. You've got to *shame* him, that's what you've got to do."

Mathilde Donoghan's head jerked round. "Shame *Donoghan?*" she said. "You lost your mind?"

Miss Ramell forced a laugh; she tried to make her voice ingratiating. "Darling, I don't mean *that*. I mean you've got to shame him in *her* eyes. You're going to have to find yourself another man. You've got a real cute figure, and you're still young—you're only thirty-nine. There's lots and *lots* of men —why, all you'd have to do is let them *see*—you know. That's what I'd do, I'd give him a good taste of his own medicine." She panted now; her words came tripping on each other's heels. "Do—do you think she'd want him—if she saw—saw that you didn't care at all?"

Slowly and gently, Mrs. Donoghan lowered the dark *kukri* to her lap. Slowly, she drew her hands along her hips, her waist. With them she cupped and felt her small, round breasts. She *was* attractive, her body still a magnet for men's eyes. She knew that what Miss Ramell said was true. "How would she find out?" she asked, still in the same flat voice.

Miss Ramell hesitated, at a loss; she seized the first idea that came to mind. "Honey, she's got that boy. *He'll* tell her. You'll let her know through him."

"Through *him?* He won't know anything. He's just a kid!"

"He's big," Mona Ramell said, "and he's fifteen. I've been watching him. He—he's *in*terested. You ought to see the way he looks at women, dear—even at me. So all you've got to do is hire him, to carry messages once you've found a man, to carry notes and things, and you can pay him not to tell, especially not your husband, dear. Then, if you leave the notes unsealed, and make them *intimate* enough—well, you won't need to worry, she'll find out."

She posed there, excited by the unplanned subtlety of her design.

In the gathering darkness, Mathilde Donoghan regarded her. Then, "You do not want to punish him," she said, picking the *kukri* up again. "You want to save his life. You want to save him because he screwed you when you first moved in."

Mona Ramell gasped; she had never thought about the episode in quite those terms; now it was spread before her, naked, unwashed. "But, Tilda! Honey! We-we've *discussed* all that!"

Mrs. Donoghan stood up. Her voice, out of her twisting mouth, was still a monotone. "You bitch. You soft, white bitch. Because I've stood for it for all these years, do you think I can't feel anything? Listen, I *married* Donoghan. We married in the Church. All right, he's no damn' good. But does that mean I got to be like him and you? you and your goddam itchy crotch. That's what *he* said—only he wasn't so polite. And now you want me to go out and lay some guy, so all of us can all be just alike. You think my doing that would send him back to *you?*" She was rigid now, *kukri* in one hand, scabbard in the other, trembling. "I'll never do it. I'll never give my marriage up like that. You hear? And *she* shan't have him. Tonight I'll give him one more chance. I'll tell him. He's got to throw her *out*. And then—then if he won't—" She paused. Her nostrils flared. She drove the *kukri* back into its sheath. "And now get out. Get out, *you!*"

Tears ran down from Mona Ramell's violet lids over her wide, white cheeks. She stood there, blubbering.

"Get out!"

She stumbled backwards, turned, and fled as she had come, her spike heels taking her as silently as they had brought her in. As the door closed to behind her, far-away lightning forked the air; the summer storm clouds hung low and heavily, athirst for thunder; and, from the room below, the rich, high laughter of the Gypsy woman welled, soared, and died again.

For several minutes, as though rooted there, Mrs. Donoghan remained on her feet. Then, slowly, she sat down, returned the *kukri* to the scuttle, set her clasped hands sedately in her lap, and began her wait.

Sometimes, as the night hours wore on, she rose and walked around the shop, staring from the windows into the leaden darkness that surrounded her, thinking her thoughts and listening to the sounds. Occasionally, remembering Mona Ramell, she tiptoed to the door, turned the knob, peered out. But always the hall was empty, and then she would return and sit again.

It was after three when Donoghan returned. His tread shook the wooden steps that led to the shop's street door. Swearing, he fumbled his key into the lock, turned it clumsily, pushed the door open. His wife could tell that he was drunk, tired out, and ugly. Six feet from the doorway, she confronted him.

In the pale light of the distant streetlamp, he saw the wavering pallor of her face. "Hey, what the hell?" he grunted, to himself; then, reaching back a hand, he found the switch. "For Chris'sake, what *you* want?"

She said, without inflection, "This is my house. You bought it with my money. From my mother, who the Gypsies killed." Sharply her voice rose. "You can have all the women that you want. But this one—*no*. I will not let you keep this Gypsy here."

Donoghan said nothing whatsoever. He took one of her wrists in each of his two hands and forced her to her knees. Then, so swiftly that she had no time even for a cry of protest, he hit her, one great backhanded blow across the mouth that sent her crashing down, knocking the scuttle over with its load, to fall against his chair and an adjoining cabinet. Growling, he stared at her for a moment as she lay there half stunned, broken glass around her, blood starting to ooze down from her ruptured lips.

Mona Ramell, listening intently behind her darkened, half-inch-open door far down the hall, heard not the blow but its result; she heard the sound of Donoghan's hard, heavy footsteps as he left the shop; finally, long after he had entered his apartment, she heard his wife get up, and rearrange the fallen things around her, and softly, quietly, come down the hall to bed. Then, having wiped her own tear-ringed eyes, smiling a momentary, secret smile, she at last closed her door.

Jim Donoghan could be completely charming, when he wanted to or when instinct told him that it would be worthwhile. Something in his cruel hammer of a mind was naturally attuned to people; almost invariably, it told him what they wanted him to say, to think, to be; and chameleon-like, he would oblige them, echoing their interests and admirations, his manner, his intonation, his choice of words shaping spontaneously to suit his purposes. Or, if the person happened to be someone weaker for whom he had no use, someone despised, then his brutality would drive as quickly to make the deepest wound. It was a useful talent. Often it had enabled him to appraise objects about which he knew nothing whatsoever from the informed reactions of collectors, of other dealers, who wanted them—to put on extemporaneous shows of *expertise* just by avoiding pitfalls and volleying back the shreds of information served at him. Because of it, with few exceptions, he had kept the friends and customers he wished to keep, and had gathered only unimportant, helpless enemies. Only when he was deeply drunk did it become first erratic, then inoperative. Scarcely aware of it himself, he trusted it implicitly.

Next morning, shaved, showered, breakfasted, he opened up the shop at his accustomed hour, eleven o'clock. For a few minutes, he stood outside the door, watching the last few scattered clouds drift through the sky, stretching to let the rain-washed sunlight warm him. Massive, big-bellied, pink-cheeked under his thick white hair, he seemed the soul of geniality. Only his eyes, examined very carefully, betrayed him; they were a shark's eyes, small and bluish-gray, flat, merciless.

He yawned. He flexed the stevedore muscles of his arms. He scratched the still-red thatch of hair at the open neck of his Hawaiian-flowered sports-shirt. When the postman brought him up his mail, remarking that it was real fishin' weather, he offered cheerfully to take his route so he could go out to the kelp-beds after yellowtail. And when the man enquired how his Mrs. was, he winked and said that she'd gone back to bed—it was that time of the month.

The postman said his wife had just got over it; with her it always lasted pretty near a week.

Donoghan laughed at him. "Lucky they don't all have the rag on the same time," he said. "We'd be out chasing sheep!"

Then, still chuckling, he went back in, opened his mail, threw most of it away, and made his half-dozen morning calls to buyers, sellers, and upholsterers, interrupting them only to sell a cleverly repaired Imari bowl to a dental surgeon's wife for three times its worth. By the time Ambejian came, at ten past twelve, he was already in his chair, the chessmen all arrayed in front of him.

Sarkis Ambejian was gaunt, with enormous bones. There was no weakness in him anywhere, but he disturbed nothing in his passage; no woman startled, no beast bared its teeth, no bird awakened. His strength, having won all its battles, had no need for more. Donoghan liked him a little, hated him frequently, and grudgingly respected him.

"Well, you're on time, anyhow," grunted Donoghan.

Ambejian's great, hard face smiled slightly, softly. "Always I am on time, Jim," he answered, folding himself down into the chair, placing his vast hands on the table-top, relaxed and still. His long accustomed glance took in the marks of anger and of recent drunkenness, added the scraped, swollen knuckles; and instantly he knew what had occurred. "And Madame?" he asked politely. "How is she?"

For a moment, Donoghan cursed him with his eyes. Then his glance dropped, to those hands formed by a lifetime of striving against rugs—tying their tight knots from dawn to dusk as a boy in Constantinople, stretching them, sewing them, washing, rolling, wrestling them. Saying nothing, he shuffled a white pawn and a black, held out his hands.

Ambejian picked the black. Donoghan opened. They played, a bold and quite unsound development of the Queen's Gambit, the sort of thing one might expect from players of imagination and intelligence who wouldn't bother to read books on chess.

Sarkis Ambejian made his moves slowly, deliberately, enjoying them. But under the surface of his mind, he thought of his own undeviating loyalty to wife and church, and asked himself, *Why do I come here to play chess with this man? Often I beat him. Sometimes he beats me. When I have beaten him too often, I arrange that he will win. I am his friend, but is he mine? No, I do not think so. He is his own friend—that is all. I hope he has not hurt her very much.*

He knew, of course, that the Gypsy was involved. Donoghan had bragged to him already of her endowments and accomplishments, and he himself had often heard Mathilde relate the story of her mother's death. Now he said no word, for life, he knew, was full of tragic happenings from which —as from the Sultan's soldiers pillaging a street—men of good sense must stand aside.

Silently, in the sweet sunlight, the game went on. In fifteen minutes, Donoghan was two pawns up. His mood brightened; he began to joke and boast, secretly planning a knight sacrifice to gain at least a rook and one more pawn. Then suddenly the little silver bell pealed on its spring above the opening door.

Donoghan's fingers halted on his king; his face assumed the look, half hunger, half suspicion, that signaled his appraisal of a customer. Then he relaxed again; grunted in mock disgust, "Oh, Jesus Christ—the fuzz."

The plainclothesman was young, dark and plump. The hardness his job required was beneath the surface, showing itself only when it was needed. He winked at Donoghan, "Hi, Jim. How's the tradin' post?" And then his voice warmed as, for a moment, he let his hand rest on Ambejian's shoulder. "How're you doing, Uncle Beje? How's everything at home?" He had lived next door to the Ambejians, played with their kids, gone to the same schools, dated their two daughters once in a while. Even as they exchanged small news of friends and families, Ambejian could feel Donoghan, across the table, stiffen at the difference in the policeman's tone.

Donoghan picked up a pawn. "Well, what can I do for you, boy?" he said. "No Patersons today, no flintlock duelers. No guns *at* all."

Colhoun had one knee on a chair. He folded his arms over its back and smiled. "It's not my gun-collecting day," he answered. "Jim, I'm here on business."

Donoghan's brows lowered. "Godalmighty! What'd I do now—buy a stolen pisspot?"

Colhoun gestured downwards with a thumb. "It's that Gypsy sign. The Captain says it's got to go."

The pawn fell. "What you mean it's got to go? Why tell me? What the hell—you think I look like Madame Zelda?"

"I think you look like Madame Zelda's boy friend."

Donoghan gripped the chair arms. His face flushed, but neither Ambejian nor the policeman missed the cold instant of evaluation before he spoke. "No goddam punk cop's going to tell me—"

Colhoun's expression did not change. "Listen, Donoghan. The Captain's doing you a favor. This isn't 1925—there's a city ordinance. You want us to just come and pick her up?"

"Ah, *crap*," said Donoghan. "She's got to make a living, doesn't she?"

"She'll get by. She can call herself a spiritual adviser, maybe a psychological consultant, put an ad in Personals— that's what they mostly do." He stood abruptly, grinning. "Come off it, Jim. How many guys are making out as good as you? I wish *I* was. Let's get this over with. Take me on down and we'll meet the lady."

Donoghan accepted the compliment to his virility. Grumbling, he hoisted himself to his feet. "Okay, we'll go below. Beje, you watch the shop."

They said nothing to each other as they walked down the steps and the few feet to the apartment door. Donoghan knocked—a personal, prearranged tattoo. A woman's voice called something unintelligible. There were steps, the door opened, and Madame Zelda stood before them.

She was a startling sight. Gypsy she perhaps was, but she seemed darker, even more exotic, as though harking back to her race's ancient origins. She wore a great and complex necklace of gold coins, and gold coin earrings. Otherwise there was no hint of Romany attire. Her jet black hair was

piled high in a strange modern hairdo. Her face and figure
were those of a temple dancer on a Hindu frieze: the nose
aquiline, broad nostriled; the dark red lips too coarse. Her
sequinned, blue-black blouse, her silver stretch-pants, fitted
breasts, belly, buttocks like another skin. On her naked feet,
she wore scuffed golden slippers with high heels. She flashed
a welcome with her eyes, her teeth.

Colhoun tried not to show astonishment. He stared at her
intense, pneumatic body. *Boy, can she carry weight, this
girl!* he thought. *It'll take even more than Donoghan to ride
her to a frazzle.*

Donoghan kissed her half-open mouth. Then they walked
into a living-room typical of furnished rentals, its papered
walls, carpet, pictures, miscellaneous furniture all without
character. Beside the window stood a Mission table with a
soiled cloth, a frilled lamp on a pseudo-Chinese pottery base,
a crystal ball, a deck of cards. On the day-bed, propped
against a cushion, lay a limp rabbit-doll, hideously pink-
cheeked, with long eyelashes and red rosebud mouth—half
beast, half baby. Next to it, Pete was stretched out, watching
the TV, a lumpy boy, big with overweight, dark and sullen
under his coarse, curly hair.

Donoghan switched his program off. "Beat it, kid," he
ordered.

Pete glowered for a moment; then a peremptory gesture
from his mother sent him on his way.

"Meet Danny Colhoun," Donoghan said.

"He is your friend?" Her eyes and smile flashed; she held
out her hand.

"Known him for years." Donoghan's voice was jocular
again. "A real keen cat, Zell. Without his handcuffs nobody'd
ever guess he was Sergeant Fuzz."

Colhoun took her hand. It did not move; it did not close.
He felt the suddenness of its rigidity, as though a handcuff
had just closed around her wrist. Her expression did not
change; it froze.

While he spoke politely about being glad to meet her,
his mind, well programmed, shuffled the possibilities. Her origins? Her record. Her intentions? He released her hand. He
sat. A Gypsy? Her kid looked more like he had something
else besides. Most likely she was a Gypsy, outcast from her
tribe. That could be bad. That could mean she was alone
against the world—a world of stupid women just waiting for
the pigeon drop, of married men horny enough to fall into a

blackmail trap. He thought of Donoghan getting blackmailed and almost laughed aloud.

He had intended only to crack a joke or two, make sure she took the sign down, and get on to his next assignment. Now, automatically, he started asking questions. Where was she from? And before that? Married? Okay, where was he now? Routine stuff.

At every question, he saw her glance at Donoghan, react ever so slightly to his infinitesimal signals; and he felt Donoghan's resentment rising sullenly, held in check only by the threat of his authority. Her background was unclear; she had been somewhere in the Middle West, before that in Canada; before that she had lived down in Brownsville, Texas, for a year or two, and on the Border generally. Was she a U.S. citizen? She told him that she was, born near Elizabeth, New Jersey.

Colhoun hesitated. Temporarily, he shelved the question of whether he ought to mention her to Immigration. He rose, stretched, grinned. "Okay," he said. "I'll tell the Captain you've got the sign out. No sweat. Well, I'd best get on my horse. Nice meeting you." He turned to Donoghan. "You coming, Jim?"

"No."

"Have fun," Colhoun said, closing the apartment door behind him. He went off whistling to his car, thinking that after this Donoghan ought to give him a real break on the next cap-and-ball Colt that came along.

Donoghan did not follow for twenty minutes. He poured himself two quarter-tumblers full of bourbon, gave the Gypsy woman some long kisses and a quick rubdown, warned her against talking to anyone but him, and finally went upstairs.

He listened to Ambejian's account of who had come and gone almost without comment, and resumed his play. Ambejian beat him easily. Donoghan sent for Pete to run out for a sandwich, and ate it over their second game, raging at Dan Colhoun for a goddam narrow-minded fink cop. Ambejian looked and listened, and saw him struggling in the strait, blank-walled prison of his soul, and beat him again very badly. At four they parted, as they often had, with scarcely a goodbye.

Sarkis Ambejian observed, as he left the stairs, that the sign was gone, and he thought that this was good.

Later, when she came home from work, Mona Ramell saw it too. Although it dulled the edge of her anxiety, she hungered after what had happened in her absence, and knew that there was no way she could ask.

Mathilde Donoghan did not see it until the morning after. Then, for a moment only, her heart sang.

Every summer, Mona Ramell took two weeks vacation from her job as drapery supervisor at Holzheimer's Department Store, and rode the Greyhound up the coast to Pismo Beach, where she had an aunt, a Mrs. Prewett, who ran an auto court. It was exactly that, built in the early 'twenties before the term *motel* was born, and its string of pink stucco cabins was patched and puttied, streaked and stained. Nowadays it drew the overflow from its more prosperous and pretentious neighbors. To Miss Ramell, it represented a release. She looked forward to bickering with her aunt, to the stream of life in and out of the ten cabins, to the men she sometimes met, and to the eventual independence which would be hers when her aunt died and she inherited.

Her trip was still three weeks away, and she lived the greater part of those weeks anguished and apprehensive about what might occur, afraid that it might happen while she wasn't there, tempted more than once to try and change her dates. She had learned soon enough that the Gypsy had not vanished with her sign, that Donoghan still went to her— but that was all she learned. For ten days or more, Mathilde Donoghan avoided her completely, pretending not to hear her on the one occasion when she tried to speak, pretending not to see her in the hall. She thought of questioning Donoghan, of going down to see the Gypsy and have her fortune told, dismissed both notions as imprudent. As far as she could see, things had come back to normal. There were no further sounds of violence in the night.

Then, after nearly a fortnight had elapsed, Mrs. Donoghan began to speak to her again. A small, cold smile, a cold good morning—enough to lull her fears and to dispel her awful feeling of exclusion. A few days more, and they were once again conversing—a little more stiffly, a little artificially, for there was that one vital subject that neither touched.

Finally, only a day or two before she was to leave, Miss Ramell noticed suddenly that something really interesting was going on. For the first time, Mathilde Donoghan's nails were now bright red. For the first time, she wasn't wearing a brassiere under her tight blouse, and her firm nipples stood out assertively. For the first time since the Gypsy came, she sang again. She sang the songs of Provence still, but they no longer were the songs of childhood. Though Miss Ramell could not understand their language, she recognized that they were songs of love and hate, of triumph and tragedy. When twice in quick succession she saw Mathilde whispering to Pete, giving him money, obviously sending him on errands, she knew at once what had occurred.

"Well," she said, powdering herself before her mirror after her bath, "she's followed my advice! I'd like to see his face when he finds out! I wonder who she's found?" She raised her breasts a little, admired them. Luxuriously, savoring Donoghan's humiliation, she ticked off in her mind the men they knew. She thought of Mr. Hamm, the C.P.A. renting the top floor front; he spent three or four nights a week with his divorcée in Chula Vista, who didn't want to lose her alimony. In the house, too, there were the *boys,* Mr. Timperman, who wore a blonde toupée and was a decorator, and his roommate, Mr. Vascals, who vaguely studied art; they—she giggled—didn't count. There were men living at Mrs. Weatherbleak's, two houses down, and men who came and went, and friends of Donoghan's. There was Ambejian.

The idea grew on her. While she dressed, she fondled it, turning it over, discovering bright new facets of seeming pertinence. Ambejian could speak French. She'd heard them talking it together. She'd heard Mathilde tell laughingly how, when he spoke it, all his other accents were obscured by the persisting accent of Marseilles, near where she'd come from. Besides, he was a big, tall man, like Donoghan, like Uncle Léonard. And then there was his wife: Mrs. Ambejian was huge and fat and dark, with untidy half-gray hair, plum-colored lips, and swollen ankles. She was nobody's sex symbol, certainly. The chances were they hadn't been together in a bed for years.

Considering all these points, Mona Ramell dressed and went out to the Chinese restaurant for dinner. She came home, packed her things, and finally slept. When she awakened, beautifully refreshed, suspicion in her mind had swelled to certainty. On the way to the bus depot, she stopped off at Ambejian's shop, talking too much, pretending to look at Persian runners for her aunt, turning the conversation a little shrilly to drop hints, then darting sudden sidelong glances to trap any involuntary betrayal on his face. She had him show her fourteen rugs—the last half-dozen at her insistence and reluctantly—and finally left, no wiser than before but doubly reinforced in her conviction. She left Sarkis Ambejian dismayed and angry, suspecting that somehow he was being embroiled in Donoghan's unclean private life but uncertain how, and thoroughly disliking her; and all the way, as the bus sped up Highway 101, she played the situation over to herself, from that first night when she and Mathilde Donoghan had listened to the insulting sounds beneath their feet, to this last interview when—she was sure—Ambejian had shown all the signs of guilt and the resentment born of it.

That night, over their TV dinners, she told her aunt about it. Then afterwards, during commercials or when the screen failed to hold their interest, they picked it over carefully; and the shrewd old woman, pouring out white port, agreed that certainly Ambejian must be the man. "Ramona honey," she declared in her worn Middlewestern voice, "even if she was raised in a convent she *is* French. They're not like *us;* they know their way around in all these things just naturally. That's why she picked her husband's friend—there's nothing makes a man more jealous, dear. Besides, you'd never guess it, but those Armenians are very strongly sexed."

They shared the story, the wine, the TV with several of Mrs. Bobsie Prewett's closest cronies, all in the same business or retired from it, who dropped in. The evening, thoroughly successful, set the tone of Mona Ramell's whole vacation. Now that she was no longer in the dark, her fears had vanished; she could enjoy each retelling, each speculation, every new picture of what was going on that her imagination produced for her. Twice, she picked up men—or *met* them, anyway—and her aunt, as always, said nothing to her, not even on the way to church on Sunday morning. And even when the second time—he was a cemetery sales manager from near Oceanside, who knew some people whom she'd met—she woke up naked in her half-empty, disordered bed, and found a twenty-dollar bill folded into her highball glass—even then she did not feel, as she would otherwise have done, that it was anything but complimentary. She, she herself, had set the course of what was happening four hundred miles away; she was the prime mover, no longer just a passive instrument of forces out of her control. She savored Donoghan's humiliation in advance, vague where its precise nature was concerned, but certain now that it was preordained.

She shone. All her Aunt Bobsie's guests commented on how clever her ideas about it were, especially when her aunt had told them, in *strictest* confidence, about a few of her affairs. They said politely that, well, you had to meet the world on its own level to really understand it, didn't you? They listened to her every word attentively, applauded, exchanged their winks and heavy sidelong glances when they could, and usually, blind to the mirror-image of their own frustrations, envied her. They even gave a party for her the night before she left; and all during the long ride back she alternated between remembering all of this and imagining what had happened in her absence. For her, it was a very pleasant ride indeed.

Mona Ramell returned on the Sunday. She took a taxi from the depot up the hill. Ordinarily, she would have let it turn the corner to the front door, but she saw that Donoghan was on his shop porch, absorbing the last late warmth of the setting sun, and so she told the driver to stop there. Opening the window, she called out, "Hello! See, I'm back!"

She was a little disappointed to see him grin, to see no signs of anguish on his face. "All in one piece?" he shouted back.

She blushed; once, long ago, it had been part of a private joke between the two of them.

"Come on back when you've dumped your stuff—I'll buy the beer."

She accepted eagerly, gestured to the driver to go on, overtipped him as he let her out, and delayed only long enough in her apartment to freshen up a bit. Then she went down the hall, hearing and seeing nothing of Mathilde, and entered the shop by the back door. Donoghan had already brought and opened up two cans of beer. He gave her one, indicating a rosewood love seat, new since she'd been gone. She sat.

"Well, Mothers for Morality!" he said, lifting his can.

They drank. They smiled at one another; he from the comfort of his slippered feet, his slouching body; she from the sharp imperative to know what she herself had brought about.

"I—I didn't see Mathilde," she said. "I—hope she's well?"

"She's doing fine," he answered. "She's gone to church. Late Mass."

"*This* late?" Miss Ramell asked.

"Yeah. They been doing it since that new guy got in. John the Umpty-ump—the one that died. Anyhow, she's been

hanging round the church a lot. Lot more'n she used to do."
He drank his beer, and chuckled deeply, a muted belly-laugh.
"This time, I guess she's maybe getting something to confess
worth listening to. She's got herself a boy friend."

Mona Ramell tasted it. She savored every word of it
again. She drew her breath in hungrily, and licked her lips.
Her smile exposed her panoply of flat, white teeth. "Ambejian!" she whispered. "I—I *knew* it—it's Ambejian!"

For an instant, he only looked at her. Then the belly-laugh
broke out; he shook with it; it shook the room. He reached
and grasped her thigh, high up. "You're off your rocker," he
exclaimed, still quaking. "Godalmighty, Beje doesn't savvy
what a woman's for, except his wife. You don't think Tilda'd
try to work on that old thug? Christ, when I said 'boy
friend,' I meant *boy*. She's making after Pete."

"Pete?" said Mona Ramell stupidly, as all the stage-sets of
the world began to fall around her ears. "Wh-who's Pete?"

"*Pete!* Zell's kid. What's wrong with you?"

She dropped her beer can; it leaked its final yellow tea-
spoonful onto the naked floor. "But, *Jim*—" She forgot her
comments to Mathilde three weeks before; her voice grew
shrill. "She *can't*. He's just a—a *child!*"

"Don't kid yourself," laughed Donoghan. "That kid can
get a hard-on like a horse." His fingers began to knead the
flesh within their grasp. "She's not got much of anywhere
yet," he said. "He's sort of scared. All she's been doing is
buying him a lot of girlie magazines. He takes 'em in the
john—boy, does he have himself a ball! You can hear him
in the living-room. But lately she's been feeling around a
little more. I'll give you even money she's had her finger in
his fly." Again the chuckle came. "Lolito, that's what I call
him—Lolito, get it?"

Mona Ramell looked at him in utter disbelief. Her first
reaction had been simple shock. Then the swift thought had
crossed her mind that Mathilde Donoghan had been more
subtle in applying her idea than she herself; wouldn't any
man feel his manhood slighted if his wife cheated on him
with a pimply kid? The answer, now, was plain before her.
Donoghan didn't give a damn.

"*Jim!*" she cried out. "You *can't*. You can't just let her do
it. He—he's a minor. What'll his *mother* say? You've simply
got to *stop* it, Jim!"

Donoghan's joviality dissolved. "What's wrong with you?
She'll make a man of him. It's how the French do things—the

married women get the kids broke in. Hell! She'll maybe have some fun, and while he's at it she'll be off our backs. Zell feels like I do. Jesus, the first time in twenty years she's not been ridin' me—you think I'm going to stick my oar in? You're nuts."

It's wrong! It's wrong! It's wrong! screamed Mona Ramell's mind. The sense of wrongness inundated her, as vast and undefined as a tsunami on a moonless night. "You—*you can't!*" she said.

Donoghan's fingers bit into her thigh, his splayed thumb pulling at the pubic hairs under her girdle's edge.

Mouth working, she jerked back. "She—she'll *kill* you, Jim!"

His hand pursued her. "Chris' sake," he grunted, "you sleep around the way you want. Don't try to screw things up for me." Then suddenly he shouted, *"Beat it, you dimwit! Go out and find yourself a life to lead!"*

His hand released her. Slowly, uncertainly, she stood. She tottered for an instant on her high, sharp heels. Fear, outrage, insult—beneath all these she recognized the justice of his thrust, his cold exposure of her nothingness.

She left, edging around his outstretched feet, backing away from him, silently, biting her lower lip. At the door, she turned and fled, rushed through the dreadful shadows of the hall and through her door, locked and bolted it.

Behind her, Donoghan belched thunderously, and opened up another can of beer.

At first, Mathilde Donoghan seemed unaware that Mona Ramell had returned, that she had ever been away. Immersed in her preoccupation, her design, she moved as though only she herself had any true identity, conferring it by virtue of her own intensity on Pete, on Donoghan, and on the Gypsy woman unseen beneath her feet. She cooked, she cleaned, she dusted in the shop; each day she went to Mass—but every moment she could spare was dedicated to the seduction of the boy.

It was a strange, and not an easy task. Not only was he obviously afraid; self-love consumed him, turning his hungers inward with the assistance of his fear. In the beginning, when he was simply running errands and when she started giving him the magazines, he would snatch them from her like a starved cur snapping dangerous meat and almost run for the locked haven of the downstairs bathroom—which Donoghan, guffawing, called his lovenest. Presently, though, he began to hesitate, to listen to her whispered words about his size and strength, to tell her how he thought of girls, to let her tense, gentle hand guide his own, first simply round her waist then to the mystery of her breasts, where it could touch the warm excitements of her heart. She did not talk to him of sex directly. She suggested nothing. She praised him, and she listened, a woman more than of his mother's age with whom, he gradually discovered, he could discuss matters banned by the mother-son relationship. His body first learned that she was more than that. One day it told him suddenly that she was sweet and naked underneath her housecoat, reddening his dark face, sending him running off, magazines held concealingly in front of him. One night it brought her to him in a dream, a spasm of swift hunger and white thighs, her mouth on his, a too-abrupt fulfillment. He wakened writhing in it. He did not dare go upstairs for nearly two full days. Then, when she summoned him, he almost crept to her—and, while they spoke, coarsely and clumsily kissed her on the lips, holding his loins away from her so that she might not be too angered by his readiness.

She felt his fear and shame and selfishness, and used her weapons unobtrusively: her knowledge of his need, his body's knowledge of where that need could readily be filled, propinquity.

Donoghan kidded her about it, friendly and almost sympathetic now. How was Lolito making out? he'd ask occasionally, usually when he had stamped upstairs at two or three A.M. It was a quiddity of his that with the Gypsy woman he never stayed the night, as though the ceremony of his coming home and waking up his wife was somehow necessary to the affair. Then he would ask his questions; and she, torn from the surcease of her dreams, would wink at him deliberately out of the dead cavern of her eyes, smile, toss her head, and answer that the kid was maybe sort of scared —but what could you expect? As he came to bed, Donoghan would tell her how *he* could have been expected to perform when he had been that age, and what a slob Pete's father must have been, because he sure as hell didn't take after his ma. And Mathilde, turning her back to him, would try to sleep again.

During this month-long culmination of her courtship, she was indeed aware of Mona Ramell's ghostly, brief intrusions into the edges of her busy world. The after-supper encounters in the hall, the weekend blunderings (covered by giggles and hysterical apologies as though they really had been unintentional) into her moments of intimacy with Pete—she ignored all of these, counting them only in the archives of her mind. It was only when from being the pursuer she changed inevitably to the pursued, when—as she had planned so carefully—she found herself warding off Pete's importunities —only then did she once more present Miss Ramell with a role.

She chose a Saturday when Donoghan, taking the Gypsy with him, had gone off on a buying trip up La Jolla way. She knocked lightly on Miss Ramell's door at ten o'clock, and mentioned that they hadn't been seeing much of one another, and how she missed their talks—and maybe Mona could have lunch with her? at noon? She'd fix a salad and a casserole, and set a table in the patio, by the french windows so that she wouldn't have to close the shop.

Miss Ramell looked at her, at her long crimson nails and demanding breasts. She looked into her eyes and felt the unrelenting claws of her intensity, and knew that something dark was hovering over them. She was afraid now, with a new, cold, and terrible fear. But she did not dare refuse; she smiled and simpered, and said she'd simply love to come.

At noon, Mathilde admitted her into the shop, squeezing her hand, murmuring cheerful unimportances, leading her out past Donoghan's huge chair, out to the sunlight and the summer breeze. The table was of wrought iron with a thin marble top, pretty with Haviland set out on soft blue Guatemalan linens; the casserole, on its electric warmer, sent out a message about tender chicken, herbs, mushrooms, and white wine—a message which Miss Ramell's cold nostrils scarcely noticed.

She ate mechanically. Mechanically, she drank her glass of chilled Chablis, ate her dessert, sipped at her demitasse, and listened to Mathilde chattering about the little things of life—who had bought what, who had moved in or out of Mrs. Weatherbleak's, what was on special at the Safeway Store. She listened, each nerve, each tendon tightening for the blow.

It finally came. Mathilde replaced her cup precisely in its little saucer. "How few real friends we have," she said. Her eyes were hard and bright. "Friends like you, Mona dear." She paused; the heavy silence stood between them there. She laughed. "When I was small, there was a Sister in the convent who took care of me, Sister Thérèse her name was. She used to lecture me against the world, against the people who, well, know their way around, like Donoghan. And I believed her all those years, until you wised me up." She saw Miss Ramell's mouth begin to move, and raised her hand. "Oh, yes you did. You gave me that advice, that I could get myself what he was getting, that I could have as good a time as you or him. God knows what I might of done to him, the way I felt. Maybe—maybe you saved his li—"

She broke off. Mona Ramell's head and eyes had turned involuntarily, to stare an instant at the brass scuttle standing by Donoghan's black chair. Her loose white features left no doubt at all that she recalled the *kukri* lying there.

Mathilde leaned forward. Her voice was harsh and low. "I *sold* it, Mona dear. I couldn't stand to see it still around."

And Mona Ramell, looking in her eyes, knew that she lied.

Then it was like that moment at a séance when, by some accounts, warmth drains abruptly from the circle, from the room, and a chill more than body-deep enters with whatever has arrived.

Mathilde's hand reached out and stroked her arm. "I owe it all to you. To you. I know you know about it, because *he* said he'd told you. This time, for me, it won't be like it was with him. The boy is young and strong; he does not drink. Perhaps he lacks experience, but I shall teach him, I. At that age, dear, imagine it—five times perhaps, just in one night."

Miss Ramell closed her eyes. She swallowed hard. "You—you haven't *yet?*" she whispered finally.

"I've held him off. To—to celebrate. You see"—Mathilde's red nails held Miss Ramell's arm—"the twenty-third's our anniversary. That'll be when I let him first. It's fifteen years since Donoghan remembered even, let alone gave me anything. Well, Pete's an anniversary present from him to me. From me to him. But it's you who really gave him to me—you. I want to thank you, dear."

For an instant, her high, clear laughter rose again, like its own ghost released, before it was cut off.

An hour before, Mona Ramell had lamented her exclusion, her utter impotence. Now she was stamped with quite a new identity: that of one forced to cause without wanting to, without knowing how or why. Her mind rejected the idea of Mathilde and Pete hot in each other's arms in bed,

Mathilde enjoying it. Her mind rejected it, presenting her instead with a much harder certainty—that soon, because of her, Donoghan would be dead.

She withdrew her hands, to keep their trembling from the table-top; the image of the *kukri,* razor-edged, hung there before her eyes. Her tongue licked out around her teeth to wet her lips. "But Tilda, *Pete's a Gypsy!*" she cried out.

Silence fell. Somewhere within its folds, Mathilde remained, answering not a word. A moment passed. Then, without notice, as though nothing serious had been touched upon, she once again was gossiping inconsequentialities.

That was the twentieth, and three short days lay everlastingly ahead. Miss Ramell's mind accepted such simplicities as infidelity and jealous rage, blows struck in anger, the threat of murder in a heat of hate—which she herself could taste through the sharp sauce of ordinary fear. But now the looming brief eternity held something much more deeply, much more darkly born, a vengeance not content with the destruction of its object, but hungry for the torture of its instrument—a vengeance seeking to enmesh her too. She struggled now between the two imperatives: that somehow she must stop Mathilde from killing Donoghan, or else, accepting her unasked responsibility, her guilt, must stand aside and let things take their course. Or, strangely, both.

Actually, she never stated it as clearly as all that. Her mind turned and twisted, darting at false hopes, recoiling from one absurd solution to another. On Sunday, she wasted several dollars on a long distance call to Pismo Beach, to tell her aunt about it and beg advice. She received scant comfort. "It's like I said, Ramona," came her aunt's acid voice, "you're a fool for having got involved. Honey, if something happens and they call the police, you don't know *anything*—you just remember now!"

On Monday afternoon, at work, she suddenly perceived that Donoghan must be persuaded not to go down there to see his Gypsy that one night. This, this, she repeated to herself, *this* was the key. She left the store before it closed and hurried home, to find him sitting monstrous in his chair, among the relics of so many lives, relics which once had spoken to her of old loves and sweet, forgotten scenes and dear nostalgias. Now, all around him, they told her of betrayals and abandonments lost in the night of time; they echoed tears long shed; they breathed the dust and the decay of outworn violences. Seeing them there, she understood the uselessness of what she'd come to say. With a new wrench of terror, she saw that maybe—*maybe* he hadn't even planned to go tomorrow night; that any plea of hers, disastrously, might make him change his mind.

Donoghan greeted her good-humoredly. "Hey, kid, you wanta buy a duck?" He pointed to the table at his side; there the duck stood, a piece of Meissen porcelain, caught by the potter's cheerful eye and hand, complete with duckling brood. "It's Eighteenth Century," he declared, greed working on his face. "I'll sell it for a mint."

She tried to praise it, incoherently; stammered that she had just dropped by, to say hello because she'd—well, she'd just wanted to. She forced herself to make a show of listening to him brag how he had conned another dealer out of it. Finally, twisting wet hands together behind her back, somehow she escaped.

That night she dreamed there was a coffin there, surrounded by a white-faced wall of black-winged nuns, the nuns who long ago had taught Mathilde to cook and sew. They would not let her look inside. Their smooth, immobile faces held her there. *They* knew what she had thought, what she had done. Somewhere behind them a large, old-fashioned radio kept blaring out, "You wanta buy a duck?" and laughing at its own inanity. There was no other sound. Then, from the coffin's middle suddenly, the *kukri* rose, vast, menacing—

She wakened with a cry, sweating, ice-cold. She leaped from bed, made coffee, paced the floor, the dream still riding her, spurring her apprehensions and imaginations. Somehow she struggled through the hour till dawn, then heated up a butterhorn and ate a third of it. At seven-thirty, when the switchboard opened, she called the store and left a message that she had migraine and would not be in. She took two sleeping pills and slept till noon. At one o'clock, in desperation, she phoned Ambejian. He listened to her quietly, if resentfully, and, with a sigh, agreed to her request that she come down and tell him everything.

When she arrived, he was in back, sitting cross-legged on his bench, mending a soft, red, ancient carpet from the steppes. He put it down, and rose politely, patiently, doing his best to hide his deep distaste, and brought her up a chair. He heard her out, saying not a word, ignoring sensibly her punctuating tears. He asked some questions; sat silent for a while, eyes closed, his features hard with thought. Eventually he said, "I know that much of what you say is true. Perhaps all of it is—even about the boy. But what would Mrs. Donoghan reply if you explained it to her as you have to me? What do you think Jim Donoghan would say?"

Her silence answered him.

"Yes," he continued, "*that* is what they would say—and that is also what they'd say to me. Mind your own business, old Ambejian. Go back and darn your rugs!" He picked his needle up. "There are some people, Mona Ramell, you can argue with. There are others who can go one way only. Donoghan is like that; maybe he now has also made his wife the same. What can we do?"

"There—there must be *something*," Mona Ramell screamed. "The boy's a minor! It's against the law."

Ambejian brightened. "Then I shall phone my friend, Danny Colhoun. He is a policeman and is very smart in all such things. He will know what to do."

"I—I don't think we ought to bring *them* into this," she tried to argue. "I—well, I mean, it could be so embarrassing for everyone."

Ambejian soothed her, explaining how Colhoun had grown up practically in their home, a member of the family. He called the station and left word with the radio clerk. Then, during the twenty minutes or so they had to wait, he plied his needle and talked to her about the roses he so carefully grew.

Danny Colhoun called out, "Hello, Uncle Beje!" as he came in. He told Miss Ramell that he was glad to meet her, seated himself comfortably on the platform's edge, and lit a cigarette. Uneasily, she felt his young, experienced eyes appraising her, and flushed, tongue-tied momentarily.

With a few quiet questions, Colhoun brought her out of it. Her name was Mona Ramell, with two L's? She lived at Donoghan's, in one of their apartments? She worked downtown? And she had something she wanted help about?

Soon she was voluble again, though with a greater effort at control. The story tumbled from her, and she was not aware how Colhoun's interjected questions focussed it and cut its length in half. Occasionally, he glanced at Ambejian for confirmation of something that she'd said. Finally, he asked them both if Donoghan had ever hinted at being scared, if he or the boy's mother had complained, if anyone besides Miss Ramell had heard Mathilde make threats or seen her making passes at the kid. Seemingly no one had; Ambejian had only heard a nasty crack or two about Mathilde and Pete from Donoghan.

"And cracks from Donoghan don't prove a thing," Colhoun remarked, smiling at Mona Ramell. Without warning, then, he asked, "Lady, are you mixed up with this in any way?"

"Certainly *not!*" she answered—and knew at once that she had been too shrill. She dropped her eyes.

Colhoun exchanged glances with Ambejian, and shrugged. He asked her, "What do you want that we should do?"

"You've got to stop him!" she exclaimed. "He *can't* go there tonight. You've got to make Mathilde lay off Pete! If you don't stop them, there's going to be a—a crime! Don't you *see?*"

Colhoun stood up. "You want to come down to the station and sign a complaint?"

She hesitated for a moment. It wasn't like she had a record, really. Besides, she hadn't been involved with Donoghan for years and years. But— She stood there silent, staring at the floor, unpleasant possibilities flooding through her mind.

"They usually don't," said Dan Colhoun aside. "I'm sorry, Uncle Beje, but there's no real evidence. There's nothing we can do." Briefly, they talked about their families. He told Miss Ramell again that he was sorry, and suggested that, if she was right about the situation, it was one she ought to stay well clear of.

Mona Ramell did not return to her apartment until nine o'clock. Ambejian, touched by her despair, had tried to reassure, to comfort her. He'd even promised that, when he could, he'd talk to Donoghan. Neither comforted nor reassured, she had wandered the downtown streets for aimless hours, moving from shop window to shop window without seeing what they held. She had taken in a Swedish adult movie, hoping that it might take her mind off things, and left it when it was half over, remembering none of it. She had picked up a cup of coffee and a tasteless snack. Only then had the awful certainty of what was now to come drawn her back. She took the bus. She walked on up the hill past the bright windows of the Gypsy's living room. The night was warm, and one of them was open; and, as she passed, the sound of Donoghan's deep laughter floated out to her.

She went around to the front door, unlocked it, and made her cautious way to her apartment, alert for any sounds across the hall. She did not think that Pete would yet have dared to come; she knew that he was frightened of himself and scared of Donoghan. She also knew that guilt and fear would keep him from coming the back way, up through the garden, where Donoghan might hear. She entered her apartment, leaving the door on its chain but open half an inch. She poured herself a highball and, in the darkness, settled down to wait. Within ten minutes, she heard the front door click. She darted to her own, just in time to see Pete passing it on tip-toe. She watched him going down the hall, and knocking softly, fearfully, on Mathilde's door. She saw it open. She caught a flash of bare white flesh, a naked arm, and heard Mathilde's soft laughter as she drew him in. It closed. It sealed them in its silence. Panting, she drew back. She turned her light on, and wondered how to wait.

She thought of the TV, but realized that all its noise would mask the sounds she would be listening for. Then she undressed, decided not to bathe, powdered herself, renewed her makeup, repairing the ruined violet of her eyes. She used deodorants, depilatories. Once, in her frantic preoccupation with herself, she quite forgot the present, and found her glass again reflecting the private smile with which, not long before, she had anticipated torments not her own. The smile died when it was recognized, and the real world swept in on her again. She sat there, wearing gartered stockings, slippers, nothing more. Sometimes, caught by a throb of fear, she'd rise, pace back and forth, listen intently for five minutes, ten; then, scarcely aware of what she did, return to her machine-like admiration of herself. Her hands trembled; the level of her bourbon bottle went down and down; occasionally she closed her eyes and sobbed.

At fourteen minutes after one, she thought she heard a whisper of soft feet go through the hall, but when she reached the door all was empty. Dread filled her. She dressed herself hurriedly, reluctantly, in furred slippers and frothy negligee. She waited. Nothing stirred. She pictured Donoghan returning home, finding the Gypsy boy—as Mathilde meant him to, and—and— Her mind produced a flash of steel, a terrible choking cry—

At three minutes after two, Miss Ramell heard two doors bang shut below, and voices, footsteps. She knew that Donoghan would now be coming home. She ran out through the hall, through the front door, down to the corner and around it, down the hill. When Donoghan reached the steps that led up to the shop, she was already waiting there.

She seized his hands. "Jim!" she cried. "Jim dear—don't go up there! Oh, *please* don't go. She—she's going to kill you, Jim!"

He glared at her. "Oh, crap!" he answered, almost wearily. "Don't you ever learn?" He broke her grip, placed his right hand flat between her breasts, and pushed. She fell away from him, tripping over the low hedge around the little lawn, sprawling into the hydrangeas that grew there.

Donoghan took his key out of his pocket as he went up the steps. The porch light wasn't on, and, muttering, he tried to find the lock. He had forgotten Mona Ramell instantly.

The key went in and turned. He pushed the door open ahead of him. Inside, the light was on.

Mathilde stood there.

Her hair was loose and flowing down her back. She wore a nightgown of virginal white lace, the one which she had worn just once before, on her wedding night. She faced him, her face as smooth and as unlined as any nun's. She held the naked *kukri* in her hand.

Donoghan stopped dead. The color drained abruptly from his cheeks.

"It is our anniversary," she told him, in her light, clear voice. "I have a present for you, Jim."

She took a step towards him. He leaped back. But then she stopped, and dropped the terrible *kukri* at his feet.

It lay there. He saw that it was wet.

And then, with a strange small curtsy, a little whimpering laugh, she danced aside. She did not tell him why—

So that he could pass her. So that he could walk on through the hall to the apartment where they lived.

So that he could look down at the slaughtered thing that lay in their blood-drenched bed.

TOWN WANTED

FREDRIC BROWN

*Whenever I think of this short-short, "Town Wanted,"
I'll always think of Tony Boucher, because it was probably the first story of mine he ever read. It was written
way back when, in 1940, and when I first met Tony a
few years after that, he remembered it well and had
many nice things to say about it. I have a hunch that
it may have been his praise of the story that caused it
to become the second most lucrative story per word
that I have ever written; it was reprinted quite a few
times and was also adapted for radio and later for tele-
vision.*

ON MY WAY IN, I looked into the back room. The boys
were there.

Alderman Higgins had a pile of blue chips in front of him
and was trying to keep his greasy little mug from looking
sap-happy.

Lieutenant Grange was there too. He was half tight. He
had beer spots on the front of his blue uniform shirt. His
hand shook when he picked up the stein.

The alderman looked up and said, "Hi, Jimmy. How's
tricks?"

I gave him a grin and went on upstairs. I pushed on into
the boss's office without knocking.

He looked at me sort of queerly. "Everything go okay?"

"They'll find him when the lake dries up," I told him.
"We won't be around then."

"You covered all the angles, Jimmy?"

"All what angles?" I asked him. "Nobody's going to investigate. A guy won't pay his protection, and Annie Doesn't Live Here Any More. Now the rest of them will lay it on the line."

He took out a handkerchief and wiped the sweat off his bald spot. You could see the guy was squeamish. That's no way to handle things. It would be different, I figured, when I took over.

I sat down and lighted a cigarette. "Listen," I said, "this town is worth twice the take we're getting. Who do we move in on next?"

"We're letting it ride awhile, Jimmy. Things are hot."

I got up and started for the door.

He said softly, "Sit down, Jimmy."

I didn't, but I went back and stood in front of him. "Well?" I asked.

"About the boys you've lined up to buck me, Jimmy. When do you think you're going to take over?"

I guess I'd underestimated him. You can't run rackets and be a shlemiel.

I sat down. "I don't get you, boss," I stalled.

"Let's settle this, Jimmy," he said. There were beads of sweat on his bald spot again and he wiped them off. I kept my yap shut and looked at him. It was his move.

"You're a good guy, Jimmy," he went on. "You've been a big help to me."

There wasn't any malarkey in that. But he was just winding up and I sat back and waited to see what he was going to pitch.

"But six months ago I saw it couldn't last, Jimmy. You got big ideas. This burg isn't large enough for you to stay in second spot. Right?"

I waited for him to go on.

"You think you've bought four of the boys. You've got only two. The other two leveled with me. They're set to gum your works."

That was bad listening. He *did* know; four was right. And I didn't know which two ratted. All right, I thought, this is showdown.

"Go on," I said. "I'm listening."

"You're too ambitious for me, Jimmy. I was satisfied to run the slot machines and the joints. Maybe just a little on the protection societies. You want to run the town. You want to collect taxes. And your trigger finger's too jittery, Jimmy. I don't like killing, except when I have to."

"Lay off the character reading," I told him. "You've called the shots. Add it up."

"You could kill me now, maybe. But you wouldn't get away with it. And you're too smart, Jimmy, to stick your neck out unless it's going to get you something. I'm counting on that. I'm ready for you. You wouldn't get out of here alive. If you did, you'd have to blow. And if you blow, what's it get you?"

I walked over to the window and looked out. He wouldn't draw on me, I knew. Hell, why should he? He held the cards; I could see that now. He'd wised up a little too soon for me.

"You've been a big help, Jimmy," he went on. "I want to break fair with you. In the last year I've made more dough than I'd have made without you. I want you to leave. But I'll give you a stake. Pick a town of your own and work it. Leave me this one."

I kept looking out the window. I knew why he wouldn't bump me. There'd been too many killings; the cops were beginning to take it on the chin. The boss wanted to pull in his horns.

And from his point of view, I could see it all right. He could even drop the protectives. The slots, the joints, the semi-legit stuff paid enough to suit him. He'd rather play safe for a small take. I'm not that way.

I turned and faced him. After all, why not another town? I could do it. If I picked one that was ripe.

"How much?" I asked him.

He named a figure.

And that was that.

You can see now why I'm in Miami. I figured I could use a vacation before I picked out a spot. A swell suite, overlooking the sea. Women, parties, roulette and all that. You can make a big splash here if you're willing to blow a few grand.

But I'm getting restless. I'd rather see it coming in.

I know how I'll start, when I've picked my town. I'll take a tavern for a front. Then I find which politicians are on the auction block. I'll see that the others go out. Money can swing that. Then I bring in torpedoes and start to work.

Coin machines are the quickest dough. You pyramid that into bookie joints, sporting houses and the rest; and when you're strong enough, the protective societies—where the merchants pay you to let them alone. That's the big dough racket, if you're not squeamish. It's big dough because you don't have to put out anything for what you take in.

If you know the angles and work it so you don't have to start liquidating the opposition until you've got control, it's a cinch. And I know the angles.

Plenty of towns would do, but some are easier than others. If you pick one that's ripe, it goes quicker. If you can buy enough of the boys in office, you won't have to get the others out.

I'm looking them over. I'm tired of loafing.

How's your town? I can tell if you answer me a question. Last time there was an election did you really read up both sides of things, with the idea of keeping things on the up and up? Or did you go for the guy with the biggest posters?

Huh? You say you didn't even get to the polls at all?

Pal, that's the town I'm looking for. I'll be seeing you.

THE GENTLEMAN FROM PARIS

JOHN DICKSON CARR

*"The Gentleman from Paris" was written at Mamaro-
neck, New York, in 1949, the hundredth anniversary
of Poe's death; and, somewhat to my surprise, it won
first prize in Ellery Queen's contest the same year. At
that time, so far as I recall, Tony Boucher made no
comment. It was not until the late 1950s—Tony visiting
New York, I shuttling back and forth between England
and America—that he dropped some word of praise for
the story when we met again. "To use Poe as the detective," I said, "seemed a pretty obvious move." "Possibly so," he replied, "and yet sometimes, as those who
laugh at Dr. Watson ought to remember, the obvious
seems obvious only after somebody has done it." I
could have asked for no higher compliment.*

Carlton House Hotel
Broadway, New York
14th April, 1849

MY DEAR BROTHER:

Were my hand more steady, Maurice, or my soul less agitated, I should have written to you before this. *All is safe*: so
much I tell you at once. For the rest, I seek sleep in vain;
and this is not merely because I find myself a stranger and a
foreigner in New York. Listen and judge.

We discussed, I think, the humiliation that a Frenchman

must go to England ere he could take passage in a reliable ship for America. The *Britannia* steam-packet departed from Liverpool on the second of the month, and arrived here on the seventeenth. Do not smile, I implore you, when I tell you my first visit on American soil was to Platt's Saloon, under Wallack's Theatre.

Great God, that voyage!

On my stomach I could hold not even champagne. For one of my height and breadth I was as weak as a child.

"Be good enough," I said to a fur-capped coachman, when I had struggled through the horde of Irish immigrants, "to drive me to some fashionable place of refreshment."

The coachman had no difficulty in understanding my English, which pleased me. And how extraordinary are these "saloons"!

The saloon of M. Platt was loud with the thump of hammers cracking ice, which is delivered in large blocks. Though the hand-coloured gas-globes, and the rose-paintings on the front of the bar-counter, were as fine as we could see at the Three Provincial Brothers in Paris, yet I confess that the place did not smell agreeably. A number of gentlemen, wearing hats perhaps a trifle taller than is fashionable at home, lounged at the bar-counter and shouted. I attracted no attention until I called for a sherry cobbler.

One of the "bartenders," as they are called in New York, gave me a sharp glance as he prepared the glass.

"Just arrived from the Old Country, I bet?" said he in no unfriendly tone.

Though it seemed strange to hear France mentioned in this way, I smiled and bowed assent.

"Italian, maybe?" said he.

This bartender, of course, could not know how deadly was the insult.

"Sir," I replied, "I am a Frenchman."

And now in truth he was pleased! His fat face opened and smiled like a distorted, gold-toothed flower.

"Is that so, now!" he exclaimed. "And what might your name be? Unless"—and here his face darkened with that sudden defensiveness and suspicion which, for no reason I can discern, will often strike into American hearts—"unless," said he, "you don't want to give it?"

"Not at all," I assured him earnestly. "I am Armand de Lafayette, at your service."

My dear brother, what an extraordinary effect!

It was silence. All sounds, even the faint whistling of the gas-jets, seemed to die away in that stone-flagged room. Every man along the line of the bar was looking at me. I was conscious only of faces, mostly with whiskers under the chin instead of down the cheek-bones, turned on me in basilisk stare.

"Well, well, well!" almost sneered the bartender. "You wouldn't be no relation of the *Marquis* de Lafayette, would you?"

It was my turn to be astonished. Though our father has always forbidden us to mention the name of our late uncle, due to his republican sympathies, yet I knew he occupied small place in the history of France and it puzzled me to comprehend how these people had heard of him.

"The late Marquis de Lafayette," I was obliged to admit, "was my uncle."

"You better be careful, young feller," suddenly yelled a grimy little man with a pistol buckled under his long coat. "We don't like being diddled, we don't."

"Sir," I replied, taking my bundle of papers from my pocket and whacking them down on the bar-counter, "have the goodness to examine my credentials. Should you still doubt my identity, we can then debate the matter in any way which pleases you."

"This is furrin writing," shouted the bartender. "*I* can't read it!"

And then—how sweet was the musical sound on my ear!— I heard a voice addressing me in my own language.

"Perhaps, sir," said the voice, in excellent French and with great stateliness, "I may be able to render you some small service."

The newcomer, a slight man of dark complexion, drawn up under an old shabby cloak of military cut, stood a little way behind me. If I had met him on the boulevards, I might not have found him very prepossessing. He had a wild and wandering eye, with an even wilder shimmer of brandy. He was not very steady on his feet. And yet, Maurice, his manner! It was such that I instinctively raised my hat, and the stranger very gravely did the same.

"And to whom," said I, "have I the honour . . . ?"

"I am Thaddeus Perley, sir, at your service."

"Another furriner!" said the grimy little man in disgust.

"I am indeed a foreigner," said M. Perley in English, with an accent like a knife. "A foreigner to this dram-shop. A foreigner to this neighbourhood. A foreigner to—" Here he paused, and his eyes acquired an almost frightening blaze of loathing. "Yet I never heard that the reading of French was so *very* singular in accomplishment."

Imperiously—and yet, it seemed to me, with a certain shrinking nervousness—M. Perley came closer and lifted the bundle of papers.

"Doubtless," he said loftily, "I should not be credited were I to translate these. But here," and he scanned several of the papers, "is a letter of introduction in English. It is addressed to President Zachary Taylor from the American minister at Paris."

Again, my brother, what an enormous silence! It was interrupted by a cry from the bartender, who had snatched the documents from M. Perley.

"Boys, this is no diddle," said he. "This gent is the real thing!"

"He ain't!" thundered the little grimy man, with incredulity.

"He is!" said the bartender. "I'll be a son of a roe (*i.e., biche*), if he ain't!"

Well, Maurice, you and I have seen how Paris mobs can change. Americans are even more emotional. In the wink of an eye hostility became frantic affection. My back was slapped, my hand wrung, my person jammed against the bar by a crowd fighting to order me more refreshment.

The name of Lafayette, again and again, rose like a holy diapason. In vain I asked why this should be so. They appeared to think I was joking and roared with laughter. I thought of M. Thaddeus Perley, as one who could supply an explanation.

But in the first rush towards me M. Perley had been flung backwards. He fell sprawling in some wet stains of tobacco-juice on the floor, and now I could not see him at all. For myself, I was weak from lack of food. A full beaker of whisky, which I was obliged to drink because all eyes were on me, made my head reel. Yet I felt compelled to raise my voice above the clamour.

"Gentlemen," I implored them, "will you hear me?"

"Silence for Lafayette!" said a big but very old man with faded red whiskers. He had tears in his eyes, and he had been humming a catch called "Yankee Doodle." "Silence for Lafayette!"

"Believe me," said I, "I am full of gratitude for your

hospitality. But I have business in New York, business of immediate and desperate urgency. If you will allow me to pay my reckoning . . ."

"Your money's no good here, monseer," said the bartender. "You're going to get liquored-up good and proper."

"But I have no wish, believe me, to become liquored-up! It might well endanger my mission! In effect, I wish to go!"

"Wait a minute," said the little grimy man, with a cunning look. "What *is* this here business?"

You, Maurice, have called me quixotic. I deny this. You have also called me imprudent. Perhaps you are right; but what choice was left to me?

"Has any gentleman here," I asked, "heard of Madame Thevenet? Madame Thevenet, who lives at number 23 Thomas Street, near Hudson Street?"

I had not, of course, expected an affirmative reply. Yet, in addition to one or two snickers at mention of the street, several nodded their heads.

"Old miser woman?" asked a sportive character, who wore chequered trousers.

"I regret, sir, that you correctly describe her. Madame Thevenet is very rich. And I have come here," cried I, "to put right a damnable injustice!"

Struggle as I might, I could not free myself.

"How's that?" asked half a dozen.

"Madame Thevenet's daughter, Mademoiselle Claudine, lives in the worst of poverty at Paris. Madame herself has been brought here, under some spell, by a devil of a woman calling herself . . . Gentlemen, I implore you!"

"And I bet you," cried the little grimy man with the pistol, "you're sweet on this daughter what's-her-name?" He seemed delighted. "Ain't you, now?"

How, I ask of all Providence, could these people have surprised my secret? Yet I felt obliged to tell the truth.

"I will not conceal from you," I said, "that I have in truth a high regard for Mlle. Claudine. But this lady, believe me, is engaged to a friend of mine, an officer of artillery."

"Then what do you *get* out of it? Eh?" asked the grimy little man, with another cunning look.

The question puzzled me. I could not reply. But the bartender with the gold teeth leaned over.

"If you want to see the old Frenchie alive, monseer," said he, "you'd better git." (*Sic*, Maurice). "I hearn tell she had a stroke this morning."

But a dozen voices clamoured to keep me there, though this last intelligence sent me into despair. Then up rose the big and very old man with the faded whiskers: indeed, I had never realised how old, because he seemed so hale.

"Which of you was with Washington?" said he, suddenly taking hold of the fierce little man's neckcloth, and speaking with contempt. "Make way for the nephew of Lafayette!"

They cheered me then, Maurice. They hurried me to the door, they begged me to return, they promised they would await me. One glance I sought—nor can I say why—for M. Thaddeus Perley. He was sitting at a table by a pillar, under an open gas-jet; his face whiter than ever, still wiping stains of tobacco-juice from his cloak.

Never have I seen a more mournful prospect than Thomas Street, when my cab set me down there. Perhaps it was my state of mind; for if Mme. Thevenet had died without a sou left to her daughter: you conceive it?

The houses of Thomas Street were faced with dingy yellow brick, and a muddy sky hung over the chimney-pots. It had been warm all day, yet I found my spirit intolerably oppressed. Though heaven knows our Parisian streets are dirty enough, we do not allow pigs in them. Except for these, nothing moved in the foresaken street save a blind street-musician, with his dog and an instrument called a banjo; but even he was silent too.

For some minutes, it seemed to me, I plied the knocker at number 23, with hideous noise. Nothing stirred. Finally, one part of the door swung open a little, as for an eye. Whereupon I heard the shifting of a floor-bolt, and both doors were swung open.

Need I say that facing me stood the woman whom we have agreed to call Mademoiselle Jezebel?

She said to me: "And then, M. Armand?"

"Madame Thevenet!" cried I. "She is still alive?"

"She is alive," replied my companion, looking up at me from under the lids of her greenish eyes. "But she is completely paralysed."

I have never denied, Maurice, that Mlle. Jezebel has a certain attractiveness. She is not old or even middle-aged. Were it not that her complexion is as muddy as was the sky above us then, she would have been pretty.

"And as for Claudine," I said to her, "the daughter of madame—"

"You have come too late, M. Armand."

And well I remember that at this moment there rose up, in the mournful street outside, the tinkle of the banjo played by the street-musician. It moved closer, playing a popular catch whose words run something thus:

> Oh, I come from Alabama
>   With my banjo on my knee;
> I depart for Louisiana
>   My Susannah for to see.

Across the lips of mademoiselle flashed a smile of peculiar quality, like a razor-cut before the blood comes.

"Gold," she whispered. "Ninety thousand persons, one hears, have gone to seek it. Go to California, M. Armand. It is the only place you will find gold."

This tune, they say, is a merry tune. It did not seem so, as the dreary twanging faded away. Mlle. Jezebel, with her muddy blond hair parted in the middle and drawn over her ears after the best fashion, faced me implacably. Her greenish eyes were wide open. Her old brown taffeta dress, full at the bust, narrow at the waist, rustled its wide skirts as she glided a step forward.

"Have the kindness," I said, "to stand aside. I wish to enter."

Hitherto in my life I had seen her docile and meek.

"You are no relative," she said. "I will not allow you to enter."

"In that case, I regret, I must."

"If you had ever spoken one kind word to *me!*" whispered mademoiselle, looking up from under her eyelids, and with her breast heaving, "one gesture of love—that is to say, of affection—you might have shared five million francs."

"Stand aside, I say!"

"As it is, you prefer a doll-faced consumptive at Paris. So be it!"

I was raging, Maurice; I confess it; yet I drew myself up with coldness.

"You refer, perhaps, to Claudine Thevenet?"

"And to whom else?"

"I might remind you, mademoiselle, that the lady is pledged to my good friend Lieutenant Delage. I have forgotten her."

"Have you?" asked our Jezebel, with her eyes on my face and a strange hungry look in them. Mlle. Jezebel added, with more pleasure: "Well, she will die. Unless you can solve a mystery."

"A mystery?"

"I should not have said mystery, M. Armand. Because it is impossible of all solution. It is an Act of God!"

Up to this time the glass-fronted doors of the vestibule had stood open behind her, against a darkness of closed shutters in the house. There breathed out of it an odour of unswept carpets, a sourness of stale living. Someone was approaching, carrying a lighted candle.

"Who speaks," called a man's voice; shaky, but as French as Mlle. Jezebel's. "Who speaks concerning an Act of God?"

I stepped across the threshold. Mademoiselle, who never left my side, immediately closed and locked the front doors. As the candleglimmer moved still closer in gloom, I could have shouted for joy to see the man whom (as I correctly guessed) I had come to meet.

"You are M. Duroc, the lawyer!" I said. "You are my brother's friend!"

M. Duroc held the candle higher, to inspect me.

He was a big, heavy man who seemed to sag in all his flesh. In compensation for his bald head, the greyish-brown moustache flowed down and parted into two hairy fans of beard on either side of his chin. He looked at me through oval gold-rimmed spectacles; in a friendly way, but yet frightened. His voice was deep and gruff, clipping the syllables, despite his fright.

"And you—" *clip-clip;* the candle-holder trembled—"you are Armand de Lafayette. I had expected you by the steam-packet today. Well! You are here. On a fool's errand, I regret."

"But why?" (And I shouted it at him, Maurice.)

I looked at mademoiselle, who was faintly smiling.

"M. Duroc!" I protested. "You wrote to my brother. You said you had persuaded madame to repent of her harshness towards her daughter!"

"Was that your duty?" asked the Jezebel, looking full at M. Duroc with her greenish eyes. "Was that your right?"

"I am a man of law," said M. Duroc. The deep monosyllables rapped, in ghostly bursts, through his parted beard. He was perspiring. "I am correct. Very correct! And yet—"

"Who nursed her?" asked the Jezebel. "Who soothed her, fed her, wore her filthy clothes, calmed her tempers, endured her interminable abuse? *I* did!"

And yet, all the time she was speaking, this woman kept sidling and sliding against me, brushing my side, as though she would make sure of my presence there.

"Well!" said the lawyer. "It matters little now! This mystery . . ."

You may well believe that all these cryptic remarks, as well as reference to a mystery or an Act of God, had driven me almost frantic. I demanded to know what he meant.

"Last night," said M. Duroc, "a certain article disappeared."

"Well, well?"

"It disappeared," said M. Duroc, drawn up like a grenadier. "But it could not conceivably have disappeared. I myself swear this! Our only suggestions as to how it might have disappeared are a toy rabbit and a barometer."

"Sir," I said, "I do not wish to be discourteous. But—"

"Am I mad, you ask?"

I bowed. If any man can manage at once to look sagging and uncertain, yet stately and dignified, M. Duroc managed it then. And dignity won, I think.

"Sir," he replied, gesturing with the candle towards the rear of the house, "Madame Thevenet lies there in her bed. She is paralysed. She can move only her eyes or partially the lips, without speech. Do you wish to see her?"

"If I am permitted."

"Yes. That would be correct. Accompany me."

And I saw the poor old woman, Maurice. Call her harridan if you like.

It was a square room of good size, whose shutters had remained closed and locked for years. Can one smell rust? In that room, with faded green wall-paper, I felt I could.

One solitary candle did little more than dispel shadow. It burned atop the mantelpiece well opposite the foot of the bed; and a shaggy man, whom I afterwards learned to be a police-officer, sat in a green-upholstered arm-chair by an unlighted coal fire in the fireplace grate, picking his teeth with a knife.

"If you please, Dr. Harding!" M. Duroc called softly in English.

The long and lean American doctor, who had been bending over the bed so as to conceal from our sight the head and shoulders of Madame Thevenet, turned round. But his cadaverous body—in such fashion were madame's head and shoulders propped up against pillows—his cadaverous body, I say, still concealed her face.

"Has there been any change?" persisted M. Duroc in English.

"There has been no change," replied the dark-complexioned Dr. Harding, "except for the worse."

"Do you want her to be moved?"

"There has never been any necessity," said the physician, picking up his beaver hat from the bed. He spoke dryly. "However, if you want to learn anything more about the toy rabbit or the barometer, I should hurry. The lady will die in a matter of hours, probably less."

And he stood to one side.

It was a heavy bed with four posts and a canopy. The bed-curtains, of some dullish-green material, were closely drawn on every side except the long side by which we saw Madame Thevenet in profile. Lean as a post, rigid, the strings of her cotton nightcap tightly tied under her chin, Madame Thevenet lay propped up there. But one eye rolled towards us, and it rolled horribly.

Up to this time the woman we call the Jezebel had said little. She chose this moment again to come brushing against my side. Her greenish eyes, lids half-closed, shone in the light of M. Duroc's candle. What she whispered was: "You don't really hate me, do you?"

Maurice, I make a pause here.

Since I wrote the sentence, I put down my pen, and pressed my hands over my eyes, and once more I thought. But let me try again.

I spent just two hours in the bedroom of Madame Thevenet. At the end of the time—oh, you shall hear why!—I rushed out of that bedroom, and out of number 23 Thomas Street, like the maniac I was.

The streets were full of people, of carriages, of omnibuses, at early evening. Knowing no place of refuge save the saloon from which I had come, I gave its address to a cab-driver. Since still I had swallowed no food, I may have been lightheaded. Yet I wished to pour out my heart to the friends who had bidden me return there. And where were they now?

A new group, all new, lounged against the bar-counter under brighter gaslight and brighter paint. Of all those who smote me on the back and cheered, none remained save the ancient giant who had implied friendship with General Washington. *He,* alas, lay helplessly drunk with his head near a sawdust spitting box. Nevertheless I was so moved that I took the liberty of thrusting a handful of bank-notes into his pocket. He alone remained.

Wait, there was another!

I do not believe he remained there because of me. Yet M. Thaddeus Perley, still sitting alone at the little table by the pillar, with the open gas-jet above, stared vacantly at the empty glass in his hand.

He had named himself a foreigner; he was probably French. That was as well. For, as I lurched against the table, I was befuddled and all English had fled my wits.

"Sir," said I, "will you permit a madman to share your table?"

M. Perley gave a great start, as though roused out of thought. He was not sober: this I saw. Indeed, his shiver and haggard face were due to lack of stimulant rather than too much of it.

"Sir," he stammered, getting to his feet," I shall be— I shall be honoured by your company." Automatically he opened his mouth to call for a waiter; his hand went to his pocket; he stopped.

"No, no, no!" said I. "If you insist, M. Perley, you may pay for the second bottle. The first is mine. I am sick at heart, and I would speak with a gentleman."

At these last words M. Perley's whole expression changed. He sat down, and give me a grave courtly nod. His eyes, which were his most expressive feature, studied my face and my disarray.

"You are ill, M. de Lafayette," he said. "Have you so soon come to grief in this—this *civilized* country?"

"I have come to grief, yes. But not through civilization or the lack of it." And I banged my fist on the table. "I have come to grief, M. Perley, through miracles or magic. I have come to grief with a problem which no man's ingenuity can solve!"

M. Perley looked at me in a strange way. But someone had brought a bottle of brandy, with its accessories. M. Perley's trembling hand slopped a generous allowance into my glass, and an even more generous one into his own.

"That is very curious," he remarked, eyeing the glass. "A murder, was it?"

"No. But a valuable document has disappeared. The most thorough search by the police cannot find it."

Touch him anywhere, and he flinched. M. Perley, for some extraordinary reason, appeared to think I was mocking him.

"A document, you say?" His laugh was a trifle unearthly. "Come, now. Was it by any chance—a letter?"

"No, no! It was a will. Three large sheets of parchment, of the size you call foolscap. Listen!"

And as M. Perley added water to his brandy and gulped down about a third of it, I leaned across the table.

"Madame Thevenet, of whom you may have heard me speak in this café, was an invalid. But (until the early hours of this morning) she was not bedridden. She could move, and walk about her room, and so on. She had been lured away from Paris and her family by a green-eyed woman named the Jezebel.

"But a kindly lawyer of this city, M. Duroc, believed that madame suffered and had a bad conscience about her own daughter. Last night, despite the Jezebel, he persuaded madame at last to sign a will leaving all her money to this daughter.

"And the daughter, Claudine, is in mortal need of it! From my brother and myself, who have more than enough, she will not accept a sou. Her affianced, Lieutenant Delage, is as poor as she. But, unless she leaves France for Switzerland, she will die. I will not conceal from you that Claudine suffers from that dread disease we politely call consumption."

M. Perley stopped with his glass again half-way to his mouth.

He believed me now; I sensed it. Yet under the dark hair, tumbled on his forehead, his face had gone as white as his neat, mended shirtfrill.

"So very little a thing is money!" he whispered. "So very little a thing!"

And he lifted the glass and drained it.

"You do not think I am mocking you, sir?"

"No, no!" says M. Perley, shading his eyes with one hand. "I knew myself of one such case. She is dead. Pray continue."

"Last night, I repeat, Madame Thevenet changed her mind. When M. Duroc paid his weekly evening visit with the news that I should arrive today, madame fairly chattered with eagerness and a kind of terror. Death was approaching, she said; she had a presentiment."

As I spoke, Maurice, there returned to me the image of

that shadowy, arsenic-green bedroom in that shuttered house; and what M. Duroc had told me.

"Madame," I continued, "cried out to M. Duroc that he must bolt the bedroom door. She feared the Jezebel, who lurked but said nothing. M. Duroc drew up to her bedside a portable writing-desk, with two good candles. For a long time madame spoke, pouring out contrition, self-abasement, the story of an unhappy marriage, all of which M. Duroc (sweating with embarrassment) was obliged to write down until it covered three large parchment sheets.

"But it was done, M. Perley!

"The will, in effect, left everything to her daughter, Claudine. It revoked a previous will by which all had been left (and this can be done in French law, as we both know) to Jezebel of the muddy complexion and the muddy yellow hair.

"Well, then . . !

"M. Duroc sallies out into the street, where he finds two sober fellows who come in. Madame signs the will, M. Duroc sands it, and the two men from the street affix their signatures as witnesses. Then *they are gone*. M. Duroc folds the will lengthways, and prepares to put it into his carpet bag. Now, M. Perley, mark what follows!

" 'No, no, no!' cries madame, with the shadow of her peaked nightcap wagging on the locked shutters beyond. 'I wish to keep it—for this one night!'

" 'For this one night, madame?' asks M. Duroc.

" 'I wish to press it against my heart,' says Madame Thevenet. 'I wish to read it, once, twice, a thousand times! M. Duroc, what time is it?'

"Whereupon he takes out his gold repeater, and opens it. To his astonishment it is one o'clock in the morning. Yet he touches the spring of the repeater, and its pulse-beat rings one.

" 'Madame!' cries M. Duroc, shocked to the very fans of his beard. 'That would not be correct.'

" 'Yes, you are right,' says madame. And never, swears the lawyer, has he seen her less bleary of eye, more alive with wit and cunning, more the great lady of ruin, than there in that green and shadowy and foul-smelling room.

"Yet this very fact puts her in more and more terror of the Jezebel, who is never seen. She points to M. Duroc's carpet-bag.

" 'I think you have much work to do, dear sir?'

"M. Duroc groaned. 'The Good Lord knows that I have!'

" 'Outside the only door of this room,' says madame, 'there is a small dressing-room. Set up your writing-desk beside the door there, so that no one may enter without your knowledge. Do your work there; you shall have a lamp or many candles. Do it,' shrieks madame, 'for the sake of Claudine and for the sake of an old friendship!'

"Very naturally, M. Duroc hesitated.

" '*She* will be hovering,' pleads Madame Thevenet, pressing the will against her breast. '*This* I shall read and read and read, and sanctify with my tears. If I find I am falling asleep,' and here the old lady looked cunning, 'I shall hide it. But no matter! Even *she* cannot penetrate through locked shutters and a guarded door.'

"Well, in fine, the lawyer at length yielded.

"He set up his writing desk against the very doorpost outside that door. When he last saw madame, before closing the door, he saw her in profile with the green bed-curtains drawn except on that side, propped up with a tall candle burning on a table at her right hand.

"Ah, that night! I think I see M. Duroc at his writing-desk, as he has told me, in an airless dressing-room where no clock ticked. I see him, at times, removing his oval spectacles to press his smarting eyes. I see him returning to his legal papers, while his pen scratched through the wicked hours of the night.

"He heard nothing, or virtually nothing, until five o'clock in the morning. Then, which turned him cold and flabby, he heard a cry which he describes as being like that of a deaf-mute.

"The communicating door had not been bolted on Madame Thevenet's side, in case she needed help. M. Duroc rushed into the other room.

"On the table, at madame's right hand, the tall candle had burnt down to a flattish mass of wax over which still hovered a faint bluish flame. Madame herself lay rigid in her peaked nightcap. That revival of spirit last night, or remorse in her bitter heart, had brought on the last paralysis. Though M. Duroc tried to question her, she could move only her eyes.

"Then M. Duroc noticed that the will, which she had clutched as a doomed religious might clutch a crucifix, was not in her hand or on the bed.

" 'Where is the will?' he shouted at her, as though she were deaf too. 'Where is the will?'

"Madame Thevenet's eyes fixed on him. Then they moved down, and looked steadily at a trumpery toy—a rabbit, perhaps four inches high, made of pink velours or the like—which lay on the bed. Again she looked at M. Duroc, as though to emphasize this. Then her eyes rolled, this time with dreadful effort, towards a large barometer, shaped like a warming-pan, which hung on the wall beside the door. Three times she did this before the bluish candle-flame flickered and went out."

And I, Armand de Lafayette, paused here in my recital to M. Perley.

Again I became aware that I was seated in a garish saloon, swilling brandy, amid loud talk that beat the air. There was thumping noise from the theatre above our heads, and faint strains of music.

"The will," I said, "was not stolen. Not even the Jezebel could have melted through locked shutters or a guarded door. The will was not hidden, because no inch of the room remains unsearched. *Yet the will is gone!*"

I threw a glance across the table at M. Perley.

To me, I am sure, the brandy had given strength and steadied my nerves. With M. Perley I was not so sure. He was a little flushed. That slightly wild look, which I had observed before, had crept up especially into one eye, giving his whole face a somewhat lopsided appearance. Yet all his self-confidence had returned. He gave me a little crooked smile.

I struck the table.

"Do you honour me with your attention, M. Perley?"

"What song the Sirens sang," he said to me, "or what names Achilles assumed when he hid himself among women, although puzzling questions, are not beyond *all* conjecture."

"They are beyond *my* conjecture!" I cried. "And so is this!"

M. Perley extended his hand, spread the fingers, and examined them as one who owns the universe.

"It is some little time," he remarked, "since I have concerned myself with these trifles." His eyes retreated into a dream. "Yet I have given some trifling aid, in the past, to the Prefect of the Parisian police."

"You are a Frenchman! I knew it! And the police?" Seeing his lofty look, I added: "As an amateur, understood?"

"Understood!" Then his delicate hand—it would be unjust to call it claw-like—shot across the table and fastened on my arm. The strange eyes burned towards my face. "A little more detail!" he pleaded humbly. "A little more, I beg of you! This woman, for instance, you call the Jezebel?"

"It was she who met me at the house."

"And then?"

I described for him my meeting with the Jezebel, with M. Duroc, and our entrance to the sick-room, where the shaggy police-officer sat in the arm-chair and the saturnine doctor faced us from beside the bed.

"This woman," I exclaimed, with the room vividly before my eyes as I described it, "seems to have conceived for me (forgive me) a kind of passion. No doubt it was due to some idle compliments I once paid her at Paris.

"As I have explained the Jezebel is *not* unattractive, even if she would only (again forgive me) wash her hair. Nevertheless, when once more she brushed my side and whispered, 'You don't really hate me, do you?' I felt little less than horror. It seemed to me that in some fashion I was responsible for the whole tragedy.

"While we stood beside the bed, M. Duroc the lawyer poured out the story I have recounted. There lay the poor paralytic, and confirmed it with her eyes. The toy rabbit, a detestable pink colour, lay in its same position on the bed. Behind me, hung against the wall by the door, was the large barometer.

"Apparently for my benefit, Madame Thevenet again went through her dumb-show with imploring eyes. She would look at the rabbit; next (as M. Duroc had not mentioned), she would roll her eyes all around her, for some desperate yet impenetrable reason, before fixing her gaze on the barometer.

"It meant . . . what?

"The lawyer spoke then. 'More light!' gulped out M. Duroc. 'If you must have closed shutters and windows, then let us at least have more light!'

"The Jezebel glided out to fetch candles. During M. Duroc's explanation he had several times mentioned my name. At first mention of it the shaggy police-officer jumped and put away his clasp-knife. He beckoned to the physician, Dr. Harding, who went over for a whispered conference.

"Whereupon the police-officer sprang up.

"'Mr. Lafayette!' And he swung my hand pompously. 'If

I'd known it was you, Mr. Lafayette, I wouldn't 'a' sat there like a bump on a log.'

" 'You are an officer of police, sir,' said I. 'Can *you* think of no explanation?'

"He shook his head.

" 'These people are Frenchies, Mr. Lafayette, and you're an American,' he said, with somewhat conspicuous lack of logic. '*If* they're telling the truth—'

" 'Let us assume that!'

" 'I can't tell you where the old lady's will is,' he stated positively. 'But I can tell you where it ain't. It ain't hidden in this room!'

" 'But surely . . . !' I began in despair.

"At this moment the Jezebel, her brown-taffeta dress rustling, glided back into the room with a handful of candles and a tin box of the new-style Lucifer matches. She lighted several candles, sticking them on any surface in their own grease.

"There were one or two fine pieces of furniture; but the mottled-marble tops were chipped and stained, the gilt sides cracked. There were a few mirrors, creating mimic spectral life. I saw a little more clearly the faded green paper of the walls, and what I perceived to be the partly open door of a cupboard. The floor was of bare boards.

"All this while I was conscious of two pairs of eyes: the imploring gaze of Madame Thevenet, and the amorous gaze of the Jezebel. One or the other I could have endured, but both together seemed to suffocate me.

" 'Mr. Duroc here,' said the shaggy police-officer, clapping the distressed advocate on the shoulder, 'sent a messenger in a cab at half-past five this morning. And what time did we get here? I ask you and I tell you! Six o'clock!'

"Then he shook his finger at me, in a kind of pride and fury of efficiency.

" 'Why, Mr. Lafayette, there's been fourteen men at this room from six this morning until just before you got here!'

" 'To search for Madame Thevenet's will, you mean?'

"The shaggy man nodded portentously, and folded his arms.

" 'Floor's solid.' He stamped on the bare boards. 'Walls and ceiling? Nary a inch missed. We reckon we're remarkable smart; and we are.'

" 'But Madame Thevenet,' I persisted, 'was not a complete invalid until this morning. She could move about. If she be-

came afraid of' "—the name of the Jezebel choked me—" 'if
she became afraid, and *did* hide the will . . .'

" 'Where'd she hide it? Tell me!'

" 'In the furniture, then?'

" 'Cabinet-makers in, Mr. Lafayette. No secret compart-
ments'

" 'In one of the mirrors?'

" 'Took the backs of 'em off. No will hid there.'

" 'Up the chimney!' I cried.

" 'Sent a chimney-sweep up there,' replied my companion
in a ruminating way. Each time I guessed, he would leer at
me in friendly and complacent challenge. 'Ye-es, I reckon
we're pretty smart. But we didn't find no will.'

"The pink rabbit also seemed to leer from the bed. I saw
madame's eyes. Once again, as a desperate mind will fasten
on trifles, I observed the strings of the nightcap beneath her
scrawny chin. But I looked again at the toy rabbit.

" 'Has it occurred to you,' I said triumphantly, 'to examine
the bed and bedstead of Madame Thevenet herself?'

"My shaggy friend went to her bedside.

" 'Poor old woman,' he said. He spoke as though she were
already a corpse. Then he turned round. 'We lifted her out,
just as gentle as a newborn babe (didn't we, ma'am?). No
hollow bedposts! Nothing in the canopy! Nothing in the
frame or the feather-beds or the curtains or the bedclothes!'

"Suddenly the shaggy police-officer became angry, as
though he wished to be rid of the whole matter.

" 'And it ain't in the toy rabbit,' he said, 'because you can
see we slit it up, if you look close. And it ain't in that
barometer there. It just—ain't here.'

"There was a silence as heavy as the dusty, hot air of this
room.

" 'It is here,' murmured M. Duroc in his gruff voice. 'It
must be here!'

"The Jezebel stood there meekly, with downcast eyes.

"And I, in my turn, confess that *I* lost my head. I stalked
over to the barometer, and tapped it. Its needle, which already indicated, 'Rain; cold,' moved still further towards that
point.

"I was not insane enough to hit it with my fist. But I
crawled on the floor, in search of a secret hiding-place. I
felt along the wall. The police-officer—who kept repeating
that nobody must touch anything and he would take no re-

sponsibility until he went off duty at something o'clock—
the police-officer I ignored.

"What at length gave me pause was the cupboard, already
thoroughly searched. In the cupboard hung a few withered
dresses and gowns, as though they had shrivelled with Madame Thevenet's body. But on the shelf of the cupboard . . .

"On the shelf stood a great number of perfume-bottles:
even today, I fear, many of our countrymen think perfume
a substitute for water and soap; and the state of madame's
hands would have confirmed this. *But,* on the shelf, were a
few dusty novels. There was a crumpled and begrimed copy
of yesterday's New York *Sun.* This newspaper did not contain a will; but it did contain a black beetle, which ran out
across my hand.

"In a disgust past describing, I flung down the beetle and
stamped on it. I closed the cupboard door, acknowledging
defeat. Madame Thevenet's will was gone. And at the same
second, in that dim green room—still badly lighted, with only
a few more candles—two voices cried out.

"One was my own voice:

" *'In God's name, where is it?'*

"The other was the deep voice of M. Duroc:

" *'Look at that woman! She knows!'*

"And he meant the Jezebel.

"M. Duroc, with his beard-fans a-tremble, was pointing to
a mirror; a little blurred, as these mirrors were. Our Jezebel
had been looking into the mirror, her back turned to us. Now
she dodged, as at a stone thrown.

"With good poise our Jezebel writhed this movement into
a curtsy, turning to face us. But not before I also had seen
that smile—like a razor-cut before the blood comes—as well
as full knowledge, mocking knowledge, shining out of wide-
open eyes in the mirror.

" 'You spoke to me, M. Duroc?' She murmured the reply,
also in French.

" 'Listen to me!' the lawyer said formally. 'This will is *not*
missing. It is in this room. You were not here last night.
Something has made you guess. You know where it is.'

" 'Are you unable to find it?' asked the Jezebel in surprise.

" 'Stand back, young man!' Mr. Duroc said to me. 'I ask
you something, mademoiselle, in the name of justice.'

" 'Ask!' said the Jezebel.

" 'If Claudine Thevenet inherits the money to which she is .

entitled, you will be well paid; yes, overpaid! You know Claudine. You know that!'

" 'I know it.'

" 'But if the new will be *not* found,' said M. Duroc, again, waving me back, 'then you inherit everything. And Claudine will die. For it will be assumed—'

" 'Yes!' said the Jezebel, with one hand pressed against her breast. 'You yourself, M. Duroc, testify that all night a candle was burning at madame's bedside. Well! The poor woman, whom *I* loved and cherished, repented of her ingratitude towards me. She burnt this new will at the candle-flame; she crushed its ashes to powder and blew them away!"

" 'Is that true?' cried M. Duroc.

" 'They will assume it,' smiled the Jezebel, 'as you say.' She looked at me. 'And for you, M. Armand!'

"She glided closer. I can only say that I saw her eyes uncovered; or, if you wish to put it so, her soul and flesh together.

" 'I would give you everything on earth,' she said. 'I will not give you the doll-face in Paris.'

" 'Listen to me!' I said to her, so agitated that I seized her shoulders. 'You are out of your senses! You cannot give Claudine to me! She will marry another man!'

" 'And do you think that matters to me,' asked the Jezebel, with her green eyes full on mine, 'as long as you still love her?'

"There was a small crash as someone dropped a knife on the floor.

"We three, I think, had completely forgotten that we were not alone. There were two spectators, although they did not comprehend our speech.

"The saturnine Dr. Harding now occupied the green arm-chair. His long thin legs, in tight black trousers with strap under the boot-instep, were crossed and looked spidery; his high beaver hat glimmered on his head. The police-officer, who was picking his teeth with the knife when I first saw him, had now dropped the knife when he tried to trim his nails.

"But both men sensed the atmosphere. Both were alert, feeling out with the tentacles of their nerves. The police-officer shouted at me.

" 'What's this gabble?' he said. 'What's a-gitting into your head?'

"Grotesquely, it was that word 'head' which gave me my inspiration.

" 'The nightcap!' I exclaimed in English.

" 'What nightcap?'

"For the nightcap of Madame Thevenet had a peak; it was large; it was tightly tied under the chin; it might well conceal a flat-pressed document which—but you understand. The police-officer, dull-witted as he appeared, grasped the meaning in a flash. And how I wished I had never spoken! For the fellow meant well, but he was not gentle.

"As I raced round the curtained sides of the bed, the police-officer was holding a candle in one hand and tearing off madame's nightcap with the other. He found no will there, no document at all; only straggly wisps of hair on a skull grown old before its time.

"Madame Thevenet had been a great lady, once. It must have been the last humiliation. Two tears overflowed her eyes and ran down her cheeks. She lay propped up there in a nearly sitting position; but something seemed to wrench inside her.

"And she closed her eyes forever. And the Jezebel laughed.

"That is the end of my story. That is why I rushed out of the house like a madman. The will has vanished as though by magic; or is it still there by magic? In any case, you find me at this table: grubby and dishevelled and much ashamed."

For a little time after I had finished my narrative to M. Perley in the saloon, it seemed to me that the bar-counter was a trifle quieter. But a faint stamping continued from the theatre above our heads. Then all was hushed, until a chorus rose to a tinkle of many banjos.

> Oh, I come from Alabama
>   With my banjo on my knee;
> I depart for Louisiana . . .

Enough! The song soon died away, and M. Thaddeus Perley did not even hear it.

M. Perley sat looking downwards into an empty glass, so that I could not see his face.

"Sir," he remarked almost bitterly, "you are a man of good heart. I am glad to be of service in a problem so trifling as this."

"Trifling!"

His voice was a little husky, but not slurred. His hand slowly turned the glass round and round.

"Will you permit two questions?" asked M. Perley.

"Two questions? Ten thousand!"

"More than two will be unnecessary." Still M. Perley did not look up. "This toy rabbit, of which so much was made: I would know its exact position on the bed?"

"It was almost at the foot of the bed, and about the middle in a crossways direction."

"Ah, so I had imagined. Were the three sheets of parchment, forming the will, written upon two sides, or upon only one?"

"I had not told you, M. Perley. But M. Duroc said: upon one side only."

M. Perley raised his head.

His face was now flushed and distorted with drink, his eyes grown wild. In his cups he was as proud as Satan, and as disdainful of others' intelligence; yet he spoke with dignity, and with careful clearness.

"It is ironic, M. de Lafayette, that I should tell you how to lay your hand on the missing will and the elusive money; since, upon my word, I have never been able to perform a like service for myself." And he smiled, as at some secret joke. "Perhaps," he added, "it is the very simplicity of the thing which puts you at fault."

I could only look at him in bewilderment.

"Perhaps the mystery is a little *too* plain! A little *too* self-evident!"

"You mock me, sir! I will not . . ."

"Take me as I am," said M. Perley, whacking the foot of the glass on the table, "or leave me. Besides—" here his wandering eye encountered a list of steam-sailings pasted against the wall—"I—I leave tomorrow by the *Parnassus* for England, and then for France."

"I meant no offence, M. Perley! If you have knowledge, speak!"

"Madame Thevenet," he said, carefully pouring himself more brandy, "hid the will in the middle of the night. Does it puzzle you that she took such precautions to hide the will? But the element of the *autré* must always betray itself. The Jezebel *must not* find that will! Yet Madam Thevenet trusted nobody—not even the worthy physician who attended her. If Madame were to die of a stroke, the police would be there and must soon, she was sure, discover her simple device. Even if she were paralysed, it would ensure the presence of other persons in the room to act as unwitting guards.

"Your cardinal error," M. Perley continued dispassionately, "was one of ratiocination. You tell me that Madame Thevenet, to give you a hint, looked fixedly at some point near the foot of the bed. Why do you assume that she was looking at the toy rabbit?"

"Because," I replied hotly, "the toy rabbit was the only object she could have looked at!"

"Pardon me; but it was *not*. You several times informed me that the bed-curtains were closely drawn together on three sides. They were drawn on all but the 'long' side towards the door. Therefore the ideal reasoner, without having seen the room, may safely say that the curtains were drawn together at the foot of the bed?"

"Yes, true!"

"After looking fixedly at this point represented by the toy, Madame Thevenet then 'rolls her eyes all round her'—in your phrase. May we assume that she wishes the curtains to be drawn back, so that she may see something *beyond* the bed?"

"It is—possible, yes!"

"It is more than possible, as I shall demonstrate. Let us direct our attention, briefly, to the incongruous phenomenon of the barometer on another wall. The barometer indicates, 'Rain; cold.' "

Here M. Perley's thin shoulders drew together under the old military cloak.

"Well," he said, "the cold is on its way. Yet this day, for April, has been warm outside and indoors, oppressively hot?"

"Yes! Of course!"

"You yourself," continued M. Perley, inspecting his fingernails, "told me what was directly opposite the foot of the bed. Let us suppose that the bed-curtains are drawn open. Madame Thevenet, in her nearly seated position, is looking *downwards*. What would she have seen?"

"The fireplace!" I cried. "The grate of the fireplace!"

"Already we have a link with the weather. And what, as you have specifically informed me, was in the grate of the fireplace?"

"An unlighted coal fire!"

"Exactly. And what is essential for the composition of such a fire? We need coal; we need wood; but primarily and above all, we need . . ."

"Paper!" I cried.

"In the cupboard of that room," said M. Perley, with his disdainful little smile, "was a very crumpled and begrimed (mark that; not dusty) copy of *yesterday's* New York *Sun*. To light fires is the most common, and indeed the best, use for our daily press. That copy had been used to build yesterday's fire. But something else, during the night, was substituted for it. You yourself remarked the extraordinarily dirty state of Madame Thevenet's hands."

M. Perley swallowed the brandy, and his flush deepened.

"Sir," he said loudly, "you will find the will crumpled up with ends most obviously protruding, under the coal and wood in the fireplace grate. Even had anyone taken the fire to pieces, he would have found only what appeared to be dirty blank paper, written side undermost, which could never be a valuable will. It was too self-evident to be seen—Now go!"

"Go?" I echoed stupidly.

M. Perley rose from his chair.

"Go, I say!" he shouted, with an even wilder eye. "The Jezebel could not light that fire. It was too warm, for one thing; and all day there were police-officers with instructions that an outsider must touch nothing. But now? *Madame Thevenet kept warning you that the fire must not be lighted, or the will would be destroyed!*"

"Will you await me here?" I called over my shoulder.

"Yes, yes! And perhaps there will be peace for the wretched girl with—with the lung-trouble."

Even as I ran out of the door I saw him, grotesque and pitiful, slump across the table. Hope, rising and surging, seemed to sweep me along like the crack of the cabman's whip. But when I reached my destination, hope receded.

The shaggy police-officer was just descending the front steps.

"None of us coming back here, Mr. Lafayette!" he called cheerily. "Old Mrs. What's-her-name went and burnt that will at a candle last night—Here, what's o'clock?"

The front door was unlocked. I raced through that dark house, and burst into the rear bedroom.

The corpse still lay in the big, gloomy bed. Every candle had flickered almost down to its socket. The police-officer's clasp-knife, forgotten since he had dropped it, still lay on bare boards. But the Jezebel was there.

She knelt on the hearth, with the tin box of Lucifer matches she had brought there earlier. The match spurted, a bluish fire; I saw her eagerness; she held the match to the grate.

"A Lucifer," I said, "in the hand of a Jezebel!"

And I struck her away from the grate, so that she reeled against a chair and fell. Large coals, small coals rattled down in puffs of dust as I plunged my hands into the unlighted fire. Little sticks, sawed sticks; and I found it there: crumpled parchment-sheets, but incontestably madame's will.

"M. Duroc!" I called. "M. Duroc!"

You and I, my brother Maurice, have fought the Citizen-King with bayonets as we now fight the upstart Bonapartist; we need not be ashamed of tears. I confess, then, that the tears overran my eyes and blinded me. I scarcely saw M. Duroc as he hurried into the room.

Certainly I did not see the Jezebel stealthily pick up the police-officer's knife. I noticed nothing at all until she flew at me, and stabbed me in the back.

Peace, my brother: I have assured you all is well. At that time, faith, I was not much conscious of any hurt. I bade M. Duroc, who was trembling, to wrench out the knife; I borrowed his roomy greatcoat to hide the blood; I must hurry, hurry, hurry back to that little table under the gas-jet.

I planned it all on my way back. M. Perley, apparently a stranger in this country, disliked it and was evidently very poor even in France. But *we* are not precisely paupers. Even with his intense pride, he could not refuse (for such a service) a sum which would comfort him for the rest of his life.

Back I plunged into the saloon, and hurried down it. Then I stopped. The little round table by the pillar, under the flaring gas-jet, was empty.

How long I stood there I cannot tell. The back of my shirt, which at first had seemed full of blood, now stuck to the borrowed greatcoat. All of a sudden I caught sight of the fat-faced bartender with the gold teeth, who had been on service that afternoon and had returned now. As a mark of respect, he came out from behind the bar-counter to greet me.

"Where is the gentleman who was sitting at that table?"

I pointed to it. My voice, in truth, must have sounded so hoarse and strange that he mistook it for anger.

"Don't you worry about that, monseer!" said he reassuringly. "*That's* been tended to! we threw the drunken tramp out of here!"

"You threw . . ."

"Right bang in the gutter. Had to crawl along in it before

he could stand up." My bartender's face was pleased and vicious. "Ordered a bottle of best brandy, and couldn't pay for it." The face changed again. "Goddelmighty, monseer, what's wrong?"

"*I* ordered that brandy."

"*He* didn't say so, when the waiter brought me over. Just looked me up and down, crazy-like, and said a gentleman would give his I.O.U. Gentleman!"

"M. Perley," I said, restraining an impulse to kill that bartender, "is a friend of mine. He departs for France early tomorrow morning. Where is his hotel? Where can I find him?"

"Perley!" sneered my companion. "That ain't even his real name, I hearn tell. Gits high-and-mighty ideas from upper Broadway. But his real name's on the I.O.U."

A surge of hope, once more, almost blinded me. "Did you keep that I.O.U.?"

"Yes, I kepp it," growled the bartender, fishing in his pocket. "God knows why, but I kepp it."

And at last, Maurice, I triumphed!

True, I collapsed from my wound; and the fever would not let me remember that I must be at the dock when the *Parnassus* steam-packet departed from New York next morning. I must remain here, shut up in a hotel-room and unable to sleep at night, until I can take ship for home. But where I failed, you can succeed. He was to leave on the morrow by the *Parnassus* for England, and then for France—so he told me. You can find him—in six months at the most. In six months, I give you my word, he will be out of misery forever!

"*I.O.U.*," reads the litttle slip, "*for one bottle of your best brandy, forty-five cents. Signed: Edgar A. Poe.*"

I remain, Maurice,

Your affectionate brother,

Armand

THE MOORS MURDERS

MIRIAM ALLEN deFORD

*Although he wrote relatively little in the true crime field,
it was one of Anthony Boucher's chief interests, and he
did deal with it extensively in his magazine, newspaper
and radio book reviews. This ghastly English murder
case especially aroused his curiosity, and after the article
was published in the* Saint Mystery Magazine, *I sent
him for his own files all the clippings from London
papers and other source material on which I had based
my account. I also quoted him in the article itself.*

MULTIPLE MURDERS ARE FAR from uncommon—there have
been at least four striking instances of them in this country
within the past year. Murder for the thrill of killing is as old
as human nature. What differentiates the Moors Murders in
England from the common run of other wanton and motive-
less cases of the destruction of human life is the character
and personality of the two perpetrators set against the particular period in which these young people were born and have
grown up. Sick eras produce sick people.

Strictly speaking, the main crime for which Ian Brady
and Myra Hindley are now serving life sentences was not a
Moors Murder at all, though Brady had planned to bury the
corpse of Edward Evans in the Pennine Moors, near the
graves of his other victims, if he had not been forestalled by
the panic-stricken appeal to the police by his *soi-disant* broth-

er-in-law, David Smith—himself perhaps an accomplice and fundamentally a victim also of Brady's corrupting influence. Evans was killed in the house in Hattersley, near Manchester, in which Brady lived with his mistress, Myra Hindley, and her grandmother, Mrs. Maybury. The two other known victims, 12-year-old John Kilbride and 10-year-old Lesley Ann Downey, probably also were killed elsewhere and then buried a few hundred feet apart in the wild and desolate moors which were the guilty couple's "home away from home" where they spent much of their leisure time from their office jobs, sometimes all night long.

Brady himself is almost a case history in alienated youth. The illegitimate son of a waitress in Glasgow, his father unknown, he was reared by a foster mother in the Gorbal slums. She was kind and motherly and treated him well. He was a bright child who did well at school, but already the aberrant streak in him was manifest; he tortured animals, bullied his schoolmates, and as a child of 11 he was already obsessed with Nazism, with the Storm Troopers as his ideals. Also, he had started his career as a thief and housebreaker, his first arrest and probation coming at 13, in 1951. He left school at 14 and went to work as a butcher's assistant, and after two more arrests and probation periods the Glasgow authorities decided he was beyond his foster mother's control and sent him south to Manchester to his mother, who had married and moved there. He was not yet 15.

To his thieving propensities and his delight in Nazism he had by now added an obsessive preoccupation with torture and sexual perversion; he had discovered de Sade. To his companions he was known as "Dracula." He could not change his nature, but at first he seems to have made some effort toward normality; he changed his name to his stepfather's and went to work. But soon he was back in his old habits, and in 1955 he was sent to Borstal (the boys' reform school) for three years. Eight months after his release he got a job as an invoice clerk at a small chemical works in Gorton, another Manchester suburb. (He was a very satisfactory employee.) Two years later, he met there a new stenographer named Myra Hindley.

Psychopaths frequently have superior mentality; Brady reminds one constantly of Richard Loeb. He was good at his job, his interests were intellectual, but he was utterly antisocial. He worshiped naked power and made no secret of his leanings. It was his misfortune that he was born in the wrong country—he would have gone far under Hitler. As it was, his only outlet was the corruption of and hatred and contempt for those inferiors, all other human beings. A generation earlier he would have been a disciple of a misunderstood version of the philosophy of Nietzsche.

This was the man with whom a wilful, undisciplined girl fell so madly in love that she remade herself into his image, became his devoted slave, followed him into murder, and proudly proclaimed in the witness box that she still loved him —while he did not even glance at her. So far as a psychopath can care for anyone except himself she did become Brady's absorbing interest; she was his creature.

Myra Hindley is four years Brady's junior. When she was four years old her sister Maureen was born, and her working mother handed her over to her own mother, Mrs. Maybury, to rear: the two lived near each other. Myra grew up a tomboy, but essentially very much like other girls in a poor industrial neighborhood. What she most admired was strength. Brady was far from strong physically, but emotionally he fulfilled her dreams. She threw over a fiancé and devoted herself to winning Brady's attention. It took her a long time. But after her grandmother moved to Hattersley, Brady moved in too (ostensibly he was still living with his mother and stepfather), and the two became inseparable.

No consideration of the two principals in this case would be complete without some reference to David Smith, who married Maureen Hindley when he was 16 and she was 17, and thus became Myra's brother-in-law. Whether Smith actually took part in the murder of Edward Evans is open to question; he turned Queen's evidence and was free from prosecution. He probably brought Lesley Ann Downey to the house where she met her death—it is unlikely that there was any truth in Brady's assertion that he took her away again, alive. He is weak and vicious, with an easy acceptance of criminality, but he has none of the driving force of Ian Brady. When they planned a robbery together, Smith wanted blank cartridges in the guns. Brady would never have panicked, as Smith did, after the murder of Evans. By the time of the trial he had recovered his aplomb; he was brash and impudent on the stand, acknowledging proudly that he was being paid £1000 by a newspaper for his story—"Money is gorgeous stuff." His pregnant young wife, Myra's sister, was a mere bystander. Once she and Myra were close friends; they are no longer on speaking terms.

The first known murder was that of 12-year-old John Kilbride, who disappeared from a movie on November 23, 1963, and whose body was dug up on the moor, close to the grave of Lesley Ann Downey, and identified by the clothing. (Brady is still being questioned about the disappearances of other young people in this part of the North of England during the past few years. He had boasted to Smith that he had committed "three or four" murders and would be committing another soon. But the moors are vast, and if Brady had not photographed Myra, with her dog, staring at the spot they frequented where Lesley Ann lay buried, these two might never have been discovered, either.)

The boy had been sexually abused before his death. It was impossible to tell just how he had been killed, but in all probability—and in the case of the little girl also—he was suffocated. Smith certainly had no connection with this murder, and neither did Myra Hindley, though she was convicted of "harboring" Brady knowing that he had killed John Kilbride.

There was much more circumstantial evidence in the murder of Lesley Ann. Among Brady's chief hobbies was photography, including pornographic photography. There is no doubt that the child, who had gone to a local fair with sixpence to spend, was picked up by somebody—probably Smith—and persuaded to go with him to Myra's grandmother's house to have her picture taken. (They were complete strangers.) She would have been promised some small sum, perhaps was flattered to be told that she was pretty enough to be wanted as a subject, and went innocently to a scene of horror that makes this one of the unpleasantest murders on record.

Most of the English newspapers forebore to publish all of the heartbreaking tape recording which Brady and Myra callously set going to preserve Lesley Ann's dreadful experience. The jury and the auditors in court heard her screams and protests, her pitiful plea that she must get back home in time for tea, her vain appeals. She had been stripped naked and either raped or otherwise abused. Her captors took photographs in obscene poses, which were with the tape in a suitcase they had packed with this and other incriminating material and checked. When she kept on screaming she got on Myra's nerves; she slapped the girl and then they stuffed her mouth with rags to gag her. To finish off the recording in style they tuned in to a radio broadcast of Christmas music

—it was Boxing Day, the day after Christmas, in 1964. She was buried as she died, naked. When a neighbor's girl they made a protegée of read aloud the newspaper account of a reward offered for Lesley Ann's recovery by her distraught mother, Myra made a flippant remark and laughed.

The murder of Edward Evans was of a very different nature. Brady remarked to Smith that this one was "out of turn" and didn't count. Evans, only 17, was an overt homosexual. Brady had seen him once before in a "drag club" in Manchester; Ian used to visit such places "for fun," to laugh at the habitués. In the course of his indoctrination of David Smith—they were planning a hold-up at the time—he thought David should have some personal experience in crime; for a start, how about "rolling a queer"? "The point was that if anything did go wrong, this person was unlikely to complain to the police, so there was no risk."

On the evening of October 6, 1965, Ian and Myra drove to Gorton for some wine and then on to the Central Station at Manchester; Brady couldn't drive and Myra always drove them in her own car. There Brady saw Evans and decided to take him home with them, ostensibly for a drink. Why he thought a young apprentice engineer would have any money worth stealing is a problem; another version of his story is that this was just practice for Smith, in preparation for the robbery the next Saturday.

So Smith had to be brought into the picture. It was past midnight by now and presumably David was asleep at his nearby home with Maureen. Brady sent Myra to his house with a supposed message for Maureen from their mother; then she asked Smith to "walk her home" and pick up some wine bottles they had for him. Smith, who had been undressing to go to bed, did as she asked, and she left him standing inside the front door while she went "to get the bottles." His story is that he heard thumping sounds and Myra called, "Dave, come and help me." He went into the room and found a young man unknown to him writhing and screaming on the floor while Brady kept hitting him with a hatchet.

Brady had not waited for Smith's arrival. There is evidence that while Myra was gone he and Evans had had intimate relations, though Brady denied it; but just what precipitated his attack on Evans is unknown. From that point on, with Myra in and out of the room, there is no doubt that Brady kept slashing at Evans with the hatchet until the youth collapsed—Brady said Smith helped him by hitting Evans with his stick, Smith says he simply stood and watched, horrified. Finally, to stop his "gurgling," Brady strangled Evans with a cord.

Blood was everywhere, and they all three set to with cloths and mops to clean up. Then they tied the corpse in a polythene sheet and blankets. Their first idea was to carry it out between them, drive to the moor, and bury the victim at once, but they were afraid of a trail of blood, so they carried him to an upstairs bedroom—where the police found him. (They also found a cryptic "plan" for disposing of a murder victim among Brady's belongings.)

One may ask, where was Mrs. Maybury, the 77-year-old grandmother, during all this? She had been visiting Myra's uncle over Christmas, and Myra had refused to drive her home that night on the grounds that the roads were too bad.

All this practical demonstration had been too much for David Smith. He got himself home somehow, washed, vomited, and tried to sleep but couldn't, so he woke Maureen and told her what had happened. By this time they were both terrified. They armed themselves for protection with a knife and a screwdriver and, since they had no telephone, went to a nearby booth, where they phoned the police. It was the beginning of the end for Ian Brady and Myra Hindley.

The preliminary hearing was held in December, the trial in April and May of 1966. The judge was Justice Fenton Atkinson; the case was prosecuted, with two assistants, by Sir Elwyn Jones, Q.C., the Attorney General; Brady's chief counsel was Emlyn Hooson, Q.C., Liberal M.P. for Montgomery, and Hindley's was Geoffrey Heilpern, Recorder of Salford. (During the trial Heilpern's sister-in-law was murdered in her dress shop in London by someone unknown.) Four of the 12 first picked for the jury were women, but they were all challenged by the defense and the jury was all male. No photographs were allowed, and the names of children who testified in the Kilbride and Downey cases were not published.

The jury took two hours and 14 minutes to convict Brady of all three murders and Hindley of the Downey and Evans murders and of harboring Brady in the Kilbride case. (For this last she received seven years.) This was the first important murder trial after the abolition of capital punishment in Britain; both defendants received concurrent life sentences on the murder charges.

Brady is in Durham Gaol, in solitary confinement at his

own request; Myra Hindley, whose appeal was rejected, is in
Holloway. (Her appeal was based on the fact that she was
not given a separate trial. Brady did not appeal.) She took
the rejection unemotionally, as both took their sentences;
it was noted that the synthetic blonde Myra has by now become a brunette. (An odd reflection is that Brady, slender
and dark-haired, would never be noticed in a crowd; Hindley, with her wedge-shaped jaw and cavernous eyes, is much
nearer the Lombrosan picture of a born criminal, though in
actuality it is Brady who is the born criminal, if such a thing
exists, and if they had never met there is no likelihood that
Myra would ever have deviated from the conventional
norm.)

So what is one to make of this sorry case? Has it any
relevance to our troubled and chaotic time? Among the
books which were Brady's Bibles, besides the works of de
Sade and Hitler's "Mein Kampf," were volumes about
Goering and Eichmann and descriptions of Nazi genocide;
there were also books with such titles as "Kiss of the Whip,"
"Pleasures of the Torture Chamber," "The History of Torture and Cruelty," and "Corporal Punishment through the
Ages." As David Ware remarked in *Punch,* "the pages devoted to Sade are the best thumbed . . . in the Reading Room
of the British Museum." Doubtless some of the crowd who
shrieked "Kill them!" as Brady and Hindley were taken to
prison have been among those readers—but they have committed no murders. The Moors Murders are no argument for
censorship; despite the complacency with which one London
newspaper stated that the books the two read and passed on
to Smith were "the drugs" that "poisoned their minds,"
Anthony Boucher has commented that this is the first sadistic
murder on record in which there was any evidence that the
murderer had ever actually read de Sade!

People like Ian Brady have existed in all times and all
places. What developed his evil potentialities and brought
them to fruition was the world into which he was born. This
is a sick world in a sick age. There is hope for humanity's
recovery, but there is no use in pretending that all is well with
us. Perhaps if it were made possible for *no* child to be born
unwanted, there would be fewer like Brady. But *any* child
born in an urban slum has a tremendous handicap to start
with. Just because he had so good a mind and so frustrated a
personality, Ian Brady seized on his one means of fulfillment
—the relentless pursuit of individual power and domination.

In a healthy civilization, his bent would have been recognized early and he would have had assistance toward and opportunity for socially desirable ways to prove his superiority. We threw him away, after we had let him corrupt and ruin at least two other human beings.

A statement by the managing director of Madame Tussaud's Waxworks throws inadvertently a flood of light on the thin veneer of our normality. Brady and Hindley will not appear in the Chamber of Horrors, he says: in fact, the Chamber is now complete. "However nasty the murders were, they were at least executed, which gave them a touch of glamor." While murder, either private or by the State, is popularly considered glamorous, we cannot call ourselves civilized, or justify amazement and revulsion at the emergence of an Ian Brady.

As Pamela Hansford Johnson said, "A wound in the flesh of society. . .(has) cracked open."

[Addendum: In 1968, Ian Brady, in the maximum security wing of the prison, took and passed (at 0 level) his examination for a General Certificate of Education—in German. He has not changed.]

THE COMPETITORS

RICHARD DEMING

Tony Boucher seemed particularly to enjoy a private eye character named Manville Moon who was featured in my early books. The appeal, according to one of his reviews, lay in what he called "a genial, half-humorous, medium-boiled style."

I was rather at a loss to pick a crime story which would somehow relate to Tony Boucher, since I had never sold him such a story. Then I went back to my scrapbook, found that particular line, and instantly thought of "The Competitors" as just the type of story he would enjoy most.

THE VILLAGE OF SHANNON wasn't big enough for two funeral parlors, Sam Potter thought morosely. One for each fifteen hundred population. Even if he and Dave continued to get their fair half of the available business, future prospects were gloomy. Particularly since Shannon natives tended to live to such discouraging old age.

This was largely because of the nature of the community, Sam reflected as he paused in his raking of the already immaculate lawn to examine without pleasure the sedate sign reading: *Potter and Clemson Mortuary.* A sleepy Western New York State village on the shore of Lake Erie, Shannon had no large industries to provide hazardous occupations, so little crime there hadn't been a murder in thirty years, and a disgustingly healthy climate.

If only Harry Averill had been content to stick to the furni-

111

ture business and hadn't decided, three years back, to branch out into the funeral business also, Sam thought resentfully, he and Dave would still have a comfortable living. After enjoying a monopoly for fifteen years, it was a little hard to see half your business snatched away by a man who already had a way to make a living. Then in grudging fairness Sam had to admit it was Averill's son insisting on studying to be an embalmer which had induced the elder Averill to enter the field, and not pure avarice.

He went back to his raking, a short, round little man in his forties whose normal expression was a benign smile instead of the frown his face now wore.

Dave Clemson came from the funeral home's garage, where he had been tinkering with the engine of the ancient hearse, and walked across the lawn toward Sam. Glad of an excuse, Sam again stopped his raking and leaned on the rake handle as his partner approached.

Dave Clemson was the same age as Sam Potter, also a bachelor, and for business purposes had cultivated an identically benign expression. But there the resemblance ended. Dave was four inches taller than Sam and as thin as a rail.

When he reached Sam, Dave stopped and said in a discouraged voice, "It's no use. She's finally done."

"The hearse?" Sam asked.

"What else?" the thin man snapped at him.

"You don't have to bite my head off," Sam said mildly. "Maybe it's not as bad as you think."

"It's as bad as I think," Dave assured him. "The cylinders are too big now to bore out again, the pistons are warped and the head's almost eaten through. Nothing but a new motor would ever make her run again. Also the transmission's shot and the rear end is ready to go out. After eighteen years, what could you expect?"

Sam asked, "What are we going to do?"

"Either buy a new hearse or fold up."

"A new hearse!" Sam said, appalled. "Where do we get the sixty-five hundred bucks?"

"I figure eighty-five hundred. For a combination hearse and ambulance."

Sam's voice rose to a squeak. "A combination job! What in the devil do we need with an ambulance?"

"I've had it in mind for some time," Dave said. "Come inside and we'll talk it over."

By tacit agreement they went to the casket display room in

the basement, as it was the coolest room in the building. And as always before a business conference, Dave got some ice from the refrigerator in the embalming room, squeezed a couple of the lemons he always kept in the same refrigerator and made two tall glasses of lemonade. Neither man spoke until they were both comfortably seated, had their pipes going and had sampled their drinks.

Then Dave said, "Like I said, I've been thinking this over for some time, Sam. And the way I see it, we're never going to get out of the red waiting for Shannon natives to die."

"So how will spending eighty-five hundred bucks we haven't got help us?"

"We've got to rake up business from outside of Shannon. And that's where the ambulance idea comes in. I been checking up on a few things. You know how many accident calls that broken-down fire-department ambulance made last year?"

The plump man shook his head.

"A hundred and eight," Dave Clemson said in an impressive voice. "Better than two a week."

Sam looked surprised, but not particularly impressed. "So?"

"So I happen to know their ambulance is as close to falling apart as our hearse. The chief plans to go before the common council Monday night and ask for a new one. Suppose we show up too, tell the council we plan to buy a new hearse, and as a public service would just as soon make it a combination ambulance-hearse? Then the village wouldn't need one any more. We could guarantee twenty-four-hour service and charge a set fee. We'd bill patients able to pay, and charge the village for charity cases. I think the common council would jump at it."

Sam looked at his partner in astonishment. Finally he said, "So do I. Look at the money they'd save. But I don't see any profit for us. We couldn't charge more than ten or fifteen dollars a call, and even if we got fifteen dollars, a hundred and eight calls comes to only . . ." He paused to gaze at the ceiling a moment, then said, "Sixteen hundred and twenty dollars a year. And the outfit would cost us two thousand dollars more than a plain hearse. Figuring depreciation . . ."

"You don't get the idea," Dave interrupted. "I don't plan to make any profit from ambulance calls. It's an investment in good will."

Sam examined his partner with an expression indicating he thought the thin man had lost his mind. Instead of answering, he took a long and sarcastic pull on his lemonade.

"Just listen me out," Dave said insistently. "You know what most local ambulance calls are for?"

"Auto accidents, I suppose."

"Almost all of them," Dave agreed. "Usually involving out-of-town people. Not many Shannon people get hurt in accidents, because they never move fast enough to do more than dent a fender. But an awful lot of tourists passing by town smash up. Since they built the two new highways both sides of town, hundreds of out-of-staters whiz past us every day. And at least a couple a week crack up. I checked with the hospital the other day, and of the hundred and seventy-eight accident victims brought in last year by the hundred and eight ambulance calls I mentioned, thirty-three people were either DOA, or died in the hospital later. But we only got two of those bodies. And of course both those were split fees with the undertaker in the deceaseds' home towns, since neither was from around here."

Sam Potter began to look more interested. "What are you getting at, Dave?"

"I've been doing a lot of thinking about why Harry Averill got thirty-one of those bodies while we only got two. Us being the older firm, you'd think it would be the other way. I finally figured it out."

"How?" Sam asked blankly.

"Just put yourself in the place of the next of kin of an accident victim. Maybe you've rushed in from out of town when the hospital called you, or maybe you were in the accident too, but weren't killed. Maybe you're hurt, maybe not, but at least you're upset, you're not thinking too clearly, and you don't know a soul in town. When the charge nurse at the hospital asks what you want done with the body, what do you do?"

Sam said slowly, "Why, ask the nurse who the undertakers in town are, I guess."

"And does the nurse recommend one?"

"No, of course not. They're not allowed to do that. I suppose she'd give me the names of both funeral homes and let me take my pick."

"Or, more likely, just hand you a phone book opened to the proper page in the classified section."

Sam stared at his partner. "Yeah. And . . ." He stopped

and his eyes widened. "My God! I don't know anything about either of them, so naturally I'd take the first one in the book. Averill got all that business simply because his name starts with A!"

"Exactly," Dave said, pleased with his pupil. "Probably the only reason we even got two was because Averill's phone was busy or something when the next of kin tried to reach him."

Sam was now so interested, he had allowed his pipe to go out and the ice in his lemonade to melt. Setting the glass on the floor next to his foot, he leaned forward with his elbows on his knees.

"So get back to your good will idea," he said.

"It's simple," Dave said. "With an ambulance, we'd be in on the ground floor. Every time we bring in an accident victim, we leave a card. If the victim dies, his next of kin isn't going to look in any phone book. He's going to phone those nice, sympathetic ambulance attendants who did everything possible to save the victim's life by rushing him to the hospital, and who also happen to run a funeral home."

Sam regarded his thin partner with admiration. "We'd get all of them," he breathed. "Over thirty a year." He paused, then went on reflectively, "Of course some of them would just be embalmings, because some families would want their home town undertakers to handle details." Then he brightened. "But at least half ought to buy caskets from us."

"At least," Dave agreed. "And tourists are quite likely to have money. I happen to know Averill unloaded a fifteen-hundred-dollar casket in one of the thirty-one accident fatalities he got last year."

"Eighty-five hundred dollars for a combination job," Sam Potter said with a faraway look in his eyes. "We could mortgage the funeral home . . ."

When word got around the village that Potter and Clemson had taken over the responsibility for furnishing ambulance service for the community, Harry Averill used the rumor as an excuse to needle his competitors a little. The incident occurred at the weekly luncheon meeting of the Shannon Businessmen's Club.

Harry Averill was a bland, portly man of about fifty, and had once been regarded as a good friend by both Sam Potter and Dave Clemson. During the past three years, ever since Averill's son Harry Jr. had graduated from a New York City embalmer's school and the elder Averill had added the funeral business to his already thriving furniture business, their relations remained the same on the surface, but underneath there was the bitterness of business rivals. This particular luncheon meeting Averill made a point of sitting directly across the table from the two partners.

He deliberately waited until mealtime conversation had subsided somewhat, then said in a friendly voice, but one which carried from one end of the table to the other, "Hear you fellows are buying an ambulance."

"Combination ambulance-hearse," Sam Potter said. "Matter-of-fact, it arrived this morning."

Averill beamed. "Probably a wise move. Ambulance fees will help carry you over rough spots when the funeral business is bad."

Both partners beamed back as genially as their competitor was beaming.

Dave Clemson said in a loud voice, "We don't even hope to break even on ambulance calls. It's just a service to the community."

"Well, that's certainly civic-minded of you boys," Averill said in an equally loud voice. "When I heard you were going in for additional revenue because your business had slipped, I knew it was just a malicious rumor."

"We're getting along fine," Sam Potter said in a comfortable tone which effectively hid his rage.

It took Harry Averill a full two months to discover the effect the new ambulance service was having on his business. During that time there were four automobile accident deaths at the local hospital, but Averill didn't get a single one. But when he finally realized what was happening, he took action to correct the situation at once.

He dropped the news in the partners' laps like a bombshell at a meeting of the Businessmen's Club.

"Got a new hearse yesterday," he announced casually. "Combination ambulance-hearse, like yours."

Only eighteen years in a business where public relations demanded an ability to control facial expression prevented the partners from gaping at him in consternation. Instead they both managed to look delighted.

"Shannon will have better ambulance service than most cities," Sam Potter remarked with a wide grin.

But when they got back to the funeral home, neither partner felt it necessary to conceal his gloom from the other.

"We're licked," Sam said. "Jimmy Straight, the Hose One pump truck driver, is Averill's brother-in-law. Every call that comes into the fire department will be relayed on to him instead of to us."

"Yeah," Dave said dispiritedly. Then he brightened. "On the other hand, Tommy Johnson on the night desk at the police station is my cousin. I think I can fix it to have *us* called first by the police."

This information cheered Sam a little. "Then at least we'll have an even break," he said thoughtfully. "It'll just be a question of which ambulance can get to the scene first."

That was the way it worked out. Since the police station and the fire department had a joint switchboard, both learned about automobile accidents simultaneously. And as a result the two funeral homes learned of them simultaneously. During the next few weeks both ambulances roared to every accident scene.

But since in no case were there more than three victims requiring hospitalization as a result of any one accident, and each ambulance was equipped to handle up to three stretcher cases, one ambulance always returned home empty. Neither managed to gain an edge, each garnering roughly half the available business.

At the end of six weeks Harry Averill made a visit to the Potter and Clemson Mortuary. He caught the partners in the act of laying out an elderly woman who had tried to pass a semi-trailer on a hill.

"Competent-looking job so far," Averill commented judiciously. "Though Harry Jr. would be a better judge of that than me. He handles all this end of the business, you know, while I work out front."

Neither partner felt as constrained to be polite to their competitor in private as they did in public. Sam Potter said with a trace of condescension, "We know you're not an embalmer," and Dave Clemson asked bluntly, "What do you want?"

"Thought it time we had a little business discussion," Averill said. "Did you know the whole village is beginning to talk about our races to accident scenes?"

Both partners looked at him. They not only knew it, they had worriedly discussed the possible effect such bad publicity might have on both funeral homes.

But all Sam Potter said was, "So?"

"So up to now people just think it's funny. They just

think we're competing for ambulance fees. It hasn't occurred to anyone that we're also trying to line up . . ." He paused, discarded the phrase he had started to use and changed it to, "Trying to create good will."

When Sam and Dave merely continued to look at him, Averill coughed delicately. "It occurred to me that if the general public ever suspects our . . . ah . . . good-will reason for rushing to accident scenes, people might consider it a trifle ghoulish."

The partners looked at each other, then went back to work. Sam carefully injected a little paraffin into the withered left cheek of the corpse, rounding it out prettily. As he moved to the other cheek, Dave lightly touched the left one with rouge.

"In a town this small, that sort of talk could ruin both of us," Averill said.

Sam asked bluntly, "What you driving at?"

"I suggest we split the business. You fellows take all calls one week, we'll take them the next. That way we won't be going out on unnecessary calls, there won't be any danger of talk and, best of all, we'll each only be on twenty-four-hour call half the time. I don't imagine you fellows like having to stick near a phone all the time any more than I do."

Sam and Dave silently continued working on the corpse for some minutes. Finally Dave said, "I think he's got a point, Sam."

"I guess so," Sam said reluctantly. "Maybe we ought to try it at least for a while."

Neither partner mentioned to Harry Averill that they had discussed going to him with the identical proposition.

For the next six months the cooperative agreement between Averill's Funeral Home and the Potter and Clemson Mortuary worked without friction. On alternate weeks the combination ambulance-hearses of each rushed to accident scenes alone. And while some weeks the traffic toll was heavier than others, over a period of time each made approximately the same number of trips.

However, when Dave Clemson made one of the statistical studies he was so fond of at the end of the six months, his findings upset him.

"We've had twenty-four calls in six months," he told Sam. "Averill's had twenty-seven. We brought in forty-nine people and he only brought in forty. In every case where a victim from out of town died, the next of kin called the funeral home whose ambulance brought the deceased to the hospital."

"Sounds fair enough to me," Sam said.

"But out of his forty people, twelve of Averill's died. Only seven of our forty-nine did. He got five more embalmings than we did."

"It'll work out even over the years," Sam assured him. "Next six months we'll probably get more embalmings than Averill."

"We better," Dave said darkly. "Even with this extra tourist business, we're barely keeping up payments on that eighty-five hundred loan. If things get *worse* instead of better, we're sunk."

. . .

But things didn't get worse. Fortunately for the shaky financial status of the mortuary, Sam Potter's prophecy came true. During the next six months, despite ambulance calls being fairly evenly split, only five of those accident victims brought in by Averill died, while eighteen delivered to the hospital by Sam and Dave expired.

"See?" Sam said, when Dave had reported to him the results of his semi-annual statistical study. "Now we're eight embalmings ahead of Averill." Then his face turned gloomy. "Which means the percentages are we'll drop way down during the next six months."

But this time Sam's prophecy was not correct, for the partners' luck held for the whole of the next six-month period. The accident victims they rushed to the hospital continued to die with much more gratifying frequency than those brought in by Averill.

By now the partners' procedure on emergency calls had settled into a routine. On the way to accident scenes Dave Clemson invariably drove. Coming back Sam Potter always drove while his thin partner sat in back with the patients. After delivering their cargoes to the hospital, they switched again and Dave drove home.

This might have gone on indefinitely without change had it not been for Sam Potter mistaking a car seat cushion for a body one dark night.

The call came in about eleven P.M., reporting a bad accident on the main highway about two miles beyond town. Within three minutes they were roaring to the scene with the siren wide open.

When they approached the accident scene, the first thing the partners saw was a ditched semi-trailer with a cluster of people gathered about it, then an overturned sedan fifty yards beyond. As usual Dave was driving, and since from previous experience he knew that in arguments between semis and passenger cars it was normally the occupants of the passenger car who were most in need of attention, he slid by the semi and brought the ambulance to a stop near the sedan.

A large number of cars had stopped, and so many curious on-lookers were wandering around, it was impossible to determine which, if any, group surrounded an injured person. As Sam slid out of the right-hand side of the ambulance, he spotted a seat cushion lying in the ditch near the overturned sedan, and in the dark mistook it for a body.

As the cushion was still some yards beyond where the ambulance had halted, Sam ran around the front of the vehicle instead of the rear. But when he reached a point near the left front fender, he saw his mistake and turned to look for Dave. Then he saw that Dave had stopped the ambulance right next to an injured man lying on the shoulder, and was already pulling open the rear doors.

Reversing himself, Sam rushed back along the left side of the vehicle, catching his shoulder sharply on the side-view mirror as he passed. It gave him a painful bruise, but in the flurry of helping Dave load the injured man into the ambulance he forgot about it.

There was only one injured person, and he was unconscious. As always Sam Potter drove to the hospital while Dave sat in back with the patient. They had almost reached the village line before Sam grew conscious of his shoulder aching. Then he remembered bumping the side-view mirror and glanced at it reproachfully.

The ambulance's siren had pulled all other traffic to the sides of the road, but one truckman had neglected to dim his highway lights. Just as Sam glanced at the sideview mirror, the ambulance interior was flooded with light. And to his surprise Sam noted that his jostling the mirror had turned it so that he had a full view of the back.

Then his surprise changed to horror as he saw the reflection of his partner's raised arm. What looked like a small blackjack was in Dave's hand. In the momentary illumination Sam saw it descend in a vicious arc onto the already injured head of their passenger.

Sam was so shocked by what he had seen, it didn't even occur to him to demand an explanation from Dave. With his mind in a turmoil, he roared on to the hospital.

He said nothing to Dave as they carried the stretcher inside, nor anything while they waited outside the door of the emergency room for the doctor's verdict.

He continued to remain silent when the doctor came out and announced laconically, "DOA." The doctor handed Dave a wallet and said, "Seems to be plenty of identification in there."

While Dave counted the money and wrote out a receipt which he gave the charge nurse, Sam thought over the appalling sight he had seen. He examined his partner carefully, but could detect nothing in his manner indicating a guilty conscience.

Prior to the advent of the new ambulance service, it had been the chief nurse's duty to contact accident victims' next of kin, but since both Averill and Clemson and Potter had volunteered to take this unpleasant task off her shoulders for cases they brought in, she had gladly relinquished the responsibility. Now Sam had another wait while Dave made a long-distance call from the superintendant's office.

Sam didn't go in with him. He didn't want to listen to his partner's sympathetic voice as he broke the news, nor to his respectful explanation that it was the Potter and Clemson Ambulance Service and Mortuary calling. Particularly he didn't want to hear Dave's question as to what disposition the next of kin wanted made of the body.

He still had not spoken to Dave when they returned to the ambulance. By force of habit he climbed in the right side of the cab, as he always did when they left the hospital, leaving the driver's seat for Dave. The first thing Dave did was glance at the side-view mirror.

Looking puzzled, Dave reached through the window to straighten it, then paused and carefully studied its present angle. When he saw it gave a full view of the rear, he gave Sam a quick sideglance.

Sam nodded his head and said in a dispirited voice, "I saw it."

Dave made no comment, merely starting the engine and driving away. But several times during the short trip home he glanced surreptitiously at his partner. Even in the dark Sam could tell that the thin man's face was pale.

When they pulled into the garage, Dave could stand the

suspense no longer. "What are you going to do, Sam?" he asked in a slightly high voice.

"I'm going to think awhile before I do anything," Sam said heavily.

He climbed out of the cab and made straight for the casket display room, leaving Dave to close the garage doors alone. When Dave came down a few moments later, Sam was seated with his pipe going and was staring off into space.

Dave's face was now very pale. After watching Sam hesitantly for a minute or two, he disappeared into the embalming room. Five minutes later he returned with two glasses of lemonade. Sam accepted one mutely and waited until Dave had his pipe going before he spoke.

Then he said, "This wasn't the first one, was it, Dave?"

Without looking at him, Dave shook his head.

"We've been averaging two to one over Averill," Sam said.

"Maybe they'd all have died anyway," Dave said in a low voice.

Sam looked at him steadily until Dave said in a defensive tone, "It's paid off the hearse and got us back on our feet. Without all those extra cases, we'd be bankrupt by now."

Sam drew thoughtfully on his pipe. "There's that of course," he conceded.

He continued to puff his pipe for some minutes. Finally he took it from his mouth and drained a quarter of his lemonade.

"If I called the police," he said reflectively, "I guess the business would be finished. Even if they electrocuted you and cleared me, the mortuary would never survive such a scandal."

Dave said nothing.

"Maybe they *would* all have died anyway," Sam said.

Dave said with a faint note of relief, "Of course they would have, Sam."

Sam drained the rest of his lemonade and tapped some of the ashes from his pipe to make it draw better. In a brisk tone he said, "I guess the best thing to do is change our procedure a little. You shouldn't have all the responsibility. Hereafter I'll ride in back half the time."

He looked up and met Dave's eyes. The two men smiled at each other.

THE QUESTION

STANLEY ELLIN

"The Question" was first published in Ellery Queen's
Mystery Magazine *in 1962. When, some time after this,
I met Tony at a Mystery Writers of America banquet—
these annual banquets were the only occasions when
we did meet—he told me that he had powerful feelings
about capital punishment, and that of all the polemics
against it he had ever read, none was as effective as
this short piece of fiction.*

*Coming from Tony, the compliment was as good as
a Pulitzer Prize for a short story. And it not only made
it easy for me to select a story of mine he particularly
liked, but made clear, through his preference, his depth
of humanity. He was, in every way, a very special man.*

I AM AN ELECTROCUTIONER . . . I prefer this word to executioner; I think words make a difference. When I was a boy,
people who buried the dead were undertakers, and then
somewhere along the way they became morticians and better
off for it.

Take the one who used to be the undertaker in my town.
He was a decent, respectable man very friendly if you'd let
him be, but hardly anybody would let him be. Today, his
son—who now runs the business—is not an undertaker but
a mortician, and is welcome everywhere. As a matter of fact,
he's an officer in my Lodge and is one of the most popular
members we have. And all it took to do that was changing
one word to another. The job's the same but the word if dif-

123

ferent, and people somehow will always go by words rather than meanings.

So, as I said, I am an electrocutioner—which is the proper professional word for it in my state where the electric chair is the means of execution.

Not that this is my profession. Actually, it's a sideline, as it is for most of us who perform executions. My real business is running an electrical supply and repair shop just as my father did before me. When he died I inherited not only the business from him, but also the position of state's electrocutioner.

We established a tradition, my father and I. He was running the shop profitably even before the turn of the century when electricity was a comparatively new thing, and he was the first man to perform a successful electrocution for the state. It was not the state's first electrocution, however. That one was an experiment and was badly bungled by the engineer who installed the chair in the state prison. My father, who had helped install the chair, was the assistant at the electrocution, and he told me that everything that could go wrong that day did go wrong. The current was eccentric, his boss froze on the switch, and the man in the chair was alive and kicking at the same time he was being burned to a crisp. The next time, my father offered to do the job himself, rewired the chair, and handled the switch so well that he was offered the job of official electrocutioner.

I followed in his footsteps, which is how a tradition is made, but I am afraid this one ends with me. I have a son, and what I said to him and what he said to me is the crux of the matter. He asked me a question—well, in my opinion, it was the kind of question that's at the bottom of most of the world's troubles today. There are some sleeping dogs that should be left to lie; there are some questions that should not be asked.

To understand all this, I think you have to understand me, and nothing could be easier. I'm sixty, just beginning to look my age, a little overweight, suffer sometimes from arthritis when the weather is damp. I'm a good citizen, complain about my taxes but pay them on schedule, vote for the right party, and run my business well enough to make a comfortable living from it.

I've been married thirty-five years and never looked at another woman in all that time. Well, looked maybe, but no more than that. I have a married daughter and a granddaughter almost a year old, and the prettiest, smilingest baby in town. I spoil her and don't apologize for it, because in my opinion that is what grandfathers were made for—to spoil their grandchildren. Let mama and papa attend to the business; grandpa is there for the fun.

And beyond all that I have a son who asks questions. The kind that shouldn't be asked.

Put the picutre together, and what you get is someone like yourself. I might be your next-door neighbor, I might be your old friend, I might be the uncle you meet whenever the family gets together at a wedding or a funeral. I'm like you.

Naturally, we all look different on the outside but we can still recognize each other on sight as the same kind of people. Deep down inside where it matters we have the same feelings, and we know that without any questions being asked about them.

"But," you might say, "there is a difference between us. You're the one who performs the executions, and I'm the one who reads about them in the papers, and that's a big difference, no matter how you look at it."

Is it? Well, look at it without prejudice, look at it with absolute honesty, and you'll have to admit that you're being unfair.

Let's face the facts, we're all in this together. If an old friend of yours happens to serve on a jury that finds a murderer guilty, you don't lock the door against him, do you? More than that: if you could get an introduction to the judge who sentences that murderer to the electric chair, you'd be proud of it wouldn't you? You'd be honored to have him sit at your table, and you'd be quick enough to let the world know about it.

And since you're so willing to be friendly with the jury that convicts and the judge that sentences, what about the man who has to pull the switch? He's finished the job you wanted done, he's made the world a better place for it. Why must he go hide away in a dark corner until the next time he's needed?

There's no use denying that nearly everybody feels he should, and there's less use denying that it's a cruel thing for anyone in my position to face. If you don't mind some strong language, it's a damned outrage to hire a man for an unpleasant job, and then despise him for it. Sometimes it's hard to abide such righteousness.

How do I get along in the face of it? The only way possible —by keeping my secret locked up tight and never being tempted to give it away. I don't like it that way, but I'm no fool about it.

The trouble is that I'm naturally easygoing and friendly. I'm the sociable kind. I like people, and I want them to like me. At Lodge meetings or in the clubhouse down at the golf course I'm always the center of the crowd. And I know what would happen if at any such time I ever opened my mouth and let that secret out. A five-minute sensation, and after that the slow chill setting in. It would mean the end of my whole life then and there, the kind of life I want to live, and no man in his right mind throws away sixty years of his life for a five-minute sensation.

You can see I've given the matter a lot of thought. More than that, it hasn't been idle thought. I don't pretend to be an educated man, but I'm willing to read books on any subject that interests me, and execution has been one of my main interests ever since I got into the line. I have the books sent to the shop where nobody takes notice of another piece of mail, and I keep them locked in a bin in my office so that I can read them in private.

There's a nasty smell about having to do it this way—at my age you hate to feel like a kid hiding himself away to read a dirty magazine—but I have no choice. There isn't a soul on earth outside of the warden at state's prison and a couple of picked guards there who know I'm the one pulling the switch at an execution, and I intend it to remain that way.

Oh, yes, my son knows now. Well, he's difficult in some ways, but he's no fool. If I wasn't sure he would keep his mouth shut about what I told him, I wouldn't have told it to him in the first place.

Have I learned anything from those books? At least enough to take a pride in what I'm doing for the state and the way I do it. As far back in history as you want to go there have always been executioners. The day that men first made laws to help keep peace among themselves was the day the first executioner was born. There have always been lawbreakers; there must always be a way of punishing them. It's as simple as that.

The trouble is that nowadays there are too many people who don't want it to be as simple as that. I'm no hypocrite, I'm not one of those narrow-minded fools who thinks that every time a man comes up with a generous impulse he's some kind of crackpot. But he can be mistaken. I'd put most of the people who are against capital punishment in that class. They are fine, high-minded citizens who've never in their lives been close enough to a murderer or rapist to smell the evil in him. In fact, they're so fine and high-minded that they can't imagine anyone in the world not being like themselves. In that case, they say anybody who commits murder or rape is just a plain, ordinary human being who's had a bad spell. He's no criminal, they say, he's just sick. He doesn't need the electric chair; all he needs is a kindly old doctor to examine his head and straighten out the kinks in his brain.

In fact, they say there is no such thing as a criminal at all. There are only well people and sick people, and the ones who deserve all your worry and consideration are the sick ones. If they happen to murder or rape a few of the well ones now and then, why, just run for the doctor.

This is the argument from beginning to end, and I'd be the last one to deny that it's built on honest charity and good intentions. But it's a mistaken argument. It omits the one fact that matters. When anyone commits murder or rape he is no longer in the human race. A man has a human brain and a God-given soul to control his animal nature. When the animal in him takes control he's not a human being any more. Then he has to be exterminated the way any animal must be if it goes wild in the middle of helpless people. And my duty is to be the exterminator.

It could be that people just don't understand the meaning of the word *duty* any more. I don't want to sound old-fashioned, God forbid, but when I was a boy things were more straight-forward and clear-cut. You learned to tell right from wrong, you learned to do what had to be done, and you didn't ask questions every step of the way. Or if you had to ask any questions, the ones that mattered were *how* and *when*.

Then along came psychology, along came the professors, and the main question was always *why*. Ask yourself *why, why, why* about everything you do, and you'll end up doing nothing. Let a couple of generations go along that way, and you'll finally have a breed of people who sit around in trees like monkeys, scratching their heads.

Does this sound far-fetched? Well, it isn't. Life is a complicated thing to live. All his life a man finds himself facing one situation after another, and the way to handle them is to live by the rules. Ask yourself *why* once too often, and you can find yourself so tangled up that you go under. The show must go on. Why? Women and children first. Why? My country, right or wrong. Why? Never mind your duty. Just keep asking *why* until it's too late to do anything about it.

Around the time I first started going to school my father gave me a dog, a collie pup named Rex. A few years after Rex suddenly became unfriendly, the way a dog will sometimes, and then vicious, and then one day he bit my mother when she reached down to pat him.

The day after that I saw my father leaving the house with his hunting rifle under his arm and with Rex on a leash. It wasn't the hunting season, so I knew what was going to happen to Rex and I knew why. But it's forgivable in a boy to ask things that a man should be smart enough not to ask.

"Where are you taking Rex?" I asked my father. "What are you going to do with him?"

"I'm taking him out back of town," my father said. "I'm going to shoot him."

"But why?" I said, and that was when my father let me see that there is only one answer to such a question.

"Because it has to be done," he said.

I never forgot that lesson. It came hard; for a while I hated my father for it, but as I grew up I came to see how right he was. We both knew why the dog had to be killed. Beyond that, all questions would lead nowhere. Why the dog had become vicious, why God had put a dog on earth to be killed this way—these are the questions that you can talk out to the end of time, and while you're talking about them you still have a vicious dog on your hands.

It is strange to look back and realize now that when the business of the dog happened, and long before it and long after it, my father was an electrocutioner, and I never knew it. Nobody knew it, not even my mother. A few times a year my father would pack his bag and a few tools and go away for a couple of days, but that was all any of us knew. If you asked him where he was going he would simply say he had a job to do out of town. He was not a man you'd ever suspect of philandering or going off on a solitary drunk, so nobody gave it a second thought.

It worked the same way in my case. I found out how well it worked when I finally told my son what I had been doing on those jobs out of town, and that I had gotten the warden's permission to take him on as an assistant and train him to handle the chair himself when I retired. I could tell from the way he took it that he was as thunderstruck at this as I had been thirty years before when my father had taken me into his confidence.

"Electrocutioner?" said my son. "An *electrocutioner?*"

"Well, there's no disgrace to it," I said. "And since it's got to be done, and somebody has to do it, why not keep it in the family? If you knew anything about it, you'd know it's a profession that's often passed down in a family from generation to generation. What's wrong with a good, sound tradition? If more people believed in tradition you wouldn't have so many troubles in the world today."

It was the kind of argument that would have been more than enough to convince me when I was his age. What I hadn't taken into account was that my son wasn't like me, much as I wanted him to be. He was a grown man in his own right, but a grown man who had never settled down to his responsibilities. I had always kept closing my eyes to that, I had always seen him the way I wanted to and not the way he was.

When he left college after a year, I said, all right, there are some people who aren't made for college, I never went there, so what difference does it make. When he went out with one girl after another and could never make up his mind to marrying any of them, I said, well, he's young, he's sowing his wild oats, the time will come soon enough when he's ready to take care of a home and family. When he sat daydreaming in the shop instead of tending to business I never made a fuss about it. I knew when he put his mind to it he was as good an electrician as you could ask for, and in these soft times people are allowed to do a lot more dreaming and a lot less working than they used to.

The truth was that the only thing that mattered to me was being his friend. For all his faults he was a fine-looking boy with a good mind. He wasn't much for mixing with people, but if he wanted to he could win anyone over. And in the back of my mind all the while he was growing up was the thought that he was the only one who would learn my secret some day, and would share it with me, and make it easier to bear. I'm not secretive by nature. A man like me needs a thought like that to sustain him.

So when the time came to tell him he shook his head and said no. I felt that my legs had been kicked out from under me. I argued with him and he still said no, and I lost my temper.

"Are you against capital punishment?" I asked him. "You don't have to apologize if you are. I'd think all the more of you, if that's your only reason."

"I don't know if it is," he said.

"Well, you ought to make up your mind one way or the other," I told him. "I'd hate to think you were like every other hypocrite around who says it's all right to condemn a man to the electric chair and all wrong to pull the switch."

"Do I have to be the one to pull it?" he said. "Do you?"

"Somebody has to do it. Somebody always has to do the dirty work for the rest of us. It's not like the Old Testament days when everybody did it for himself. Do you know how they executed a man in those days? They laid him on the ground tied hand and foot, and everybody around had to heave rocks on him until he was crushed to death. They didn't invite anybody to stand around and watch. You wouldn't have much choice then, would you?"

"I don't know," he said. And then because he was as smart as they come and knew how to turn your words against you, he said, "After all, I'm not without sin."

"Don't talk like a child," I said. "You're without the sin of murder on you or any kind of sin that calls for execution. And if you're so sure the Bible has all the answers, you might remember that you're supposed to render unto Caesar the things that are Caesar's."

"Well," he said, "in this case I'll let you do the rendering."

I knew then and there from the way he said it and the way he looked at me that it was no use trying to argue with him. The worst of it was knowing that we had somehow moved far apart from each other and would never really be close again. I should have had sense enough to let it go at that. I should have just told him to forget the whole thing and keep his mouth shut about it.

Maybe if I had ever considered the possibility of his saying no, I would have done it. But because I hadn't considered any such possibility I was caught off balance, I was too much upset to think straight, I will admit it now. It was my own fault that I made an issue of things and led him to ask the one question he should never have asked.

"I see," I told him. "It's the same old story, isn't it? Let somebody else do it. But if they pull your number out of a hat and you have to serve on a jury and send a man to the chair, that's all right with you. At least, it's all right as long as there's somebody else to do the job that you and the judge and every decent citizen wants done. Let's face the facts, boy, you don't have the guts. I'd hate to think of you even walking by the death house. The shop is where you belong. You can be nice and cozy there, wiring up fixtures and ringing the cash register. I can handle my duties without your help."

It hurt me to say it. I had never talked like that to him before, and it hurt. The strange thing was that he didn't seem angry about it; he only looked at me puzzled.

"Is that all it is to you?" he said. "A duty?"

"Yes."

"But you get paid for it, don't you?"

"I get paid little enough for it."

He kept looking at me that way. "Only a duty?" he said, and never took his eyes off me. "But you enjoy it, don't you?"

That was the question he asked.

You enjoy it, don't you? You stand there looking through a peephole in the wall at the chair. In thirty years I have stood there more than a hundred times looking at that chair. The guards bring somebody in. Usually he is in a daze; sometimes he screams, throws himself around and fights. Sometimes it is a woman, and a woman can be as hard to handle as a man when she is led to the chair. Sooner or later, whoever it is is strapped down and the black hood is dropped over his head. Now your hand is on the switch.

The warden signals, and you pull the switch. The current hits the body like a tremendous rush of air suddenly filling it. The body leaps out of the chair with only the straps holding it back. The head jerks, and a curl of smoke comes from it. You release the switch and the body falls back again.

You do it once more, do it a third time to make sure. And whenever your hand presses the switch you can see in your mind what the current is doing to that body and what the face under the hood must look like.

Enjoy it?

That was the question my son asked me. That was what

he said to me, as if I didn't have the same feelings deep down in me that we all have.

Enjoy it?

But, my God, how could anyone *not* enjoy it!

THE ADVENTURE OF
THE ADAM BOMB

ROBERT L. FISH

*No critic was ever kinder to an author than was Tony
in introducing my collection,* The Incredible Schlock
Homes. *His remarks tell more about this story—and
Tony—than anything I could ever say.*

*"There have been parodies and pastiches of Sherlock
Holmes for very nearly as long as there have been Sherlock Holmes stories. . . . I have several times stated
publicly that these Fish stories are the best of all the
mock-Holmesian literature in the sixty-odd years since
Robert Barr; and I have yet to hear a murmur of dis-
sent from such informed authorities as Ellery Queen or
Vincent Starrett. . . . Not merely are they unpardonably
and outrageously funny; they are small masterpieces of
adroit and devious plotting. . . ."*

I HAD BEEN PURSUING an errand for my friend Mr. Schlock
Homes in the small village of Elbow Twisting, Herts., when
the fateful telegram arrived. I do not have it before me as
I write but it is not necessary, since its tragic message is
engraved upon my memory. It read: "MR. HOMES PASSED
AWAY YESTERDAY. INTERMENT AT 4 P.M. PORTLAND CEME-
TERY," and was signed by our housekeeper, Mrs. Essex. It
was in complete shock that I threw my few possessions
into my bag and caught the first train for London. There I

133

transferred to a hansom and proceeded directly to the cemetery, my mind a blank.

As we rattled through the dismal streets, I remembered that Homes had insisted upon doing research on a rare virus; so rare, he had informed me, that no known case of the disease had as yet been discovered. I had warned him of the dangers of such investigation, but he had passed it off with his usual disregard for either personal danger or the advice of others, and had now apparently fallen victim to the very germ he had been seeking. It was with heavy heart that I descended at the cemetery, barely able to think coherently.

There was a large group gathered about the open casket, and I forced myself to step forward for a last look at the frozen profile I had known so well. His brother Criscroft came forward and grasped my hand wordlessly. In silence I stepped back and observed the crowd about the grave. There I could see many police agents whom Homes had assisted in past cases; many persons of high estate who owed a great deal to my dead friend for their present state of well-being; and included in the crowd I could also see the smirking faces of many criminals to whose downfall Homes had been dedicated. I could not help myself; tears formed in my eyes and fell unhindered to the ground. Feeling more alone than at any time in my life, I watched the undertaker's men bolt the cover into place and begin the sad task of lowering the casket into the waiting earth.

A sudden elbow in my ribs caused my attention to turn to a short, stocky figure at my side. He was a cockney, poorly dressed, and with a long scarf wrapped about his neck, and a huge straggling mustache covering half of his face.

"Good riddance to bad rubbish! Eh, wot, Guv'nor?" said this vile apparition in a high whining voice, once again nudging me with his sharp elbow.

"Hold your foul tongue and be off with you, you miserable specimen!" I cried, brandishing my stick. "No finer person ever breathed the clean, sweet air of Putney, and I shall tolerate no word against his memory! Be off, I say, or you shall suffer the worse for it!"

"My, my, Watney, such devotion would better to have been deserved," came the voice of my friend Schlock Homes with a low chuckle. "No, do not look now, but meet me in fifteen minutes at the Uppin Arms in Jermyn Street!"

I could not help myself; I turned in astonishment but the

small figure had disappeared and I was left with my mind awhirl, watching the coffin lowered into the cold grave.

I found my way to Jermyn Street after the funeral, but to this day I do not know how. It was difficult to believe that I had not been dreaming, for I had seen his body with my own eyes; yet the memory of that voice in my ear left me no choice. Afraid of what I might find, I pushed open the heavy door of the pub and entered into the gloom. The cockney, still with scarf, but lacking his grotesque mustache, confronted me from a corner booth, and his twinkling eyes could belong to nobody in this world except my old friend Schlock Homes!

"Homes!" I cried, sinking into the seat opposite as my legs weakened under me. "How is it possible? What is the reason for this macabre joke? Why have you given this terrible shock to all of your friends?"

"Only to you, I am afraid, Watney," replied Homes. "It was essential to a case I am engaged upon that I disappear, and ever since the time I disappeared in that tavern in Switzerland for several months, only a buried corpse could have satisfied my enemies. Both Criscroft and the police agents were aware of the scheme, and I believe I have made Mrs. Essex quite happy by allowing her to play a role in one of my cases. You, however, are too honest and open in your feelings, and any of my enemies, seeing your countenance, would have known at once it was a trick. I am indeed sorry, Watney, for the shock you have suffered today, but believe me, it was of vital necessity!"

"And your sending me to Elbow Twisting?"

"A part of the same plan, I am afraid. I had planned to die of a virulent disease, and I was sure that I could scarcely hope to deceive you on that score!"

"But the body, Homes! I saw it myself!"

"An excellent example of Madame Tussaud's art, Watney. They have owed me a favor since the time I foiled those two miscreants who concealed themselves on the premises for the purpose of robbing the safe during the night. You, yourself, chronicled the case in 'The Adventure of the Waxed Pair.' "

"But your appearance, Homes! Your extra weight!"

"Only stuffing; actually, one of Mrs. Essex's pillows."

"And your height, Homes! You are fully a foot shorter!"

"Special shoes. But this involved procedure was not formulated either to demonstrate my ability at disguise, nor to needlessly cause you anguish, Watney. No, it was necessary as, if you will allow me, I shall explain at once."

We ordered drinks, and once they were before us, Homes leaned back and proceeded to explain the strange events of the past few weeks.

"You are, of course, acquainted with my brother Criscroft," said he, "and you know of his important position in the Home Office. You must also be familiar with the high regard in which I hold him, not only for his intelligence, but also for his almost infallible sense of prescience.

"Well, some three weeks ago, while you were out on a call, Criscroft appeared in our rooms on Bagel Street. He had not sent any previous notice of his coming, which in itself was highly unusual, and he was not his usual calm self. He wandered about the room making small talk, as if reluctant to state the purpose of his visit. I waited patiently for him to approach the subject, but he continued with his evasions.

" 'You were familiar with the Brace-Partridge plans?' he asked, obviously making conversation.

" 'Certainly; a lovely couple,' I replied. 'Unfortunately, I was unable to attend the nuptials.'

" 'But you sent a fish slice?'

" 'Of course. Halibut, I believe. However, I am sure that you did not remove yourself from your busy desk in Whitehall for the purpose of discussing London's social season with me. Pray tell me what is actually bothering you!'

"He threw himself into a chair and stared at me broodingly. 'If only I knew,' he replied. 'In truth I have nothing to go on but a feeling of foreboding, and I hate to interrupt your schedule with something which could well be only a wild-goose chase!'

" 'Simply state the facts and let us proceed from there,' I said. 'You have never given me cause for complaint until now.'

" 'Very well, then,' said he. 'The facts are these: Quite recently a person giving his name as Frederic Adam appeared at the War Office and claimed to have invented a new type infernal machine which he wished to patent under the name of the Adam Bomb. The War Office wanted more detailed information; he refused to disclose any of his secrets. They then offered him the use of the Sussex Proving Grounds for him to demonstrate his new invention, but he declined on the basis that the proving grounds were too small, and that the test would jeopardize near-by residents. Since the Sussex

Proving Grounds are fully four acres in size, the War Office considered his excuse quite spurious, and sent him about his business.'

" 'I should tend to agree with their action.'

" 'I am not so sure. Well, a few days later a colleague of mine in the Explosives Section happened to mention the case to me in our club, not for action, but merely in idle conversation as demonstrating the type of annoyance they suffered at the hands of cranks. For some reason a feeling of foreboding seemed to overcome me, and I pressed him for all details of the man and their conversations, but other than the facts which I have just stated, he was unable to be of further assistance.'

" 'What did you do then?'

" 'Actually, there was little that I could do officially. However, unofficially I began making inquiries into Mr. Frederic Adam's past, and while I could find nothing actionable in his activities, I did discover that while a student he had studied under Professor Marty, who, as we both know, is not only a brilliant scientist, but the most dangerous criminal in all England.'

" 'Professor Marty, you say? You interest me deeply!'

" 'I thought I should. Well, my investigation seemed to show that there had been no contact between them since Adam graduated University, but this in itself means nothing. Adam, it appears, had private means, and established a laboratory near Glasgow, where he pursued his researches, and from whence he traveled when he appeared at the War Office.'

" 'And since that time?'

" 'He has recently purchased an abandoned coal mine near Newcastle in Northumberland County and is even now moving his scientific equipment into it. It is heavily guarded, extensively fenced, and quite impossible to enter. Other than his previous acquaintance with Professor Marty, and this feeling of foreboding which I have, I admit to small basis for further investigation, but I cannot rid myself of the conviction that it is vital that we know what he is planning!'

" 'And what do you wish me to do?'

" 'I suggest that you attempt to gain entrance to this mine in one of your inimitable disguises. Since I know that you are under constant surveillance by the criminal element of London, you must first convince them that you have taken sick and succumbed to your illness. You will then be free to pursue your investigation without undue suspicion on their part.'

"We therefore decided on the plan which you are now witnessing. I am very sorry that it was necessary to include you among the victims of the deception, Watney, but the assurance of every scoundrel in England tonight that Schlock Homes is safely disposed of beneath six feet of earth owes much to your touching performance at the grave!"

"But, Homes," I inquired, "is this not basically a matter for the police? Can they not demand entrance to this mine and see what deviltry is afoot?"

Homes smiled at me pityingly. "The police," said he, "may serve to locate something of the size of an elephant, assuming the area of search were sufficiently proscribed; but in the first place, there is no evidence that Mr. Adam is engaged in anything nefarious, which would seriously complicate the possibility of obtaining search warrants. In the second place, I doubt if the police would be in a position to recognize a clue should they encounter one. No, Criscroft is right. I shall have to go down there myself and attempt to gain entrance to this mysterious mine in some fashion."

"And what is my role in all this?"

Homes leaned forward impressively. "This mine which Adam has purchased," said he, "is located at Seldom-on-Tyne, a suburb of Newcastle, in Northumberland County. We shall select a country inn on the river, sufficiently distant from the mine to avoid suspicion, but close enough to allow easy travel. There we shall share quarters, for I am certain to have errands for you to do. Besides, it is always well to have a friend in the vicinity when one is working underground."

"And our luggage?"

"All has been arranged. Even now your baggage and mine are awaiting us at King's Cross. Our reservations on the sleeper are being held at the ticket office. I suggest we dine at some small restaurant where my disheveled appearance will not cause comment, and then, if you wish, we can pass the hours until train time in shilling seats at Queen's Hall, where the Minsk dancers are performing."

"I should like that!" I cried with enthusiasm. "I have always wanted to see the Russian Minsk dancers!"

"Actually," said Homes, "I believe these are the Harold Minsk dancers from the United States."

"But, Homes," I said in disappointment, "this is misrepresentation!"

"Yes," replied Homes thoughtfully, "I suppose you might call it a ballet ruse, but we do have the time to pass in some manner, and I understand that their talent is quite revealing."

The following morning I found myself ensconced in a fairly clean inn at Skeleton Quay, but a few miles from the heavily guarded mine. Homes had separated from me at the station, selecting to hire a ramshackle bicycle and pedaling off along the road ahead of my trap. I was amazed at his appearance; with his cap pushed back, his scarf waving in the breeze, his mustache rampant, and his shrill whistle, he appeared in all respects to be what he pretended to be, a Tyneside worker on his way to the job.

It was evening when he came whistling up the stairs to our room and entered the door. As soon as it was closed, he quickly locked it and fell into a chair, laughing.

"There was little to it, Watney," he said. "I managed to combine the stupidity of a natural with the native cunning of the local folk, and this, plus my pure Geordie accent, did the job. They hired me at once! You are now looking at the new sweeper in the Adam mine."

"A sweeper?" I asked in amazement. "Certainly you could have obtained a better position than that!"

"I am not there to make a living," he remarked dryly, "and the sweeper, my dear Watney, is one person who has access to all parts of the installation. Also, in order not to interfere with the work, my duties require me to be in places when the other workers are having meals, which will allow for opportunities for observation which might otherwise be difficult.

"It is an interesting operation, and one which must have cost a pretty penny. Huge equipment is arriving constantly and being unpackaged. My duties take me to many parts of the mine, and I find it to be far more extensive than I should have imagined. I suggest, Watney, that tomorrow you take a trap into Newcastle and visit the local Coal Board for the purpose of obtaining a copy of the original survey of this mine. I am beginning to have a glimmer of the aim behind this tremendous imposture, and I shall need to be familiar with the terrain!"

When Homes had left the following morning on his bicycle, I arranged transportation and went into Newcastle.

While the Coal Board would not permit the original drawing to leave the premises, there was no difficulty in arranging to trace the underground map comprising the various tunnels of the old, abandoned mine. With the tracing safely concealed on my person, I returned to Skeleton Quay and spent the remainder of the day strolling along the river and admiring the fortitude of the brave people who could tolerate such a place.

The usual whistle announced the arrival of my friend, and once in the room I could tell from the excited gleam in his eyes that he was on the trail of some interesting discovery.

"We are getting warmer, Watney!" he exclaimed. "You have the underground map?"

"A tracing of it," I replied. "It is indeed extensive. Some of the tunnels cover many miles."

"Fine! Please spread it out on this table and allow me to study it!"

Taking a standard one-inch map from his jacket, he laid it side by side to my tracing, and began to pore over the two maps with the greatest of concentration. Finally he shoved them to one side and leaned back.

"I begin to see light, I believe, Watney. Let me tell you of an interesting discovery which I made today. During the lunch hour it is my duty to clean the offices while the staff are eating, and I naturally took the opportunity to make a thorough search of the desks and drawers, as well as of the papers lying about. I found them to be covered with many scientific symbols, and I knew that if the solution to our problem lay in decoding all of these, our task would be a difficult one indeed! However, there was one formula which was recurrent, appearing at the head of each sheet of paper, and I memorized it, rather than take the chance of having it discovered during the nightly search which all employees must endure on leaving the premises."

"And what is this formula, Homes?" I asked breathlessly.

He leaned over the table and scrawled on a piece of paper. I stared at the figures in bewilderment, for he had written: $E = Mc^2$!

"You believe that this strange formula might throw light on our problem?" I asked in amazement. "But it is so short that it barely permits of decoding!"

"True, but still it is the only formula repeated on all the papers, and must therefore be vital to our case. As to its lack of length, I have solved shorter. I once located the body of a murdered man with nothing more to go on than the single letter X which appeared mysteriously on a newspaper diagram of the scene of the killing."

He rubbed his hands together nervously, in that gesture which I well knew indicated a desire to be alone with an interesting problem. "And now, if you will excuse me, Watney," he said, "I shall get right to it while the events are fresh in my mind, for I feel that I have all of the necessary facts within my possession!"

The following morning I awoke to find Homes pacing the floor in smiling satisfaction, and he chuckled at my startled expression, for he was no longer in disguise.

"Yes, Watney," said he in high good humour, "the masquerade is over! The problem is solved! I am afraid that Mr. Adam will have to apply to the Labour Board for a new sweeper, although in truth I doubt if they will be in business long enough to require such services!"

"But, Homes," I exclaimed in awe, "do you mean that with the little information which you showed me last night you have managed to arrive at an answer to this mystery?"

"The importance of information is in direct relationship to our ability to interpret it," he replied. "Come to this table and allow me to show you the connexion between the facts which we were able to collect."

Spreading the one-inch district map upon the table, he placed the mine tracing over it and carefully oriented the two until they were properly superimposed.

"I began my cogitation," he said, "by considering the possible reasons Mr. Adam might have for locating his so-called scientific experiment in a mine. In the papers which I perused during my search of the office, I recalled reading something about a 'mushroom cloud,' and mines, of course, because of their dampness and constant temperature, are ideal for the cultivation of mushrooms; but since I was—and am—convinced that these papers were spurious in intent, I disregard this line of thought.

"I then considered what more logical reason he might have for this odd selection of location. Suddenly a possibility struck me! Mine tunnels, Watney, run for many miles underground, and are a perfect means of getting from one place to another without detection! I immediately began to trace the various tunnels, comparing their location with the surface objects under which they passed. And then I had it!" He placed a long tapering finger on one spot of the superimposed maps and continued. "Here, Watney, is the answer! Tunnel No. 5 runs in a northeasterly direction, passing beneath nothing more important than farm country and several small villages, until it reaches here, at which point, you will note, *it stops directly beneath Eastland Prison!*

"It was now quite obvious that the *E* of the formula stood for *Eastland,* and I therefore returned with even greater enthusiasm to the study of the remainder of these mysterious symbols: Mc^2! I attempted to rationalize the *M* for either miles or meters, or the *c* for either cubits or cells, but the answer refused to appear. It was only after many hours of pondering that I realized that I was being unnecessarily complex in my reasoning. The equal sign in the formula clearly indicated that the symbols were mathematical in nature, and I therefore reapplied my efforts to the problem, studying it from a purely mathematical approach. And then I finally saw it! Do you recall from your school days what the small 2 above the *c* stands for in mathematics, Watney?"

"The square, does it not?" I hazarded.

"It does indeed," said Homes, his eyes twinkling. "But is it not also called the *power?"*

And then, suddenly, I saw the answer. "McPowers!" I cried. "Angus McPowers, the Glasgow assassin!"

"Precisely! The man known in thieves' argot in Glasgow as the 'Scotch Cooler!' His execution at Eastland Prison is scheduled for next week, and his friends and criminal associates have sworn they would arrange his escape at all costs! In the mine, Watney, I also came across a large machine which was marked 'Cyclatron,' and which can only be an electrically operated cycle of some new scientific design intended to spirit this murderer beyond reach once they have tunneled him to freedom! But I am afraid they did not plan on the interference of Schlock Homes when they designed this ingenious escape!"

"A brilliant tour de force, Homes!" I exclaimed, grasping his hand. "What do you plan to do now?"

"It is already done, Watney," he replied simply. "Early this morning I entered the mine in my sweeper's disguise and reversed the electrical connexions on their high-powered cycle. Then, upon my return here, I sent telegrams to both Criscroft and Scotland Yard advising them of the situation. Even now the watch on McPowers is being doubled, and the Adam gang are under twenty-four hour surveillance. Mc-

Powers will go to his Maker as the judge ordered—that I promise!"

The following morning, back once again in our quarters in Bagel Street, Homes entered the breakfast room just as I was finishing my perusal of the daily journal.

"Is there anything of interest in the headlines this morning?" he inquired genially, sitting down to his breakfast and drawing a napkin languidly into his lap.

"A rather curious disappearance in the north," I replied, reading further into the article.

Homes sat back in alarm, breakfast forgotten. "Do not tell me that despite all of my efforts the police have allowed McPowers to disappear!" he cried.

"Not exactly," I said, handing him the journal folded to the article. "It seems that sometime during the night the whole of Northumberland County disappeared."

"Northumberland County, eh?" said Homes, relaxing and accepting the newspaper. "Ah, well, at least there should be no need for us to become involved. Northumberland County is of sufficient size that even the police should be able to discover it!"

IN THE SHADE OF
THE OLD APPLE TREE

FLETCHER FLORA

> *This writer's relationship with Anthony Boucher was restricted, so to speak, to an occasional pat on the head or rap on the knuckles. Both were administered verbally, by remote control. In brief, being a volunteer exile in the hinterland, a stranger to the literary meccas of East Coast and West alike, the former never had the pleasure of meeting the latter, or of knowing him in any way other than by his work and published judgments. Nevertheless, there is reason to believe that the following story was one of Mr. Boucher's favorites among the writer's inventory. The writer, at any rate, hopes so.*

IT'S APRIL AGAIN. THE frail pink blossoms of the flowering crab shower to earth in the slightest stirring of the languid air to lie like pastel snow among the clustered headstones of the Canning dead. Already the fruit is forming where the blossoms hung, and in a little while, after the swift passing of spring, toward the end of summer's indolent amble, the small red apples will fall in turn to lie where the blossoms lie. The seasons come and the seasons go . . .

The nicest thing about Connie was that she was, so to speak, sort of in and out of the family at the same time. What I mean is, she wasn't really a Canning at all, although she used the name for the lack of another. As a matter of fact, she was someone Uncle Wish (a happy compromise with Aloysius) picked up in Italy after the late great war and managed, by hook or crook, to appropriate and spirit home. She was, Uncle Wish had explained with tears in his voice, a homeless waif foraging among the rubble of an ancient world, her poor little body emaciated and filthy, her cute little nose chronically snotty. Anyhow, he brought her home and left her with Grandfather, after which, having euphemistically borrowed a substantial sum of money, he was off again to some other place to see what else he could find.

Grandfather saw to it that Connie's body was washed and her nose wiped. He believed, I think, that Uncle Wish's bootleg adoption of Connie was a good sign. He took it as an indication that Uncle Wish was developing a sense of commitment to the serious problems of life. Nothing, of course, could have been more absurd. Uncle Wish was simply a compassionate scoundrel who was always prepared to indulge his humanity if there was someone else at hand to pay the price over the long haul. Most of the girls he picked up in the places he went were well-washed and well-fed and, after Uncle Wish was finished with them, well-paid. It should be said, moreover, that they were invariably older than Connie was. And much less permanent. Uncle Wish may have been willing to be an absentee father, but he had absolutely no intention of becoming a husband, absent or present.

So Grandfather paid for Uncle Wish's grand gesture over the long haul, but don't shed any tears in your beer because of that. Having accumulated most of the money in an area approximately a hundred miles wide running roughly from Chicago to Denver, he was adequately equipped for it. And Connie blossomed in his tender care. I saw her for the first time in the summer of 1949, when I made my annual visit to Grandfather's country estate. He was a great family man, Grandfather was, and I was invited every summer for a visit of three month's duration. The invitation was, in fact, by implication a command, and in view of the high price of disfavor, I appeared faithfully near the first of every June, bearing the fulsome greetings of my father, Grandfather's son and Uncle Wish's brother, and mindful of the fierce admonitions, delivered in private just before my departure, to for God's sake be very careful to say or do nothing that would jeopardize our position in Grandfather's will. My father was extremely sensitive about our position in Grandfather's will, but I never blamed him for that. Inasmuch as he never earned a dime in his life, living quite richly on an allowance Grandfather made him, it was perfectly understandable.

It was, as I said, nice to have Connie in and out of the family at the same time. Being in, she was, so to speak, handy. Being out, she was, as it were, available. What I mean is, there were none of the messy complications and taboos ordinarily imposed upon blood relationships. That very first summer, in 1949, I was introduced to the advantages of our anomalous connection. While foraging among the rubble of an ancient civilization, it became quickly apparent, Connie had acquired a seamy sort of intelligence far beyond her years in matters that would have, if he had known it, set Grandfather's few remaining hairs on end. She was ten at the time, and I was twelve, but she in effect was ages older. She was as old as Nero, and she spoke a language older than Latin. Her English was hardly more than a few key words and phrases, but the eyes and the hands have a vocabulary and a grammar of their own. She had much to teach me, and I must say that I was an apt pupil. I anticipated eagerly my annual pilgrimage to Grandfather's house.

Cleaned up, Connie was a pretty little girl. Grown up, she was a beauty. She grew along lovely lines to intriguing dimensions, and when she reached the intriguing dimensions, she simply quit growing. As she mastered English she forgot Italian, but she never forgot her other ancient language. She lived with Grandfather until she was ready for college, and after college she established herself in an apartment in Chicago, where she was, she claimed, working seriously at painting. I never visited the apartment and never saw any of her work, and I suspect that the reason I never saw any was that there never *was* any. As with me and Father and Mother and Uncle Wish, as with us all, Grandfather paid the freight over the long haul. I was happy to learn, the first summer after her establishment in the Chicago apartment, that her command appearance at Grandfather's was to run, for the most part, concurrently with my own.

In the summer of 1964, I was twenty-seven and Connie was twenty-five. Grandfather was eighty-six. Father and Mother and Uncle Wish were dead. All dead. Father had died suddenly under Grandfather's roof of what was diagnosed by Grandfather's doctor, also an octogenarian, as a coronary. Mother, remaining after Father's death, had soon followed him to heaven as a result of an overdose of sleeping medicine, which sad event was popularly supposed to have been incited by grief. I was present on both occasions, as was Connie, and I remember expressing to her a proper astonishment at discovering, on the first occasion, that Father had any heart at all, let alone a weak one, and, on the second, that Mother was capable of grief for anyone, let alone for Father. But small matter. Every loss has its compensatory gain. Uncle Wish having previously come a fatal cropper in a distant land, from which his mortal remains were shipped home for burial, Connie and I remained as the only heirs in Grandfather's last will and testament. His estate, I believe, amounted to something like seventy million dollars, which is, you must agree, a tidy sum.

And so, when I arrived at Grandfather's house last June, there was Connie to meet me. As I tooled up the long drive from the road between tall and lithesome poplars, she came out of the house and across the veranda and down into the drive, and by the time I had brought my black Jag to a halt, she was in position to lean across the passenger bucket and give me a kiss. Contact, minimum. Effect, below standard.

"Hello, Buster," she said. "Crawl out of that thing and get kissed properly."

I crawled out and was kissed properly. Or improperly, depending on your point of view.

"Very stimulating," I said. "I believe your technique has improved, if possible."

"Do you think so? It's sweet of you to say it."

"No doubt you've been practicing. I must remember to call on you in that apartment of yours sometime."

"No chance. The summer is sufficient, darling. I don't believe I'd care for you in off-seasons. You might become tiresome."

"That's true. There's nothing to be gained from too much of a good thing. Where's Grandfather?"

"He's on his daily pilgrimage to the Happy Hunting Grounds. He's communing with Canning ghosts."

"A dreary practice, surely. It was, all in all, a dreary practice even when the ghosts were alive and kicking. I refer especially to Father."

"Well, you know Grandfather. He's very devoted to his

little family, dead or alive. Fortunately, I might add, for you and me."

"True again. Darling, you have the most devastating knack of getting directly to the crux. I suppose I had better go up there and check in immediately."

"I was about to suggest it. I'll just go along for company, if you don't mind."

"I'd be delighted. Perhaps, along the way, we can trifle for a while in some leafy glade."

"It's entirely possible. I have no special preference for leafy glades, but I am, as you know, addicted to occasional trifling."

Leaving the Jag in the drive, my bag in the Jag, we went around the big Colonial house, past the garages in the rear, and so onto a path that ran up a gentle slope among maples and oaks and sycamores to the crest of the rise, and down again among more of the same into a hollow where, under the flowering crab, Grandfather had gathered in a private plot the latter members of the Canning clan, deceased. There side by side, or end to end, lay Grandmother and Uncle Wish and Father and Mother. There in good time would Grandfather lie, a patriarch among them. There also was room reserved for me, and for Connie by my side. An unpleasant prospect, surely, but hopefully remote. What was pleasant and immediate was the fact that Connie and I were side by side and hand in hand already, very much alive and with a prospect of trifling.

Unfortunately for the prospect, however, we met Grandfather on his way back. As we reached the crest of the rise, we could see him on the slope below us, ascending briskly among the trees. I must say candidly that Grandfather, for an octogenarian, was depressingly spry. He lifted his knees high when walking, and in fact his gait was a kind of prance that seemed about to break any second into a trot. Now, seeing us above him, he gave out with a shrill cackle of greeting and lifted an arm in salute. A soft warm breeze stirred the white fuzz on his head.

"Good to see you again, Buster," he said, approaching. "Welcome home."

"Thank you, Grandfather. You're certainly looking fit."

"Feel fit. Am fit. You were coming at once to say hello to your old Grandfather, hey? Good boy."

"As you see, Connie and I came looking for you first thing."

"Good girl, Connie. Considerate. I've been to visit my children. Pay them a visit every decent day. Just on my way back. Got a project in hand that I must get to work on. Work on it two hours every day, decent or not."

"Is that so? What are you doing?"

"Writing a history of this county. Many fascinating things have happened here. Know many of them firsthand. Consulting sources for the rest."

"It sounds like quite a project. How long do you think it will take to finish it?"

"Five years. Got it worked out on a schedule. Two hours a day for five years."

"Five years!"

If my dismay was apparent in my voice, Grandfather didn't seem to notice it. My exclamation was literally wrenched out of me, of course, and small wonder. After all, I mean, five and eighty-six are ninety-one!

"That's right," he said. "Five years will see it done. Must keep at it, though. Must get at it now. You'll excuse me, I hope."

"We'll walk back to the house with you."

"Wouldn't hear of it. Since you've come this far, you'll want to go on and pay your respects to your father and mother. Connie will go with you."

"Thanks, Grandfather. It's very thoughtful of you."

"Not at all, not at all. Make yourself at home, my boy, as usual. The place is yours. I'll expect to have you until September at least. You and Connie both."

He pranced over the crest and out of sight down the far slope. I sighed and groped for Connie's hand, which I had released to shake Grandfather's.

"To tell the truth," I said, "I am singularly uninterested in paying my respects to Father and Mother."

"Grandfather expects it, and you mustn't disappoint him."

"Nevertheless, I find the idea uninviting."

"Perhaps I can make things a little more interesting for you. When you stop to consider it, the Happy Hunting Ground is as nearly a leafy glade as any other spot we are likely to find."

"As a matter of fact," I said, "I am more interested already."

The blossoms were gone, gone a month or more, and the crab was hung along the bough with little red apples. The small headstones sought and achieved a neat and charming simplicity, enclosed and isolated from unkempt indigenous growth by iron pickets painted green. The grass within the enclosure had been clipped, and the mower was at rest with spade and hoe and rake and shears in the tool shed, also painted green, that stood aside from the assembled dead outside the iron pickets. Sunshine filtered through apple leaves to fashion a random pattern of light and shade. Light lay lightly on Connie's eyes, which were closed. Shade made a mystery of her lips, which were smiling.

"Do you know the trouble with Grandfather?" she said.

"I wasn't aware that he had any," I said.

"The trouble with Grandfather," she said, "is that he won't die."

The warm air was filled, if one bothered to listen, with a thousand sleepy sounds. Among the leaves of the crab there was a flash of yellow wings.

"It's true," I said, "that's he's taking his time about it."

"He's absolutely interminable, that's what. You heard what he said about that dreary book he's writing about things that are surely of no consequence to anyone. Five years, he said."

"I heard."

"Do you think he can possibly live five years longer?"

"It's my opinion that he can."

"It's positively obscene. Here are Uncle Wish and your mother and father, all dead and decently buried, and all years and years younger than Grandfather. Damn it, Buster, there ought to be some kind of decent order in dying."

"Death is often disorderly. It's peculiar that way."

"It doesn't seem fair for things to be so badly managed."

"Oh, I don't know. You must admit, my lovely waif, that you and I have profited from the disorder. A split two ways has obvious advantages over a split five ways."

"It does, doesn't it? I've been thinking about that."

"Thinking is bad for you. As someone said about metaphysics, it befuddles you methodically."

"Just the same, it was odd how your mother and father died."

"How, odd?"

"Well, how your father just up and died all at once of something that was diagnosed by a senile octogenarian doctor as a heart condition. I never dreamed that there was anything wrong with his heart. Did you?"

"No, I didn't."

"And then how your mother presumably committed suicide in her presumed grief. I never saw any evidence that your mother was inordinately fond of your father. Did you?"

"Not a shred."

"I've also been thinking about something else odd."

"What else?"

"You were here for both deaths, darling. Don't you think that's odd?"

I raised myself on an elbow and looked at her. She lay on her back and did not move. Her eyes were still closed in the light. Her lips still smiled in the shade. The shade moved as the leaves that cast it moved.

"As odd," I said, "as your own attendance at those unhappy events."

She laughed instantly in some strange, contained delight. Opening her eyes, she sat up. Her laughter was more motion than sound, hardly louder than a whisper. In her voice, when she spoke, was a kind of mock wonder.

"Darling," she said, "I do believe we suspect each other."

"Impossible. One of us suspects; the other *knows.*"

"That's so, isn't it? You're very logical, darling."

"Logical enough to know that the quotient increases as the divisor gets smaller."

"Of course. That's elementary."

"As you say, elementary. Even a child could see it. Even you."

"Thank you. I'm really quite clever at arithmetic when you come right down to it. I understand clearly, for instance, that this all remains academic, a kind of textbook exercise, until the dividend is available for division."

"In good time. Five years will pass in five years. Meanwhile, let us enjoy our summers."

"I'm sick of our summers. At this instant, if I weren't on orders and rations, I might be in Rio or Mexico City or some other exciting place."

"If you were, I'd be desolate."

"No, you wouldn't darling. You're a summer habit. We'd make arrangements."

"I'm reassured. However, you must admit that Grandfather, for all his irritating devotion and familial despotism, is exceedingly generous with his money. He has always cheerfully supported us all. Some fair day after the detestable county history is finished, you and I shall have what he leaves behind."

"How can you be so certain?"

"There's nothing deceptive about Grandfather. He's fanatically devoted to his family, even though they neither sow nor reap. You know that."

"For all his generosity, however, he's a straight-laced and sensitive old moralist in his way. Suppose we did something to offend him and got cut out of the will."

"Don't even think of such a horrible contingency. We must take care to avoid any such thing."

"That's easily said, but I know you, and you know me, and we both know that either of us could come a cropper anytime. All I can say is, it's a good thing Grandfather doesn't have access to our detailed case histories this minute."

She lay down again upon the neat green grass, and I lay down beside her. The grass, lately cut, smelled sweet and good. Closing my eyes, I listened to the thousand summer sounds. Beside me, Connie's voice was drugged with drowsy dreams.

"It isn't remarkable when an old man dies," she said.

"If he has seventy million dollars and dies in the company of his two remaining heirs," I said, "it may attract remarkable notice."

"Nonsense. One only needs to be clever and careful."

"I'll think about it," I said.

While I was thinking, June passed. In July, the first two weeks of it, it was too hot to think. Then, the third week, we began to get thundershowers every day, and the temperature became tolerable, and it actually began to seem as if it might be almost possible to reach a decision and to accomplish something exceptional. I must admit that I greatly admired Connie during this trying period. She never pushed; she never nagged; she never even mentioned, not once, Grandfather's distressing longevity. She left me strictly to my lonely thoughts regarding that critical matter, and it was only now and then that I caught her looking at me with a wary, watchful expression in her ancient Florentine eyes. Otherwise, we played tennis, we lay in the sun, we took walks, we drank gin and tonic, we trifled when we chose. It was, all in all, a pleasant summer, albeit dull in spots.

Even the rains, when they came, were rather pleasant. They broke the heat and cleared the mind and stimulated the

imagination. Some days of that third July week broke bright
and clear, but always in the morning the thunderheads would
begin to pile up in the southwest and in the afternoon would
come boiling over with the wind roaring and the thunder
crashing and great jagged bolts of lightning splitting the sky.
Connie responded intensely to these gaudy displays of ele-
mental pyrotechnics. She would stand or sit very erect, her
nostrils flaring, her eyes dilated and shining, and I could see
her small, alert breasts rise and fall in a cadence of contained
excitement. We always watched from the front veranda of
the house. Sometimes the rain blew in and wet us down.
That's where we were one afternoon when the week had
nearly passed, and the rains with the week. The clouds had
just rolled over, and the deluge had stopped. The sun, breaking through scattered remnants, transformed the shadowed
earth to an Eden of shimmering green and gold.

"Let's take a walk," Connie said.

"Now?" I said.

"Yes, now."

"We'll get our shoes wet."

"We'll take our shoes off."

She was wearing loafers on bare feet, and she kicked the
loafers off and went down off the veranda and across the
yard. I took off my tennis shoes and socks and followed. She
was walking swiftly, and she was around the house and past
the garages and onto the path beyond them before I caught
up. She took my hand and held it tightly, as if she were
trying by the pressure to transmit a message, and we walked
on up the slope and over the crest and down the slope on
the other side. Skirting the Happy Hunting Ground, we
walked on through thicker trees and denser growth until
we came to the far side of the estate where a narrow creek
ran between deep banks. Ordinarily, the creekbed carried
little water, but the heavy rains had drained into it from the
slopes, and now it was nearly full. We walked along it until
we reached a place where the banks were lower and the
water spread and became shallower and rushed in a rapids
over worn rocks. A chain of large stepping-stones had been
strung across the creekbed here, but now they were submerged, and the water boiled around them. We sat down together on the trunk of a fallen tree.

"How could we do it?" I said.

"It would be easy." She picked up my thought as if there
had been a pause of only minutes instead of weeks in our

conversation. "He's an old man. It's time for him to die. Who would suspect?"

"It would have to be done just so. At best, it would be a terrible risk."

"Hardly any risk at all. I have a plan."

"I confess that I feel a certain reluctance, quite aside from the risk, to do Grandfather in. It's true, however, that his unreasonable tenacity incites it."

"There would be no pain, no violence. In the end, he wouldn't even know. He would simply die in his sleep."

"Neat enough, if it could be arranged. How could it?"

"Surely you have thought of it a hundred times yourself, Buster. You couldn't have helped yourself."

"The nightcap?"

"You see? I knew you'd thought of it."

The reference was to an old habit and a minor family ritual. The old quack who had been Grandfather's doctor for ages had recommended years ago that he take a nightcap of good bourbon and water every night upon retiring. This was supposed to calm his nerves, pep up his circulation, and act upon him generally as a salubrious tonic. Grandfather was by no means addicted to the bottle, but his nightcap became a habit entrenched, and a minor ritual, as I said, developed around it. I don't know what adjustments were made when I was not in the house, but when I was there I was expected at Grandfather's bedtime to make the highball and deliver it to him in his room, where I usually found him waiting on the edge of his bed in his nightgown. I made the highball in the kitchen from 100-proof stuff that he kept tucked away in the cabinet for his private consumption. In the beginning, the highball had been a mild thing, mostly water, but it grew stronger as time passed, and currently it was quite the other way round, mostly bourbon in a water tumbler with one small ice cube and a quick pass under the tap. It was enough, indeed, to blow the top off an ordinary man's head, but Grandfather had approached it slowly for a long time, and I suppose he had sort of immunized himself to it by small and regular increases of the dosage, as Mithridates is said to have done with poisons.

"The thought has crossed my mind," I said. "As you remarked, it affords altogether such a beautiful opportunity that I could hardly fail being tempted."

"Why have you never done it?"

"Poison is so treacherous. It has a way of getting found in the innards."

"Only if there's an autopsy."

"Poison has a nasty way of leaving various signs that arouse suspicions and make autopsies inevitable."

"Not always. Buster, you simply haven't taken the trouble to inform yourself sufficiently, that's all."

"Perhaps you would care to inform me sufficiently now."

"I'd be delighted. You simply lace his nightcap with chloral hydrate. In brief, you slip him a gigantic Micky Finn. A large dose would be fatal, I assure you, and it would have definite advantages from our point of view. He would merely pass out and die without recovering consciousness, which would have the virtue of making him appear to have died in his sleep, surely not an uncommon occurrence with men so old. Moreover, besides being merciful, the drug disappears from the system quickly and is extremely difficult to detect."

"That last point is particularly important. You *are* well-informed, aren't you, darling? I'm happy, I must say, that you aren't devising a scheme for murdering *me*. Or are you?"

"Don't be absurd, Buster. How could I dream for an instant of murdering someone I've been so friendly with? You must think I'm a perfect monster."

"Haven't you been friendly with Grandfather?"

"That's different. Grandfather and I have hardly been friendly in the same way."

"I should hope not. Returning to your plan, however, it seems to me that it would be difficult, as well as risky, to acquire a lethal dose of chloral hydrate."

"You needn't concern yourself with that. My contacts in Chicago are rather diversified, to say the least. I'm always getting interested in all sorts of odd people who have access to lots of things. I happen to have some chloral hydrate in my possession."

"Here?"

"Yes, here."

"Where, exactly?"

"Never mind that. If you decide sensibly to put it in Grandfather's nightcap, I'll get it for you at once."

"Your service is excellent, darling. I'll have to give you that."

"I try to be helpful."

"Your plan, so far as I can see, is practically flawless. Simple and direct. No fancy complications."

"Will you do it?"

"Maybe."

"Tonight?"

"Maybe."

"Darling, it would be so easy."

"Damn it," I said, "I've got mud between my toes."

When the time came, it wasn't. Easy, that is.

We were in the library, Grandfather and Connie and I. Grandfather was dozing in his chair. Connie was listening to muted jazz. I was playing solitaire. The library clock struck ten, and Grandfather stood up.

"I'll say good-night, children," he said. "Buster, my boy, will you bring my nightcap?"

He pranced out. I looked at Connie, and Connie looked at me. Turning away, I went out to the kitchen and made Grandfather's nightcap according to recipe. When I turned around, Connie was in the doorway watching me. We stood there looking at each other for a long minute. She was excited. She was filled with the strange, contained excitement she had felt on the veranda when the thunderheads rolled over.

"Now?" she said.

I didn't answer. Carrying the nightcap, I went upstairs to Grandfather's room.

When I came down, Connie had disappeared.

The next day, there was another thunderstorm. It came early in the afternoon, just after lunch. Grandfather had withdrawn to the library to put in his daily labor on the cursed county history, and I was on the veranda to watch the black roistering masses roll overhead to the deafening detonations of the thunder and the forked flashes of lightning and the great rush of wind-blown rain. The storm, this day, was brief. Fifteen minutes after the rain began, it was all over. I kept waiting for Connie to join me on the veranda, but she never did. Not, that is, while the storm lasted.

She came out afterward and down the steps into the yard. She was wearing a pair of white shorts and a white cotton blouse, and her feet were bare. She didn't look at me or speak, and I went over to the steps and down into the yard after her.

"Where have you been?" I said.

"Upstairs in my room," she said.

"I've been waiting for you."

"Poor boy. Waiting is a tedious business, isn't it? One gets so sick of it after a while."

"Are you angry with me?"

"Not at all. A little disappointed in you, perhaps. It is perfectly clear that nothing extraordinary can be expected of you."

"You must give me a little more time, that's all."

"Take all the time you want. Take forever."

She had turned to face me, and now she turned away again and started across the yard. I followed a few steps behind.

"Where are you going?"

"I'm going for a walk."

"I'll come with you."

"No, thanks. I don't care to have you."

"Why not?"

"Life is dull enough around here at best. You'd only make it worse."

"You never seemed to find me so dull before."

"I thought you were better than nothing, darling. Now I'm not so sure."

I stopped where I was and watched her go. She had broad shoulders and a narrow waist and long golden legs. For a moment, watching her, I had a hard and hurting sense of intolerable loss. Then I turned back to the house and went inside and upstairs to my room.

I opened my windows and lay down on the bed, and the cool wet air blew in across me. I could hear the dripping of rain and the chittering of birds and the rustling of leaves in what was left of the wind. After a while I sank into a strange sort of lassitude, a passive submission to fragmentary dreams between waking and sleeping, and then, some time later, I went to sleep soundly and slept through the afternoon, and it was, when I woke, after five o'clock. I washed my face and went downstairs and found Grandfather, after a brief search, standing behind the house looking off in the direction of the slope beyond the garages.

"There you are, Buster," he said. "I've hardly set eyes on you all day long. Where have you been keeping yourself, my boy?"

"I went upstairs after lunch and fell asleep. I slept longer than I intended."

"Where's Connie?"

"She went for a walk right after the storm. Isn't she back yet?"

"Can't find her. Can't find her anywhere."

"Maybe she's in her room."

"Knocked. Got no answer."

"Well, she wasn't in a very good humor. Probably she's off sitting somewhere until she recovers. She'll be along in good time."

"I walked to the cemetery. Didn't see her along the way."

"I dare say she's over by the creek."

"I'm a bit concerned, my boy. Can't deny it. She may have hurt herself. Sprained an ankle or something. May be out there waiting for help."

"If it will make you feel better, Grandfather, I'll go look for her."

"Do that, my boy. Relieve your old grandfather's anxiety."

"All right. I'm sure I'll be back with her shortly, if she doesn't get back ahead of me."

"Meanwhile, I'll go in and change my shoes. Soaking wet. Hurry back, my boy."

He turned toward the house, and I walked up the slope and over the crest and down into the hollow and past the cemetery and on through grass among the trees toward the creek. The sky had cleared, and the sun was out, and the light of the sun lanced through the trees. The earth was scrubbed and rinsed and sparkling green. I could hear ahead of me the rushing sound of the swollen creek. My canvas shoes were soon soaked. At the creek's bank, I turned toward the rapids.

That was the last day of the thunderstorms. The next morning broke clear, and the clouds never formed, and every day thereafter for a long time was bright and dry. It was like that over in the hollow, bright and dry and still in sunshine and shade, the day we buried Connie.

The service was private. Only a handful of people were present. Grandfather and I were the only mourners, and after the sad and definitive ceremony was finished beside the grave, we walked back alone to the house. The house without Connie seemed vast and empty and filled with whispered echoes. I had not yet got used to her being gone, and I truly missed

her, although I knew my loneliness wouldn't last. Add to
thirty-five million an equal amount, and you have what may
be called an antidote to lasting sorrow.

In the house I went upstairs to my room and lay down on
the bed and tried to think of certain things in order to avoid
thinking of certain others. This was not very successful, and
I began to wish that Connie were there to distract me,
which was no more at most than half an ambivalence. I got
up and went downstairs again after an hour or so, and there
was Grandfather in the library with a visitor. The visitor was
a short thin man with pale limp hair and a furrowed face
and a vaguely deferential manner. I had met him once before, which was once too often, and I knew him already as
well as I ever wanted to. His name was Drake, and he was a
captain of county detectives.

"There you are, my boy," Grandfather said. "Come in,
come in."

"I don't want to intrude," I said.

"No intrusion. None at all. I was just about to send for
you. In fact, Captain Drake wants to talk with you."

"I don't know why," I said. "I've already told Captain
Drake all I know."

"I know you have, my boy. I know that well enough. He
merely wants to clarify some points and get his report in
order. Isn't that so, Captain?"

"That's so," Drake said. "I'm sorry to intrude again on a
day so sad as this one. Won't you please come in and sit
down, Mr. Canning? This will take only a few minutes."

I went in and sat down on the edge of a chair.

"What do you want to know?" I said.

"I'd appreciate it if you'd go over your account again.
Just one more time."

"Why? I've already gone over it and over it."

"I know. I'm sorry. If you will just indulge me, please."

"Well, as I've said, it was the day of the last thunderstorm.
When the storm was over, Connie went out for a walk. I offered to go along, but she wouldn't have me. I guess she
just wanted to be alone. Anyhow, I went upstairs and took a
nap. When I woke up, it was late, and Connie wasn't back,
and Grandfather was worried. So I went out to look for her.
I walked to the creek and along the creek to the place we've
always called the riffles. There the water spreads out and
becomes shallow and flows through a lot of rocks. Stepping-
stones have been placed across the bed, and Connie was there

in the water, face down, and her body had lodged between two of the stepping-stones. She was barefooted, wearing shorts, and I suppose she tried to wade the creek. It wasn't very deep there, even after all the rains, but the current was very swift, and it must have swept her feet out from under her. She struck her head on a boulder and drowned, that's all. I can't tell you any more."

He was leaning forward in his chair in a posture of intent listening, but his eyes were abstracted, remote, and he seemed to be hearing, if he heard anything, some private voice subliminal to all but him. Aware after a moment that I had finished, he sighed and stirred.

"Quite so. The story as before. Well, it's reasonable. It's possible. There's only one thing that disturbs me."

"What's that?"

"She struck her head, you say, and she must have done so. But it's puzzling. There was only one contusion on her head, and it was high up, near the crown. It could have caused unconsciousness, certainly, but it's difficult, all factors considered, to see how it could have been acquired in falling. It looks very much, in fact, as if she'd been struck deliberately by a rock in someone's hand." He fell silent and seemed to be listening again to the private subliminal voice. Then he added, almost casually, "It would help if the blow had killed her. If she had been dead when she entered the water, I mean. But that's no good. There was water in her lungs."

"You're distorting things," I said. "You've got too much imagination."

"I dare say you're right. I've been told that it's a fault of mine." He turned abruptly to Grandfather. "The young lady who drowned was not your natural granddaughter, I understand. Would you mind telling me if she was one of your heirs?"

"She was. She was to share equally with my other principal heir."

"And the other principal heir is young Mr. Canning here?"

"Naturally."

"And now he will become your *sole* principal heir. Is that correct?"

Grandfather rose from his chair, and the white fuzz seemed to bristle on his head. The old boy, when he chose, could be as hard as diamond and as cold as ice.

"Captain," he said, "I consider that question an intrusion on my personal affairs. It requires me to commit myself, and is therefore unwarranted. Moreover, sir, it is impertinent and offensive."

Captain Drake sighed again and stood up. His vaguely deferential manner was suddenly pronounced, but his voice remained, somehow, impersonal and invulnerable.

"Yes. Yes, of course. Sorry." He crossed to the library door, his wilted cord suit hanging limply on his thin frame, and paused with his hand on the knob to look back at us. "I hope that young Mr. Canning is not planning to leave this house in the immediate future."

"Buster will be my guest until September at least," Grandfather said coldly.

"Let us hope so," Drake said. "Let us earnestly hope so."

There was a knock on my door, and immediately afterward, before I could answer, the door was pushed open and Grandfather entered the room carrying a tray with two glasses on it. The glasses were filled with dark amber liquid, and a small ice cube floated in each. I had been negligent, clearly, of what I referred to lightly as my thirty-five million dollar duty. Now, with luck, seventy.

"Grandfather," I said, "I've forgotten your nightcap. I'm sorry."

"Think nothing of it, my boy. It has been a trying day for you, what with Drake's impertinence on top of poor Connie's funeral, and I'm more than happy to serve you for a change."

"It's very thoughtful of you."

"Not at all, my boy, not at all. As you see, I've brought along my own nightcap. We shall have our drinks together tonight."

"Thank you, Grandfather. I'll enjoy that."

I cleared a place on my bedside table, and Grandfather set the tray there. He picked up one of the glasses and handed it to me, keeping the other for himself.

"Grandfather," I said, "I don't like that detective. He worries me."

"Drake? He's a clever man, but he forgets his proper place. He is sometimes, as I said, impertinent."

"Impertinence is a mild word for what was practically an accusation of murder."

"Oh, he didn't actually accuse you of murder, my boy. His suspicions have been aroused by a seeming incongruity in conjunction with what appears to be a powerful motive and ample opportunity. That's all there is to it."

"All! Isn't that enough?"

"Don't worry about it, my boy. I shall see that no harm comes to you. I shall care for you and keep you secure, just as I have always cared for the members of my family."

Grandfather had pulled a chair near the bed, and now he sat down in the chair and sipped his nightcap. I sat on the edge of the bed and took a long drink of my own. It was, as its color indicated, very strong.

"I must say that you've made me feel better, Grandfather," I said.

"Trust me, my boy. Trust your old grandfather, just as all the others trusted me. Haven't I brought them all home? Haven't I given them all peace and lasting security? They were charming children, all charming children, but not one who was not helpless. Not one who didn't need my constant loving care. The tragic end of your Uncle Wish convinced me finally of that. Could I leave the others to comparable ends or worse? Could I trust life to those who couldn't even be trusted with a dollar? Could I go away, when my time comes to go, and leave them all behind to their own frail and futile devices? Well, they are all secure now. All secure in the hollow beyond the crest. All at rest beneath the flowering crab."

Grandfather leaned forward and patted me on the knee, watching me closely with his inexhaustible loving care. I started to say something, but it was so much easier to say nothing at all.

"How do you feel, my boy? It will be over quickly, I promise you, as it was with dear little Connie, and soon you will be safe forever. Let Drake think what he pleases. If he thinks, as he surely will, that you took in fear the easy way to evade him, what matter? He will quietly close his case on all the wrong assumptions, and we shall just as quietly have the last good laugh. Leave it to me, my boy. Leave it all to your old grandfather."

He patted my knee again, tenderly, and I was dimly aware that my hands were empty and that I must have carelessly dropped my glass. I started to rise, but it was so much easier simply to lie down.

It's April again. The frail pink blossoms of the flowering crab shower to earth in the slightest stirring of the languid air to lie like pastel snow among the clustered headstones of the Canning dead. Already the fruit is forming where the blossoms hung, and in a little while, after the swift passing of spring, toward the end of summer's indolent amble, the small red apples will fall in turn to lie where the blossoms lie. The seasons come, and the seasons go . . .

But Grandfather, it seems, endures forever.

FILE #4: LINCOLN
SEDAN DEADLINE

JOE GORES

As a man, I rejoiced in Tony and I mourn his passing. As a writer, I feel profoundly grateful to him. In April, 1966, while still a working private detective, I gave a talk on investigative techniques to the Northern California Chapter of Mystery Writers of America. Afterward, Tony suggested that I try a group of stories using factual private-eye procedures.

From this came the File Series for EQMM.

Tony found the stories about my fictional agency "moving and uncompromising," and called the series "something completely new" in detective fiction..

If this is so, the credit belongs not to me, but to Tony. The conception, after all, was his.

DAN KEARNY LAUGHED AND said, " 'Bye!" in a bright and jocular voice. Then he tossed the receiver toward the phone and cursed aloud in his basement cubbyhole at DKA. That made it just a perfect morning.

Item: the new receptionist had blithely let in a process server, and Kearny had been slapped with a damage-suit summons.

Item: Marty Rossman had lost a repossessed auto from the tow-bar coming down Cathedral Hill, and had wiped out three parked cars.

Item: Kathy Onoda, Office Manager ever since Kearny

had quit Walter's Auto Detectives nearly eight years before to form Daniel Kearny Associates, was off sick again. Hell, she was rundown from a full-time job, two kids, and supporting a deadbeat husband, but it still put them in a bind. Now this!

Kearny jabbed Giselle Marc's intercom button viciously; as it buzzed upstairs in clerical, he shook a cigarette from his pack and lit it. He was a hard, pugnacious man with a square face and icy gray eyes; his slightly bent nose and massive jaw gave him the look of an aging middleweight club fighter.

"Yes, Dan," said Giselle musically. She was a tall stimulating blonde, 24 years old, whose looks kept most men from realizing that her wits matched her other attractions. Kearny was one of the few who wasn't fooled.

"Who's the field agent on this Jennifer Poteet skip?"

"Larry Ballard."

"Where the hell is—" He broke off; through the one-way glass of his cubbyhole he had seen Ballard entering the garage. "Skip it."

"Dan, don't you jump on Larry! This is a Gypsy case, and you know what Gypsy cases are."

"Somebody oughta tell Lou Cassavette at Crescent Lincoln-Mercury what Gypsy cases are so he doesn't get on the horn to blow smoke at me about making California-Citizens Bank eat this one because it won't be back before the deadline. So I—" He caught himself, but not in time.

"Dan, did you bet Lou Cassavette that we'd have that car back?"

"Bet?" he asked innocently. "Why, I—yeah. Fifty iron men. Hell, I won at the track Saturday." Over her expostulations he hung up, buzzed Ballard. "Get in here—with your case file," he growled.

Larry Ballard, tall and energetic and in his mid-twenties, had a surfer's build and sun-bleached hair. He reminded Kearny of himself twenty years before at the same age: smart, ready to work around the clock, slowly gaining the successful investigator's necessary detachment. In his nine months with DKA, Ballard had become a damned good field agent; but he still didn't know how to really dig on skip cases. He'd learn on this one.

Kearny offered a cigarette, began silkily, "Ballard, what are *you* DOING ON *JENNIFER POTEET?*" His voice thumped the words like a ring opponent's jaw.

"I—well, er—that's a tough one, Da—Mr. Kearny."

"It's a deadline deal, Ballard." Kearny's voice was deceptively soft. He suddenly roared: *"AT ONE MINUTE PAST TWELVE TOMORROW NIGHT CAL-CIT BANK IS GOING TO HAVE TO EAT THAT CAR!"* His voice dropped. "The dealer recourse expires then, three months since initial delinquency, and Lou Cassavette isn't about to take back a seven-thousand-dollar car once it's gone over the wire. Not from a Gypsy."

Ballard hadn't really *forgotten* the Poteet Lincoln sedan, just had—well, let it slip by. A bounced down payment, three months delinquent. Now a deadline deal, with the deadline just 38 hours away.

"Dan, I can't get a live lead on this one."

"Ballard, I don't care if you boot one," said Kearny coldly "Everyone does. But none of *my* men tell me they 'can't.' "

Reviewing the Jennifer Poteet file under Kearny's critical eye, Ballard mentally cringed. The reports were pathetic. *Followed to given address, cruised the area. Vehicle not in sight. Returned several times during late evening and early morning hours without success.* A dozen such reports in the file, all written by himself. All he'd really discovered was that the 28-year-old subject was gone from her residence address in the Mission district, and that she had walked off her job at a North Beach topless joint.

Dropping a dime for Information would have told them that much.

"We also know she's a John clan Gypsy," Kearny pointed out.

"How can we be sure of that?"

"The residence address is a storefront joint where only John clan Gyps live. If I'd seen this file sooner—" He looked up. "Why didn't I?" It was just a question, not badgering.

"This is the first Gypsy file I've worked."

"It isn't the first one Giselle's worked."

Private investigators, law-enforcement officers, auto dealers, and retail credit men all know there is a flourishing Gypsy subculture in this country, with its own royalty, its own unique clan structure, and a moral code relating only to other Gypsies. Punishments for those who break the code can range up to ritual murder. Piercing this spider web is not impossible, for money talks as loudly to Gypsies as to anyone else; but it takes time. And time was just what Kearny didn't have.

"Let's get at it," he growled. "Deadline's tomorrow night."

To Larry Ballard the hours until midnight, with sandwiches sent in, were a crash course in skiptracing as opposed to field work. They also explained why the DKA phone bill ran twenty grand a year.

Kearny began with long-distance calls to the motor vehicle departments of Georgia and Mississippi, where cars sometimes are licensed without actual proof of ownership. No record. Then he called Louisiana, where such fraudulently registered vehicles sometimes get a clear title which bypasses original lien holders such as Cal-Cit Bank. No record.

"So it probably still has California plates," said Kearny.

Ballard learned that the seven main western Gypsy clans —John, Miller, Ristick, Costello, Ephrem, Ellis, and Steve— use some fifty regular aliases and, on fraudulent credit applications, such supposed occupations as boilermakers, brass workers, coppersmiths, church vestment salesmen, silversmiths, photographers, and many others.

"Did you ask around that go-go joint in North Beach where the subject was supposed to be the house photographer?"

"She worked at the club, Dan," said Ballard, "But as a topless waitress. She was so kooky that they were glad to see her leave."

Kearny gave him a list of Sheriffs, State Police agencies, repossessors, skiptracers, and local cops to phone around the country. He discovered that the Jones and Stanley clans were attending the funeral of a Gypsy prince in Toledo, Ohio; that the Blake clan had been operating a florist shop in Buffalo, New York, to establish credit for a big color TV-set haul; that the Nicholas and Mitchell clans were in Clearwater, Florida, waiting for the carnival season to open; and that more than 50 wanted Gypsy vehicles had been discovered on a farm near Clear Lake, Indiana. Of Jennifer Poteet, however, he discovered nothing.

At 3:30 p.m. he got his first break: an Arizona policeman once had arrested the subject for operating a fraudulent mitt camp at a County Fair midway. With this information, Kearny learned from another fortuneteller near Santa Rosa that the subject had a brother named Rudolph Marino. Then the lead seemed to die.

At 8:00 p.m. Marino's wife, reached by phone at Portland, explained that Marino had been in the Oregon state pen for nearly a year on a charge of assault with a deadly weapon while in commission of a felony.

At midnight Kearny leaned back and knuckled his reddened eyes. The desk was littered with papers, the ashtrays were overflowing, the soundproofed office was close and stale.

Ballard rubbed the back of his neck. "What do we do now? Punt?"

"We keep digging. Cassavette has the idea we can't produce; he wants to be sitting in his used car lot tomorrow at midnight when we *don't* bring in that Lincoln sedan. Which wouldn't help us at the bank one damned bit." He grinned wolfishly. "Be here at six in the morning."

It was 6:01 a.m. Although DKA wouldn't open for another hour and a half, Giselle Marc stuck her gleaming blonde head into Kearny's cubbyhole. "Any luck, guys?"

"What are you doing here?" In the same tone Kearny said to Ballard, "Larry, this is the girl I was telling you about."

"No kidding? And she looks like such a sweet kid, too."

"All right, you cats—" began Giselle.

"We haven't turned up a thing," Kearny said. "Did you see Kathy last night?"

She nodded. "I'm worried about her, Dan. She looks terrible but she won't see a doctor. Says she's just tired."

When she left, Kearny pushed aside his very real concern for Kathy Onoda. He began, "Poteet must not be using any common Gypsy alias." His eyes suddenly gleamed. "Larry, what was that number for Marino's wife in Portland?"

Ballard told him, objecting, "But Marino's in the pen, Dan."

"His wife isn't." Kearny used the area code so that it would seem like a local call. "Hello? Mrs. Marino? This is Morning Wake-Up from station KXWR in Portland. Have you been listening . . . my phone call woke you up? Well, Mrs. Marino, you—can I call you something besides Mrs?— Neya? A lovely name. And for being such a good *sport*, Neya, we are giving you an electric carving knife *ab*solutely free—you just have to pick it up here in Studio C at KXWR. Oh, could we have your maiden name for identification purposes? That's right, Neya. And could you spell that? Z-L-A-T-C-H-I. Fine. Thanks and 'bye, Neya."

Ballard shut his mouth, which had been hanging open

wide enough to catch flies. "What if she'd asked for the studio address?"

"I'd have made one up," said Kearny airily. "Like I made up the studio." He leaned forward to pluck a cigarette from the pack on the desk. "The subject was busted once for running a fortunetelling skam, right? She's not traveling with other Gyps or our informants would have turned her up, right? So what's she doing for eating money? We start checking for a palm reader named Madame Neya or Madame Zlatchi."

"Seems like an awfully long shot, Dan."

"We don't have any short ones left," grunted Kearny.

His third phone call broke the case. A San Pedro Gypsy informant, grumbling about being got out of bed, said a Madame Neya was reading tea leaves at a joint a few miles from Palm Springs.

"We've got a field agent in Riverside—" Ballard began.

"—who's too brittle to find the Lincoln and get it back up here in seventeen and a half hours. No." Kearny jerked his wallet from his inside jacket pocket. "Here's fifty bucks, Larry. I'll drive you to the airport, you get the jet shuttle to L.A.—it only takes forty minutes. You can catch the eight-twenty Palm Springs flight from there." He stood up, gesturing impatiently. "C'mon. Let's move."

They moved. Larry Ballard was in Palm Springs by 9:14 a.m.

From the airport he called San Francisco. Kearny came on. "I've contacted The Green Cactus, Larry. They only know that the subject has a shack in a date grove near Rancho Mirage, and that she shows up for work at six o'clock every night. You'll have to find that shack if you're to get the Lincoln back here in time."

On the blacktop beyond the airport Ballard pushed his rented Mustang up to 70; but an open Cadillac deVille rocketed past him like an errant moon probe, its pilots a pair of bleached blondes goggled with wrap-around sunglasses. They waved airily; marvelous what sunshine and an assured income did for your outlook, Ballard thought.

At a stationery store in the rich, still somnolent town he got a blowup map of the area, and at a gas station he got directions to the nearest firehouse. The red trucks gleamed in a driveway still puddled from their morning bath. A lean browned man in heavy rubber boots like a buccaneer's was wiping the chrome grille of a truck.

"Dirt roads through the date groves near Rancho Mirage that might have shacks on 'em?" He dropped his chamois into his bucket and dried his hands. "Let's go inside and take a look at the wall map.

Twenty minutes later Ballard was on his way, his head full of local lore and his map full of wavy pencil squiggles, on one of which he hoped to find Madame Neya.

It took him just under two hours.

He had turned off a dirt road between the Thunderbird Club and the Shadow Mountain Club on a pair of hardened ruts meandering off into the date groves. Clouds of tan dust swirled around the car when he drove across a dry wash and then stopped abruptly. Just ahead, some 30 yards, the tail of a black Lincoln sedan protruded from behind a date palm.

He drove on, slowly. Yes. The Lincoln had the correct license number, and the shack was there, too, like something out of the Oklahoma migrations of the 'thirties. 12:01 p.m.: eleven hours, 59 minutes left.

Ballard returned to the highway, locked the Mustang, and laid the keys on top of the left-rear wheel. Then he walked back, trying to steel himself. Mustn't blow it by being soft. One girl he'd been soft with, Jocelyn Mayfield, had ended up killing herself.

Palm fronds tickled the roof drily; his shoes were soundless in the soft dust. As he quietly opened the door of the Lincoln the screen door on the porch slammed. The woman was as tall as Ballard, nearly six feet, with a striking face—straight nose, high cheekbones, thin lips.

She pointed a carmine-tipped finger. "You are accursed!" Her deep, rich, angry voice raised the hairs on the back of Ballard's neck.

"Miss Jennifer Poteet?"

"I am Madame Neya," she intoned.

Thin loops of beaten gold gleamed in her pierced earlobes, and set inside the edges of the ears, which also were pierced, were small beads of gold. Her legs were superb, and her plunging neckline suggested that she wore no brassiere. Her very femaleness lessened her impact.

"Madame Neya, huh?" said Ballard. "Jennifer Poteet to the bank."

"Ah." She expelled a breath, again drawing his eyes to her

neckline. "You have come to take poor Madame Neya's car."

"That's it—come all the way from San Francisco."

She led him through a living room, furnished only with a beaten-down couch, a new color TV, and a dozen garish hippie posters, through a small dark bedroom, and into the kitchen. It was very dirty, with dishes piled high in the sink. She leaned back against the stove, arms crossed; her eyes were such a deep blue they were nearly violet.

"Now, Mr. Car Thief man, what can I do to keep my Lincoln?"

"You should have done it four months ago. All you can do now is to remove any personal property and give me the keys. I have to get it back to San Francisco by midnight."

She smiled warmly; her eyelashes were very long and very dark. Outside a desert bird called brokenly in the noonday heat. "Don't you want to go to bed with me?" she purred.

Ballard was not really successful in putting boredom into his voice; she was a lot of woman. "Where are the keys, Jennifer?"

She realized then that he actually meant to take the car, and her face got momentarily ugly; her eyes flashed and her fingers worked, like a cat sheathing and unsheathing its claws. Then she suddenly laughed.

"So. You take Madame Neya's beautiful car. I gave them the good run for it, eh?" She turned to the stove, her face calculating but her eyes dancing with some arcane Gypsy delight. "Anyway, a cup of coffee before you go, eh? To show there is no hard feeling?"

"Okay." She obviously was playing for time—for the arrival of a friend, perhaps; but the coffee already was hot. She added half-and-half and a lump of sugar for Ballard, drank hers black like a woman conscious of her figure. Ballard knew he certainly was conscious of it.

"Still not too late to change your mind, Mr. Car Thief man."

Maybe she really *was* a mind reader; but Ballard said, "Sorry, Jennifer, just the coffee. But I can give you a ride to work."

She shrugged, finally giving up. "My boy friend picks me up every day. I thought maybe today he would come early."

He'd been right about her stalling for time. He guzzled his coffee, which was vile, just remembering that he'd left the coil wire in the Lincoln instead of removing it as he should have.

"You giving me those keys, Jennifer?"

Her face was sullen again. "They're on the counter."

He got to the living room before she called out behind him. The odd resonance of her voice turned him almost against his will. She was standing in the center of the dim bedroom like a nighttime animal in its den; her violet eyes gleamed ferally, her magnificent breast heaved.

"You hope to get that car to San Francisco by midnight? You will not get it there . . . *at all.*" Her eyes rolled up and her voice rose, to pierce his eardrums like an eagle's cry. "Oh, ye who sow discord, where are you? Ye who infuse hatreds and propagate enmities, I conjure you: fulfill your work—so that *never again shall this man go in peace.*"

Ballard tried to speak, but his throat was dry; he tried to laugh, but her voice still echoed in his brain. She was rigid, one arm extended, a blood-tipped finger pointing him out for her private Evils.

Then the spell was broken and Ballard was through the door and off the sagging, unpainted porch. His shadow seemed to hunch at his feet uneasily as he scuffed through the dust toward the Lincoln; he drove away with his eyes unconsciously fixed on the rear-view mirror.

Jennifer Poteet. Some woman. He checked the time: over eleven hours to drive 500 miles. At a gas station he filled up, made out the vehicle condition report, and called the Sheriff about the repo, the rental agency about the Mustang. He felt better once he was on the open highway. How about that chick? *Cursing* him! And in broad daylight!

It started about an hour later—a little after 2:00 p.m. At first he thought it was just the broiling sun, so he switched on the air conditioner. It didn't help. His palms were sweaty and when he took a hand from the wheel it was tremoring. He kept his mind carefully away from the curse; after all, how silly could you get?

But the sun *was* intense. Why? What did it have against him? He was squinting. This time of year the sun set about 4:30; he'd be glad when it was gone. The Lincoln whispered down the freeway at 80. The damned thing was *drinking* gas. What reason did it have?

Ballard began to laugh softly. A curse, huh? He said aloud,

"What are you laughing at?" To reassure himself he added, "Don't worry, I'm not laughing at you."

The last five minutes by the dashboard clock had been longer than the preceding five minutes. This struck him as funny, so he laughed once more. Why worry about getting the car to San Francisco before midnight when the minutes were getting steadily longer?

On a sudden whim he pushed down the automatic door lock. No use taking chances. At this speed it was doubtful if anything dangerous could get into the car with him, but it paid to be sure. He felt a slight chill at the thought, and thrust his hands into his pockets to warm them, and the perverse Lincoln swerved wildly. He grabbed the wheel. What the hell was going on? He shook his head to clear it of the light dancing from the chrome-work of approaching cars. Marvelous colors in that supposedly silver gleam of reflected sunlight—and how loud the sound of his tires was on the pavement! By stretching his ears he could even hear the tires of approaching autos.

Los Angeles. Intensely vivid streets. And then, waiting at a light, he saw Madame Neya. She was tiny, viewed through a telescope turned wrong-end to, but even at this distance he could see her great violet eyes. Eyes? Or empty sockets?

The head whipped toward him at sickening speed. It was huge. Then the lights changed, and the cars behind began to blare their hostility; but how could he drive right through that giant balloon face bobbing right in front of his windshield? Had to. Gritting his teeth, he jammed down the accelerator. The tires shrieked.

No, not the tires. Madame Neya, rolling over and over in his rearview mirror, her mouth distended, her teeth gleaming, her larynx working to form the screams. The words, rather.

ye who infuse hatreds—fulfill your work—never go in peace

Jocelyn Mayfield, screaming for peace, had slashed both her wrists because Ballard had taken her car and her man had beaten her

a Lincoln—he looked about the car—*this* Lincoln?

in San Francisco

Strength flowed through him. He had to get to San Francisco, help Jocelyn. Tell her not to do it. San Francisco by midnight

Somehow he got through Los Angeles

Serenity brushed him with gentle wings as he climbed into the darkening Tehachepi mountains on The Grapevine. How had he let a curse frighten him so? Jennifer, after all, was behind him, run down in Los Angeles, bleeding in a gutter—only Jocelyn was ahead—Jocelyn dead—but death, birth, decay—all were natural processes

Staring at the great clustered rock formations flanking the highway he realized that even stone decayed. It was a monotheistic universe: God was good, God was everywhere. But how to reach Him? How to say "sorry" to Him?

Ballard glanced at the gas gauge, and terror shattered serenity. Nearly EMPTY. Only a theistic, vengeful God would do that to Larry Ballard—Larry Ballard—guilty—guilty

don't panic—He regarded the gauge cunningly. Had to stop for gas, had to act natural. Station ahead. Breathe deeply—*don't panic*

He pulled in on the cement apron and waited while the attendant came around to the driver's side. Through the closed window he mouthed the words, "Fill 'er up." He watched the attendant set the hose, wash the windshield. The wrist of the hand wiping the paper towels back and forth was delicate, like a woman's. Like Jocelyn Mayfield's wrist. My God! The wrist was bleeding—green blood was washing down the glass.

"Okay under the hood, sir?"

"What?" The blood was gone. "Oh. Yes. Okay. Fine."

"Eight-fifty, sir."

He was just a kid; how did they corrupt them so young? Ballard touched the button to lower the window an inch. It took twenty minutes, but the attendant did not hold out his hand. Hiding that slashed wrist—then as he reached for Ballard's ten-dollar bill his left eye popped out on his cheek—Ballard could see into the socket—into the brain—could see the thoughts forming sluggishly in the convoluted lobes

accursed—the word glowed redly

The grease-rimed fingers took an hour to close over the bill and all that time the eyeball swayed gracefully on its cable of optic muscle—the fingers moved away with the bill—the eye swayed

Ballard slyly had left the ignition key on to check that the tank actually was filled. Now he saw his chance. He twisted the key, slammed the accelerator to the floor while he snapped the transmission into DRIVE. Fishtailing wildly, the Lincoln screamed back out onto the highway. Safe.

Time, which was eternity, stretched ahead to midnight and the deadline. Darkness had come. Lights. From the cavern of his headlights, thrown down the blackness ahead, came life— from Cambrian seas to Devonian slime to Carboniferous forests.

He drove on—one hundred and fifty million years passed in a single hour by his watch—then with a sudden sob Ballard admitted it all—he was guilty—accursed.

when the night of action has arrived, the operator shall gather up his goatskin, the stone called Ematille, two vervain crowns, two candles of virgin wax, and four nails from the coffin of a dead child

Time passing. Half-remembered greenglow freeway signs. Bakersfield. Fresno. Modesto. Must have stopped for gas again—gauge all right. He couldn't make it—had to atone— had to save Jocelyn—but the razor blade was laid full-edge against the pulsing blue veins on the wrist of the girl seated beside him on the front seat

No, Jocelyn! Not because of an *automobile!* I won't

A sudden convulsive movement—blood bubbling up and running down the slim white arm—glowing eyes solemn beneath dark brows gazing sadly into his as her blood ran free

Staring in terror, Ballard suddenly became aware that the top of the car had begun lowering, like the canopy of that terribly strange bed in that story he'd read in high school. It was pressing on his head now—intolerable pressure

He began sobbing—the flesh was melting from his hands— what had begun as a soft suety look around the edges of his fingernails had become drops of hot tallow running down his wrists—like the blood down Jocelyn's wrists to the cold tiles of the bathroom floor

He wrenched the wheel over. Had to stop before the flesh was gone, before the marrow dried and the bones fell apart. Had to atone for Jocelyn for Jennifer for a hundred others. He was accursed damned. Had to stop get out walk in front of the next passing car

he waited

Better now—areas of the headlights which had been detached and revolving like mobiles, giving him glimpses of the eyeless sockets from which they had come, had begun to steady. Soon now he would atone. He watched the headlights through closed, opaque lids. Soon now—Soon

The door, jerked open, nearly spilled Ballard on the ground.

The overhead light dazzled him, but the headlights now were normal. So was the gruff voice, demanding, "Hey, buddy, you okay?"

"What? Huh?" His head ached slightly. "Oh." He could see the gleaming leather belt and starchly crisp uniform of the highway patrol.

"I said, you okay, buddy?" The patrolman's nose was quivering, trying to smell booze. As Ballard watched, the nose began to lengthen and hair began to sprout on the man's cheeks—he was turning into a fox—

Ballard rubbed his eyes. The face was normal again.

"Sure. Thanks, officer. I got—sleepy." He yawned involuntarily. "Thought I'd better pull off the road. What time is it?"

"Ten forty-five."

Ten forty-five? Urgency shook him. "How far to San Francisco?"

"Just under seventy miles; you're right out of Manteca."

Ballard watched the lights of the parked police car in his rear-view mirror as he pulled away. If that cop hadn't stopped—What the hell had happened? Jennifer's curse? He shuddered. As he roared on through the night, holding the big Lincoln sedan at 85, occasional demons still lurched beyond his arc of headlights; but they dissolved when he turned his face to meet them.

Would he make the deadline? He used Highway 50, taking the MacArthur freeway rather than the Nimitz. After the tricky interchanges at Oakland he swept down to the Bay Bridge's gold-lit toll plaza. On the bridge he shattered the 50 m.p.h. speed limit; using the Ninth Street off-ramp gave him a straight shot across Market and over to Van Ness Avenue.

At 11:56 p.m. he turned sedately into the Crescent Motors used-car lot on Van Ness and Eddy, cut the motor and lights, and got the condition report from the glove compartment. The small shed at the rear of the lot spilled out light; he needed only carry the condition report up those three wooden steps, get it signed, and he'd make the deadline.

But he couldn't move. His hands shook on the wheel with delayed reaction; his body refused to function. Sweat stood out on his face.

Then from the darkness came a Negro. He was grinning. The breadth of his shoulders and the thickness of his chest gave an impression of bulk, but his hips were narrow and he moved with the grace of an athlete. Ballard released a

long sigh. Bart Heslip, ex-boxer, for three years a DKA field
agent. He'd trained Ballard, and was Ballard's best friend.
Heslip opened the door.

"Hey, dad, what the hell you doin'? Waiting for the deadline to pass?" Ballard didn't speak. "What's the matter,
man, you stoned?"

Then he saw the sweat on Ballard's face. He grunted,
reached in to grab the condition report, and strode away
without looking back.

Inside the shed a broad, heavy man in his thirties was
reading a girlie magazine, one leg cocked on the dusty surface of his desk. A dead cigar jutted from a corner of his
mouth. Heslip opened the door.

"Yeah?" The cigar switched corners without apparent vo-
lition.

"Cassavette?"

"Me." The big man stood up and yanked the cigar from
his mouth and was balanced easily on the balls of his feet in
one smooth movement.

"DKA's man. The Jennifer Poteet repo is outside. Keys
are in it."

"I'll be a bird." From the doorway he looked out at the
black gleaming auto. "I'll be a *dirty* bird. I tried to turn up
this chick myself; would have sworn *nobody* could find her
before the deadline—"

"How about kind of checking it in now?"

"Yeah, yeah," he muttered absently, scrawling his name
and the magic numerals 11:59 p.m. scross the bottom of the
condition report. "Hey, look, where the hell did you find
her?"

"It'll all be in the field report," said Heslip smoothly.

Ballard had finally got out and was leaning against the
fender, wiping his face on his jacket sleeve. Heslip punched
him lightly on the arm in passing, and they walked away,
leaving Cassavette shaking his head over the DEALER copy of
the condition report.

Heslip silently drove the company car out through the
darkened Western Addition on Fell street. He'd planned to
drive over to his apartment on Steiner, where Corinne Jones
was waiting for them; but it seemed better now to get Larry
out to his own place on Lincoln Way near the Park. Corinne
could wait. When you worked this job, your woman did a lot
of waiting.

Finally he turned to Ballard. "Okay, baby. Give."

Ballard gave, his voice quickening over the recital, becoming compulsive, almost hysterical; he talked as fast as he could form the words. The curse. The strange derangements of the drive up.

"Cursed, huh? And you feel good now? Just a little headache?"

"Yeah. Bart, this Madame Neya said—"

"It started with sweaty palms, irritation at light, anxiety, physical disorientation, feelings of guilt and oppression—"

"That's it," Ballard exclaimed excitedly. "Do you suppose—"

"Don't suppose. *Know*. That wasn't any curse, baby. You've been on a bad trip."

"Bad trip?" Ballard's face had gone slack with surprise.

"LSD. Acid. Lysergic acid diethylamide tartrate. She gave it to you in the sugar cube, and an hour later—*VOOM!* Tripsville."

"But *why*, Bart? I could have smashed up the car, been killed—"

"Just what she wanted; hell, *she'd* lost it anyway. She *wanted* you to think you'd been cursed. Mumbo-Jumbo, god of the Congo, all that jazz." He shook his head admiringly. "Chick plays *rough*, man."

When the light at Stanyan stopped them, Ballard suddenly realized where they were going. "Hey!" he exclaimed, "isn't Corinne waiting for you over at your place? I don't want you to—"

"Cool it, dad, I'll get you home, pour some coffee into you—"

"*Coffee?*" exclaimed Larry Ballard. His face suddenly was sick.

Heslip looked over at him. After a moment Heslip began to shake. Then he couldn't hold it in and let out a roar of laughter. Yeah, man! The Lincoln sedan car was in the barn by the deadline, all right, and Larry Ballard had put it there. But Larry Ballard, boy acid-head, was going to be hearing about curses, and sugar in his coffee, for a long, long time around DKA. Bart Heslip would see to that.

REUNION

EDWARD D. HOCH

I met Tony Boucher only once, at a crowded MWA cocktail party in New York some eight or ten years ago. His comments on my stories over the years were always most encouraging, and revealed a depth of perception that is gratifying to any author. "Reunion" was the first of four stories by me which he reprinted in his annual Best volumes. He called it a "nostalgic mood piece" with a "delicately elegiac tone." It was largely through Tony's efforts on the MWA awards committee that I received their 1968 Edgar for the best short story of the preceding year. The award was made on April 26, just a few days before his death.

CAPTAIN LEOPOLD'S OFFICE WAS tucked away at the rear of the second floor in the dingy, smoke-scarred building that served as police headquarters, and perhaps for this reason he was rarely bothered by social callers. The detectives, like Fletcher, who worked under him would occasionally stop in for a chat or a gripe, and when election time neared, the politicians came out of their holes. But mostly those who occupied the worn straight-backed chair opposite his desk were there on the most specific of business. They were there because they were suspected of murder.

Harry Tolliver was not a cop or a politician—nor, so far as Leopold knew, was he a murderer. He was, actually, a boiler salesman—and Leopold had not seen him in almost twenty-five years.

"You haven't changed a bit," he was saying. "I'd still know you anywhere."

Leopold smiled and offered him a cigarette. "Well, my hair is a bit thinner on top. And I'd hate to think that my middle bulged like this in high school."

Harry Tolliver waved away the cigarette. "Stopped smoking three years ago, when I turned forty. This stuff you read in the papers scares you after a while."

"In my business, Harry, walking down a dark street at night scares you more."

"Yeah. You're head of the homicide squad or something, aren't you?"

Leopold smiled at the popular misconception of his position. "Not really. There's no such thing in this city. It's more of a violent crimes squad, I suppose. But most of the cases do seem to be murders of one sort or another. Let's not talk about me, though. It's a dull subject. What about yourself? What brings you around to see me?" He had a half-day's work waiting, and Harry Tolliver had never been that good a friend, even in high school.

"Well, it's been twenty-five years."

Leopold looked blank. "Since what?"

"Since we graduated from high school. Some of us got together and decided we should have a reunion of the whole class, all the guys and gals."

"Oh?"

"Sure. Sounds great, doesn't it?"

Leopold tried to think back twenty-five years, to recapture those faces and names so buried now in his memory. He'd traveled in different circles during those intervening years—away to college, and the army, and a job with a police department out west, then back east for ten years of marriage that didn't work, until finally he'd found himself a middle-aged captain of detectives, back in his old home town. He liked it here, always had. He liked the breeze off the Sound in the summertime, and even the occasional heavy snows of winter. Perhaps, he sometimes thought, being back home made him feel less lonely—at least until moments like this.

"I don't know how it sounds," he answered frankly.

"We were thinking of a big picnic at Venice Park, just like the old days. Wives and kids and everything."

"I'm afraid I don't have any family to bring."

"Oh. Well, come anyway. It'll be great to see the old

crowd. Hell, my kids probably won't even come themselves. They're all in high school now."

"When is this going to be?"

"First Saturday in June, right close to the actual graduation date—just a few days early."

"I'll think about it, Harry."

"Hell, I want you to do more than just *think* about it. I want you to help us find people, contact them."

"Well, I really don't have much time . . ."

"Sure you do. Look, I brought along my old yearbook." He bent to a zipped brief-case and produced from it the slick-papered volume with thickly padded covers which had all but vanished from Leopold's memory. "Remember?"

"I remember."

Harry Tolliver ran his fingers lovingly over the imitation leather with its gold stamping now dulled and blurred by age. "Those were the days, boy! Those really were. So look, what we want you to do is take a few names—just a dozen or so—and contact the people. Hell, if anyone can find them you should be able to! You're a *detective!*"

"Yeah. Well, you see . . ."

"Come on! For the old crowd!"

Leopold looked into those middle-aged eyes and knew it would be useless to refuse. "All right. Maybe I can call a few people for you."

"Good, good. Look, why don't you take everyone whose name starts with *F* and *G*? There are only thirteen of them."

"Sure. You better leave me your book, though. I doubt if I could find mine any more."

Tolliver passed over the book a bit regretfully. "Take good care of it, huh? I wouldn't want anything to happen to it."

Leopold nodded. "I'll see if I can get a list of names typed up from it. Then I can give it back to you."

"Thanks. You'll get right on this? We've only got about five weeks, you know."

"Sure, Harry. Don't you worry about it."

Tolliver stood up and shook hands. "Good to see you again, Leopold, after all these years."

"I'll be in touch with you."

The little man nodded. "Say, when they going to give you a new building? This place is getting pretty shabby."

"Talk to the city council, Harry. They probably think it's pretty plush."

For a time after Tolliver left, Leopold sat alone at his

desk, letting the pages flip through his fingers, stopping now and then at some familiar face, some scrawled greeting addressed to Harry Tolliver. The class of George Washington High School, in that good year just before the coming of war.

He remembered how it was, and the memory depressed him.

During the next two days, Leopold ran quickly through eleven of the names on the list he'd made. Eight of them were men whose names were still in the phone book, and a ninth phoneless man was located through the city directory. Two of the women had been tracked down with some help from Tolliver, and Leopold had phoned one of them in New York City to convey the invitation. Each phone call was an adventure of sorts, even when he hardly remembered the people. It made him feel old, but he'd never been one to close his eyes to reality.

The man without a phone was named Jim Groves, and he lived in an apartment on the west side of town. Leopold stopped to see him one sunny afternoon on his way home, and caught him just as he was leaving for the night trick at a nearby factory. Jim Groves in his day had been the star quarterback of the Washington High football team, and even Leopold remembered him well. The man hadn't changed much in twenty-five years.

"Leopold! Sure, I remember you. God, it's been a long time."

They shook hands and Leopold told him quickly about the reunion plans. "Venice Park, the first Saturday in June. And bring the wife and kids if there are any."

Jim Groves was suddenly glum. "They're with her family up in Boston. We're separated."

"I'm sorry to hear that."

"One of those things. After all these years she decided she'd married a failure."

"You'll come to the reunion anyway?" Leopold urged. Somewhere along the line he'd caught the fever of the thing.

"Sure. It'll be good to see them all. The team and all. You finding everybody O.K.?"

Leopold glanced at his list. "Harry Tolliver's contacting most of them. I've got all but two on my list. Maybe you know something about them. It'll save me another call to Harry."

"I see a few of them once in a while. Who you looking for?"

"Shirley Fazen . . ."

"Sure. She married Quain, the class president. Remember? Chuck Quain? They live in town somewhere. He went to college and got an engineering job of some sort. They got a big house out in the suburbs."

Leopold made a note. "Thanks. One more—George Fisher."

For a moment, Groves didn't answer. He only looked at Leopold, his face troubled and intent. "Don't you remember? Don't you remember what happened to George Fisher? He drowned on the senior picnic at Venice Park."

"Yes," Leopold said slowly, wondering how he could ever have forgotten that night, even after so many years. "I never knew him well, and his picture was in the yearbook. I forgot it was him."

"Sure," Groves went on. "The yearbooks were already out by that time. I remember we were all signing them at the picnic. Poor George! You know, I always thought there was something funny about his death. I always thought maybe somebody pushed him out of that boat."

"It was a long time ago," Leopold answered carefully.

"Yeah. Well, I gotta get to work before that whistle blows. Keep me informed on the plans and I'll be there."

"All right," Leopold answered.

"Poor George," Groves mused as he turned away. Then, as an afterthought, he asked, "What are you doing these days, anyway, Leopold? You were always the brains of the class."

"I'm with the city, Jim," Leopold answered, starting down the stairs. "I'm a detective."

Chuck and Shirley Quain had made it big. Their house perched on top of a small hill, just a bit higher than the others in the suburban subdivision, and to Leopold's untrained eye it appeared to be in the fifty-thousand-dollar class. As he climbed out of the car he wished he'd worn a better necktie.

They remembered him, because he'd "hardly changed at all," and he remembered them. Shirley Fazen had been the best-looking girl in the senior class, and looking at her in the doorway Leopold could still remember why. Her cheer-leading at the football games had been a major attraction, and even the somewhat dull swimming meets were well attended by boys anxious for a look at Shirley Fazen in a bathing suit.

Leopold was a bit surprised to find that she'd married Chuck Quain. He'd been elected president of the senior class after a hard-fought, dirty campaign that seemed to mark him as a future politician but little else. The house on the hill showed that he'd made it to something else, but Leopold couldn't help wondering if he was still using the same tactics.

"Come in, come in," Quain urged. "You remember Shirley, surely. Ha, ha!" That must have been his favorite joke. "Drink? Scotch, rye, rum, vodka, anything you name. We live the good life out here." Behind him, the setting sun was streaking through a window, turning his grey hair momentarily reddish.

Leopold followed them into a sunken living-room a bit too full of the good life. "You have a nice place here," he managed to say.

"We like it." Quain lit a cigar without offering one to Leopold. "How about that drink, or are you on duty?"

"I see you've kept up on me more than I have on you."

"How could I miss? Every time there's a murder Captain Leopold gets his name in the papers. Isn't that right, Shirley?"

She nodded agreement and came over to perch on the arm of Leopold's chair. She was wearing tight orange pants that did youthful things for her figure, and Leopold had to remind himself that she too must now be forty-three years old. "But I don't imagine the Captain's here on business," she purred. "Are you, Captain? I'll bet it's about the big reunion. Harry Tolliver has already talked to Chuck about it."

Leopold smiled up at her. "Then my trip was for nothing."

"Not if you'll take a drink."

"All right," he said with a sigh. "Scotch and water—but just one."

Chuck Quain produced the drink from a little bar at one end of the living-room. "The good life does have its drawbacks," he said. "The kids are getting old enough now to sneak a swig of the booze when we're not around. But I guess that's the only way to learn about it. I guess I did things like that myself when I was young."

"You're an engineer, aren't you?" Leopold asked.

"That's right. That's where the money is these days. I could tell you . . ."

"Chuck, no shop talk, please. We haven't seen him for

twenty-five years! I want to hear about this reunion, any-way."

"You probably know as much as I do, from Tolliver. He's the one who roped me in on it. Venice Park's the place, right where we had our senior class picnic."

"Yeah," Chuck muttered. "I remember that."

"Funny thing, I'd completely forgotten about George Fish-er drowning that day. I stopped by to see Jim Groves this afternoon and he reminded me."

"It's not the sort of thing you like to remember," Shirley said.

"But the three of us were right there when it happened," Leopold said. "I can remember it now as if it were just yesterday. You saw him fall in, didn't you, Chuck?"

Quain nodded. "I got there a minute later, anyway. I was taking the canoe back to the boathouse, and I guess he was doing the same thing. He was always ahead of me on the creek, just around the bend, when I heard a yell and a splash. He'd fallen out of the damned canoe and was thrash-ing around in the water. God, it was awful!"

"Then why talk about it?" Shirley asked. "It was awful for all of us. I was practically engaged to George at the time."

"You helped pull him out, didn't you?" Leopold asked.

She nodded. "Some of us had been swimming earlier, and I still had my suit on. We heard Chuck yelling for help and came running. It was pitch dark, of course, but he shouted that George had capsized his canoe and gone under. A bunch of us dived in, and finally we found him. Not in time, though."

The details were growing more vivid in Leopold's memory as she spoke. He'd never been a good swimmer himself, and the black of the water had been too frightening that night. But he remembered running to one of the footpath bridges directly above the tragic spot, remembered looking down with flashlights playing over the water as Shirley and someone else pulled the body onto the grassy bank of the creek. The place was called Venice Park because of these creeks and footbridges, and it was a perfect setting for picnics and canoeing—a bit of Venice in New York State. For the most part, the creeks were barely six or seven feet deep, hardly enough to be very dangerous. That night, though, they'd been dangerous—deadly—to George Fisher. They'd worked over him for an hour before admitting what they all must have known. He was dead, and the senior picnic had been ended by sudden tragedy.

"Who else helped you pull him out, anyway?" Leopold asked.

"I think it was Jim Groves."

Leopold nodded. "I thought it might have been. Funny he didn't mention it today."

"What *did* he say about it?" Chuck Quain asked.

"Oh, nothing really. Just that he thought there might have been something funny. Something not quite right."

Shirley Quain laughed. "Are you going to make a murder case out of it after all these years, Captain?"

He joined her with a chuckle. "Hardly."

Chuck studied the damp end of his cigar. "It would be too late now anyway, wouldn't it? After twenty-five years?"

"Well, there's no statute of limitations on murder, if that's what you mean."

"Let's find a pleasanter subject," Shirley suggested. "How about another drink, Captain?"

"No, no. I really have to be going. I didn't mean to be talking shop either. Just wanted to tell you about the reunion."

"Do you think under the circumstances that Venice Park is a very good place to have it?" Chuck asked.

Leopold got to his feet. "I'll bring up the point with Harry Tolliver. He might have forgotten about Fisher too."

"Everyone seems to have."

Leopold nodded. "Everyone but Jim Groves. He still remembers it."

That night, later, Leopold phoned Harry Tolliver at his home. The man was a bit overly jovial, as if he might have been drinking. "Hi, boy! How you doing? Did you reach everyone?"

"All but George Fisher. He's dead."

"George . . . Oh, sure. I didn't know his name was on the list."

"Harry?"

"Yeah?"

"Do you think we should consider moving the reunion to some other location? Venice Park might bring back unpleasant memories."

"Why? What do you mean?"

"Well, Fisher and all."

"Everybody's forgotten that."

"Some people haven't. Some people even think his death might not have been accidental."

"*What?* God, Leopold, stop letting that badge go to your head! I asked you to call a few people, that's all."

"Sorry." Leopold hung up and lit a cigarette. For a long time he sat staring at the frosted glass of his office door. What was it? Was he just trying to be a big man with his former classmates? Was he overdoing the detective bit? He was forty-three years old—hardly a child any more. He'd forget about the thing. Right now!

But the next afternoon he went to see Jim Groves again.

Groves was blinking sleepy eyes as he opened the door. "Hey! We don't see each other for twenty-five years, and then bingo—two days in a row!"

"Sorry to bother you again," Leopold said.

"Come on in. I got some cold beer in the icebox."

"No thanks. I just wanted to ask you something, Jim. Yesterday you said something about George Fisher's death. You said you thought someone may have pushed him out of that boat. Why?"

"You're working now, aren't you? You're going to solve the damn thing after twenty-five years!"

"If there's anything to solve. It was a long time ago."

"There's something to solve, all right. Fisher was never much of a swimmer, but the damned creek was only ten feet wide!"

"How deep?"

"Six feet, maybe. He could almost have walked out."

"But he didn't."

"Darn right he didn't! Because somebody pushed him out of the canoe."

"Somebody walking on the water?"

"Maybe somebody in another canoe," Groves answered.

Leopold lit a cigarette. "You've got quite a memory. What else do you remember? Who else had a canoe out that night?"

"Quain. Chuck Quain was right behind him when it happened."

"Were they friends?"

"That's hard to say." He went into the kitchen for a moment and returned with a frosty bottle of beer. "Hard to say. They both were hot for that Shirley Fazen. I remember the football games when she used to cheer. She was really built."

"Wasn't just about everybody hot for Shirley, as I remember it?"

"Yeah, I guess so. Even me, once."

"Was George with Shirley that day?"

"Not too much as I remember it. He had this other chick on the string. Marge Alguard. Remember her?"

"Vaguely. Short girl, dark hair?"

"That's the one."

"What's she doing these days?"

"I don't think she ever got married. I see her around town once in a while. She works at one of the department stores."

"Thanks a lot, Jim. You've got quite a memory."

"Listen, if you've got some time, let me tell you about one or two of my best games. Remember the time I ran eighty-five yards for a touchdown against Tech?"

"I remember, Jim. Maybe I can come again some time and we can talk about it. Right now you'd better start getting ready for work."

"What? Yeah, it is getting late." He downed the rest of his beer. "See you around. In June if not before."

"Sure." Leopold left him there, feeling vaguely sorry for Jim Groves, feeling that nobody should be cursed with that good a memory of the better days.

Marge Alguard's name didn't start with *F* or *G*, but Leopold went to see her anyway. He found her working behind the candy counter of the city's largest department store, scooping multi-colored jelly beans into little plastic bags. Easter was only a few weeks past, and he imagined this was the unsold remainder. He found himself wondering if they melted down the chocolate rabbits, too.

"Pardon me. Miss Alguard?"

"Yes?" She still had a pleasant smile, though she was too obviously a woman in her forties.

"You probably don't remember me after all these years. My name's Leopold and I went to high school with you."

She hesitated a moment and then her tiny face lit up. "Why yes, I remember you! How *are* you?"

"Fine. I'd like to talk to you a few minutes if I could. Do you get a coffee break or anything?"

"I'm in charge of the department," she answered with a superior smile, signaling to one of the other girls. "I'd be happy to have coffee with you. I see so few of the old crowd any more."

Over coffee in the store's gaudy restaurant they talked of old times and people they'd known, and finally after a decent interval of casualness Leopold asked her, "Remember George Fisher? The fellow that drowned at the senior picnic?"

"Oh yes, George Fisher." Her eyes seemed suddenly to blur.

"I was thinking about that day, trying to figure what really happened. You were with George, weren't you?"

"Not when he died."

"No, no. I meant earlier."

"It's hard to remember. Twenty-five years next month. You know, Harry Tolliver called me the other day about a class reunion."

"I know."

"Yes, I guess I was with George most of that day. I remember he rented the canoe and we paddled all over the park, up and down those creeks and streams, under the bridges, through the branches of the trees where they touched the water."

"Then what happened?"

"Oh, I don't know. We rested for a time on the bank. I remember how nice the grass was, how soft. Then it was dark, and he said he had to return the canoe. I never saw him alive again. I heard the shouting and ran down and saw them trying to revive him. It was horrible."

Leopold wanted to leave her in peace, but there was one other question he had to ask. "When . . . when you rested on the bank, did he kiss you, neck with you?"

"Say, what is this?" Her blurred eyes were suddenly sharp with suspicion. "Why are you asking me all these questions?"

"I'm looking into Fisher's death."

"Are you a cop or something?"

"It's not an official investigation," he said quickly, but he saw that he had already lost her. He had gone too far with his casual questions. She finished her coffee and hurried back to the candy counter with hardly a good-bye.

Leopold sighed and ordered a second cup of coffee. He should forget the thing, then and there. Nothing good could come of what he was doing. He was just stirring up a lot of memories better left buried after twenty-five years. At times he had too much of the detective's mentality—the ability to see evil where no evil lurked. Perhaps this was one of those times.

That night Harry Tolliver—an alarmed Harry Tolliver—phoned Leopold at his apartment. His voice over the telephone had lost now all of the friendly charm he'd tried to show that first day.

"Leopold, what in hell are you trying to do?"

"About what?"

"You know. George Fisher. You've got everybody all upset."

"Oh? Who?"

"Marge Alguard, just to name one. She found out you were with the police and she's scared half out of her wits. What did you ask her, anyway?"

"Nothing special."

"Her name wasn't on your list, even. What in hell are you trying to stir up?"

"Just the truth."

"After twenty-five years there isn't any truth, only memories. Stop bothering these people. Stop bothering *me!*"

"You?"

"I want this reunion to be a success. You think anyone'll show up if you turn it into a murder investigation?"

"No one's mentioned murder. No one till now."

"Look, just forget I ever approached you about the reunion. Forget everything, huh?"

"That's difficult to do at this point. Memories linger."

Tolliver hung up in disgust. Leopold felt a bit sorry for the man, as he did for most people, but the thing was almost out of his hands. He had the decided feeling that wheels had been set in motion, wheels which could not now be stopped until they had ground exceedingly fine.

That night Leopold's dreams were troubled, and he awoke at the first hint of dawn with a cool layer of sweat covering his body. By some trick of memory he was back there, back on that stone bridge over the creek, remembering it all as clearly as if it were yesterday. Yes, the lights playing on the water, the wet stone beneath his hands as he clutched the parapet and peered down; it was all too vividly clear. There was Shirley Quain—Shirley Fazen then—the bathing suit clinging to her strong young form, helping to pull the limp, sodden body from the water. And there too was Jim

Groves, aiding her, though his clothes were soaked and his shoes lost somewhere in the creek.

Leopold came suddenly awake. Jim Groves, for all his remarkable memory, had not mentioned to Leopold that he'd helped recover Fisher's body from the creek. Why not? Was it simply that he hadn't been asked?

Leopold rolled out of bed and dressed quickly. He wanted to get down to headquarters, away from his thoughts, away from the memories. When he reached his desk he rang for Fletcher and asked at once for an account of the night's activities.

"Morning report's not ready yet," Fletcher said. "What's the trouble this morning, Captain?"

Leopold ran a hand over his eyes. "I don't know. Talk to me about something, will you? What about that jewel robbery yesterday?"

Fletcher's smile broadened. "We cracked that one. The bird they grabbed outside the building finally confessed."

"What did he do with the diamond rings?"

"Damnedest thing you ever heard of! He's got a girl friend working in the building and he had it set up that she'd leave her office and go down for coffee at exactly three o'clock. He staged the robbery when he saw her coming back along the hallway with her paper cup full of coffee. As he ran by her he just dropped the rings into the coffee and kept going. It was perfect."

"Not quite perfect," Leopold said.

"What?"

"You caught him."

"Yeah, but if he hadn't broken down and talked we'd never have gotten wise to the way he worked it."

The conversation depressed Leopold. Everything seemed to depress him. "Fletcher, perfect crimes can become an obsession with detectives sometimes. I wonder if that's what's happening to me."

"What's the trouble, Captain?"

"Twenty-five years ago an eighteen-year-old boy drowned at Venice Park during a class picnic. I was practically a witness to the thing. Now I'm wondering about it, wondering if someone might have killed him."

"Take my advice and forget it, Captain. We have enough new murders coming in every day without worrying about anything that old."

Leopold sighed and swiveled around to look out the window. These first few days in May were always among his favorites, a special time when the earth seemed alive again not just with spring but with an electric impulse to accomplish the strident tasks of winter. Perhaps it was the weather that was against him this day. "Fletcher, I value your opinion, but I just can't accept it. Go down to the records room and dig me out what they've got on this drowning, will you?"

"*How* long ago did you say it was?"

"Twenty-five years next month, but we must have something on it. The boy's name was George Fisher. He was a senior at Washington High."

"That stuff's probably in the basement, under a ton of dust."

"See what you can find," Leopold said. "Just to humor me."

Fletcher was gone for the better part of an hour, and when he returned his brow was streaked with a line of dust. He collapsed into Leopold's straight-backed chair and blew more dust from a thin legal-sized folder. "I hope you're satisfied, Captain."

Leopold smiled through tight lips. "I don't think anything could satisfy me today. What've you got?"

"Who knows? I only hope the paper hasn't all crumbled into dust. Weren't they talking about putting all this old stuff on microfilm?"

"They'll do that about the same time they give us a new building," Leopold said. He was now suddenly anxious to see these old reports, anxious to delve into this page from his past. He wondered if somewhere on these pages his own name might even appear, like a ghostly vision of another, forgotten life. "What've you got, Fletcher?"

"Not too much, really. Let's see—autopsy report, statements by some of the kids, and the report of the investigating detective."

"Detective?" Leopold sat up straighter in his chair. "Why a detective?"

"Don't know. Nothing to indicate why, but apparently they thought something was funny at first."

"Yeah. The autopsy—what were the findings?"

"Death by drowning. Nothing irregular there."

"Any other marks or wounds on the body?"

"Not a thing. Some hair pulled out, but that probably happened when they tried to rescue him."

Leopold stared off into space. "Do you have a statement by Chuck Quain there?"

Fletcher flipped through the papers. "Here it is . . . He was in a canoe about a hundred feet behind Fisher. It was dark, but there was an occasional moon through the clouds. He hadn't been with Fisher, but had seen him earlier in the boat with a girl named Marge Alguard . . ."

Leopold nodded. "What about the drowning?"

". . . Well, Quain heard a yell and a splash from around a bend in the creek. By the time he reached the spot, he saw Fisher struggling in the water. Quain couldn't swim, and hesitated about going in after him. He shouted for help, and some of the others came running. It was hard to see anything, and by that time Fisher had gone under for good. But after a moment or two Shirley Fazen and Jim Groves found him and pulled him out. They applied artificial respiration, but it was too late."

"What are the other statements?"

"Let's see . . . Shirley Fazen—she was the only one who still had her bathing suit on, and she was the first to reach the creek and go in after Fisher. But she couldn't find him until Groves joined her after a moment. He was fully dressed, but he dived in anyway and they pulled Fisher out together."

"What did Groves say?"

"About the same thing. He'd been swimming earlier in the evening with Shirley Fazen, and she stayed in the water while he dried off and got dressed. This was at a pool about a hundred yards from the creek. The first thing he knew he heard Quain shouting for help and he started to run towards the sound. He dived into the creek and found that Shirley was already there, searching for Fisher. They found him together."

"Is Marge Alguard mentioned anywhere?"

"In Quain's statement."

"Yeah. Anywhere else?"

"Here's a very brief statement by her, just to the effect that she'd been in the canoe with Fisher earlier."

"How about Harry Tolliver?"

Fletcher skimmed over the last remaining sheet of paper. "Nothing on him. This is just the detective's conclusions."

"That should be interesting."

"It should be, but it isn't. He figures Fisher was standing up in the canoe and fell in. That's all."

"Why would he stand up?"

Fletcher shrugged. "Beats me." He fumbled for a cagarette and lit it. "But then I can't figure out why you're so interested in making this a murder, Captain."

"Shouldn't I be? Isn't it my job?"

"After all this time?"

"If it was murder then, it's still murder today."

Fletcher frowned into the cigarette smoke, blue against the morning sunshine filtering through the dirty window. "Yeah. But if it's murder, then you could be one of the suspects yourself."

Leopold blinked. He hadn't really thought of that.

In the afternoon he called again at the candy counter where Marge Alguard worked. He waited patiently while she conducted business with three tiny children, then stepped into her line of vision.

"You again?" she said between tight lips. "I don't want any coffee today, thanks."

"I just wanted to ask you a question."

"Didn't you ask enough already?"

"Maybe not the right ones. That day in the park—did you have a fight with Fisher for any reasons?"

She stepped very close to him, so no one else could hear her words. "Look, get out of here. Get out of here with your dirty little questions! What's the trouble—trying to get your kicks this way? You were never much with the girls back in school, were you?"

"Marge . . ."

"No, I didn't have a fight with George that day. That day was about the happiest in my life, until he died, and your questions aren't going to turn it into something dirty. I don't have much to remember any more, at my age, but I remember George Fisher."

There was nothing more for Leopold to say, except, "I'm sorry. I won't bother you again." He went away, wondering if he'd already bothered too many lives with his needless prying. Perhaps it didn't really make any difference, after all these years.

That night, under a clear but moonless sky, a brick fell from the roof of Leopold's apartment building as he was entering, just missing his head. It might have been toppled by the wind, except that there was no wind. He hurried to the roof with his revolver drawn, but there was nothing to be seen. Down in the back alley, at the foot of the fire escape, he caught a split-second glimpse of a running man, who vanished around a corner. Leopold slept the rest of the night with the gun under his pillow, something he'd never done before.

Fletcher turned the unmarked police car into Venice Park, narrowly avoiding a group of bicycling teenagers on a day's outing. "A Saturday in May," he said, not unkindly. "Brings 'em all out."

Leopold was smoking an old pipe he'd resurrected that morning from his dresser drawer. He watched the kids on their bicycles until they were out of sight around a curve, then said, "I guess that's what parks are for."

"That, and lovers after dark, and maybe sometimes a killing or two."

They crossed a stone bridge over one of the creeks and Leopold asked him to stop. "It was in this area somewhere, I'm sure. The swimming pool's still just over there."

"I thought you said it was a footbridge."

"It was, then. But times change." He opened the door on his side and slid out. "Let's walk awhile, Fletcher. It's a nice day."

The detective fell into step at his side. "You really think one of them tried to kill you last night, Captain?"

"It's hard to say. I've acquired a good many enemies in my life. But this is the only thing I've really been working on all week." And even that thought troubled him. Would he have devoted so much time to the drowning of George Fisher in a week when a major murder or two had occurred? Weren't they all mere victims of time and circumstance, ultimately?

Fletcher lit a cigarette. "I had a couple of the boys check the roof this morning like you suggested, but they didn't come up with anything. Not even an old butt."

Leopold felt a sudden surge of excitement. They'd crossed a graveled path which led from the direction of the pool to a narrow stone bridge over the creek. "This is it, Fletcher. I'm sure!"

He remembered it now as if the events had happened only yesterday. There was the bridge, with its engraved metal plaque in tribute to the W.P.A., its carefully placed stones now showing the wear of some thirty years' travel by foot and cycle. Leopold stood in the very center and looked down once more into the dark waters below.

Fletcher climbed down the grassy bank to the water's edge and took out a twelve-foot tape measure. He tossed one end to Leopold and watched the point where the other end, weighted by its round metal case, cut the water. "O.K., Captain. Nine feet from the top of the bridge to the water."

"How far from the bottom? How much clearance is there?"

Fletcher stretched his long body out over the water, clinging to a jutting stone with one precarious handhold. "I make it just under six feet. Maybe about five-ten."

Leopold nodded. "So if he'd been standing in the canoe he might have hit his head going under."

"Who stands in canoes?"

"People who get drowned. Did you check on the detective who wrote that original report?"

Fletcher nodded. "He retired seven years ago and moved to Florida. Died a couple years back."

"He probably wouldn't have remembered it anyway," Leopold decided. "Just a drowning. Toss your measure into the water and see how deep we are at this point, Fletcher."

The detective joined Leopold on the bridge and they played out the full twelve feet. By leaning far over the edge Fletcher was able to touch bottom. "It's around six feet," he said finally, after some quick mathematics. "Deep enough to drown in."

"Fisher was tall. Just about that tall. Why didn't he just walk to shore. It's only a few feet."

"He panicked in the dark. People do, you know. Maybe it was deeper then."

Leopold shook his head. "These creeks rise in the spring, but by June it would be lower than it is now."

"Maybe he hit his head, like you suggested. Knocked himself out."

"But the autopsy showed no marks on his head. And Chuck Quain's story had him struggling in the water, obviously conscious."

"Well, what then?"

Leopold was running his hand over the smooth dry stone of the bridge, remembering something from long ago. "Fletcher, what do we have back in the car that's big enough to make a splash?"

"Huh?"

"Something . . . the spare tire! Get the spare tire, will you?"

Moments later, Fletcher returned with a puzzled frown, rolling the tire before him. "You're sure this is what you want, Captain?"

"It'll have to do," Leopold answered with a smile, "unless you'd like to jump in."

"No thanks, Captain. Say, what are you up to, anyway?"

Leopold was lifting the tire to the stone ledge. "Just trying something, Fletcher." He let the tire fall, then watched as the water splashed up in return. "See if you can fish it out for me and we'll try once more."

Fletcher broke a thin branch off a nearby tree and used it to coax the floating tire in to shore. "I hope you know what you're doing."

Leopold tapped his pipe against the stone while he waited. "I suppose it will be good to see them all again at the re-union," he mused. "Funny how the years separate us so much, by occupation and economics. Back in those days I don't think we were so different. But now I'm a detective, and Harry Tolliver is a salesman, and Marge Alguard is a clerk. Shirley married Chuck Quain, and he's a successful engineer. Groves is a factory worker."

"And Fisher's dead."

"Yes, and Fisher's dead. I guess that's life. Some of us get happy and some of us get dead." He let the tire fall again, but the splash was no greater than the first time.

"Satisfied, Captain?"

"Satisfied. I wanted to see if the water could splash up to the top of this railing. It can't."

"What does that prove?"

Leopold shrugged and said nothing. It was too soon for answers, even after twenty-five years.

Later in the day, he had still another phone call from the increasingly distraught Mr. Harry Tolliver. "Look, Leopold," he began without preamble, "Some of us are having a meeting tonight about the reunion. We'd like you to come."

"Where?"

"Chuck Quain's place. We want to get things out in the open, find out just what you're up to."

Leopold sighed into the mouthpiece. "All right, I'll be there. What time?"

"A little after eight."

At eight-thirty that evening, Leopold turned his car into the Quain driveway once more, and was surprised to see only one other vehicle ahead of him. The meeting, he soon discovered, had so petered out that only the Quains and Tolliver and Marge Alguard were present, all looking quite unhappy.

Shirley Quain, wearing the same orange slacks, served him a martini that he didn't really need, and he settled down into an uncomfortable purple chair opposite Marge. He wondered if it was a sign of the new sophistication to serve martinis this late in the evening. "This all that's coming?" he asked.

"I asked Jim Groves, but he's working," Tolliver mumbled.

Reminded of Groves' night job, Leopold wondered if he had been there the previous evening. He didn't really need to check, though. He thought he knew who'd tried to kill him. "Well, what seems to be the problem?"

"You, I guess," Chuck Quain answered, not quite managing a laugh. "Marge here says she won't come to the reunion because of the questions you've been asking, and some of the others feel the same way."

"Oh?"

"I told you to lay off," Tolliver said.

"I was going to, but something changed my mind."

"You really think George Fisher was . . . killed?" This question came from Shirley Quain, who'd just returned from the kitchen with another tray full of cocktails.

"I think he was killed, yes. I think the police were suspicious at the time, but they were unable to prove anything."

"You can prove something?" Tolliver asked.

"I don't know."

"But you intend to continue this foolish investigation?" Quain had left his chair to begin pacing the floor. He reminded Leopold of a caged tiger waiting to be fed.

"I intend to continue," he said. "In fact, I'm going out to Venice Park when I leave here, just to refresh my memory of things."

"At night?" Shirley Quain questioned, somewhat startled.

"It happened at night," he answered. The thing had occurred to him on the spur of the moment, then the words were out almost before he realized it. All right, he was saying to one of them, come and get me.

If he was wrong, if it was Jim Groves after all, then there was no harm done. He downed his drink and made motions towards leaving.

"Wait a minute!" Harry Tolliver insisted. "We haven't settled anything. What about the reunion?"

"Count me out," Marge said. "I've had enough questions and prying about the past."

"See what I'm up against?" Tolliver pleaded. "Nobody'll come, the way things are."

"I'm sorry," Leopold told him. And he was sorry. Not for the reunion, but for Harry Tolliver.

Leopold waited for an hour at the edge of the creek, lounging up against the stone coldness of the bridge as he smoked his pipe and waited for death to visit him, to brush up against his flesh. He had no doubt that the man would try again, but somehow as the hour grew into two his supreme confidence began to fade. Perhaps he couldn't get away from the meeting, or perhaps Leopold had been wrong. What if it had been Jim Groves after all, or someone else?

As the second hour neared its end, he knocked the glowing embers of his pipe into the muddy creek and started to leave. It was then that he became aware of the dark figure standing near a tree some twenty feet away. A chill of anticipation ran down his spine. "Hello, there," he said. "I've been waiting for you."

Chuck Quain stepped out of the shadows, letting the pale lights of night fall full across his face. "You knew I'd come?"

"I knew."

"I've got a gun this time," Quain said, and Leopold saw the weapon flash in the moonlight.

"It's better than a brick, but I don't think you'll use it."

"Why not?"

"Because you're not a murderer. Because killing me won't keep your wife's secret. It was Shirley who killed George Fisher, all those years ago. Wasn't it?"

Chuck Quain never even noticed when Leopold signaled Fletcher to come out of his hiding place. He was suddenly like a man with the life crushed from his body, and he offered no resistance when they took the gun from his hand.

"Let's go back to the car," Leopold suggested. "We can talk there."

"How did you know about Shirley? How?"

When they reached the car, Leopold signaled Fletcher to switch on the tape recorder. They could get Quain's signature on a statement later. "Memories, I think. Memories and a lot of guessing. It was fantastic that Fisher could have drowned so quickly in that shallow creek, unless he was unconscious. And yet there was no bump on his head and we had your own statement that he'd been struggling in the water. Was there another possiblity? Yes. Someone could have held him under the water."

Chuck Quain shivered with a sudden chill, or perhaps a memory. "After all these years," he said simply.

"Now, was there any confirming evidence of this theory?" Leopold went on. "There was. Fisher's hair—some of it had been pulled out. He'd spent the whole evening with Marge Alguard and she hadn't done it, so who had? It might have happened when they pulled him from the water, but I doubted if they'd use that violence in the act of rescuing a man. It seemed more likely to me that a murderer had held Fisher under the water by the hair, until he drowned. The next question was *who?* And I remembered that Shirley Fazen had been Fisher's girl, although he spent the day of the picnic with Marge. It could have been a motive."

Fletcher stirred in the back seat and lit a cigarette. Outside, the night was very quiet.

"When I began piecing together Shirley's movements for that evening in my own mind, I came up with something a bit odd. She'd been swimming with Jim Groves, and he'd left her in the pool. Apparently no one saw her leave it, but next thing we know she's in the creek with Fisher's body. And you, Chuck, were the only one who claimed to have seen her dive in after him. If someone did hold Fisher underwater by the hair until he drowned, it almost had to be one of his would-be rescuers. Either Shirley Fazen or Jim Groves."

"Why?" That was all. Just *why.*

"Because the murderer must have gotten soaked through to the skin, and nobody else would have been wet. They'd all gotten dressed except Shirley. And then somewhere along the line I remembered something from that evening, something buried in my own memory. When I stood on that stone bridge and watched them pulling Fisher from the water, the railing of the bridge was wet—not damp but actually wet. It hadn't rained, there was a moon that night and only a few clouds. And Fisher's struggles couldn't have splashed water up that far. No, it was wet because the killer had perched there before leaping down onto George Fisher's unsuspecting head as he passed under the bridge in his canoe. But Jim Groves had just put on dry clothes. Everyone else had on dry clothes. Only Shirley was still in her bathing suit, and just out of the pool. Only Shirley could have left wet stones behind on the bridge when she dropped onto Fisher's canoe."

"It wasn't really like that," Chuck Quain said, and his words were almost a moan. "She didn't plan it. She saw him taking the canoe back and ran to the bridge in the darkness. She was sitting there, with her feet dangling over the edge, when he paddled along. They said a few words. She asked about Marge Alguard and he made a statement that infuriated her—something about Marge being better at necking. Shirley just . . . just jumped on him. I don't think she ever meant to kill him."

Leopold sighed into the darkness. It might have been twenty-five years ago. This, right now, was their reunion. "And you came along and saw it. And kept her secret all these years. Is that why she married you, Chuck? Did you blackmail her into marriage?"

But that question would never be answered. His mind and memory were still back there by the creek. "She didn't know her own strength," he said, almost to himself now. "She was so at home in the water, on the swimming team, that she didn't realize Fisher was almost helpless in her hands. She was a strong girl. She still is."

"We'll have to go see her," Leopold said quietly.

"Yes." Then, "What do you intend to do?"

"I don't know. I just don't know."

He knew too well that it would be an impossible case to prove. How many could remember Shirley in the water that night? How many could have said even then, in the confusion of darkened events, whether she was rescuer or murderer? All Leopold had was Chuck Quain's statement, and the fact that their guilty secret had nearly turned Chuck into a killer himself.

In a book, they would have found her a suicide when they returned to the house on the hill. But instead there was only a haggard woman of forty-three coming down the stairs, looking suddenly old—as if the mere sight of Leopold had told her all she needed to know.

"One of the children was crying," she said simply to them both. "He was having a nightmare."

HANGOVER

JOHN D. MacDONALD

I share with many others a lasting benefit which Anthony Boucher created through his insistence, over many years in his reviewing, that novels of mystery and suspense which contain those same ingredients which give validity to the "straight" novel must be given the same recognition and acceptance by the critical establishment as the "straight" novel of merit receives. He blurred that unfair and arbitrary demarcation which labeled a whole area of work inferior because of the authors' choice of subject matter. He drew the line between good and bad, regardless of genre, and that, of course, is where it belongs and will stay.

HE DREAMED THAT HE had dropped something, lost something of value in the furnace, and he lay on his side trying to look down at an angle through a little hole, look beyond the flame down into the dark guts of the furnace for what he had lost. But the flame kept pulsing through the hole with a brightness that hurt his eyes, with a heat that parched his face, pulsing with an intermittent husky rasping sound.

With his awakening, the dream became painfully explicable—the pulsing roar was his own harsh breathing, the parched feeling was a consuming thirst, the brightness was transmuted into pain intensely localized behind his eyes. When he opened his eyes, a long slant of early morning sun dazzled him, and he shut his eyes quickly again.

This was a morning time of awareness of discomfort so

202

acute that he had no thought for anything beyond the appraisal of the body and its functions. Though he was dimly aware of psychic discomforts that might later exceed the anguish of the flesh, the immediacy of bodily pain localized his attentions. Even without the horizontal brightness of the sun, he would have known it was early. Long sleep would have muffled the beat of the taxed heart to a softened, sedate, and comfortable rhythm. But it was early and the heart knocked sharply with a violence and in a cadence almost hysterical, so that no matter how he turned his head, he could feel it, a tack hammer chipping away at his mortality.

His thirst was monstrous, undiminished by the random nausea that teased at the back of his throat. His hands and feet were cool, yet where his thighs touched he was sweaty. His body felt clotted, and he knew that he had perspired heavily during the evening, an oily perspiration that left an unpleasant residue when it dried. The pain behind his eyes was a slow bulging and shrinking, in contrapuntal rhythm to the clatter of his heart.

He sat on the edge of the bed, head bowed, eyes squeezed shut, cool trembling fingers resting on his bare knees. He felt weak, nauseated, and acutely depressed.

This was the great joke. This was a hangover. Thing of sly wink, of rueful guffaw. This was death in the morning.

He stood on shaky legs and walked into the bathroom. He turned the cold water on as far as it would go. He drank a full glass greedily. He was refilling the glass when the first spasm came. He turned to the toilet, half-falling, cracking one knee painfully on the tile floor, and knelt there and clutched the edge of the bowl in both hands, hunched, miserable, naked. The water ran in the sink for a long time while he remained there, retching, until nothing more came but flakes of greenish bile. When he stood up, he felt weaker but slightly better. He mopped his face with a damp towel, then drank more water, drank it slowly and carefully, and in great quantity, losing track of the number of glasses. He drank the cold water until his belly was swollen and he could hold no more, but he felt as thirsty as before.

Putting the glass back on the rack, he looked at himself in the mirror. He took a quick, overly casual look, the way one glances at a stranger, the eye returning for a longer look after it is seen that the first glance aroused no undue curiosity. Though his face was grayish, eyes slightly puffy, jaws soiled by beard stubble, the long face with its even, undistinguished features looked curiously unmarked in relation to the torment of the body.

The visual reflection was a first step in the reaffirmation of identity. You are Hadley Purvis. You are thirty-nine. Your hair is turning gray with astonishing and disheartening speed.

He turned his back on the bland image, on the face that refused to comprehend his pain. He leaned his buttocks against the chill edge of the sink, and a sudden unbidden image came into his mind, as clear and supernaturally perfect as a colored advertisement in a magazine. It was a shot glass full to the very brim with dark brown bourbon.

By a slow effort of will he caused the image to fade away. Not yet, he thought, and immediately wondered about his instinctive choice of mental phrase. Nonsense. This was a part of the usual morbidity of hangover—to imagine oneself slowly turning into an alcoholic. The rum sour on Sunday mornings had become a ritual with him, condoned by Sarah. And that certainly did not speak of alcholism. Today was, unhappily, a working day, and it would be twelve-thirty before the first Martini at Mario's. If anyone had any worries about alcoholism, it was Sarah, and her worries resulted from her lack of knowledge of his job and its requirements. After a man has been drinking for twenty-one years, he does not suddenly become a legitimate cause for the sort of annoying concern Sarah had been showing lately.

In the evening when they were alone before dinner, they would drink, and that certainly did not distress her. She liked her few knocks as well as anyone. Then she had learned somehow that whenever he went to the kitchen to refill their glasses from the Martini jug in the deep freeze, he would have an extra one for himself, opening his throat for it, pouring it down in one smooth, long, silvery gush. By mildness of tone she had trapped him into an admission, then had told him that the very secrecy of it was "significant." He had tried to expalin that his tolerance for alcohol was greater than hers, and that it was easier to do it that way than to listen to her tiresome hints about how many he was having.

Standing there in the bathroom, he could hear the early morning sounds of the city. His hearing seemed unnaturally keen. He realized that it was absurd to stand there and conduct mental arguments with Sarah and become annoyed at her. He reached into the shower stall and turned the faucets and waited until the water was the right temperature before stepping in, just barely warm. He made no attempt at first

to bathe. He stood under the roar and thrust of the high noz-
zle, eyes shut, face tilted up.

As he stood there he began, cautiously, to think of the
previous evening. He had much experience in this sort of
reconstruction. He reached out with memory timorously, an-
ticipating remorse and self-disgust.

The first part of the evening was, as always, easy to remember. It had been an important evening. He had dressed
carefully yesterday morning, knowing that there would not
be time to come home and change before going directly from
the office to the hotel for the meeting, with its cocktails,
dinner, speeches, movie, and unveiling of the new model. Because of the importance of the evening, he had taken it
very easy at Mario's at lunchtime, limiting himself to two
Martinis before lunch, conscious of virtue—only to have it
spoiled by Bill Hunter's coming into his office at three in the
afternoon, staring at him with both relief and approval and
saying, "Glad you didn't have one of those three-hour
lunches, Had. The old man was a little dubious about your
joining the group tonight."

Hadley Purvis had felt suddenly and enormously annoyed.
Usually he liked Bill Hunter, despite his aura of opportunism,
despite the cautious ambition that had enabled Hunter to
become quite close to the head of the agency in a very short
time.

"And so you said to him, 'Mr. Driscoll, if Had Purvis can't
go to the party, I won't go either.' And then he broke down."

He watched Bill Hunter flush. "Not like that, Had. But
I'll tell you what happened. He asked me if I thought you
would behave yourself tonight. I said I was certain you
realized the importance of the occasion, and I reminded him
that the Detroit people know you and like the work you did
on the spring campaign. So if you get out of line, it isn't
going to do me any good either."

"And that's your primary consideration, naturally."

Hunter looked at him angrily, helplessly. "Damn it,
Had . . ."

"Keep your little heart from fluttering. I'll step lightly."

Bill Hunter left his office. After he was gone, Hadley
tried very hard to believe that it had been an amusing little
interlude. But he could not. Resentment stayed with him.
Resentment at being treated like a child. And he suspected
that Hunter had brought it up with Driscoll, saying very
casually, "Hope Purvis doesn't put on a floor show tonight."

It wasn't like the old man to have brought it up. He felt that the old man genuinely liked him. They'd had some laughs together. Grown-up laughs, a little beyond the capacity of a boy scout like Hunter.

He had washed up at five, then gone down and shared a cab with Davey Tidmarsh, the only one of the new kids who had been asked to come along. Davey was all hopped up about it. He was a nice kid. Hadley liked him. Davey demanded to know what it would be like, and in the cab Hadley told him.

"We'll be seriously outnumbered. There'll be a battalion from Detroit, also the bank people. It will be done with enormous seriousness and a lot of expense. This is a pre-preview. Maybe they'll have a mockup there. The idea is that they get us all steamed up about the new model. Then, all enthused, we whip up two big promotions. The first promotion is a carnival deal they will use to sell the new models to the dealers and get them all steamed up. That'll be about four months from now. The second promotion will be the campaign to sell the cars to the public. They'll make a big fetish of secrecy, Davey. There'll be uniformed company guards. Armed."

It was as he had anticipated, only a bit bigger and gaudier than last year. Everything seemed to get bigger and gaudier every year. It was on the top floor of the hotel, in one of the middle-sized convention rooms. They were carefully checked at the door, and each was given a numbered badge to wear. On the left side of the room was sixty feet of bar. Along the right wall was the table where the buffet would be. There was a busy rumble of male conversation, a blue haze of smoke. Hadley nodded and smiled at the people he knew as they worked their way toward the bar. With drink in hand, he went into the next room—after being checked again at the door—to look at the mockup.

Hadley had to admit that it had been done very neatly. The mockup was one-third actual size. It revolved slowly on a chest-high pedestal, a red and white convertible with the door open, with the model of a girl in a swimming suit standing beside it, both model girl and model car bathed in an excellent imitation of sunlight. He looked at the girl first, marveling at how cleverly the sheen of suntanned girl had been duplicated. He looked at the mannekin's figure and thought at once of Sarah and felt a warm wave of tenderness for her, a feeling that she was his luck and, with her, nothing could ever go wrong.

He looked at the lines of the revolving car and, with the glibness of long practice, he made up phrases that would be suitable for advertising it. He stood aside for a time and watched the manufactured delight on the faces of those who were seeing the model for the first time. He finished his drink and went out to the bar. With the first drink, the last traces of irritation at Bill Hunter disappeared. As soon as he had a fresh drink, he looked Bill up and said, "I'm the man who snarled this afternoon."

"No harm done," Hunter said promptly and a bit distantly. "Excuse me, Had. There's somebody over there I have to say hello to."

Hadley placed himself at the bar. He was not alone long. Within ten minutes he was the center of a group of six or seven. He relished these times when he was sought out for his entertainment value. The drinks brought him quickly to the point where he was, without effort, amusing. The sharp phrases came quickly, almost without thought. They laughed with him and appreciated him. He felt warm and loved.

He remembered there had been small warnings in the back of his mind, but he had ignored them. He would know when to stop. He told the story about Jimmy and Jackie and the punch card over at Shor's, and knew he told it well, and knew he was having a fine time, and knew that everything was beautifully under control.

But, beyond that point, memory was faulty. It lost continuity. It became episodic, each scene bright enough, yet separated from other scenes by a grayness he could not penetrate.

He was still at the bar. The audience had dwindled to one, a small man he didn't know, a man who swayed and clung to the edge of the bar. He was trying to make the small man understand something. He kept shaking his head. Hunter came over to him and took his arm and said, "Had, you've got to get something to eat. They're going to take the buffet away soon."

"Smile, pardner, when you use that word 'got.' "

"Sit down and I'll get you a plate."

"Never let it be said that Hadley Purvis couldn't cut his own way through a solid wall of buffet." As Hunter tugged at his arm, Hadley finished his drink, put the glass on the bar with great care, and walked over toward the buffet, shrugging his arm free of Hunter's grasp. He took a plate and looked at all the food. He had not the slightest desire for food. He looked back. Hunter was watching him. He shrugged and went down the long table.

Then, another memory. Standing there with plate in hand. Looking over and seeing Bill Hunter's frantic signals. Ignoring him and walking steadily over to where Driscoll sat with some of the top brass from Detroit. He was amused at the apprehensive expression on Driscoll's face. But he sat down and Driscoll had to introduce him.

Then, later. Dropping something from his fork. Recapturing it and glancing up to trap a look of distaste on the face of the most important man from Detroit, a bald, powerful-looking man with a ruddy face and small bright blue eyes.

He remembered that he started brooding about that look of distaste. The others talked, and he ate doggedly. They think I'm a clown. I'm good enough to keep them laughing, but that's all. They don't think I'm capable of deep thought.

He remembered Driscoll's frown when he broke into the conversation, addressing himself to the bald one from Detroit and taking care to pronounce each word distinctly, without slur.

"That's a nice-looking mockup. And it is going to make a lot of vehicles look old before their time. The way I see it, we're in a period of artificially accelerated obsolescence. The honesty has gone out of the American product. The great God is turnover. So all you manufacturers are straining a gut to make a product that wears out, or breaks, or doesn't last or, like your car, goes out of style. It's the old game of rooking the consumer. You have your hand in his pocket, and we have our hand in yours."

He remembered his little speech vividly, and it shocked him. Maybe it was true. But that had not been the time or place to state it, not at this festive meeting, where everybody congratulated each other on what a fine new sparkling product they would be selling. He felt his cheeks grow hot as he remembered his own words. What a thing to say in front of Driscoll! The most abject apologies were going to be in order.

He could not remember the reaction of the man from Detroit, or Driscoll's immediate reaction. He had no further memories of being at the table. The next episode was back at the bar, a glass in his hand, Hunter beside him speaking so earnestly you could almost see the tears in his eyes. "Good Lord, Had! What did you say? What did you do? I've never seen him so upset."

"Tell him to go do something unspeakable. I just gave them a few clear words of ultimate truth. And now I intend to put some sparkle in that little combo."

"Leave the music alone. Go home, please. Just go home, Had."

There was another gap, and then he was arguing with the drummer. The man was curiously disinclined to give up the drums. A waiter gripped his arm.

"What's your trouble?" Hadley asked him angrily. "I just want to teach this clown how to stay on top of the beat."

"A gentleman wants to see you, sir. He is by the cloak-room. He asked me to bring you out."

Then he was by the cloakroom. Driscoll was there. He stood close to Hadley. "Don't open your mouth, Purvis. Just listen carefully to me while I try to get something through your drunken skull. Can you understand what I'm saying?"

"Certainly I can—"

"Shut up! You may have lost the whole shooting match for us. That speech of yours. He told me he wasn't aware of the fact that I hired Commies. He said that criticisms of the American way of life make him physically ill. Know what I'm going back in and tell him?"

"No."

"That I got you out here and fired you and sent you home. Get this straight. It's an attempt to save the contract. Even if it weren't, I'd still fire you, and I'd do it in person. I thought I would dread it. I've known you a long time. I find out, Purvis, that I'm actually enjoying it. It's such a damn relief to get rid of you. Don't open your mouth. I wouldn't take you back if you worked for free. Don't come back. Don't come in tomorrow. I'll have a girl pack your personal stuff. I'll have it sent to you by messenger along with your check. You'll get both tomorrow before noon. You're a clever man, Purvis, but the town is full of clever men who can hold liquor. Goodbye."

Driscoll turned on his heel and went back into the big room. Hadley remembered that the shock had penetrated the haze of liquor. He remembered that he had stood there, and he had been able to see two men setting up a projector, and all he could think about was how he would tell Sarah and what she would probably say.

And, without transition, he was in the Times Square area on his way home. The sidewalk would tilt unexpectedly, and each time he would take a lurching step to regain his balance. The glare of the lights hurt his eyes. His heart pounded. He felt short of breath.

He stopped and looked in the window of a men's shop that was still open. The sign on the door said Open Until Midnight. He looked at his watch. It was a little after eleven. He had imagined it to be much later. Suddenly it became imperative to him to prove both to himself and to a stranger that he was not at all drunk. If he could prove that, then he would know that Driscoll had fired him not for drinking, but for his opinions. And would anyone want to keep a job where he was not permitted to have opinions?

He gathered all his forces and looked intently into the shop window. He looked at a necktie. It was a gray wool tie with a tiny figure embroidered in dark red. The little embroidered things were shaped like commas. He decided that he liked it very much. The ties in that corner of the window were priced at three-fifty. He measured his stability, cleared his throat, and went into the shop.

"Good evening, sir."

"Good evening. I'd like that tie in the window, the gray one on the left with the dark red pattern."

"Would you please show me which one, sir?"

"Of course," Hadley pointed it out. The man took a duplicate off a rack.

"Would you like this in a box, or shall I put it in a bag?"

"A bag is all right."

"It's a very handsome tie."

He gave the man a five-dollar bill. The man brought him his change. "Thank you, sir. Good night."

"Good night." He walked out steadily, carrying the bag. No one could have done it better. A very orderly purchase. If he ever needed proof of his condition, the clerk would remember him. "Yes, I remember the gentleman. He came in shortly before closing time. He bought a gray tie. Sober? Perhaps he'd had a drink or two. But he was as sober as a judge."

And somewhere between the shop and home all memory ceased. There was a vague something about a quarrel with Sarah, but it was not at all clear. Perhaps because the homecoming scene had become too frequent for them.

He dried himself vigorously on a harsh towel and went

into the bedroom. When he thought of the lost job, he felt quick panic. Another one wouldn't be easy to find. One just as good might be impossible. It was a profession that fed on gossip.

Maybe it was a good thing. It would force a change on them. Maybe a new city, a new way of life. Maybe they could regain something that they had lost in the last year or so. But he knew he whistled in the dark. He was afraid. This was the worst of all mornings-after.

Yet even that realization was diffused by the peculiar aroma of unreality that clung to all his hangover mornings. Dreams were always vivid, so vivid that they became confused with reality. With care, he studied the texture of the memory of Driscoll's face and found therein a lessening of his hope that it could have been dreamed.

He went into his bedroom and took fresh underwear from the drawer. He found himself thinking about the purchase of the necktie again. It seemed strange that the purchase should have such retroactive importance. The clothing he had worn was where he had dropped it beside his bed. He picked it up. He emptied the pockets of the suit. There was a skein of dried vomit on the lapel of the suit. He could not remember having been ill. There was a triangular tear in the left knee of the trousers, and he noticed for the first time an abrasion on his bare knee. He could not remember having fallen. The necktie was not in the suit pocket. He began to wonder whether he had dreamed about the necktie. In the back of his mind was a ghost image of some other dream about a necktie.

He decided that he would go to the office. He did not see what else he could do. If his memory of what Driscoll had said was accurate, maybe by now Driscoll would have relented. When he went to select a necktie after he had shaved carefully, he looked for the new one on the rack. It was not there. As he was tying the one he had selected he noticed a wadded piece of paper on the floor beside his wastebasket. He picked it up, spread it open, read the name of the shop on it, and knew that the purchase of the tie had been real.

By the time he was completely dressed, it still was not eight o'clock. He felt unwell, though the sharpness of the headache was dulled. His hands were shaky. His legs felt empty and weak.

It was time to face Sarah. He knew that he had seen her

the previous evening. Probably she had been in bed, had heard him come in, had gotten up as was her custom and, no doubt, there had been a scene. He hoped he had not told her of losing the job. Yet, if it had been a dream, he could not have told her. If he had told her, it would be proof that it had not been a dream. He went through the bathroom into her bedroom, moving quietly. Her bed had been slept in, turned back where she had gotten out.

He went down the short hall to the small kitchen. Sarah was not there. He began to wonder about her. Surely the quarrel could not have been so bad that she had dressed and left. He measured coffee into the top of the percolator and put it over a low gas flame. He mixed frozen juice and drank a large glass. The apartment seemed uncannily quiet. He poured another glass, drank half of it, and walked up the hallway to the living room.

Stopping in the doorway, he saw the necktie, recognized the small pattern. He stood there, glass in hand, and looked at the tie. It was tightly knotted. And above the knot, resting on the arm of the chair, was the still, unspeakable face of Sarah, a face the shiny hue of fresh eggplant.

FIND THE WOMAN

ROSS MACDONALD

*Both my wife and I knew the splendid generosity of
Anthony Boucher's mind. Margaret's novel* Beast in
View *was conceived in the Bouchers' living room in
Berkeley. Years earlier the war had brought us to San
Francisco and given us a chance to meet Tony and
Phyllis. That was the summer of Ellery Queen's first
short story contest. At Tony's urging I wrote "Find the
Woman" between San Francisco and Kwajalein. This
started my career as a private detective story writer—
a career which, like my wife's career, was sustained by
Tony's friendship. It was his eye we wrote for, and his
unfailingly human response that set the final period to
each book.*

I SAT IN MY brand-new office with the odor of paint in my
nostrils and waited for something to happen. I had been
back on the Boulevard for one day. This was the beginning
of the second day. Below the window, flashing in the morning sun, the traffic raced and roared with a noise like battle.
It made me nervous. It made me want to move. I was all
dressed up in civilian clothes with no place to go and nobody
to go with.

Till Millicent Dreen came in.

I had seen her before, on the Strip with various escorts,
and knew who she was: publicity director for Tele-Pictures.
Mrs. Dreen was over forty and looked it, but there was
electricity in her, plugged in to a secret source that time

could never wear out. Look how high and tight I carry my body, her movements said. My hair is hennaed but comely, said her coiffure, inviting not to conviction but to suspension of disbelief. Her eyes were green and inconstant like the sea. They said what the hell.

She sat down by my desk and told me that her daughter had disappeared the day before, which was September the seventh.

"I was in Hollywood all day. We keep an apartment here, and there was some work I had to get out fast. Una isn't working, so I left her at the beach house by herself."

"Where is it?"

"A few miles above Santa Barbara."

"That's a long way to commute."

"It's worth it to me. When I can maneuver a weekend away from this town, I like to get *really* away."

"Maybe your daughter feels the same, only more so. When did she leave?"

"Sometime yesterday. When I drove home to the beach house last night she was gone."

"Did you call the police?"

"Hardly. She's twenty-two and knows what she's doing. I hope. Anyway, apron strings don't become me." She smiled like a cat and moved her scarlet-taloned fingers in her narrow lap. "It was very late and I was—tired. I went to bed. But when I woke up this morning it occurred to me that she might have drowned. I objected to it because she wasn't a strong swimmer, but she went in for solitary swimming. I think of the most dreadful things when I wake up in the morning."

"Went in for solitary swimming, Mrs. Dreen?"

" 'Went' slipped out, didn't it? I told you I think of dreadful things when I wake up in the morning."

"If she drowned you should be talking to the police. They can arrange for dragging and such things. All I can give you is my sympathy."

As if to estimate the value of that commodity, her eyes flickered from my shoulders to my waist and up again to my face. "Frankly, I don't know about the police. I do know about you, Mr. Archer. You just got out of the army, didn't you?"

"Last week." I failed to add that she was my first postwar client.

"And you don't belong to anybody, I've heard. You've never been bought. Is that right?"

"Not outright. You can take an option on a piece of me, though. A hundred dollars would do for a starter."

She nodded briskly. From a bright black bag she gave me five twenties. "Naturally, I'm conscious of publicity angles. My daughter retired a year ago when she married—"

"Twenty-one is a good age to retire."

"From pictures, maybe you're right. But she could want to go back if her marriage breaks up. And I have to look out for myself. It isn't true that there's no such thing as bad publicity. *I* don't know why Una went away."

"Is your daughter Una Sand?"

"Of course. I assumed you knew." My ignorance of the details of her life seemed to cause her pain. She didn't have to tell me that she had a feeling for publicity angles.

Though Una Sand meant less to me than Hecuba, I remembered the name and with it a glazed blonde who had had a year or two in the sun, but who'd made a better pin-up than an actress.

"Wasn't her marriage happy? I mean, isn't it?"

"You see how easy it is to slip into the past tense?" Mrs. Dreen smiled another fierce and purring smile, and her fingers fluttered in glee before her immobile body. "I suppose her marriage is happy enough. Her Ensign's quite a personable young man—handsome in a masculine way, and passionate she tells me, and naive enough."

"Naive enough for what?"

"To marry Una. Jack Rossiter was quite a catch in this woman's town. He was runner-up at Forest Hills the last year he played tennis. And now of course he's a flier. Una did right well by herself, even if it doesn't last."

What do you expect of a war marriage? she seemed to be saying. Permanence? Fidelity? The works?

"As a matter of fact," she went on, "it was thinking about Jack, more than anything else, that brought me here to you. He's due back this week, and naturally"—like many unnatural people, she overused that adverb—"he'll expect her to be waiting for him. It'll be rather embarrassing for me if he comes home and I can't tell him where she's gone, or why, or with whom. You'd really think she'd leave a note."

"I can't keep up with you," I said. "A minute ago Una was in the clutches of the cruel crawling foam. Now she's taken off with a romantic stranger."

"I consider possibilities, is all. When I was Una's age, married to Dreen, I had quite a time settling down. I still do."

Our gazes, mine as impassive as hers I hoped, met, struck no spark, and disengaged. The female spider who eats her mate held no attraction for me.

"I'm getting to know you pretty well," I said with the necessary smile, "but not the missing girl. Who's she been knocking around with?"

"I don't think we need to go into that. She doesn't confide in me, in any case."

"Whatever you say. Shall we look at the scene of the crime?"

"There isn't any *crime*."

"The scene of the accident, then, or the departure. Maybe the beach house will give me something to go on."

She glanced at the wafer-thin watch on her brown wrist. Its diamonds glittered coldly. "Do I have to drive all the way back?"

"If you can spare the time, it might help. We'll take my car."

She rose decisively but gracefully, as though she had practiced the movement in front of a mirror. An expert bitch, I thought as I followed her high slim shoulders and tight-sheathed hips down the stairs to the bright street. I felt a little sorry for the army of men who had warmed themselves, or been burned, at that secret electricity. And I wondered if her daughter Una was like her.

When I did get to see Una, the current had been cut off; I learned about it only by the marks it left. It left marks.

We drove down Sunset to the sea and north on 101 Alternate. All the way to Santa Barbara, she read a typescript whose manila cover was marked: "Temporary—This script is not final and is given to you for advance information only." It occurred to me that the warning might apply to Mrs. Dreen's own story.

As we left the Santa Barbara city limits, she tossed the script over her shoulder into the back seat. "It *really* smells. It's going to be a smash."

A few miles north of the city, a dirt road branched off to the left beside a filling station. It wound for a mile or more through broken country to her private beach. The beach house was set well back from the sea at the convergence of brown bluffs which huddled over it like scarred shoulders. To reach it we had to drive along the beach for a quarter of a mile, detouring to the very edge of the sea around the south-ern bluff.

The blue-white dazzle of sun, sand, and surf was like an arc-furnace. But I felt some breeze from the water when we got out of the car. A few languid clouds moved inland over our heads. A little high plane was gamboling among them like a terrier in a henyard.

"You have privacy," I said to Mrs. Dreen.

She stretched, and touched her varnished hair with her fingers. "One tires of the goldfish role. When I lie out there in the afternoons I—forget I have a name." She pointed to the middle of the cove beyond the breakers, where a white raft moved gently in the swells. "I simply take off my clothes and revert to protoplasm. *All* my clothes."

I looked up at the plane whose pilot was doodling in the sky. It dropped, turning like an early falling leaf, swooped like a hawk, climbed like an aspiration.

She said with a laugh: "If they come too low I cover my face, of course."

We had been moving away from the house towards the water. Nothing could have looked more innocent than the quiet cove held in the curve of the white beach like a benign blue eye in a tranquil brow. Then its colors shifted as a cloud passed over the sun. Cruel green and violent purple ran in the blue. I felt the old primitive terror and fascination. Mrs. Dreen shared the feeling and put it into words:

"It's got queer moods. I hate it sometimes as much as I love it." For an instant she looked old and uncertain. "I hope she isn't in there."

The tide had turned and was coming in, all the way from Hawaii and beyond, all the way from the shattered islands where bodies lay unburied in the burnt-out caves. The waves came up towards us, fumbling and gnawing at the beach like an immense soft mouth.

"Are there bad currents here, or anything like that?"

"No. It's deep, though. It must be twenty feet under the raft. I could never bottom it."

"I'd like to look at her room," I said. "It might tell us where she went, and even with whom. You'd know what clothes were missing?"

She laughed a little apologetically as she opened the door. "I used to dress my daughter, naturally. Not any more. Be-sides, more than half of her things must be in the Hollywood apartment. I'll try to help you, though."

It was good to step out of the vibrating brightness of the beach into shadowy stillness behind Venetian blinds. "I noticed that you unlocked the door," I said. "It's a big house with a lot of furniture in it. No servants?"

"I occasionally have to knuckle under to producers. But I won't to my employees. They'll be easier to get along with soon, now that the plane plants are shutting down."

We went to Una's room, which was light and airy in both atmosphere and furnishings. But it showed the lack of servants. Stockings, shoes, underwear, dresses, bathing suits, lipstick-smeared tissue littered the chairs and the floor. The bed was unmade. The framed photograph on the night table was obscured by two empty glasses which smelt of highball, and flanked by overflowing ash trays.

I moved the glasses and looked at the young man with the wings on his chest. Naive, handsome, passionate were words which suited the strong blunt nose, the full lips and square jaw, the wide proud eyes. For Mrs. Dreen he would have made a single healthy meal, and I wondered again if her daughter was a carnivore. At least the photograph of Jack Rossiter was the only sign of a man in her room. The two glasses could easily have been from separate nights. Or separate weeks, to judge by the condition of the room. Not that it wasn't an attractive room. It was like a pretty girl in disarray. But disarray.

We examined the room, the closets, the bathroom, and found nothing of importance, either positive or negative. When we had waded through the brilliant and muddled wardrobe which Una had shed, I turned to Mrs. Dreen.

"I guess I'll have to go back to Hollywood. It would help me if you'd come along. It would help me more if you'd tell me who your daughter knew. Or rather who she liked—I suppose she knew everybody. Remember, you suggested yourself that there's a man in this."

"I take it you haven't found anything?"

"One thing I'm pretty sure of. She didn't intentionally go away for long. Her toilet articles and pills are still in her bathroom. She's got quite a collection of pills."

"Yes, Una's always been a hypochondriac. Also she left Jack's picture. She only had the one, because she liked it best."

"That isn't so conclusive," I said. "I don't suppose you'd know whether there's a bathing suit missing?"

"I really couldn't say, she had so many. She was at her best in them."

"Still *was?*"

"I guess so, as a working hypothesis. Unless you can find me evidence to the contrary."

"You didn't like your daughter much, did you?"

"No. I didn't like her father. And she was prettier than I."

"But not so intelligent?"

"Not as bitchy, you mean? She was bitchy enough. But I'm still worried about Jack. He loved her. Even if I didn't."

The telephone in the hall took the cue and began to ring. "This is Millicent Dreen," she said into it. "Yes, you may read it to me." A pause. 'Kill the fatted calf, ice the champagne, turn down the sheets and break out the black silk nightie. Am coming home tomorrow.' Is that right?"

Then she said, "Hold it a minute. I wish to send an answer. To Ensign Jack Rossiter, USS *Guam,* CVE 173, Naval Air Station, Alameda—is that Ensign Rossiter's correct address? The text is: 'Dear Jack join me at the Hollywood apartment there is no one at the beach house. Millicent.' Repeat it, please. . . . Right. Thank you."

She turned from the phone and collapsed in the nearest chair, not forgetting to arrange her legs symmetrically.

"So Jack is coming home tomorrow?" I said. "All I had before was no evidence. Now I have no evidence and until tomorrow."

She leaned forward to look at me. "I've been wondering how far can I trust you."

"Not so far. But I'm not a blackmailer. I'm not a mind-reader, either, and it's sort of hard to play tennis with the invisible man."

"The invisible man has nothing to do with this. I called him when Una didn't come home. Just before I came to your office."

"All right," I said. "You're the one that wants to find Una. You'll get around to telling me. In the meantime, who else did you call?"

"Hilda Karp, Una's best friend—her *only* female friend."

"Where can I get hold of her?"

"She married Gray Karp, the agent. They live in Beverly Hills."

Their house, set high on a plateau of rolling lawn, was huge and fashionably grotesque: Spanish Mission with a dash of Paranoia. The room where I waited for Mrs. Karp was as big as a small barn and full of blue furniture. The bar had a brass rail.

Hilda Karp was a Dresden blonde with an athletic body and brains. By appearing in it, she made the room seem more real. "Mr. Archer, I believe?" She had my card in her hand, the one with "Private Investigator" on it.

"Una Sand disappeared yesterday. Her mother said you were her best friend."

"Millicent—Mrs. Dreen—called me early this morning. But, as I said then, I haven't seen Una for several days."

"Why would she go away?"

Hilda Karp sat down on the arm of a chair, and looked thoughtful. "I can't understand why her mother should be worried. She can take care of herself, and she's gone away before. I don't know why this time. I know her well enough to know that she's unpredictable."

"Why did she go away before?"

"Why do girls leave home, Mr. Archer?"

"She picked a queer time to leave home. Her husband's coming home tomorrow."

"That's right, she told me he sent her a cable from Pearl. He's a nice boy."

"Did Una think so?"

She looked at me frigidly as only a pale blonde can look, and said nothing.

"Look," I said. "I'm trying to do a job for Mrs. Dreen. My job is laying skeletons to rest, not teaching them the choreography of the *Danse Macabre*."

"Nicely put," she said. "Actually there's no skeleton. Una has played around, in a perfectly casual way I mean, with two or three men in the last year."

"Simultaneously, or one at a time?"

"One at a time. She's monandrous to that extent. The latest is Terry Neville."

"I thought he was married."

"In an interlocutory way only. For God's sake don't bring my name into it. My husband's in business in this town."

"He seems to be prosperous," I said, looking more at her than at the house. "Thank you very much, Mrs. Karp. Your name will never pass my lips."

"Hideous, isn't it? The name, I mean. But I couldn't help

falling in love with the guy. I hope you find her. Jack will be terribly disappointed if you don't."

I had begun to turn towards the door, but turned back. "It couldn't be anything like this, could it? She heard he was coming home, she felt unworthy of him, unable to face him, so she decided to lam out?"

"Millicent said she didn't leave a letter. Women don't go in for all such drama and pathos without leaving a letter. Or at least a marked copy of Tolstoi's *Resurrection*."

"I'll take your word for it." Her blue eyes were very bright in the great dim room. "How about this? She didn't like Jack at all. She went away for the sole purpose of letting him know that. A little sadism, maybe?"

"But she did like Jack. It's just that he was away for over a year. Whenever the subject came up in a mixed gathering, she always insisted that he was a wonderful lover."

"Like that, eh? Did Mrs. Dreen say you were Una's best friend?"

Her eyes were brighter and her thin, pretty mouth twisted in amusement. "Certainly. You should have heard her talk about me."

"Maybe I will. Thanks. Good-bye."

A telephone call to a screen writer I knew, the suit for which I had paid a hundred and fifty dollars of separation money in a moment of euphoria, and a false air of assurance got me past the studio guards and as far as the door of Terry Neville's dressing room. He had a bungalow to himself, which meant that he was as important as the publicity claimed. I didn't know what I was going to say to him, but I knocked on the door and, when someone said, "Who is it?" showed him.

Only the blind had not seen Terry Neville. He was over six feet, colorful, shapely, and fragrant like a distant garden of flowers. For a minute he went on reading and smoking in his brocaded armchair, carefully refraining from raising his eyes to look at me. He even turned a page of his book.

"Who are you?" he said finally. "I don't know you."

"Una Sand—"

"I don't know her, either." Grammatical solecisms had been weeded out of his speech, but nothing had been put in their place. His voice was impersonal and lifeless.

"Millicent Dreen's daughter," I said, humoring him. "Una Rossiter."

"Naturally I know Millicent Dreen. But you haven't said anything. Good day."

"Una disappeared yesterday. I thought you might be willing to help me find out why."

"You still haven't said anything." He got up and took a step towards me, very tall and wide. "What I said was *good day*."

But not tall and wide enough. I've always had an idea, probably incorrect, that I could handle any man who wears a scarlet silk bathrobe. He saw that idea on my face and changed his tune: "If you don't get out of here, my man, I'll call a guard."

"In the meantime I'd straighten out that marcel of yours. I might even be able to make a little trouble for you." I said that on the assumption that any man with his face and sexual opportunities would be on the brink of trouble most of the time.

It worked. "What do you mean by saying that?" he said. A sudden pallor made his carefully plucked black eyebrows stand out starkly. "You could get into a very great deal of hot water by standing there talking like that."

"What happened to Una?"

"I don't know. Get out of here."

"You're a liar."

Like one of the clean-cut young men in one of his own movies, he threw a punch at me. I let it go over my shoulder and while he was off balance placed the heel of my hand against his very flat solar plexus and pushed him down into his chair. Then I shut the door and walked fast to the front gate. I'd just as soon have gone on playing tennis with the invisible man.

"No luck, I take it?" Mrs. Dreen said when she opened the door of her apartment to me.

"I've got nothing to go on. If you really want to find your daughter you'd better go to Missing Persons. They've got the organization and the connections."

"I suppose Jack will be going to them. He's home already."

"I thought he was coming tomorrow."

"That telegram was sent yesterday. It was delayed somehow. His ship got in yesterday afternoon."

"Where is he now?"

"At the beach house by now, I guess. He flew down from Alameda in a Navy plane and called me from Santa Barbara."

"What did you tell him?"

"What could I tell him? That Una was gone. He's frantic. He thinks she may have drowned." It was late afternoon, and in spite of the whiskey which she was absorbing steadily, like an alcohol lamp, Mrs. Dreen's fires were burning low. Her hands and eyes were limp, and her voice was weary.

"Well," I said, "I might as well go back to Santa Barbara. I talked to Hilda Karp but she couldn't help me. Are you coming along?"

"Not again. I have to go to the studio tomorrow. Anyway, I don't want to see Jack just now. I'll stay here."

The sun was low over the sea, gold-leafing the water and bloodying the sky, when I got through Santa Barbara and back onto the coast highway. Not thinking it would do any good but by way of doing something or other to earn my keep, I stopped at the filling station where the road turned off to Mrs. Dreen's beach house.

"Fill her up," I said to the woman attendant. I needed gas anyway.

"I've got some friends who live around here," I said when she held out her hand for her money. "Do you know where Mrs. Dreen lives?"

She looked at me from behind disapproving spectacles. "You should know. You were down there with her today, weren't you?"

I covered my confusion by handing her a five and telling her: "Keep the change."

"No, thank you."

"Don't misunderstand me. All I want you to do is tell me who was there yesterday. You see all. Tell a little."

"Who are you?"

I showed her my card.

"Oh." Her lips moved unconsciously, computing the size of the tip. "There was a guy in a green convert, I think it was a Chrysler. He went down around noon and drove out again around four, I guess it was, like a bat out of hell."

"That's what I wanted to hear. You're wonderful. What did he look like?"

"Sort of dark and pretty good-looking. It's kind of hard to describe. Like the guy that took the part of the pilot in that picture last week—*you* know—only not so good-looking."

"Terry Neville."

"That's right, only not so good-looking. I've seen him go down there plenty of times."

"I don't know who that would be," I said, "but thanks anyway. There wasn't anybody with him, was there?"

"Not that I could see."

I went down the road to the beach house like a bat into hell. The sun, huge and angry red, was horizontal now, half-eclipsed by the sea and almost perceptibly sinking. It spread a red glow over the shore like a soft and creeping fire. After a long time, I thought, the cliffs would crumble, the sea would dry up, the whole earth would burn out. There'd be nothing left but bone-white cratered ashes like the moon.

When I rounded the bluff and came within sight of the beach I saw a man coming out of the sea. In the creeping fire which the sun shed he, too, seemed to be burning. The diving mask over his face made him look strange and inhuman. He walked out of the water as if he had never set foot on land before.

I walked towards him. "Mr. Rossiter?"

"Yes." He raised the glass mask from his face and with it the illusion of strangeness lifted. He was just a handsome young man, well-set-up, tanned, and worried-looking.

"My name is Archer."

He held out his hand, which was wet, after wiping it on his bathing trunks, which were also wet. "Oh, yes, Mr. Archer. My mother-in-law mentioned you over the phone."

"Are you enjoying your swim?"

"I am looking for the body of my wife." It sounded as if he meant it. I looked at him more closely. He was big and husky, but he was just a kid, twenty-two or -three at most. Out of school into the air, I thought. Probably met Una Sand at a party, fell hard for all that glamour, married her the week before he shipped out, and had dreamed bright dreams ever since. I remembered the brash telegram he had sent, as if life was like the people in slick magazine advertisements.

"What makes you think she drowned?"

"She wouldn't go away like this. She knew I was coming home this week. I cabled her from Pearl."

"Maybe she never got the cable."

After a pause he said: "Excuse me." He turned towards the waves which were breaking almost at his feet. The sun had disappeared, and the sea was turning gray and cold-looking, an antihuman element.

"Wait a minute. If she's in there, which I doubt, you should call the police. This is no way to look for her."

"If I don't find her before dark, I'll call them then," he said. "But if she's here, I want to find her myself." I could never have guessed his reason for that, but when I found it out it made sense. So far as anything in the situation made sense.

He walked a few steps into the surf, which was heavier now that the tide was coming in, plunged forward, and swam slowly towards the raft with his masked face under the water. His arms and legs beat the rhythm of the crawl as if his muscles took pleasure in it, but his face was downcast, searching the darkening sea floor. He swam in widening circles about the raft, raising his head about twice a minute for air.

He had completed several circles and I was beginning to feel that he wasn't really looking for anything, but expressing his sorrow, dancing a futile ritualistic water dance, when suddenly he took air and dived. For what seemed a long time but was probably about twenty seconds, the surface of the sea was empty except for the white raft. Then the masked head broke water, and Rossiter began to swim towards shore. He swam a laborious side stroke, with both arms submerged. It was twilight now, and I couldn't see him very well, but I could see that he was swimming very slowly. When he came nearer I saw a swirl of yellow hair.

He stood up, tore off his mask, and threw it away into the sea. He looked at me angrily, one arm holding the body of his wife against him. The white body half-floating in the shifting water was nude, a strange bright glistening catch from the sea floor.

"Go away," he said in a choked voice.

I went to get a blanket out of the car, and brought it to him where he laid her out on the beach. He huddled over her as if to protect her body from my gaze. He covered her and stroked her wet hair back from her face. Her face was not pretty. He covered that, too.

I said: "You'll have to call the police now."

After a time he answered: "I guess you're right. Will you help me carry her into the house?"

I helped him. Then I called the police in Santa Barbara, and told them that a woman had been drowned and where to find her. I left Jack Rossiter shivering in his wet trunks beside her blanketed body, and drove back to Hollywood for the second time.

Millicent Dreen was in her apartment in the Park-Wilshire. In the afternoon there had been a nearly full decanter of Scotch on her buffet. At ten o'clock it was on the coffee table beside her chair, and nearly empty. Her face and body had sagged. I wondered if every day she aged so many years, and every morning recreated herself through the power of her will.

She said: "I thought you were going back to Santa Barbara. I was just going to go to bed."

"I did go. Didn't Jack phone you?"

"No." She looked at me, and her green eyes were suddenly very much alive, almost fluorescent. "You found her," she said.

"Jack found her in the sea. She was drowned."

"I was afraid of that." But there was something like relief in her voice. As if worse things might have happened. As if at least she had lost no weapons and gained no foes in the daily battle to hold her position in the world's most competitive city.

"You hired me to find her," I said. "She's found, though I had nothing to do with finding her—and that's that. Unless you want me to find out who drowned her."

"What do you mean?"

"What I said. Perhaps it wasn't an accident. Or perhaps somebody stood by and watched her drown."

I had given her plenty of reason to be angry with me before, but for the first time that day she was angry. "I gave you a hundred dollars for doing nothing. Isn't that enough for you? Are you trying to drum up extra business?"

"I did one thing. I found out that Una wasn't by herself yesterday."

"Who was with her?" She stood up and walked quickly back and forth across the rug. As she walked her body was remolding itself into the forms of youth and vigor. She recreated herself before my eyes.

"The invisible man," I said. "My tennis partner."

Still she wouldn't speak the name. She was like the priestess of a cult whose tongue was forbidden to pronounce a secret word. But she said quickly and harshly: "If my daughter was killed I want to know who did it. I don't care who it was. But if you're giving me a line and if you make trouble for me and nothing comes of it, I'll have you kicked out of Southern California. I could do that."

Her eyes flashed, her breath came fast, and her sharp breast rose and fell with many of the appearances of genuine feeling. I liked her very much at that moment. So I went away, and instead of making trouble for her I made trouble for myself.

I found a booth in a drugstore on Wilshire and confirmed what I knew, that Terry Neville would have an unlisted number. I called a girl I knew who fed gossip to a movie columnist, and found out that Neville lived in Beverly Hills but spent most of his evenings around town. At this time of night he was usually at Ronald's or Chasen's, a little later at Ciro's. I went to Ronald's because it was nearer, and Terry Neville was there.

He was sitting in a booth for two in the long, low, smoke-filled room, eating smoked salmon and drinking stout. Across from him there was a sharp-faced terrier-like man who looked like his business manager and was drinking milk. Some Hollywood actors spend a lot of time with their managers, because they have a common interest.

I avoided the headwaiter and stepped up to Neville's table. He saw me and stood up, saying: "I warned you this afternoon. If you don't get out of here I'll call the police."

I said quietly: "I sort of am the police. Una is dead." He didn't answer and I went on: "This isn't a good place to talk. If you'll step outside for a minute I'd like to mention a couple of facts to you."

"You say you're a policeman," the sharp-faced man snapped, but quietly. "Where's your identification? Don't pay any attention to him, Terry."

Terry didn't say anything. I said: "I'm a private detective. I'm investigating the death of Una Rossiter. Shall we step outside, gentlemen?"

"We'll go out to the car," Terry Neville said tonelessly. "Come on, Ed," he added to the terrier-like man.

The car was not a green Chrysler convertible, but a black Packard limousine equipped with a uniformed chauffeur. When we entered the parking lot he got out of the car and opened the door. He was big and battered-looking.

I said: "I don't think I'll get in. I listen better standing up. I always stand up at concerts and confessions."

"You're not going to listen to anything," Ed said.

The parking lot was deserted and far back from the street,

and I forgot to keep my eye on the chauffeur. He rabbit-punched me and a gush of pain surged into my head. He rabbit-punched me again and my eyes rattled in their sockets and my body became invertebrate. Two men moving in a maze of lights took hold of my upper arms and lifted me into the car. Unconsciousness was a big black limousine with a swiftly purring motor and the blinds down.

Though it leaves the neck sore for days, the effect of a rabbit punch on the centers of consciousness is sudden and brief. In two or three minutes I came out of it, to the sound of Ed's voice saying:

"We don't like hurting people and we aren't going to hurt you. But you've got to learn to understand, whatever your name is—"

"Sacher-Masoch," I said.

"A bright boy," said Ed. "But a bright boy can be too bright for his own good. You've got to learn to understand that you can't go around annoying people, especially very important people like Mr. Neville here."

Terry Neville was sitting in the far corner of the back seat, looking worried. Ed was between us. The car was in motion, and I could see lights moving beyond the chauffeur's shoulders hunched over the wheel. The blinds were down over the back windows.

"Mr. Neville should keep out of my cases," I said. "At the moment you'd better let me out of this car or I'll have you arrested for kidnapping."

Ed laughed, but not cheerfuly. "You don't seem to realize what's happening to you. You're on your way to the police station, where Mr. Neville and I are going to charge you with attempted blackmail."

"Mr. Neville is a very brave little man," I said. "Inasmuch as he was seen leaving Una Sand's house shortly after she was killed. He was seen leaving in a great hurry and a green convertible."

"My God, Ed," Terry Neville said, "you're getting me in a frightful mess. You don't know what a frightful mess you're getting me in." His voice was high, with a ragged edge of hysteria.

"For God's sake, you're not afraid of this bum, are you?" Ed said in a terrier yap.

"You get out of here, Ed. This is a terrible thing, and you don't know how to handle it. I've got to talk to this man. Get out of this car."

He leaned forward to take the speaking tube, but Ed put a hand on his shoulder. "Play it your way, then, Terry. I still think I had the right play, but you spoiled it."

"Where are we going?" I said. I suspected that we were headed for Beverly Hills, where the police know who pays them their wages. Neville said into the speaking tube: "Turn down a side street and park. Then take a walk around the block."

"That's better," I said when we had parked. Terry Neville looked frightened. Ed looked sulky and worried. For no good reason, I felt complacent.

"Spill it," I said to Terry Neville. "Did you kill the girl? Or did she accidentally drown—and you ran away so you wouldn't get mixed up in it? Or have you thought of a better one than that?"

"I'll tell you the truth," he said. "I didn't kill her. I didn't even know she was dead. But I was there yesterday afternoon. We were sunning ourselves on the raft, when a plane came over flying very low. I went away, because I didn't want to be seen there with her—"

"You mean you weren't exactly sunning yourselves?"

"Yes. That's right. This plane came over high at first, then he circled back and came down very low. I thought maybe he recognized me, and might be trying to take pictures or something."

"What kind of a plane was it?"

"I don't know. A military plane, I guess. A fighter plane. It was a single-seater painted blue. I don't know military planes."

"What did Una Sand do when you went away?"

"I don't know. I swam to shore, put on some clothes, and drove away. She stayed on the raft, I guess. But she was certainly all right when I left her. It would be a terrible thing for me if I was dragged into this thing, Mr.—"

"Archer."

"Mr. Archer. I'm terribly sorry if we hurt you. If I could make it right with you—" He pulled out a wallet.

His steady pallid whine bored me. Even his sheaf of bills bored me. The situation bored me.

I said: "I have no interest in messing up your brilliant career, Mr. Neville. I'd like to mess up your brilliant pan sometime, but that can wait. Until I have some reason to believe that you haven't told me the truth, I'll keep what you said under my hat. In the meantime, I want to hear what the coroner has to say."

They took me back to Ronald's, where my car was, and left me with many protestations of good fellowship. I said good night to them, rubbing the back of my neck with an exaggerated gesture. Certain other gestures occurred to me.

When I got back to Santa Barbara the coroner was working over Una. He said that there were no marks of violence on her body, and very little water in her lungs and stomach, but this condition was characteristic of about one drowning in ten.

I hadn't known that before, so I asked him to put it into sixty-four-dollar words. He was glad to.

"Sudden inhalation of water may result in a severe reflex spasm of the larynx, followed swiftly by asphyxia. Such a laryngeal spasm is more likely to occur if the victim's face is upward, allowing water to rush into the nostrils, and would be likely to be facilitated by emotional or nervous shock. It may have happened like that or it may not."

"Hell," I said, "she may not even be dead."

He gave me a sour look. "Thirty-six hours ago she wasn't."

I figured it out as I got in my car. Una couldn't have drowned much later than four o'clock in the afternoon on September the seventh.

It was three in the morning when I checked in at the Barbara Hotel. I got up at seven, had breakfast in a restaurant, and went to the beach house to talk to Jack Rossiter. It was only about eight o'clock when I got there, but Rossiter was sitting on the beach in a canvas chair watching the sea.

"You again?" he said when he saw me.

"I'd think you'd have had enough of the sea for a while. How long were you out?"

"A year." He seemed unwilling to talk.

"I hate bothering people," I said, "but my business is always making a nuisance out of me."

"Evidently. What exactly is your business?"

"I'm currently working for your mother-in-law. I'm still trying to find out what happened to her daughter."

"Are you trying to needle me?" He put his hands on the arms of the chair as if to get up. For a moment his knuckles were white. Then he relaxed. "You saw what happened, didn't you?"

"Yes. But do you mind my asking what time your ship got into San Francisco on September the seventh?"

"No. Four o'clock. Four o'clock in the afternoon."

"I suppose that could be checked?"

He didn't answer. There was a newspaper on the sand beside his chair and he leaned over and handed it to me. It was the Late Night Final of a San Francisco newspaper for the seventh.

"Turn to page four," he said.

I turned to page four and found an article describing the arrival of the USS *Guam* at the Golden Gate, at four o'clock in the afternoon. A contingent of Waves had greeted the returning heroes, and a band had played "California, Here I Come."

"If you want to see Mrs. Dreen, she's in the house," Jack Rossiter said. "But it looks to me as if your job is finished."

"Thanks," I said.

"And if I don't see you again, good-bye."

"Are you leaving?"

"A friend is coming out from Santa Barabara to pick me up in a few minutes. I'm flying up to Alameda with him to see about getting leave. I just had a forty-eight, and I've got to be here for the inquest tomorrow. And the funeral." His voice was hard. His whole personality had hardened overnight. The evening before his nature had been wide open. Now it was closed and invulnerable.

"Good-bye," I said, and plodded through the soft sand to the house. On the way I thought of something, and walked faster.

When I knocked, Mrs. Dreen came to the door holding a cup of coffee, not very steadily. She was wearing a heavy wool dressing robe with a silk rope around the waist, and a silk cap on her head. Her eyes were bleary.

"Hello," she said. "I came back last night after all. I couldn't work today anyway. And I didn't think Jack should be by himself."

"He seems to be doing all right."

"I'm glad you think so. Will you come in?"

I stepped inside. "You said last night that you wanted to know who killed Una no matter who it was."

"Well?"

"Does that still go?"

"Yes. Why? Did you find out something?"

"Not exactly. I thought of something, that's all."

"The coroner believes it was an accident. I talked to him

on the phone this morning." She sipped her black coffee. Her hand vibrated steadily, like a leaf in the wind.

"He may be right," I said. "He may be wrong."

There was the sound of a car outside, and I moved to the window and looked out. A station wagon stopped on the beach, and a Navy officer got out and walked towards Jack Rossiter. Rossiter got up and they shook hands.

"Will you call Jack, Mrs. Dreen, and tell him to come into the house for a minute?"

"If you wish." She went to the door and called him.

Rossiter came to the door and said a little impatiently: "What is it?"

"Come in," I said. "And tell me what time you left the ship the day before yesterday."

"Let's see. We got in at four—"

"No, you didn't. The ship did, but not you. Am I right?"

"I don't know what you mean."

"You know what I mean. It's so simple that it couldn't fool anybody for a minute, not if he knew anything about carriers. You flew your plane off the ship a couple of hours before she got into port. My guess is that you gave that telegram to a buddy to send for you before you left the ship. You flew down here, caught your wife being made love to by another man, landed on the beach—and drowned her."

"You're insane!" After a moment he said less violently: "I admit I flew off the ship. You could easily find that out anyway. I flew around for a couple of hours, getting in some flying time—"

"Where did you fly?"

"Along the coast. I don't get down this far. I landed at Alameda at five-thirty, and I can prove it."

"Who's your friend?" I pointed through the open door to the other officer, who was standing on the beach looking out to sea.

"Lieutenant Harris. I'm going to fly up to Alameda with him. I warn you, don't make any ridiculous accusations in his presence, or you'll suffer for it."

"I want to ask him a question," I said. "What sort of plane were you flying?"

"FM-3."

I went out of the house and down the slope to Lieutenant Harris. He turned towards me and I saw the wings on his blouse.

"Good morning, Lieutenant," I said. "You've done a good deal of flying, I suppose?"

"Thirty-two months. Why?"

"I want to settle a bet. Could a plane land on this beach and take off again?"

"I think maybe a Piper Cub could. I'd try it anyway. Does that settle the bet?"

"It was a fighter I had in mind. An FM-3."

"Not an FM-3," he said. "Not possibly. It might just conceivably be able to land but it'd never get off again. Not enough room, and very poor surface. Ask Jack, he'll tell you the same."

I went back to the house and said to Jack: "I was wrong. I'm sorry. As you said, I guess I'm all washed up with this case."

"Good-bye, Millicent," Jack said, and kissed her cheek. "If I'm not back tonight I'll be back first thing in the morning. Keep a stiff upper lip."

"You do, too, Jack."

He went away without looking at me again. So the case was ending as it had begun, with me and Mrs. Dreen alone in a room wondering what had happened to her daughter.

"You shouldn't have said what you did to him," she said. "He's had enough to bear."

My mind was working very fast. I wondered whether it was producing anything. "I suppose Lieutenant Harris knows what he's talking about. He says a fighter couldn't land and take off from this beach. There's no other place around here he could have landed without being seen. So he didn't land.

"But I still don't believe that he wasn't here. No young husband flying along the coast within range of the house where his wife was—well, he'd fly low and dip his wings to her, wouldn't he? Terry Neville saw the plane come down."

"Terry Neville?"

"I talked to him last night. He was with Una before she died. The two of them were out on the raft together when Jack's plane came down. Jack saw them, and saw what they were doing. They saw him. Terry Neville went away. Then what?"

"You're making this up," Mrs. Dreen said, but her green eyes were intent on my face.

"I'm making it up, of course. I wasn't here. After Terry Neville ran away, there was no one here but Una, and Jack in a plane circling over her head. I'm trying to figure out why Una died. I *have* to make it up. But I think she died of fright. I think Jack dived at her and forced her into the water. I think he kept on diving at her until she was gone. Then he flew back to Alameda and chalked up his flying time."

"Fantasy," she said. "And very ugly. I don't believe it."

"You should. You've got that cable, haven't you?"

"I don't know what you're talking about."

"Jack sent Una a cable from Pearl, telling her what day he was arriving. Una mentioned it to Hilda Karp. Hilda Karp mentioned it to me. It's funny you didn't say anything about it."

"I didn't know about it," Millicent Dreen said. Her eyes were blank.

I went on, paying no attention to her denial: "My guess is that the cable said not only that Jack's ship was coming in on the seventh, but that he'd fly over the beach house that afternoon. Fortunately, I don't have to depend on guess-work. The cable will be on file at Western Union, and the police will be able to look at it. I'm going into town now."

"Wait," she said. "Don't go to the police about it. You'll only get Jack in trouble. I destroyed the cable to protect him, but I'll tell you what was in it. Your guess was right. He said he'd fly over on the seventh."

"When did you destroy it?"

"Yesterday, before I came to you. I was afriad it would implicate Jack."

"Why did you come to me at all, if you wanted to pro-tect Jack? It seems that you knew what happened."

"I wasn't sure. I didn't know what had happened to her, and until I found out I didn't know what to do."

"You're still not sure," I said. "But I'm beginning to be. For one thing, it's certain that Una never got her cable, at least not as it was sent. Otherwise she wouldn't have been doing what she was doing on the afternoon that her husband was going to fly over and say hello. You changed the date on it, perhaps? So that Una expected Jack a day later? Then you arranged to be in Hollywood on the seventh, so that Una could spend a final afternoon with Terry Neville."

"Perhaps." Her face was completely alive, controlled but full of dangerous energy, like a cobra listening to music.

"Perhaps you wanted Jack for yourself," I said. "Perhaps you had another reason, I don't know. I think even a psychoanalyst would have a hard time working through your motivations, Mrs. Dreen, and I'm not one. All I know is that you precipitated a murder. Your plan worked even better than you expected."

"It was accidental death," she said hoarsely. "If you go to the police you'll only make a fool of yourself, and cause trouble for Jack."

"You care about Jack, don't you?"

"Why shouldn't I?" she said. "He was mine before he ever saw Una. She took him away from me."

"And now you think you've got him back." I got up to go. "I hope for your sake he doesn't figure out for himself what I've just figured out."

"Do you think he will?" Sudden terror had jerked her face apart.

I didn't answer her.